T0244651

PENGUIN BOOKS
THE POLITICIAN

Devesh Verma was associated with TV journalism for over twenty-two years before he turned to fiction writing. In 2004, he received the Sahitya Akademi Award for his translation, from Urdu to Hindi, of *Sakhtiyat, Pas-Sakhtiyat Aur Mashriqi Sheriyat*, an important literary and cultural theory text.

PRAISE FOR THE BOOK

'Every bit a twenty-first-century Indian English novel, it neither tries to write back to a centre nor cares for a Western reader. The novel captures both the energy and the chaos that characterize life in small towns in Uttar Pradesh, showing effortlessly both the machinations of power politics and mounds of filth'—Scroll

'From Jawaharlal Nehru's subtle handing over of the political mantle to his daughter Indira Gandhi to B.R. Ambedkar's fight for the untouchables, or his proposed Hindu Code Bill being seen as "wicked interference with the age-old Hindu personal laws of divine provenance", there is hardly any political event of significance that has escaped Verma's attention . . . The gentle and effortless unravelling of these complex minds, and the timelessness of this tragic-comic novel by Verma, who won a Sahitya Award for a translated work in 2004, deserves praise'—*Hindustan Times*

'At several points in the novel one felt the echoes of the plenitude of Hindi and Urdu voices that Devesh must have absorbed through his intellectual journey. That he can make us feel and smell those writings in an English novel is a singular achievement . . . This is a remarkable debut and one eagerly looks forward to the second instalment of what promises to be a colossal trilogy'—*Biblio*

'Devesh Verma's debut novel, *The Politician* . . . exquisitely upends [the] dominant model of the political novel that oscillates between fact and fiction and highlights the success and skulduggery of corrupt and ruthless politicians. With well-fleshed-out characters, Devesh Verma weaves a gripping narrative around a flawed hero's quest for unbridled power'—*Frontline*

THE
POLITICIAN

A NOVEL

DEVESH VERMA

PENGUIN BOOKS

An imprint of Penguin Random House

PENGUIN BOOKS

Penguin Books is an imprint of the Penguin Random House group of companies whose addresses can be found at global.penguinrandomhouse.com

Published by Penguin Random House India Pvt. Ltd
4th Floor, Capital Tower 1, MG Road,
Gurugram 122 002, Haryana, India

First published in Viking by Penguin Random House India 2020
This edition published in Penguin Books by Penguin Random House India 2024

10 9 8 7 6 5 4 3 2 1

ISBN 9780143466154

Typeset in Bembo Std by Manipal Technologies Limited, Manipal

www.penguin.co.in

For Shinaber and to the memory of her father's mother's father

'Droll thing life is—that mysterious arrangement of merciless logic for a futile purpose. The most you can hope from it is some knowledge of yourself—that comes too late—a crop of inextinguishable regrets.'

Marlow in *Heart of Darkness*

ONE

I was about to leave for work when the telephone rang. Deena was dead. He had hung himself from the ceiling fan of his sparse one-room accommodation. Though living in the same city, we had been out of touch for nearly fourteen months, an inordinate length of time given the decades-old bond between us, but then I did not realize it had been that long. Being the output head at a new TV news channel, I had my hands full, with little time for anything else. Deena too had not tried to make any contact. Besides, I thought he was hard at work on his book, a novel, his intensely valued dream for which he had relinquished his job with a Hindi newsweekly of repute.

Right from our childhood to university days, we had been so close, shared so many interests and agreed on so many things that it was inconceivable we could ever become irrelevant to each other. But that's what had happened, of which the news of his death that I could not absorb at first made me guiltily conscious. My mind flashed back to a funeral we had attended just before I seemed to have shut him out of my life. It was our last meeting.

Surveying the preparations for the cremation, Deena, with a touch of a smile, had said, 'We have heard it said so often that death is the reality, life is just a mirage, an illusion, a dream, a drop in the desert of nothingness and so on. I mean we

1

philosophize a lot about life and death, sounding grandiose, but
Kartik, don't you think we vainly let the sheer simplicity of the
phenomenon called death elude us, because of our metaphysical
bombast?' Suddenly, he spun around and started walking away
from the crowd of the mourners. I followed him. He stopped,
'I am sorry. You know how hard I had to struggle not to laugh
out loud.'

'What is there on this cremation ground to make you laugh?'
said I, a bit annoyed. 'You were talking about the significance
of death; fine, perfectly consistent with the occasion. Then
what happened?'

'I was going to add something to what I just said, which
might have caused us embarrassment.'

'What was it, by the way? Can you tell me now?'

Deena held out his hand in a placatory gesture and said,
'The way our pompous, highfalutin existence is put in its place
by an unassuming truth. Isn't it ludicrous and funny? It's like
the Pope or an Ayatollah or a Shankaracharya—any godman
or prophet I mean—suddenly hit by the urge for a crap while
pontificating on man-God business.' He again turned away and
fought not to laugh.

'But that's the beauty of it . . . If we can live pursuing
our dreams in defiance of this truth, the truth of death, is it
something to mock? Don't you think this very courage in the
face of a hostile reality marks man's presence in this world?'

'A reality against which he can never prevail . . . That's exactly
what I meant. Posing and suffering from the seriousness about
something that can have the ground cut from under its feet any
moment. It puts closure to our pursuits with such finality that it's
a mockery of life at the hands of death, the mockery of the gravity
with which we regard our precarious condition on earth.'

'What's your point, Deena?' I asked with a quiver of
exasperation. 'What should one do?

'I'm not trying to prove a point or saying something can be done about it. It's just that this whole business is so droll—'

'What business?'

'These clumsy efforts on the part of . . .' Deena paused, 'on the part of humanity . . . to hide the comical side of its solemn posture.' He made a face and said, 'Am I sounding grave?'

* * *

We came from the same village on the outskirts of Kanpur, the largest town in north India, and had spent a large portion of our childhood together. Later, as was the trend among people who had the means to graduate to city life, my family too moved to Kanpur which at the time seemed far off. But I never lost touch with Deena. We would regularly visit Parsadpur as our extended family was there.

Deena's father Ram Mohan also lived in Kanpur with Deena's siblings. He had a teaching job together with an active literary, social and political life. Deena's mother, however, had to stay back in the village to look after their fields and trees along with Ram Mohan's uncle who was Chhote Baba to his nephew's children. His wife had died young, but he had refused to remarry, withstanding all attempts to bring him around; he regarded Ram Mohan as his own son and did not want to start a separate family.

Chhote Baba was short-sighted; he would take Deena along whenever he had to go somewhere. Though very affectionate to Deena, Chhote Baba's attitude towards Deena's mother was rather harsh. He was apt to find fault with the way she handled things, and she had to handle a lot. Besides domestic chores and looking after Deena and Chhote Baba, she would have to hire people to till the fields and see the job is properly done. At harvesting time, she would have to be extra alert.

Deena's family owned several acres of cultivable land, some of which was rented out to other peasants. They also owned a mango grove apart from some isolated trees. At the time of their bearing fruit, she would arrange for them to be watched over. Chhote Baba's blurred vision came in handy in that she could go about these tasks without him getting in the way. Chhote Baba himself could not do much except grumble, but Deena's mother's main worry was that he would vilify her, as was his wont, to Deena's father during his weekly visits, leading to her being called names, beaten too sometimes.

Ram Mohan had an imperious personality. People of the village and the area were in thrall to him. He was the most educated man in the region and had a doctorate in Hindi literature. Even in Kanpur where he taught at D.A.V. College, he had earned the respect of his students, his peers, and his social circle as a gifted teacher, speaker and conversationalist. Stories of his wit and erudition would not stop doing the rounds.

Some of Ram Mohan's personality traits reminded the old villagers of his father who too had a domineering disposition and a fearsome temper. People would avoid crossing him. His influence would also get in the way of some who aspired to have their hold over the area. Deena's only Bua once told him the story of how some enemies of his Bade Baba, in order to teach him a lesson, had caught hold of ten-year-old Ram Mohan walking back from school and rubbed the front of his neck with an inverted knife. Bade Baba was beside himself. He swore not to sit quiet until he had disembowelled his son's assailants, but they were saved by Ram Mohan's inability to recognize them as they had had their faces covered during the assault. For several days, Ram Mohan, the young boy, was unable to swallow anything as his neck was hurt and swollen. Finding it unbearable, Bade Baba would publicly dare the persons responsible to show up. In time, after coming into his own, Ram Mohan too would come to believe in the importance of violence in matters not amenable to suasion. 'I am the master of arms and argumentation both,' he would declaim.

People in Parsadpur flocked to Ram Mohan for all sorts of reasons; some to seek his help in matters ranging from trivial to grave, others for the sheer pleasure of his company. An air of excitement preceded his weekly arrival in Parsadpur, and a covey of people would go to the small railway station, barely two hundred meters away, to meet him. Deena would be on the lookout for the small procession approaching the village with his father in the front and would run back to tell his mother. Deena took pride in his father's influence, and Ram Mohan would always give him something before leaving, most often a fountain pen which Deena would flaunt to his friends and classmates, taking delight in the way they would regard it, which albeit was of no practical use for them since village children wrote with reed pens on a wooden slate. Yet being in possession of the pen meant a lot to Deena; besides being a rarity in the sticks it served as a reminder of who his father was. By the time Ram Mohan visited Parsadpur again, the pen would have been lost, and Deena would await his father's departure the following day, hanging about in the proximity of the bustle marking the hour, anxious to draw his notice.

* * *

Ram Mohan's command over Hindi was formidable. To further consolidate his grip on it, he had picked up some Sanskrit on which Hindi had, for most of its vocabulary, come to depend. Ram Mohan was also taught Urdu and a little Persian in school, as was the practice in those days given the position Urdu held during the Raj. Thus, he had an additional device in his already impressive arsenal of Hindi, Sanskrit and English. His speeches and conversations would be decked with apt sayings and verses from these languages. As English remained a symbol of power, despite disgruntled voices in post-colonial north India, he made a special effort to build up a stock of difficult words of the language to impress those who mattered. 'You won't be taken lightly if some of your words go over the heads of your interlocutors.' He was often invited to preside over literary, cultural and social functions in Kanpur.

Once set on something, Ram Mohan was known not to quit, not easily. Keen that his village should become a shining specimen of development in the region, he worked tirelessly for it. In recognition of his efforts, Parsadpur was declared the first model village by the state government. Even during his student days in Kanpur, Ram Mohan had waged a relentless battle to have the railway station renamed after Parsadpur; his point being that Parsadpur was closest to the station, while the village of which the station bore the name, though much bigger in size and population, was a little further away. Eventually, the railway department gave in to his arguments, handing a tremendous boost to his self-esteem.

———————

For all his absorption in various activities, Ram Mohan's longing for women never flagged. People close to him whispered about his ability to charm the quiet consent out of a woman. He first set eyes on Kanti, Deena's mother, when she was a school girl of sixteen, whom he heard speak at a gathering organized to alert the Kurmis—people of the peasant caste—in the area to the challenges of changing times in the country. Her speech laid stress on women's education—an issue Indians had regarded for centuries as settled. It was the year when the law minister B.R. Ambedkar was pitted against the whole gamut of forces hostile to his efforts to secure some rights for Hindu women. His proposed Hindu Code Bill was viewed as a wicked interference with the age-old Hindu personal laws of divine provenance.

Kanti had hardly any idea of the raging dispute. It was her father Baijnath who had prodded her into preparing a speech espousing the cause of women's education. He was a retired military man and had served as a mounted soldier in the British army and was part of the army unit deployed in Paris during the First World War, where to his wonderment he had seen girls on the streets, with books in their hands, walking to schools, chatting and laughing. Inspired, he had resolved to have his daughters educated and to motivate others to do the same. Baijnath was also involved in organizing the gathering in question, during the preparation of which some young men of the area had come close to him, Ram Mohan being one of them. His education and manner of speaking had won Baijnath's heart.

When Kanti finished speaking, Ram Mohan, who was busy looking after the arrangements, rushed towards the makeshift platform, looking for her. She was still on stage, receiving praise and blessings from the chief guest, the chairman of the Legislative Council of Bihar, as Baijnath stood beaming at his daughter. She was short, slim and had an angular face with neatly defined features. She was attractive. She stayed with her father and one of her brothers in Kanpur, and the reason Baijnath stayed in the city with them was to ensure their education, especially that of Kanti who seemed most inclined. The rest of their family lived in the village as Baijnath, who had taken up a job as a court clerk, could not provide for his entire family in the city; some of his earnings also went into fighting the menace of child marriage among the people of his caste, some of whom he would take to court.

Kicking up clouds of dust, the crowds had more or less dispersed when Ram Mohan muttered, getting annoyed, 'What was so special about her speech that they are fussing over her!' Some people had gathered round him but he was not with them, and to avoid any forced conversation, he moved away and climbed onto the platform where a discussion was going on; the topic was the ongoing turmoil over the proposed Hindu Code Bill in the Constituent Assembly. Seeing Ram Mohan, the chief guest was reminded that he was getting late for a meeting in Kanpur, but as he manoeuvred to rise, Baijnath said, 'I know you have other engagements, but we would be grateful if you could spare a little more time to this discussion.' The chief guest settled back leaning against the bolster.

'Most of the Hindus are not in favour of this bill,' he said, and before he could elaborate, Baijnath who sat down cross-legged facing him said, 'Ambedkar seems to be an educated man. Why would he want to do something which is not in our interest?'

'Because Hindu leaders think he is subverting the authority of the traditions rooted in our sacred scriptures—'

'But Ambedkar claims the bill has not strayed from the core beliefs of the religious texts. That's what I heard on the radio,' broke in Ram Mohan, having taken his place beside Kanti.

'He says this only to douse the fire . . . Hindu leaders are not amused; they say he is stretching the obvious to the limit.'

'What exactly does this bill entail?' Baijnath asked.

'I dare say it deals broadly with rights and status of Hindu women to whom it would give some say in matters concerning their interests. Like the questions of divorce and widow remarriage . . . their share in property . . . I don't know the details yet.'

'Ambedkar should be complimented,' blurted out Baijnath. 'Our women have been denied their due for centuries. It's time we gave them a little freedom to explore their own possibilities in life.'

The chief guest was quiet for a second, then glancing towards others, said, 'But women have the most important role in the house and are held in high esteem for their dedication and sacrifice.'

Ram Mohan nodded.

'I am not saying taking care of home is something to be ashamed of . . . but they should also receive education with our encouragement and support. There should be schools for them.'

'This, I don't mind,' said the chief guest. 'An educated mother can give her children a better upbringing.'

'But this bill has nothing to do with women's education,' said Ram Mohan. 'It's about those so-called "rights" concerning ancestral property and divorce. It's like offering a razor to a monkey, with disastrous results.'

The chief guest turned to Kanti, 'You want to say something? Don't shy away. Your father's a courageous man; so should you be.'

Looking at her father and then Ram Mohan, she said, 'We have had women who could hold their own against a general aversion to their attempting something . . . something other than what's expected of them—' Catching the sneer in Ram Mohan's face, she stopped. Her father gestured her to go on, but she kept quiet.

Ram Mohan said, 'Their number is so small it doesn't denote anything . . . the number of such women, and they can be traced back to the beginning of civilization . . . So what? Can they match up to men's achievements, ever?'

'I am not saying they can be on equal terms with men,' said Kanti. 'But I believe that given the opportunity, they can come out of their backwardness; there's so much they can do to help men in their ventures.' She fell silent again.

'Who can deny a woman's importance in a man's life?' Ram Mohan said. 'They have been performing their household duties for ages. Their role is central to an Indian family; without their presence at home, it would be difficult for men to take up challenges outside.'

Mr Singh, the chief guest, said, 'We have had a long tradition of respecting our women. But some Hindu leaders think this new code bill is detrimental to the trust women have in their men. And this would destroy the Hindu idea of family.'

Baijnath frowned. He asked, 'How can it be harmful if our women are allowed some say in matters concerning them?'

Reclining on the bolster, Mr Singh held his head down for a moment looking pensive and said, 'Giving them a share in ancestral property is suggesting that their interests are not safe in men's hands . . . which would plant the seeds of mutual misgivings, leading to the souring of relations, relations that draw strength from their emotional foundations. If these foundations are to make way for personal economic interests, we can imagine what will happen to the traditional bonds of affection in Hindu society. Look at the enthusiasm with which we conduct the weddings of our sisters and daughters. The gaiety of these occasions is not lost on anyone . . . Nor the plaintiveness of the leave-taking, when our daughter or sister sets off for her husband's home. In the event of the passing of this bill, we might have to say goodbye to these affinities.'

When Baijnath did not probe any further, Mr Singh said, 'I must push off now.' Baijnath and Ram Mohan stood up to help him rise. He was dressed in khadi—homespun cloth popularized by Gandhi as a symbol of opposition to all things

foreign, which in time would come to signify power, the power
of the politician. Mr Singh was in his early fifties and rather
overweight; smoothing his kurta and readjusting the folds of his
dhoti, he continued, 'You all deserve to be commended on such
a wonderful gathering. Now that the English are out, we should
work towards developing a strong sense of solidarity among
Kurmis and fight our way to a position of political importance.
Today the majority of positions of any significance are held by
Brahmans, because the reins of the national movement were
in their hands, because for centuries their pre-eminence has
remained unchallenged.'

Baijnath said, 'You mean the Congress which was our
united effort against the Raj has served its purpose; now we as
Kurmis are on our own and have to take up our battle afresh?'

As Mr Singh started walking towards the steps of the
platform Ram Mohan motioned to the people crowding
around to step aside.

'Yes, our real struggle begins now; look at the way
Ambedkar has fought for the untouchables. And now he is
trying to implant his newfangled ideas in Hinduism through
this bill. We may support the upper castes on this issue, but as
regards our political, economic and social interests, we cannot
rely on them . . . these upper castes.'

They were off stage now. Kanti had joined the other girls
and women standing around in a small huddle several yards apart
from the men. Barring a few unmarried girls including Kanti,
most were wearing a veil. Some of them had their saris pulled
over their faces hiding them completely; others were in smaller
veils, which they coyly lifted using their index and middle
fingers just so they could see.

Some people waiting downstage followed Mr Singh who,
flanked by Baijnath and Ram Mohan, made for his Jeep parked
in the grounds of the area's solitary primary school, which by way

of solid infrastructure, only had a mud wall all around it; classes were held under the shade of a sloping thatch. The entrance had no gate, just a gap in the wall. To the right abutting on the school wall was a pond, a thick layer of moss covering most of its surface, and two water buffalos swam quietly at the far end with only their heads visible, the rest of their bodies buried under the green sheet. Open drains from various directions flowed lazily into the pond, offering thick, black sewage as libation to its otherwise precarious existence in the absence of rainwater. Three little boys nearby were struggling to remove the moss and muck stuck to their bodies after a romp in the pond.

'If Gandhi ji had picked Sardar Patel as prime minister instead of Nehru, things would be better for us, I guess,' said Baijnath. 'What do you think?' They were now entering the school grounds. The driver had started dusting off the front seats of the Jeep. On hearing the noise, the man who had been sleeping curled up in the space between the two small seats in the back woke up and got out in a hurry.

'Baijnath ji, Sardar Patel comes from Gujarat where Kurmis are not doing badly. In fact, their position there evokes as much respect as that of the forward castes. We should be proud of him, but to expect him to set aside his other national agendas for our sake wouldn't be wise.' As Mr Singh made ready to take his leave, Baijnath and Ram Mohan bent down one by one to touch his feet, but before they could complete the gesture, he gave each a hug. He blessed Kanti by placing his right hand on her head as she bowed down. Others also rushed in to show their respect.

He got in the vehicle only to get out again. The Jeep would not start. Muttering that it was the battery, the driver slid out from behind the wheel. 'It needs to be pushed,' he said addressing no one in particular. Several men came forward. The Jeep rolled out of the school, across the narrow strip of low-ground along the front boundary wall and came to a halt against the ridge, refusing to climb onto the dirt track connecting Parsadpur to the Grand Trunk Road. Sensing the need for extra hands, some more men joined in. So rutted was the dirt track that the Jeep had to bump along at a snail's pace. The children who wanted to push the Jeep were quarrelling amongst themselves; many hadn't seen a motor vehicle before. When Baijnath asked they be allowed to push it, they fell over themselves to do it. As the Jeep picked up a little speed, the driver engaged the clutch, selected the second gear, and released the clutch in a trice while pumping the accelerator furiously. The engine sputtered giving the Jeep a few jolts before dying. The driver swore under his breath. The children were shrieking in excitement. Those who did not get to push were scampering along on either side of the Jeep yelling and laughing. In the second attempt, the driver got it running. Mr Singh along with Ram Mohan, Baijnath and others had already started walking through the swirls of dust towards the Jeep. Before climbing in the Jeep, Mr Singh paused, and then assuming a serious expression said, 'Today our caste is in a decrepit state. Our path to progress is very rough. We need to unite against our backwardness; we cannot just sit and brood over it. We have got to go about setting things right; no hurdles in our way should put us off.' With a sweep of his hand, he showed the children tussling and jostling for a better view of the Jeep, 'Look at these lads . . . the eagerness and enthusiasm with which they took on the responsibility of pushing the Jeep . . . That's how we need to embark on our mission.'

Most of the children milling about were in their drawers, grimy and crumpled, made of the cheapest material. Some younger ones had nothing on except copper amulets hung from a black twine around their waists, and almost every one of them had sores or boils on their hands or legs, some developing scabs, some still fresh; two boys had their big toe badly injured, not an

unusual thing for village children running around and stubbing
it against something every now and then. They tried to keep
the injured toe off the ground as they limped their way around.
Some had to constantly sniffle to hold back the snot that would
peek through before being drawn back in quickly.

Mr Singh finally took the seat beside the driver; some party
workers travelling with him sat in the back. Ram Mohan and
Baijnath along with the others watched the Jeep lurching along
the path till it disappeared behind a thick curtain of billowing dust.

————————

Ram Mohan invited Baijnath and a few others to his house for
a snack of gur and water. Kanti had already left for Ballamgaon,
their village, from where a large contingent of men and women
had come for the event. Ram Mohan had sent word to his uncle
in his village, who was there to receive them. Slim and a little
taller than Ram Mohan, he had certain elegance about him.
It's not that the village life did not have its share in shaping his
personality but hints of culture and polish were unmistakable,
something atypical considering he had had no education. He
could barely read or write. A man of piety, he had around his
neck a string of beads; his elder brother, Ram Mohan's father,
too was a devotional man and like his younger brother wore
beads and performed the same rituals. But they did not worship
the same deity. The younger brother would count rosary beads,
evoking Ram on every bead; in the elder one's case, it was
Krishna, but Ram Mohan's father could well be considered an
educated man, a rare breed in the sticks. In addition to having a
good grasp of the Mahabharata, the Ramayana and the Puranas,
he also knew Urdu.

Of average height, slightly thickset, Ram Mohan had a
round face and a head full of hair with flecks of grey. Unlike

his father and uncle, who wore a moustache, he was clean-shaven. Since a moustache was considered emblematic of manliness, Ram Mohan invoked Nehru, Patel and Bose, the national heroes then, and said, 'Are they not manly . . .? I have doubts about those who need a moustache to prove their masculinity!' Seeing the faces of his interlocutors, he had a hearty laugh.

They were all now seated on charpoys placed on the *chabootra*, a plinth-like raised area running along the front of Ram Mohan's house with a thatch awning.

* * *

Fourteen months into Independence, the mood was still upbeat among people like Ram Mohan who had been saved from taking the brunt of India bursting through its mask of rhetoric, during Partition. The conference had smacked of this optimistic and cheerful mood. But Mr Singh's emphasis on caste solidarity was a bit of a let-down for Ram Mohan who believed nothing could thwart talent and hard work in independent India. He had made some upper caste friends while studying in Kanpur. His father too had advised him to seek the company of Brahmans, the most educated caste in the country then; he was not averse to any caste as such, let alone his own. He would say to his son, a seeker of knowledge, 'I just want to impress upon you the futility of associating with the unlettered.'

The idea of limiting the use of his abilities to merely the promotion of his caste held no romance for Ram Mohan, and those who could marvel at his hard-earned knowledge and the glaze of an educated Brahman were few in his caste. However, Baijnath had no issue with focusing on his caste, but his objective was not political but social. He wanted to turn Kurmis against child marriage and bring them round to the importance of girls'

education. The remarks made by Mr Singh and Ram Mohan
about the place of women in society had dismayed him. He had
already drawn the ire of some of his own relations and friends
for his pursuit of stopping child marriages by threatening the
culprits with Sarda Act—the Child Marriage Restraint Act—
popularly named after its sponsor Rai Bahadur Harbilas Sarda,
passed by the British–Indian government two decades before—
and Baijnath would not hesitate to drag the violators to court,
straining his meagre resources in the process.

Baijnath and others stood up when, leaning on the arms of
his son and brother, Ram Mohan's ailing father came out. He
had recently been discharged from Hallet Hospital in Kanpur
where the doctors thought he was better off home as the dusk
closed in on him. After greetings were exchanged, he was
carefully settled on the narrow *takht* on the chabootra. Baijnath
was startled to see him in that state, so much of him having
wasted away. Sunken cheeks, hollowed eyes, a specimen of
skin and bone, and the arms, once known for their unmatched
strength, hung like a burden at his sides. To those who had seen
him in his prime, the defeat was heart-rending.

'Baijnath, we are meeting after a very long time,' he said in
a weak, rattling voice, not able to control its rise and fall. 'You
mostly stay in Kanpur these days, I hear.'

'Yes Bhaiya, but every second or third week I try to come.
Two of my children stay with me. They go to school there,'
said Baijnath.

'You are doing the right thing. It's very important to educate
our children. Times are changing . . .'

Noticing the signs of fatigue in his brother, Ram Mohan's
uncle, taking the conversation on, said, 'Is there any point in
educating girls? What purpose will it serve? Ultimately they have
to serve their husband's family. The money and time should
instead be saved for their wedding.'

Baijnath just nodded. He did not want to argue, for many a time it happened that an argument with those close to him would result in certain awkwardness between them, and it was not easy to recapture the old bonhomie even after moving to more comfortable topics. The force of logic would not convince people opposed to your thinking. It would only make them dig their heels in. So now Baijnath would not press the point beyond a point.

Having eaten gur, they were now drinking water. To the right, under a neem tree, a pair of bullocks and a water buffalo tethered to the wooden stakes sat lazily. The state of their immobility was broken only when they tried to deal with the flies pestering them. The trough, a wide-mouthed earthen container embedded into the mud, was empty. The animals were still a few hours away from their sumptuous evening meal, a mixture of water, wheat chaff, husk, oilcake, and leftover crumbs of food from the previous night. Ram Mohan's house was almost at the edge of the village. Only one house, right next door, belonging to Kalla Dada, a distant relation, was closer to the main dirt track, the one taken by Mr Singh's Jeep a short while before, beyond which lay the green stretch of fields dotted with trees. Far in the distance was a big mango grove, so imposing it had monopolized the landscape. It was a late October afternoon and there was greenery all around, a burst of it, and the village was stirring as people were about to start their evening chores. Those working in the fields had begun returning. Ram Mohan's father had already gone back into the house; his uncle, whose vision was poor but not that bad yet, was busy arranging for the cattle to be fed. Ram Mohan offered to take Baijnath around Parsadpur. It was a small

village of about sixty or so households, and barring some Harijan
families all the residents were of peasant caste i.e. Kurmi.

Looking up towards a pool of brightness in the sky formed
by the sinking sun hidden behind a white cloud, Baijnath said,
'I think we'll go around the village some other day; it's already
late.' So, after a few steps down the path, they turned left into
a lane. Two men, naked to the waist and a woman, her sari
hitched up, were busy tending the three water buffalos and
two calves, tethered on one side. The older man was pouring
their forage from a large wicker basket into the manger of brick
and mud built along the wall. The younger man, armed with
a wooden rake, was scraping the dung off the ground, while
the woman, on her haunches, was struggling to free one of the
calves that had got its front leg entangled in the rope. The men
greeted Ram Mohan and Baijnath as they picked their way past
all this and had all but made it to the other side of the alley and
onto the dirt track when the last water buffalo—just as Baijnath
keeping to the edge and walking behind Ram Mohan brushed
past it—loosened its bladder full blast. Only the agility of a
former military man kept him from being drenched. Yet his
dhoti could not escape a few tiny dust balls that sprung off the
ground. Holding a fold of his dhoti, Baijnath frowned at the
stains, prompting the older man in the lane to assure him they
would go away after a wash.

'I will come with you as far as the school,' said Ram Mohan.

They were on the main dirt path now. The sun had
disintegrated behind a dense clump of trees, lending a touch of
chill to the air.

'Can you suggest a suitable boy for Kanti?' asked Baijnath.
Ram Mohan was taken aback. 'Of all my children she is most
disposed to study; I don't want her to settle for a life in the
village, bringing down the curtain on all possibilities. If it were
up to me, I would see she gets to do whatever she is capable

of, but you know it's unthinkable in the present circumstances. After marriage and the husband willing, she can pursue her dreams. Kanti's mother is only too conscious of our limitations, of what we can do. She frets a lot about it these days.'

Taking a shortcut they turned left and climbed on to a boundary mound separating the fields of paddy and sugarcane. Ram Mohan thought of his father who had been pressurizing him through his mother and uncle to marry.

'The educated young men in our caste . . . you can count on one hand,' said Ram Mohan. 'Still, I will try and make enquiries . . . but please don't let this matter unduly tax you. We will find someone answering your expectations.' The shadow of anxiety that had got the better of Baijnath's countenance yielded to the elegant features again. They walked across a field to the dirt road. The school was right in front of them.

'From here I will be home in ten minutes,' said Baijnath, and after a pause, 'Why don't you come to Ballamgaon tomorrow, Ram Mohan? We are leaving the day after. I have to start work and Kanti needs to get back to school. Let's have lunch together and discuss things.'

Ram Mohan jumped at the invitation.

'It will look odd if you go by yourself,' said Ram Mohan's mother. Ram Mohan had lied to her that it was Baijnath who had suggested that Ram Mohan could be a suitable boy for his daughter. His mother had gladly approved. 'Take somebody along, somebody reliable.' He could think of nobody else but Badri, his best pal in Parsadpur. They used to go to the only primary school in the area and were close as children. With the passing of time, the bond between them had grown stronger, even though Badri had not gone past class five; his family had

had no illusions about any life for him beyond the village; as it is, people like him were like islands with swirling waters of illiteracy all around. But Ram Mohan had gone on to obtain a BA and MA in Hindi literature from D.A.V. College in Kanpur after finishing higher secondary school in Narval, a tiny provincial town nearby.

Unlike Ram Mohan, Badri was quiet and a little withdrawn, and despite being bony and hollow-cheeked, there was something pleasant about his face, a hint of light, a suggestion of smile and leisurely alertness. 'Have you spoken to your father about it?' Badri asked as they set off for Ballamgaon the following day.

'Not yet . . . let me see how Baijnath responds. I have told my mother though.'

'He should seize the offer with both hands . . . given the kind of boy he is looking for.'

'Baijnath is a weirdo, Badri . . . I suspect he harbours the wish that she follows a career after finishing her studies . . . Would you believe it?'

'He will have to say goodbye to hopes of getting her married then. He cannot expect his son-in-law to take up the agenda he has set for his daughter . . . He should know that a woman doesn't exist outside her husband's needs. That's her destiny. Any attempt to question it would cause grief for her and her parents.'

In order to avoid a herd of pigs coming from the opposite direction, they went to the other side of the dirt track and began walking along the left side of Dahiya—the famous pond of Ballamgaon; big and deep, it seldom dried up, hence its name, meaning 'curd-like' in the local dialect. A large part of its surface was concealed beneath a carpet of water chestnut leaves. To their right, beyond Dahiya, on a hummock stood a peepul tree whose leaves, shimmering and rippling against a clear blue sky, were like swarms of eyes blinking in the breeze and sunlight.

To its right, just off the edge of the pond, set on a high plinth, was an old temple with its dome covered in large patches with dark green mould and the plaster on the outside walls cracking; a goolar tree overhung its entrance.

Ram Mohan said, 'Absolutely. To thrust roles meant for men on women would jeopardize their deity-like status; they would end up neither here nor there . . . Nehru ji's approval of what Ambedkar is up to and Sardar Patel's acquiescence, is seen as a betrayal by the upholders of Indian values.'

Badri would always listen intently to his friend's sounding off, and Ram Mohan enjoyed the gullibility of people innocent of things beyond their immediate world.

'Ram Mohan, I am not disputing what you said. I take your point. But then I also find myself sympathizing with Baijnath's sentiments. How can we rubbish his outlook just like that? He loves his daughter and wants her to break out of the tradition-ordained life. I sometimes can't help thinking that our women are simply fed to the customs whose cause we cherish more than that of our sisters and daughters. Don't you think?'

'You don't understand, Badri. These customs are meant to be of service to women, to protect them, to keep them safe from hazards of life. I agree they are apt to be misused, resulting in atrocities against women, no doubt . . . but is it right to censure ancient conventions for our failure to appreciate their intrinsic purpose?'

'I'm no answer to your intellect, Ram Mohan. After listening to you I know why many of our social norms strike me as senseless and cruel . . . because I judge them by the way they appear in practice, and I don't have your intellect to understand their essence and truth . . .'

Ram Mohan swung his arm around his friend's neck, 'There are matters that I can discuss only with you, Badri. You are good at evaluating different points of view. An assessor of knowledge is no less important than a possessor of knowledge.'

———————

As if roused by the sound of laundry at Dahiya, they quickened their pace, glancing in the direction of the two washermen in loincloth at work, standing ankle-deep in water; holding one end of a thick bunch of clothes with both hands, they swung it up over their head and dashed it down in one single, circular motion on the slab of stone that sat half-submerged, each strike synchronized with a grunt. Behind them lay a big heap of laundry. Two women and a girl were busy sorting it into small piles, their grubby worn out saris hiked up to the knees. A little distance to their right, two boys back from a bout of defecation crouched over the edge of Dahiya, splashing their bottoms.

Slowly the dirt track curved to the right, then there was a fork; the left-hand one led out of the village to the fields and a copse, and was full of life—a boy and a little girl taking a herd of goats to graze, a peasant walking behind a pair of yoked bullocks followed by a woman carrying an infant and a sickle; two village dogs were also running along, all oblivious to the dust swirling around. They took the right-hand fork that ushered them into Ballamgaon. They walked past a row of thatched houses on the right, a cluster of guava trees on the left, and into a kind of village square that had a big neem tree in the middle with a mud platform around its base.

On the chabootra of a house sat three villagers who recognized Ram Mohan; when asked the way to Baijnath's house, they all scrambled to take them there. A few yards ahead, the track wound to the left, and after passing between the rear mud walls of some houses, it turned and they came out into an open space. At the far end of the widened path, they could see Baijnath in the company of a few others, waiting. Crowding the fronts of the houses on either side of the track, were curious onlookers. Nearby, outside his house, crouched a small boy, his face red with effort, but unable to endure the sudden fuss around him, he got up and scampered back into his house, leaving two tiny mounds and a dot behind.

They were ushered into the front room of Baijnath's house; built of unfired bricks, it was plastered with mud and whitewashed irregularly. Placed against the wall facing the main door were two rickety chairs, while a takht lay squeezed into the narrow space on the left. The earthen floor bedaubed with buffalo dung was not perfectly level, and a table-lookalike in the centre seesawed if touched. The bedsheet covering the cotton mattress on the bed was stained but clean. A locked iron trunk rusting at places sat pressed to the wall under the bed; an earthen lamp occupied a niche in the front wall, with spilled mustard oil forming a black patch around it; the arch of the niche and part of the wall above and around the edges of the niche was darkened with soot. About a foot to the right hung a tacky picture of a Hindu mendicant of the previous century, wearing russet clothes and a turban, the jaw firmly set and lips finely shaped though thin. It was Swami Dayanand Saraswati. Nicknamed 'Luther of India' by some of his supporters, he had taken it upon himself to cleanse the Hindu mind of the grime accumulated through centuries of 'cardinal misunderstanding' of the original scriptures. He was unabashed about his conviction that only the Vedas contained the complete and universal truth. The later religious beliefs were mere travesties. Baijnath was offhand with this all-encompassing truth of Vedas; the only promise the Order founded by this illustrious and virulent Vedic campaigner held out was for a society free from untouchability, traditional injustices; where women too would have freedom to fly.

Ram Mohan and Badri were comfortably settled in the two chairs; those who had shown them the way were crowding the entrance. Then there was a loud voice outside enquiring about Ram Mohan. A moment later a strapping figure shoving people aside emerged in the doorway. Gulab Singh was an imposing young man with a square face, a moustache twirled up and a prominent chin adorned with a cleft. They owed their acquaintance to a vicious circumstance at a wedding they both had attended in a village nearby about a year before.

A wedding-event was a three-day long affair in those days, and to treat the bridegroom's party to song and dance by *randis* or nautch girls was not unusual among hosts who could afford it. On the occasion in question there were two such troupes, one arranged by the hosts and the other brought along by the groom's family; these events at times also served as a showcase for the sensual allure of pubescent randis primed to be deflowered by some rich client. The troupe hired by the groom's side had two such vestals during whose performances a local tough got the hots for the younger one who seemed to have hardly gone past menarche. Her pristine youth had caught his fancy. He sent his henchmen to the head of the troupe, an elderly and superannuated woman. To his dismay, her virginity was no longer available. He tried hard and offered almost double the amount she would get from the existing deal. The woman was adamantine, saying yes they were randis, it did not mean they were unscrupulous and could go back on their word, giving a bad name to the profession.

The virginity in question had already been pledged to one Shukla ji, a very respectable man in the bridegroom's party, who had been instrumental in hiring this particular group's services for the occasion. An old hand at plucking these dew-drenched, about-to-bloom flowers, it was his wish to ogle the object of his libido as she danced in public while he could savour the thought of having her entirely to himself in private. When told of this ruffian's interest in the girl, Shukla ji felt violated. He belonged to a Brahman family of note in their region, which had been at the forefront of organizing events associated with India's freedom struggle. His father had had the honour of meeting Gandhi and Nehru during a conference of Indian National Congress in Kanpur about twenty-five years ago. Besides, these randis were engaged by the bridegroom's side; it was improper on the part of someone from the host village to have an eye on them. Shukla ji was furious but could not enter into a fight over a randi in full view. He signalled to his confidant Liyaqat Argali to thrash it out, but this village thug would not be deterred. Rather attempts at persuasion stiffened his resolve.

Shukla ji was desperate. To avoid losing out on being the first, he was willing to make concessions. The headwoman of the group then suggested that he, the elder claimant to this longed-for maidenhead, shelve his earlier plan to keep the girl for a monthly retainer for a year, as was his wont if she was very young, young enough to keep his loins pulsating past a few encounters—that is after deflowering her, he should leave the girl for his contender to enjoy for whatever length of time he desired. Shukla ji agreed. But this made the village bully more alive to the girl's desirability. His mind was in a whirl. The thought of the ecstasy that this yet-to-be-smelt flower could afford, consumed him completely, so rather than backing out, he reversed the proposition. When Liyaqat Argali tried to change tone and act tough, the ruffian whose name was Bhullan flew off the handle.

* * *

It was mid-afternoon. After a heavy meal, the members of the bridegroom's party—who had been put up under a large tent pitched in a field just outside the host village—were lounging around before being dished out another round of dance and snacks, when a sudden explosion of invective startled them. They all hurried to the spot a few meters away, where under an amla tree, Liyaqat Argali appeared to be in for some rough stuff at the hands of Shukla ji's rival. Rising to the turn of events, Ram Mohan raised his hand and asked them to calm down. But the rival kept muttering expletives. Argali explained the cause of the quarrel. By then people from the bride's family had also arrived. Ram Mohan turned to the enraged man, 'You have no business laying claim to the services of persons employed by someone else.'

'I am negotiating a deal which has nothing to do with their present engagement,' the tough reacted. All those present now stood in a ring and watched the drama unfold. Coming forward, the bride's father said, 'Bhullan, guests are held like gods in our society. They deserve to be shown the utmost respect. Your behaviour will disgrace my family and bring disrepute to the whole village. So let the marriage of my daughter pass off happily.'

'But Chacha, this is between me and the randis; these people have unnecessarily barged in.'

'These randis have come with the bridegroom's party. Once they leave you can contact them.'

'They have come with them, fine. But who are these people to argue on behalf of the groom's party?'

In crashed Shukla ji, 'But you can't force them to agree to your demand, as long as they are with us. It is our duty to see they are not harassed.'

'So you want to act as their protector?' said Bhullan derisively. 'Are they related to you? And who is this whore-lover whom they have given their word?'

'It's none of your business,' said Liyaqat Argali. 'They are well within their rights if they don't want to entertain you.'

'Don't push me if you want to leave with your limbs intact.'
Bhullan's tone reeked of menace. In a circumstance calling for
initiative, Ram Mohan could not stand aside and let somebody
else carry the day. Stern yet measured in tone, he asked Bhullan
to mind his language and taking him by the hand tried to lead him
away to have a quiet word. Bhullan reacted in a manner Ram
Mohan hadn't bargained for. Jerking his hand free, he pushed
him away, warning him not to come near him. Mortified, Ram
Mohan did not know what to do. At that moment, Gulab Singh
would salvage Ram Mohan's promise, his beginnings.

Leaping into action, the Thakur from Ballamgaon, who
had been watching the scene as part of the crowd, swooped
on Bhullan with such ferocity that his henchmen took to their
heels and before anyone could realize the gravity of what was
happening, Bhullan lay unconscious, with his nose and mouth
bleeding, and hands broken.

* * *

'I didn't know you were coming,' Gulab Singh complained,
and holding his hands, Ram Mohan said he was about to send
for him. Baijnath watched the warmth between the two men
and was surprised; he did not know about their friendship. Ram
Mohan asked him to add one more to his guests for lunch.
Baijnath had already sent word to his wife. Badri eyed Gulab
Singh who sat cross-legged on the takht. He had heard about his
fearlessness and fierceness, the man who would lend the missing
dimension to Ram Mohan's public profile.

———————

'Father's calling you inside,' Kanti's brother, a boy of twelve, shyly
informed Ram Mohan and ran back. Ram Mohan made for the

door on the left at the far end of the room where the boy had disappeared. Baijnath met him on the other side and led him across the inner courtyard to a charpoy next to the open kitchen blackened with soot. Sitting before the *chulha*, the mud stove, was Kanti's mother, preparing lunch for them. She adjusted the fold of her sari on her head. 'Kanti's mother wanted to meet you,' said Baijnath.

After smiling at Ram Mohan, she began blowing air through the metal tube into the mud stove to revive the dying flame. Kanti too was in the kitchen, cowering behind her mother, and was startled when Baijnath said, 'Why don't you ask Ram Mohan the meaning of the word you wanted to know the other day'. 'Go,' said her mother nudging her with her elbow. 'Take him to the other side of the courtyard. There's so much smoke here.' Baijnath brought out a charpoy and placed it away from the kitchen, and said he would go and look after the other guests. Ram Mohan sat down and said, his heartbeat quickening, 'So what's the word?' Kanti caught hold of her younger sister and seated herself on the floor not far from him. 'Mrinaal . . . It's in a poem in my book.'

'If your face were a lotus,' Ram Mohan said, grinning, 'the rest of your body would be Mrinaal, that is, lotus-stalk . . . By the way, your father wants me to recommend a suitable boy for you,' said he, his eyes boring into her. Blushing, she affected to speak in her sister's ear, who was trying to wriggle out of her grip to join her other siblings.'

'What do you think of me? Don't I fit the bill?' said Ram Mohan smiling sheepishly before excusing himself to go back to his friends. She coloured and ran back to the kitchen. When she told her mother about what he had said, she was surprised to find her mother smiling.

Deena had once said the prospect of marriage hung over girls like a sword that would put an end to their life with their parents and siblings and friends and things associated with their growing up years. Yet it was more excruciating for a girl to be left unmarried past a certain age, reducing her status in the family to a mere burden and a source of her parents' anxiety. Kanti's mother was already showing signs of this unease. She would often broach it to Baijnath who was usually nonchalant, but lately, under pressure from people around him, he had agreed to put his mind to it. But his idea of a prospective groom for Kanti was not Ram Mohan because he, though highly educated, sounded a bit like a traditionalist with respect to women. Yet Baijnath could not say no to the proposal for want of a better alternative. Kanti took it all in a matter-of-fact manner. It would relieve them of a lot of complications. She could sense even at this tender age that to covet a path of her own would mean the struggle to cope with her father's wishes while clinging on to societal norms. She chose to stand with her mother on this and let her heart grieve for her father.

With the help of some relatives, Kanti's mother made arrangements for the proposal to be sent to Ram Mohan's family, which was greeted with warmth. Ram Mohan's mother had already obtained his father's approval, but before a suitable date could be finalized, his father's health took a turn for the worse. Ram Mohan wanted to put off the wedding. His father would have none of it and asked his *bahu* (daughter-in-law) be brought home before he closed his eyes forever. He gave them three days' time during which he promised to keep the end at bay. They had to forgo the ceremonies, and the following day Ram Mohan accompanied by Badri and Gulab Singh and a few others went to Baijnath's house. The entire process took just a few hours and after taking the ceremonial blessings of Kanti's parents, they rushed back to Parsadpur. His father not only kept his word but hung on for a few more days after that.

TWO

I picked my way through small knots of people in the quad discussing the suicide. Everybody looked polite and solemn. Gathered around two police constables were a few people, latching on to every word of the men in khaki, whose matter-of-fact manner belied the mood of grimness pervading this middle-class neighbourhood that morning. I ran up the stairs and into the austere lodgings of Deena to find the two senior policemen standing by the window poring over the suicide note; the president and the secretary of the housing society stood watching. Deena had been brought down and was laid on the floor beside the lonely bed; I could not believe what I saw. Just as I was about to move closer to him, one of the policemen, the stoutly built, called out, 'Are you Kartik?' I nodded.

He walked up to me, 'If he had not left your number, we would not have known whom to contact,' then handing over a thick envelop to me, 'I think he wrote something for you . . . Please tell us if there is anything we should know.' It had my name written on it in capital letters, my full name, Kartik Verma. Tearing it open I took out ten or twelve sheets of paper stapled together:

Dear Kartik,

I exercised the only option left to me of being delivered from a life symbolizing nothing but the wreckage of what it could have been . . .
I could have gone on if it would have been just a life to be lived, or if I had what the narrator in The Enigma of Arrival *says about the couple who looked after the manor in Wiltshire, a 'readiness for living with what came,' and whose life 'contained no idea of the vocation or achievement. It contained only this idea of getting by, of lasting, of seeing one's days out.' It was unbearable to me, this idea of life. To explain it is not easy; it involves admitting to my share of affectations . . . Hold it! Why be needlessly harsh on myself? No, 'affectations' per se is not the word. Let me rephrase it: I cannot bear the thought of being—what Russell calls—'destitute of that core of egoism without which life is impossible.' Yes, that is closer to the mark—*

'Go to the last page,' jumped in the police officer, robbed of patience.

And now about the reason I had to write this letter . . . Kartik, I wish you would write the book I have been dreaming of all these years. You're busy I know; but a novel, the kind I have in mind, would give you a further purchase on your career as a journalist. Who knows you might eventually want to become a full-time author! If not me, then you'd agree, there's nobody more qualified than you to do justice to this tale.

'I'm leaving for you several notebooks, sheets, scraps of paper and letters, packed in my only VIP suitcase—'

'Bring that suitcase here, the one on which this envelope was placed,' the police officer directed his deputy who was going through Deena's clothes; I read on:

'They're filled with enough material for a book or books. You'll find in this suitcase many an anecdote, episode, tragic incident, letter and

remembered conversation, in addition to my thoughts on all kinds of things and on people who touched my life one way or the other. I'm sure Kartik that by dint of your closeness to my family you would know how to make sense of this jumble. Besides, you can always turn to Chacha ji, your father, for more detailed information about my father's political life and other things. Then, there's in the suitcase an incredible document, poignant and honest, in the form of Gayatri Masi's journal. You know of her but little of her life. Yes, you'd have to make full use of your imagination to put it together, to fill the blanks and fictionalize the reality of my Babu ji's life, a life worthy of a novel any way you slice it . . . No, not just one novel . . . His life was so eventful you might want to look at a trilogy. You can write the first book focusing on his world as it obtained before we moved to Allahabad, leaving enough material for the remaining ones.

Love,
Deena

The police officer wanted to have a look inside the suitcase, just in case . . . I opened it; there was nothing but—as described by Deena—a jumble of sheets and notebooks.

———————

Putting the letter back into the envelope, I stepped closer to Deena. He looked younger in death. The only anomaly in his otherwise peaceful state was the ligature mark, running round his neck like a crimson band, a bit frayed at the edges; I knelt on the floor to have a closer look at the face. Tears surged into my eyes. Breaking through layers of years was Deena of Parsadpur with the same innocence and vulnerability; I don't know why at that very moment that particular incident popped into my mind, which I must recount before taking the story further.

Having recently developed a taste for meat, one of Deena's maternal uncles had had for some time an eye on the male goat kid Deena used to play with and had named Gabdu. No sooner was he back from school than he would run to the neem tree under which their goats were kept tethered during the day. That day, to his shock and surprise, he found Gabdu missing and his mother bleating. Shankariya, the son of their outcast fieldworker—who sat near the edge of the dirt lane—could not hold back. Kanti, who had just rushed out of the house, caught Shankariya gesturing in the direction of Ballamgaon. She was a trifle too late as Deena, glowering at her, evaded the grasp of her outstretched hands and charged off.

Panicked, Deena ran for his life, across the dirt track into the fields, jumped over the boundary-mounds, and soon sighted Gabdu being pulled forward by the rope around his neck by a man; the progress was in short jerks as Gabdu strained against the rope by keeping his front legs firmly on the ground; the resistance lasted only a moment before he'd buckle under the pressure. Deena seized the rope from the man, his Mama's flunkey, telling him there had been a mistake, that his mother wanted Gabdu back. Standing by the shack located amongst the fields, his Mama watched with amusement; he yelled to his man not to haggle and let Deena be.

It was a close shave. Shankariya told him they were going to cut Gabdu into pieces. Deena could not stop crying while hugging and kissing his little friend. Next morning, he went to the goat-shed to cuddle Gabdu just before leaving for school, secure in his innocent belief that once saved he would stay saved. After returning from school, he found him gone again; now without asking anybody, he threw his bag away and sprinted for the life of Gabdu once more; however, on reaching the shack, he got bewildered by a strong but alien smell of something being cooked in oil and spices. Sitting on charpoys, his Mama was joking and laughing with his friends; squatting before a clay hearth the man from the previous day was busy stirring with a ladle the contents of a wide-mouthed aluminium pot; he wore only striped drawers and, despite good weather, was drenched in sweat, then Deena's eyes fell on the bloody skin lying puckered up on one side, which at first he could not make out; just behind the man sat a big brass bowl containing pieces of flesh bathed in blood, while on a small block of bricks just outside the shack was Gabdu's head with open sightless eyes.

Deena fell to the ground. They all scrambled to their feet; his Mama sprinkled water on his face and as soon as he lifted him into his arms, he came to, but before he became fully alert they whisked him away to his mother. Deena looked as if he was going to fall sick; Kanti took him on her lap and tried to pacify him; tears ran down his cheeks quietly.

My mind goes back to the conversation we had about a month after this atrocity, Gabdu's brutal end. While playing with his goats, Deena had said, 'Why is it that whenever there's a fight between people or somebody is getting beaten, people try to stop it? Even the police can be called if it gets out of hand, and those causing trouble can be sent to jail. When these animals are tortured and murdered, there's no one to turn to, no police, nothing.' At that time, I as a child too was appalled and bewildered by this reality. Deena was to write much later, while in JNU, fleshing out his understanding of the question he'd posed after losing Gabdu:

A quick glance at the human journey through the ages makes it plain that there have always been clashes of perspectives, ideas, ideals, beliefs and so forth; and societies and cultures in general get modified by them. Hence, with the passage of time, many a social institution considered indispensable would come to be classified as unethical and

*wicked: institutions like religious crusades, the killing of women accused
of witchcraft, slavery, apartheid, foot binding, female genital mutilation
(FGM), untouchability, bonded labour, custom of sati, widows
banished to far-off places, female infanticide and foeticide, Devdasi
system, Namboodri Brahmans deflowering the young brides of lower
caste grooms, Kuleen Brahmans marrying girls generations younger to
them, et al.*

*I've picked these examples randomly across time and cultures; to
claim that all of these atrocities have been disposed of would be foolish.
Yet it would be absurd to insist that any of these is followed as widely or
at the same scale as in former times. In fact, a few of these aren't heard of
any longer, while some have lost their intensity. My point is that none of
them has been given constitutional sanction anywhere in the world . . .
which mirrors the change in human sensibility and values, resulting from
conflicts of perspectives within and between cultures. However, there
endures one gory injustice harking back to man's barbaric past, which
negates the very idea, the very spirit of compassion. Yet instead of being
recognized as savagery it's prized for its culinary or other profitable out-
turns. It's even worse than the Holocaust, argues Coetzee's Elizabeth
Costello: 'We're surrounded by an enterprise of degradation, cruelty
and killing which rivals anything that the Third Reich was capable
of, indeed dwarfs it, in that ours is the enterprise without end bringing
rabbits, rats, poultry, livestock, ceaselessly into the world for the purpose
of killing them.'*

*Nearly all humanity conspires to justify hurting and murdering
animals in cold blood, that is, general consensus can make even the
worst kind of heinous acts seem normal. No court in the world can be
moved against this terror.*

Deena and I were in the same school, the only primary school in
the area. The L-shaped school building consisted of three rooms,

two of which were used to conduct lessons for class four and five; the third one served as staff room; the school had a headmaster along with two teachers and a clerk. Three chairs, one stool, one bench, two tables and a tin trunk, these accounted for the entire furniture of the school.

The school had been moved from its earlier location in Parsadpur to a place near Dahiya and at the edge of Ballamgaon, a few months after Ram Mohan's wedding, and within a year of which Kanti had given birth to twins, Nisha and Nishant, followed by Sandhya a couple of years later; then had come a lull to be broken by Deena's arrival before the Indo-China war. Meanwhile, Ram Mohan had bagged lectureship in Hindi literature at his own alma mater, D.A.V. College of Kanpur; it was some achievement in that he became the first in his caste to have broken through the upper-caste cordon. That he deserved the job had nothing to do with his landing it. What saw him through was his use of the potent blend of pluck and cunning. His well-wishers and disparagers alike had been of the view that he should try his luck at some lowly establishment instead; they had no idea of Ram Mohan's bent for ventures promising resistance. This success also raised his profile in his own caste; the entire sequence he'd recounted in Parsadpur—

'I'd learnt of the vacancy from a candidate whose Chacha teaches at the college; this Chacha had been cultivating the principal to secure the lectureship for his nephew.'

'Shouldn't he have known better? That it might draw you into contention?' said Badri.

Ram Mohan laughed, 'During my final year of MA, it was common knowledge that relations between the chairman of the managing committee and the principal were not good. So when the time came to fill the vacancy, most of the hopefuls preferred to solicit either the principal or the chairman; no one would risk approaching both of them. There I saw a chance for myself.

Since there was nobody I could look to for help, I decided to take it up myself. First I went to the principal and humbly expressed my desire, and mentioned that I'd already sought the blessings of Chairman Sahab. His expression changed; without waiting for his response, I added, "Chairman Sahab has told me it's up to Mathur Sahab. If he agrees, there shouldn't be any problem." He was quiet for a bit, savouring, as it were, the significance of my words, then said he respected Chairman Sahab as an elder and wouldn't question his judgment.'

'What if they came to know?' asked Gulab Singh.

'I somehow had a feeling that Mathur Sahab, rather than contacting the Chairman then and there, would return his gesture at the time of the interview . . . Even if they had met, it would not have mattered, for just a day after meeting the principal, I caught hold of the chairman while he was out on his morning walk in the park across his residence. Just off the path he was strolling along I pretended to be doing yoga; as he approached I scuttled to him giving him a little start and touched his feet. He blessed me; I introduced myself. He seemed happy I had studied at his institute. Now we were walking together, talking. I told him about my candidature for the post of lectureship in his college and about my meeting with the principal. He looked at me quizzically. Then I said Mathur Sahab had made it clear that he would respect Chairman Sahab's wish on the matter.'

They gaped at Ram Mohan as he continued, 'When he spoke, his voice quivered; I could see his eyes glistening. I had no doubt this would occupy their minds and I'd be part of the picture.'

'What exactly did Chairman Sahab say?' asked Badri.

'He fell silent; then patting me on the back said they both, the principal and he, would select the most deserving candidate. I knew I'd made an impression or he wouldn't have raised the question of merit.'

'Any sign of them finding out the truth during the interview?'

'None; they were very cordial all through, and at every glimpse of brilliance in my answers, they would exchange glances.'

'How did others take it?' This was Gulab Singh.

'Like a bolt from the blue. They were all staggered. Soon there were attempts to find the cause of the calamity. Many ascribed it to the feud between the chairman and the principal, resulting in the selection of someone like me.'

Badri chuckled, 'Isn't it strange? Your candidacy ended the hostility between them.'

'That's life. Sometimes the reality is the obverse of the obvious,' said Ram Mohan philosophically. 'Though there were some who thought I was selected on merit.'

———————

A few years later Ram Mohan relocated to Civil Lines, an upmarket area in Kanpur. It was a big compound housing several houses, which belonged to Mitra brothers—Bade Babu and Chhote Babu—who lived in the big bungalow roofed with rough brown clay tiles; into a corner portion of this bungalow—the part available on rent—moved Ram Mohan; it had a big square room, a corridor with a room on the left and a small inner courtyard, on the left side of which sat a low ceiling kitchen and a shaded corner for the manservant; on the right were the bathroom and the lavatory separate but adjacent; the kitchen and the lavatory—diagonal to each other across the courtyard—Deena would later describe as the text and the subtext.

There were three more houses in the compound to the left of the big bungalow, two of them tenanted. In the corner house, just off the main road lived Zaheer Sahab, a state government servant; it was the largest of the three; the house next to his was rented by Bhatnagar Sahab, a senior teacher at an intermediate college but whose wife taught at a girls' degree college under the same management as DAV College. Crowding the rear of the compound were families of a carpenter, a plumber, an electrician, a peanut vendor and a newspaper hawker; the women and children of this dirt clot worked for these 'Sahab' families.

In the front, between the big bungalow and the boundary wall, lay a big open space with a small oval garden, hedged in by henna bushes, and the dirt track running around it served as walking path as well as children's playground, and beyond the boundary across the main road was McRobert Hospital which seemed more like a massive residential place with big landscaped gardens suggesting generations of wealth and class; marking its boundary was a stylish iron fence painted green, and set into one of the square columns supporting the big iron gates was a shiny brass plaque engraved on which in black was the name of the hospital. The terracotta colour of its building with neatly tiled roof sat elegantly with the green surroundings.

Shortly after shifting to his new residence Ram Mohan had brought to Kanpur all his children except Deena who stayed behind in Parsadpur with his mother, Dadi and Chhote Baba, and if she, their mother, had not started a primary school for girls in Parsadpur it would've been impossible for Nisha and Sandhya to get admission in the city to a grade compatible with their age. There was no school for girls in and around Parsadpur. So when Kanti, with her father's encouragement, had spoken to Ram Mohan about the need of such a school, he'd agreed. Further, he'd given permission for the school to make use of the defunct family mill just outside Parsadpur, which had one big room and a backyard full of dirt and telltale marks of its former function. Kanti along with her sister Manno had lent the structure some resemblance to a school, and despite objections to girls being exposed to the perils of modern education, Kanti's enterprise generated considerable interest in the area; to wrestle with those opposed to the idea, there was Baijnath; proud of his daughter's initiative, he could not contain himself; people would make sport of it, of his childlike enthusiasm for the school; the sight of little girls making their way to school in small peppy groups would bring tears to his eyes.

However, there was this one alloy to his joy, to his priding himself on his daughter's effort, something about which he could not do anything, about this other group of girls who, dressed in rags, would follow these peasant girls to the mill-turned-school, only to hover outside the entrance, full of curiosity. They were Harijan girls. Any attempt for their inclusion would be beyond the pale. Not only that. It could hazard the chance for non-Harijan girls to get some elementary education, whose families could not abide such intermingling.

Kanti had been working hard trying to balance her duties at home with those at school. Her sister Manno was a big help, but Baijnath knew it was temporary. He raised the problem with Ram Mohan who, however, was way too busy enriching his knowledge of Hindi literature as well as honing a distinct style of teaching it. He knew his upper-caste colleagues would grab at any chance to show him his place, and to tear Ram Mohan away from this challenge demanded an equally if not a more dynamic situation. Baijnath who had some inkling of his temperament presented it to him as a problem to fix which required extraordinary effort. He stressed if Ram Mohan could prod the district administration into giving recognition and assistance to the school, it would reinforce people's belief in him and send a message to the doubters. This was enough to kindle Ram Mohan's interest. Baijnath had found out about the people in Kanpur, who could help in the matter, but Ram Mohan had an aversion to humouring petty clerks and local politicians. He took some time and got an appointment with a top bureaucrat in Lucknow, the man who handled an important department in addition to primary education. Ram Mohan took Baijnath along to meet him.

They had to wait about an hour for their turn, sitting in the cabin of the secretary to the official. It was one of the many offices of state ministers and bureaucrats located on either side of the long corridor. 'What a thoroughfare of power, this corridor,' whispered Ram Mohan to Baijnath. He found it oddly difficult to imagine the elaborate rather imperious manner in which the authority of each one of the members of this august troupe would be on display when they went out in the province. 'This corridor is the barrel through which their power flows,' whispered Ram Mohan to Baijnath.

The big official heard them out, after which, while commiserating about their cause, explained the reasons for his inability to help. The visit gave Ram Mohan his first taste of political authority and bureaucratic leverage that kept the entire province under their sway, not to mention it was also his first encounter with a member of the flock viewed as the finest practitioner of English. Ram Mohan thought he had left a mark on the big man with his knowledge of the language; the way the latter had eyed him, surprised by his correct use of the conjunction 'lest'. Then the bureaucrat had ordered tea as if saying he was impressed. However, Baijnath was not impressed. Far from it; he was smarting from the outcome of their effort, which to him was zero. Ram Mohan on the other hand continued to gloat over the enormity of his achievement.

They had now reached the railway station to catch a train back to Kanpur. After paying the tongawallah, they started walking towards the grand façade of the building, which looked more like a palace than a railway station; and trains, surprisingly, could not be heard outside. Built by the English about half a century earlier, it had a strong trace of the architecture associated

with the tradition of nawabs of Awadh, a tradition already in
decline before being blown out of the water with the advent of
the Raj. The region, known for the beauty of its evenings, had
once been the quintessence of Indo-Persian aesthetics coalesced
into a novel cultural stream.

The day had crawled into its fag end but the sun refused
to comply. The heat was bearable only in the light of a fierce
summer ahead. Ram Mohan wanted to relieve himself before
going into the station; maybe he was reminded of the need by
the musty and unyielding stench of urine filtering through as
they neared the palatial structure. 'No, no . . . let's go there,' said
Ram Mohan, gesturing towards the only public urinal on the far
left of the station building, when Baijnath made as if to use the
boundary wall which told of a gruesome tale of being copiously
assaulted. There was never a moment when it did not have a
male organ pointed at it. Every two steps there were patches on
it in varying stages of drying; those just left behind had puddles
at the bottom, some still bubbling.

Though he knew it would be in a mess, Ram Mohan
marched on towards the public urinal, towering over which an
imposing billboard displayed the smiling prime minister with a
rosebud in the buttonhole of his white khadi waistcoat. The man
exuded taste and culture. They had hardly reached the roofless
grimy structure when the air lost the clarity of the smell of stale
urine; added to it was a more expressive dimension, producing
a miasma so intense it beggared description. Bracing himself,
Ram Mohan, his handkerchief over the mouth, peeked inside
and recoiled. Only an acute crisis coupled with an overriding
demand for cover could make one face up to the inner sanctum
of the urinal that had long become inaccessible thanks to the
clogged urine outlet. Covering the area around the footrests
was the amber stagnant liquid—which at places had begun to
congeal, a muddy algal substance showing through its surface—

while dotting the dry or partially dry patches was an assortment of faecal mounds of various sizes and colour. Obviously, some inexorable bowel movements had deconstructed it being a mere urinal, freeing it from functional fixity; completing the picture was the fact that all the corners and walls of the enclosure were splattered with gobs of chewed betel, snot and phlegm. Ram Mohan and Baijnath made for the boundary wall.

Their train was on the platform, a passenger train. There was no rush for seats. Most of the coaches were only partially filled, and the one in which Ram Mohan spotted a man in white khadi sitting cross-legged, was nearly empty. The man was not alone. On the opposite berth sat two men listening to what he was saying. Ram Mohan and Baijnath got on and took the two side seats facing each other along the aisle next to those three. Of late Ram Mohan had started thinking about active politics. The idea had first occurred to him a few years ago when Mr Singh, the politician from Bihar, had spoken about the need to join politics in independent India. It was a time when instances of politicians known for their contribution to the world of letters would abound. Dr Sampoornanand, their present chief minister, was a renowned scholar of Hindi and Sanskrit, and Ram Mohan, familiar with the man's literary and reformist writings, knew that literature and politics, contrary to being discordant, could complement each other. While political power was bound to distinguish a man of letters in literary circles, a literary and linguistic bent would mark him off from fellow politicians.

———————

'I don't think he'd give so much of his precious time even to a collector,' said Ram Mohan.

'That doesn't help, does it?' Baijnath blurted out.

'We must accept he was sympathetic and well-meaning and wanted to help. Or why did he have to elaborate on the PM's priorities for the country? What are we to such an important official? Or for that matter, what could we have done if he'd brushed us off on some pretext or the other? Yet, he gave us a patient hearing and reasons for his inability to grant our request. It's a positive sign which means he recognizes our cause.'

Their neighbour, the man in white and his two sidekicks had stopped talking, looking snared by Ram Mohan's stylish and chaste Hindi. They glanced at Baijnath and seemed flummoxed at his morose look. 'These bureaucrats,' Ram Mohan continued, 'are suffused with a sense of responsibility and strength of purpose, having long girded for helping realize the future envisioned by Nehru ji.'

'A future—' Baijnath's voice drowned in the scream of the whistle from the steam engine; then there was a jolt as the train moved off. Clearing his throat, he repeated the sentence a little stridently, 'A future with no education for girls and the poor.'

'Can anybody in their right senses accuse Nehru of neglecting education?' said Ram Mohan. 'When you have the task of rebuilding a country, your priorities have to be very clear at the outset; that's the whole point the official was trying to illustrate when he talked of the fact that Nehru ji has to push ahead with more urgent things like heavy industry, science and technology, and international affairs . . . He's a world figure now; many foreign leaders look to him for leadership.'

Listening to Ram Mohan with admiration the man in white khadi on the neighbouring berth spoke up, 'We should be proud of our PM. Our country may be very poor and full of problems but we're not short on world class leadership. Few political figures in the world can match Nehru ji's stature, his personality, erudition and knowledge of English.' Ram Mohan found the man's mien engaging; he spoke slowly and thoughtfully, with pauses acting as teasers, building up the interest of the listeners.

Kishan Lal Tiwari was slim and looked polished; his face was evocative of ancient Greek philosophers as seen sketched in history books. He came from a village on the outskirts of Fatehpur—a small town about eighty kilometres east of Kanpur—and belonged to an influential landholding Brahman family. Recently elected village chief, he had come to Lucknow to meet his political mentor, an MLA from his region, and was going to Kanpur now to visit some relation.

Baijnath looked exasperated, 'But can the issue of educating our children wait? This should be our first priority. Even the schools we have for boys are a disgrace, with no arrangements for teaching to be effective; and about the teachers the least said the better.'

Looking at Baijnath, then at Ram Mohan, Tiwari ji said, 'By the way, what do you do exactly?'

'I teach Hindi literature at D.A.V. College.'

'Forgive me for asking, but can I know your caste?' said Tiwari ji; when told he continued, 'I think you shouldn't limit yourself to being just a teacher. You'll make an impressive politician; there's hardly any Kurmi leader worth his salt in UP. It's like a void out there, waiting for you to fill. If you convince the state Congress of your usefulness to the party, I think nothing can stop you from making the big time. Once in the Assembly or Parliament, your command of language and speaking ability will ensure your success.'

Pleased at this praise, that too from a Brahman whom he hardly knew, Ram Mohan said, 'To tell the truth, I've been thinking on these lines . . . The problem is, when the Congress has solid support of Brahmans, Muslims and Harijans to get it to the throne, why would it bother to entertain other castes? They already have a winning combination in place . . . I don't believe in the caste system, and to know that at the end of the day all my hard work would stand subordinated to my caste, pains me no end.'

Tiwari ji said, 'that is why I advise you to work towards proving your electoral strength . . . that you can have your caste rally to your support. Once you get the Congress ticket and win the election, you'd have many opportunities to show your abilities acquired through personal exertions.'

'Even to prove that I'll have to contest an election . . .'

'Yes . . . But there're other ways to do that. You can organize a large gathering in your area and invite some Congress leader to address it. The leader's bound to take note. Or you can, as you say, fight an election just to show your caste following . . . as an independent, I mean. And you might also win. I'm not denying the possibility . . . If you don't win, then on the basis of your performance, you can start lobbying the Congress leadership for a ticket next time. If the party is unable to field you, it might accommodate you somewhere else . . . in the government or the party.'

Ram Mohan said, glancing at Baijnath, 'We organized a gathering soon after Independence where the chairman of Bihar Legislative Council was the main speaker. He belongs to our caste and has recently been appointed Governor of some state.'

'Orissa,' said Baijnath.

'That's fine . . . What you need now is the hand of a big Congress leader on your head; most of them are Brahmans, but given your speaking skill you can't fail to make an impression. The combination of the two, your caste base combined with patronage from a Congress leader, will put you on the road to success.'

'I'll have to look for a suitable seat,' said Ram Mohan.

'Yes, because the constituency under which your village falls is milling with Brahmans; even Thakurs outnumber you there. You can't get enough votes to force the Congress to pause and ponder.'

Baijnath nodded.

'But there's a reason why I brought up the question of your getting into politics.'

Ram Mohan sat up.

'Right next door there exists a constituency, I'd say, tailor-made for you.' Tiwari ji stopped to clear his throat. 'A sizeable chunk of voters there are Kurmi. If this potential could be tapped . . . if they could be made conscious of their strength leading them to vote en block, then even the electoral defeat can be brandished as political victory.'

'It can't be Ghatampur which is a reserved constituency,' Ram Mohan thought aloud.

'It's Fatehpur, the area I come from.'

'But some local politicians there are already making a case for themselves.'

'You call them politicians?' said Tiwari ji. 'They're myopic, small-time and petty; no one bothers about them . . . It'll take some time, no doubt. But if you feel up to it, I'm sure these people will leave the field clear for you. The next parliamentary election is far off; you have plenty of time to test the waters and lay the ground work accordingly.'

The train had entered the purlieus of the city of Kanpur; was now crossing the bridge over the Ganges; they could hear the raining of coins into the sacred river from the slow-moving train, the popular practice in the hope of greater returns.

'What about you Tiwari ji, will you support me openly if I contest?'

Tiwari ji fell into silence as though to align his thoughts.

'You might be surprised, but I'll support you with no holds barred. I know how my community will react. There'll be taunts, catcalls and yowls of derision. It'll be mortifying for my relations to have to explain my stand to people around them. And certainly, my association with your campaign will get you no Brahman votes except, of course, of my immediate family.'

Tiwari ji's two companions hadn't spoken a word all this while; now they were nodding in approval.

'But in time I can take the sting out of their opposition. I'll describe you as the one possessed of traits long identified with Brahmans. Your way of speaking, knowledge of Sanskrit, being in the teaching profession and so on and so forth; that you were born in a peasant caste but you came to acquire the qualities of Brahmans . . . Even this won't convince them, I know . . . but their hostility to me will lose some of its intensity; they'll have seen some justification for my otherwise bizarre behaviour.' This was the beginning of a life-long association, which would surprise all for its steadfastness.

———————

Leaving Ram Mohan in Kanpur, Baijnath set off for Ballamgaon, crestfallen. The thought that Kanti might have to let go of her school was very disquieting. Ram Mohan's Chacha had lately been griping about her spending more time as teacher than as bahu, though Kanti's mother-in-law was sympathetic to the venture. But Baijnath knew it might come to an end if Kanti's burden was not eased in time. Then he thought of Ram Mohan's confidence and felt his despondency giving way to hope. He'd grown appreciative of his son-in-law's ability to not let a setback put a damper on his fight. Recalling his push, while still a student, for the change of the name of their railway station, he told himself the present setback would, if anything, fire Ram Mohan with a sense of purpose. Even the idea of the renaming of the railway station had seemed unfeasible at the time, but Ram Mohan's eventual triumph had proved otherwise;

it had established him as the tallest figure in the area dominated by high castes. With his spirits up now, Baijnath could explain to Kanti the apparently futile excursion to Lucknow in more constructive terms.

Though Kanti's sister was a great help in running the school, she could not be depended on for long now that she had turned sixteen and was well into marriageable age. Their relatives were already in the wings to come down on the family for transgression; but of a different make, Baijnath could negotiate the situation with fortitude. Kanti's mother found it hard to relate to her husband's idiosyncratic ways. His only undoing was his lack of means.

Kanti's school, in addition to being short of teachers, had no funds to mention for the needed primers and stationery; to expect the students' families to provide anything other than a wooden slate would be too much, most of whom would sooner keep their daughters illiterate than go to the expense of the said items. Thus it also fell to Kanti to arrange some rudimentary material to enable her to carry on with her school business; to help her, Baijnath had to regularly squeeze some money out of his own limited budget. However, his renewed confidence in Ram Mohan was to be borne out sooner than expected. By and by the school received official recognition accompanied by ancillary support, which again led to the fanning of legends of Ram Mohan's clout with the authorities. That he would bring it off so quickly, Ram Mohan himself had had no idea; rather he was surprised by the turn of events that resulted in unexpected success.

Acting astutely, he had seized a chance presented to him circumstantially, and turned it to his advantage. It was the occasion of the first centenary of the Mutiny, to commemorate which the city administration had held a function in Nana Rao Park—named after the great hero of the revolt, Nana

Sahab—with the State's education minister Dixit ji as the chief guest; presiding over the programme was none other than the bureaucrat whom Ram Mohan and Baijnath had met in Lucknow a few months before.

Fortuitously, one of the speakers at the function was Ram Mohan, whose oration stood out from other speeches, remembering the martyrdom of the rebel sepoys. Dixit ji—the chief guest—nodded in praise. The bureaucrat also applauded; though what set the seal on the official recognition and aid for Kanti's school was not his speech but something unanticipated. In their enthusiasm the organizers had dug out descendants of two individuals whose professional services were used by Nana Sahab's men in Kanpur during the Uprising; the reference is to the incidents of Sattichaura and Bibighar that had given the Christians a taste of what Hindus and Muslims could do when it came to restoring the dignity of their culture. Nana Sahab together with his sidekicks Tantia Topi and Azeemullah had managed to entice the Britishers from General Wheeler's entrenchment. Wheeler at first acted like a tough customer. Suspicious of the rebels' intentions, he refused to come out, but seeing the plight of his men, women and children, some old and sick, he agreed to leave the camp on one condition: that Nana Sahab sign a treaty allowing them safe passage to Allahabad along the river Ganges. While Nana Sahab was at it, his spirited followers were busy gathering thousands of Hindus and Muslims at Satichaura ghat, who were to witness the great spectacle of terror and suffering, and rejoice at the hundreds of Christians being dispatched to hell.

Seeing the crowds, the survivors mistook them for curious onlookers; no sooner had they started to board the boats than the orgy of killing was set in motion. The rebel sepoys, unwavering in their resolve and cheered on by the crowds, exhibited unparalleled strength of purpose in achieving their end as they went on cutting down single-mindedly the people whose presence on their pious land was a blot on the Hindu and Islamic landscape. But despite their plan to kill them all, some did manage to swim away to safety; Nana Sahab and his men were left with only seventy-three English women and one hundred and twenty-four children, who were incarcerated in a building called Bibighar.

It was the season of the worst of the heat and humidity. Quite a few of the captives had fallen sick, some suffering from severe bouts of dysentery. Nana Sahab and his lieutenants kept dilly-dallying for nearly two weeks before deciding to kill them. Then there was another hiccup. The sepoys entrusted with the job got cold feet at the last moment; when they aimed their guns through the windows at women and children inside, they were met by excruciating screams. The frightened children had huddled around their mothers, howling incessantly, and drowned in the agonizing chaos was the constant groaning of the sick lying on the floor. Turning their guns upward, the sepoys fired a few shots at the ceiling before retreating. Nana Sahab's personal servant Begum Khanum laid into the sepoys, making full use of her reservoir of invective, which she thought might cleanse them of squeamishness. The sepoys were adamant and left. Finally one Sarvar Khan, rumoured to be her lover, was asked to organize the slaughter. The person he sent for was a famous butcher who was to lead a few others of his ilk to hack the Christian women and children to death.

This famous butcher happened to be the great grandfather of one of the two picked by the city authorities to receive honours on the occasion of the hundredth anniversary of the country's 'First War of Independence'. After being presented with the mementoes, they were called upon to share any interesting stories they might've heard about their great grandfathers. Though illiterate, the meat-seller turned out to be rather articulate and vivid. He made quite a speech.

'I was twelve when my father taught me how to butcher, skin, and cut up a goat. Before that, before the actual initiation into the business of butchery, I along with other male children in the family would be made to watch the slaughter of goats. At first, we used to cry and tremble as the animal thrashed about in mortal pain; slowly as it became a ritual, I was able to get a better hold on my feelings. Yet the day when I was to be introduced to the act of knifing a goat, smaller in size than usual, I just couldn't bring myself to rub its neck with the knife thrust into my hand; my father who held the animal down yelled at me, but I ran away crying. My old grandfather who was lying in a charpoy nearby sat up and called me. Seating me beside him, he explained that I mustn't look the animal in the eye while slaughtering it. Then he told me the story of Bibighar.

'"It was the biggest test of your great grandfather's life. Tasked with slaughtering a big group of women and children kept in a big room, stinking of urine and excrement as some of them were very sick, he led some butchers inside. Seeing big knives in their hands, the terrified captives started shrieking; children clung to their mothers who entreated my father to let them meet Nana Sahab just for once. But after giving orders, he'd left, leaving his right-hand men Tantia Topi and Azeemullah to oversee the massacre. Blessed with stouter heart than Nana Sahab, Tantia shouted at Sarvar Khan to tell his men to hurry up . . . You're scared of slaughtering a goat, son! Think of your great grandfather who didn't flinch from cutting up humans albeit they were foreigners. A duty is a duty. The sight of crying children who were pissing and shitting in their clothes had even turned the stomach of some of my father's colleagues, so your great grandfather had had to kill a large number of these children himself, many of them girls."

'This was my great grandfather . . . who was also there the morning after to supervise the removal of bodies, limbs and chunks of flesh from the room, which then, along with a boy still breathing, were thrown into this very well right here,' he pointed to its rim, the only sign left of the well—its mouth had been bricked up—overlooking which was a bust of Tantia Topi, the "master butcher" as the British would call him. 'For a hundred years my great grandfather's courage and bravery has remained in obscurity. Today I'm thankful to Collector Sahab for honouring his family.'

Even as the butcher spoke, Dixit ji and the bureaucrat had looked uncomfortable; after the speech there was momentary silence. People seemed confounded. Then, some in the audience broke into confused applause, which shortly turned into a wave as others joined in. What the man told in his speech was something entirely different from the general perception of the doings of rebels in Kanpur. The prevalent story of the covered up well in Nana Rao Park was that Nana Sahab and his men had thrown the English soldiers into it after killing them. Even Dixit ji, the bureaucrat, the collector and the likes had no idea of what the man had proudly described. The union education ministry had commissioned a book on the sepoy revolt and the Uprising, published concurrent with the centenary; the avowed aim of the book was to present an objective study of the rebellion, yet it had to be sensitive to the nationalist discourse on the matter; it could not dwell on anything that would spoil the official take. The author did mention the grisly episodes of Kanpur and condemned them in passing, but he took care to camouflage them with the atrocities of the English troops to squash the Uprising; it also sought to exonerate Nana Sahab from his complicity in the massacres, citing the lack of evidence. The Congress and other nationalist forces had already co-opted the sepoy mutiny, acquiescing to it being called India's first war of independence. The phrase was sort of lifted from the book titled 'The Indian War of Independence 1857' authored by none other than Vinayak Savarkar, the famous mastermind of the Hindutva ideology.

By telling his story, the honoured claimant to the legacy of his great grandfather had unwittingly set the cat among the pigeons. The VIP duo, Dixit ji and the bureaucrat, standing on the stage strewn with rose petals fallen from the two big-sized garlands that had been put around their necks, looked vexed; the city mayor, the collector, two police officials and some others were trying to mollify them. Ram Mohan walked up to them, as the bureaucrat, head bent, arms crossed over the chest and eyes fixed on his own feet, listened to what was being said, while Dixit ji in his sparkling white khadi was gazing in silence at the bust of Tantia Topi a few yards to his left.

'Sir, if I had known at all, I wouldn't have called the man,' the Collector said pleadingly.

'That's what makes me wonder. How can the administration decide to honour someone without knowing anything about the nature of their association with the Uprising?'

Mayor Sahab, coming to the rescue of the collector, said, 'Actually it was my idea. I thought it would impart a touch of concreteness to the remembrance; even I was ignorant of the butchery involved in the whole thing. A clerk in my office had recommended this fellow.'

Even this did not lessen the bureaucrat's chagrin.

'Mayor Sahab, there's nothing wrong in your suggesting something. It's the responsibility of the people under him,' said the bureaucrat nodding at the Collector. 'They have to ensure the persons chosen for such bestowal of honour don't say anything that can cause embarrassment.'

Dixit ji, irritated at this beating around the bush, said with a tone of finality, 'No point in going on and on in this manner. Please tell me how you people are going to keep it from reaching the ears of Delhi. I can handle it in our state where people aren't very particular about how our heroes behave while fighting for a cause. The problem is with the English-educated crop of leaders in Delhi. They would have nowhere to run if a controversy of this nature were to be aroused over the conduct of some of the great leaders of the Uprising. It would wreck the entire ethical dimension of the popular discourse of . the first war of independence . . . I am sure you people noticed the way the audience today seemed bewildered by the man's story. They might have thought it to be an anecdote made up by his grandfather to help him overcome his squeamishness.' Dixit ji stopped, and then added impishly, 'The reality of the story was more or less lost on most of them.'

Dixit ji held the education portfolio not for nothing. His explication was also an attempt to understand the gravity of the problem at hand. Conscious of the standards of provincial journalism, he was anxious about how the function would be reported in the local press. He did not want to leave the matter unattended.

'Mayor Sahab, you know how indiscreet sometimes our local journalists can be. There are occurrences in history, which if not contextualized, can cost the big picture. To appreciate the nub of something as frenzied as the great Uprising one has to avoid making an issue of these instances of savagery perpetrated by rebels, or it would unravel our attempts to give out an easy-to-understand version of our first war of independence. The general public can't be subjected to the painful complexities involved in cracking those traumatic events.'

It was almost noon. But the sun was still struggling to force its way through the clouds that had started gathering at dawn, which aided by a cool breeze, dispensed with the searing heat of the previous week, while complementing the weather was the beautiful greenery of the Nana Rao Park.

Dixit ji said to Mayor Sahab and the Collector, 'Now tell me how you're going to ensure the butcher's story . . . let alone his being honoured at my hands . . . finds no mention in the local press? Gosh, how it marred the pathos of the occasion!'

'Sir, I know the proprietor of the daily newspaper here,' said the mayor. 'In fact, he started the paper more than a decade ago to help in the national cause. I can assure you of his cooperation. But one of the weekly papers "Kanpur Vivechna" is openly hostile to me; its editor was also in the mayoral race; if he gets wind of my wish to suppress the story, he'll make it the banner headline. The other tabloids can be taken care of.'

Ram Mohan gestured to the bureaucrat; they moved away to the edge of the stage. A minute later the bureaucrat returned and introduced Ram Mohan to Dixit ji, 'Sir, this is Ram Mohan; he teaches at D.A.V. College here and is friends with the journalist who came to cover this event for this paper. He says he can persuade the journalist to not write in his report what the butcher said.'

'Wonderful. Thank you, Ram Mohan ji. We need young men like you. People should think constructively, and I'm sorry to say that members of such an august institution as journalism sometimes see their salvation only in running after controversies.'

The bureaucrat tapped Ram Mohan on the shoulder and said, 'Sir, he's also involved in social and educational issues in his village. He came to meet me some time back seeking help for the primary school for girls that his wife has started; it'll be nice if their school gets official recognition along with some funds to help them carry on the good work.'

Addressing Ram Mohan, Dixit ji said, 'As soon as you're done with the task at hand, come to Lucknow with a written application. I'll see what can be done.'

They were now walking Dixit ji and the bureaucrat to their waiting vehicles, the usual paraphernalia representing the movement of a state cabinet minister. The bureaucrat instructed his driver to follow as he got in beside the minister in his Ambassador. The red light atop the two cars had long become a beacon of power, a delicious fruit born out of the struggle against the foreign rule.

Baijnath's trust reposed in Ram Mohan was finally justified; Kanti's school, to her disbelief and relief, was soon granted some funds; it also got one more teacher to help manage things; her name was Gayatri. Now the question of how she could suitably be housed in Parsadpur needed to be addressed, and Ram Mohan, having been told of her closeness to Dixit ji, provided the answer. His house had a kind of garret where she could stay comfortably.

Gayatri's husband had died before the consummation of their marriage. A fire in a house nearby altered everything for her. He was one of those trying to douse it when a burning beam fell on him. His family could not delink the sudden death from the arrival of Gayatri, the timing of it being too close for comfort. Even her smashing looks, a matter of pride for them before the tragedy, now signalled something sinister; the clue to the catastrophe, according to the family priest, lay in the marriage not consummated. He posited that the lost soul of someone who would have been denied his rightful claim in the previous life was guarding over her. Her virginity was off-limits that is. Naturally her status changed from that of a dignified

bahu of a respectable family to one who had turned out to be
a curse.

Gayatri's father had died when she was very young; her
brothers were younger still. Her Mama eventually rescued her
from the hell she had stumbled into; he knew Dixit ji who
represented his area in the state Assembly. Sympathetic and
kind, Dixit ji had arranged for her—she was educated enough
to teach small children—to stay in Lucknow and do a one year
teacher's training programme, after which he got her this job.
Parsadpur was her first posting.

On getting word from Lucknow, Ram Mohan had reached
Parsadpur and sent Kanti along with Badri and Baijnath to meet
Gayatri at the Parsadpur railway station. And when he saw them
in the distance, he could make out Gayatri in the middle; she
was accompanied by her maternal uncle. Her face was still a
blur, yet Ram Mohan had no doubt as to the shapely figure
clad tautly in a white sari with a black border. Even the path, a
typical village dirt track, seemed to have specially been laid so
this beauty could tread on it. She was fair and had an oval face
furnished with sloe eyes, a fetching nose, a slightly broad mouth
equipped with winsomely up-curving lip; the small scar on her
left cheek failed woefully to make any dent in her arresting
attractiveness. Rather the vertical lesion touching the corner of
the mouth deepened her sensuality.

Her head as she walked appeared faintly thrown back to the
left, letting it slip to an expert eye that though a simple soul she
was not innocent of her top-drawer looks. Ram Mohan realized
wistfully how just one amiable glance from her could drive any
lovelorn soul to a desperate sense of desolation. Exerting his
will, he reined back his thoughts. Gayatri was related to the
minister. He had to be careful.

———————

Kanti being several years older treated Gayatri like a younger sister. Any sneering hint at her widowhood would invite Kanti's angry reaction. Ram Mohan's mother too was kind to her, often bemoaning the workings of the cruel hands of destiny. In time, Kanti's children—Nisha, Nishant and Sandhya—would grow very close to Gayatri, spending a lot of time in the garret playing with her. Nisha and Nishant had started school while Sandhya was still too young; Gayatri taught her the Hindi alphabet; Kanti was relieved to have Gayatri around. About a year later, Kanti gave birth to her fourth child, Deena. Nisha would not leave the baby alone; after coming back from school she tended to Deena with their grandmother watching over, which allowed Kanti to attend to other household chores, while Gayatri could stay back in school to clean the classroom and organize things for the next day.

Learning of Gayatri's schedule, Ram Mohan had advanced his weekend arrivals by a few hours; instead of taking the shuttle that reached Parsadpur in the evening, he had started travelling by the passenger train arriving in the afternoon. He would stop at the school on his way and wait for Gayatri to finish and bring her back home, though he did not have her person entirely to himself, for apart from some girl or girls with her, there would be Badri, Gulab Singh and others who invariably met him at the station. He did not resent the bargain. To be seen walking alone in the company of a young widow that too an out-and-out knockout would have caused a stir. Besides, the presence of others had helped him overcome the initial awkwardness with her. Other than that, he sparkled more naturally in a bigger audience.

So, instead of catching her alone and attempting stiffly at conversation with his heart racing—which would be fraught with the risk of losing the leverage of the colour of his personality—it was always wise to first make her conscious of his bright perky self in public, and wait, letting her think of him at her leisure, and then murmur subtly nuanced words to her in private as and when an opportunity came. Of the long passage and its pitfalls he was aware. But stepping on the gas could scuttle the project. Given the stake he did not mind the long haul and was willing to be patient before tiptoeing towards the goal that promised unimaginable depths of pleasure.

* * *

The only rival to Ram Mohan's salacity was the desire for learning. Just being known as a learned man would not do. He wanted to be intellectually feared. A few among his peers at D.A.V. College had already done a PhD; some were to receive the honour soon. He could not remain without one for long; he approached the head of the Hindi department—Trivedi ji—who he acknowledged as a scholar because of his masterly knowledge of Sanskrit. Ram Mohan's main literary adversary among his peers was one Mishra who did not have a PhD yet; they both vied for his attention though Ram Mohan had an inkling of Trivedi ji having a soft spot for his rival, and the topic he suggested to Ram Mohan for his doctorate could easily be seen as a trap by any perceptive mind.

It was an obscure poet of seventeenth century, from a saintly sect devoted to Nirgun Brahm, an ultimate unqualified being. There was little material available on him. Even his verses had not been collected, and none in the Hindi department seemed to know of anybody who could help Ram Mohan gain a toehold in the world of this poet-saint. Clearly, the task required a great deal of fieldwork in Rajasthan, the region to which the poet belonged. His predicament was one of the talking points in the department. He also suspected that the topic suggested was a ploy to keep him engaged in a pointless exercise that would gnaw away at his confidence. Had he wanted he could have backed out. Ram Mohan embraced the challenge. He would liken his nature to that of a river that revealed its real strength when prodded by obstacles.

On his next visit to Parsadpur he brought up his PhD mission during a meal. His mother as usual expressed her displeasure. She tended to disagree with anything threatening to keep her son away from her for long. She wondered in annoyance when he would finish his studies. Ram Mohan laughed and explained that this was the most important degree for anyone wanting to be taken seriously in this profession; when he told her there were people who wanted him to fail, her motherly weakness was transmuted into exhortation for him to succeed. The news of his new undertaking was directed at everyone, his mother, Chacha and Kanti, but the way he packaged it was meant exclusively for Gayatri, who was sitting on the floor beside his mother not far from where Ram Mohan and his Chacha were having food sitting cross-legged on small stools. A little self-conscious in Ram Mohan's presence, she was trying to engage Nishant and Sandhya who hovered nearby; Kanti was making chapattis in the far corner that served as kitchen. Talking in a measured tone, he was using words that made him sound dignified, which was odd in his home setting and had his mother peeved, for while talking to her and his Chacha, Ram Mohan would use the village dialect. She did not object, perhaps thinking the topic of the conversation could not be elucidated in any other manner. But Ram Mohan—with respect to his yearning—knew there was something that only his absence could achieve. He wanted the lilt of his voice and sound of his words to keep ringing in Gayatri's consciousness while he was gone. He had already embarked on his quest during one of their walks from Kanti's school, knowing that the first crucial stage of any such journey consisted in signalling one's interest to the woman so desired;

then let the idea work on her before resorting to a clearer hint to get the drift if she was game. To Ram Mohan's glee, Gayatri innocently provided him with a fortuitous moment to kick-start his expedition.

Fond of listening to the All India Radio (AIR) on the small transistor, she had heard a ghazal sung by a famous singer, one of the couplets of which had particularly charmed her; the reason was the way it sounded, not the meaning, but thanks to the style of the singer she had remembered tidbits of that particular couplet of this ghazal which Ram Mohan knew by heart, the entire ghazal, a very famous one.

Pattaa-patta, bootaa-bootaa haal hamaaraa jaaney hai,
Jaaney na jaaney, gull hi na jaaney, baagh to saaraa jaaney hai.

He told her about its poet Meer, one of the two tallest pillars of Urdu poetry, the other one being Ghalib. To Gayatri's surprise, Ram Mohan rendered most of its couplets then and there, singing in his own way, with impeccable tonal inflections, emphasizing the beauty of Urdu words. She could not curb her smile when he came to the said couplet, in which Meer laments that if indifference were not the norm among the beautiful, even the most naïve of them would have the cure for the yearnings of his heart. While explaining it, Ram Mohan took great pains not to be overtly explicit for fear it might unnerve her; he just alluded to the irony the poet wished to convey, that even a simpleton possessed the ability to soothe an ache of this nature. Unnoticed by his friends, he flicked a look at Gayatri and segued into another topic but not before catching the sudden deepening of her complexion, enough to convince him of having given her some food for thought.

And now with the way he was talking about his PhD project, he tried to present a different side of his personality—a level-headed, authentic intellectual persona—a far cry from the lovesick heart in Meer's couplet. He knew the potency of this combination with respect to seduction. The notion of important men being thus vulnerable could lend any woman with a modest background a strange sense of amour propre. He was also aware of the virtue of tempering one's sensual pursuit with an air of insouciance. His absences for reasons of some scholarly engagement would also come in handy, giving his person a gloss of gravitas.

His words of wisdom to his friends in Kanpur would often be: Do not confuse flippancy with humour while trying to impress a woman. You'll put her to flight if she is sensible and worth pursuing.

The flame of political ambition kindled by Kishan Lal Tiwari was still burning bright in Ram Mohan. It was one of the reasons Ram Mohan did not want to defer his research work any further. Parliamentary and Assembly elections might still be a few years away; he wanted to employ this time to achieve his scholarly objective, a feather in his cap; after which he could think of a way to assert his presence in the political arena as well. It could be either through contesting an election as suggested by Tiwari ji or through associating with the campaign of some important candidate of the Congress. But if he decided to be in the fray, it would not only be to prove his following. He would fight with a view to securing victory by convincing castes other than Kurmis of his merit.

The mere thought of surprising them by his ability to quote from Sanskrit classics and Tulsidas's *Ramcharitmanas* was uplifting. He was never apolitical, but his interest in politics after meeting Tiwari ji had jumped to another level; he would make it a point now to keep abreast of all important political happenings. Just the previous year, he had taken part in a public meeting in Kanpur organized to condemn the allegations of corruption against Nehru government. It was district Congress committee's answer to the protest rallies of the Communist Party and the People's Union, the right-wing Hindu party; the former had a strong support base among the workers in state-owned mills of Kanpur, the latter drew its strength from the city's Hindu shopkeepers.

Given his poor grasp of the details, Ram Mohan simply lambasted the opposition, declaring that it was a sin to even insinuate that the allegations could be true; to back up his contention, he invoked the figures of Gandhi, Patel, Nehru and the like whose values were the cornerstone of the Congress. Biting at each word, Ram Mohan wondered how a respectable member of the Union cabinet chosen by Nehru ji could be accused of any financial misconduct. His speech had brought tears to the eyes of some old Congressmen. Later however, the controversy had transformed into a monstrous scandal, brought to light by none other than Nehru's estranged son-in-law, a Congress MP. He had raised the issue in Parliament. What had seemed to have transpired was that the Life Insurance Corporation of India had ploughed a huge amount of money into a private company of tenuous reputation; the shares were bought the day the stock markets were closed and at a price much above their market-value. The resulting uproar forced the government to order a judicial enquiry, which found the finance minister guilty of making the fraudulent investment. He had no option but to resign. It was the first big instance of government corruption coming to surface in independent India, which shocked Ram Mohan into making a fetish of financial honesty and pouring scorn on people suspected of bribery.

* * *

Before Ram Mohan could plunge into research on the poet-saint, there had been a couple of more Congress-related events to engage him. Soon after the scandal, Nehru dropped the bomb of his reluctance to continue as PM, arguing the position demanded ceaseless work, leaving him with no time 'for quiet thinking'. The Congress was thrown into turmoil. Congressmen across the country were falling over themselves to issue appeals to the party to pay no heed to the hideous idea. When local congress leaders in Kanpur met to pass a resolution against Pandit ji's 'request', Ram Mohan committed a political faux pas by suggesting—to the extreme embarrassment of all the office bearers in the committee—that the resolution should also urge Nehru ji to identify and nurture an alternative leadership before he could think of quitting. Ram Mohan had to be shouted down by all those present. 'We're shocked and disgusted at this temerity,' bellowed a committee member. Anyway, the crisis blew over shortly as Nehru quit the idea of quitting by bowing down to the party's wish.

Ram Mohan could not make sense of the severity of the reaction to his innocuous rather intelligent suggestion. He had had no idea that anyone even remotely hinting that there could be an alternative to Nehru was persona non grata in the Congress, that his regularly bowing down to the party's wish suited not only his cause but that of his daughter's future, which dawned on Ram Mohan when she was elected party president at the Congress session in Nagpur. The party's decision took Nehru by surprise, apparently, and he aired his reservations about it, yet after mulling it over he would decide to 'keep apart from this business'. He did however admit that 'it has its disadvantages'; that it was rather in poor taste: his daughter being the party president while he was PM. But after Patel was gone and Rajaji quietened down, the Congress had been firmly under Nehru's sway. His wish—forgive the cliché—

was others' command. Still, on the question of his daughter
heading the Congress, Nehru preferred to bow down to the
party's wish.

To celebrate and welcome Indira Gandhi's election as party
president, the district Congress committee of Kanpur held a
function, but Ram Mohan was denied the opportunity to speak
this time. There was one more reason why he got short shrift.
In the local Congress circle, Ram Mohan was considered a
supporter of Baran Singh, an important minister in the state;
famous for his role in the abolition of zamindari system in UP,
Singh was an honest and plain-speaking Jat leader from western
UP, a leader who had the interests of peasant community
uppermost in his mind. Ram Mohan's enthusiasm had
impressed him; also the fact that he was Kurmi. It was Shukla
ji who first brought him to Baran Singh's notice. Shukla ji,
who—the reader would remember from the violent episode at
a wedding—was indebted to Ram Mohan whose intervention
had saved him from being done out of the prized virginity
of a very young nautch girl, something that he believed was
rightfully his. Active in state politics, Shukla ji now was a
member of the Legislative Assembly.

But this valued connection had now turned into a liability;
because Baran Singh had let the pickaxe of his brashness wreck
the path of his own growth in the Congress. He had voiced
objection to Nehru's proposal for cooperative farming at the
Congress session in Nagpur, dealing a blow to the general piety.
Opposed to Nehru's economic policies, he had termed the
proposal impractical; he might have thought his candour could
rub shoulders with Pandit ji's graciousness. He had not reckoned
with his daughter. Already the party president, she would have
taken note of this irreverence.

Taking its cue from Baran Singh's shaky future in the Congress, the district committee had quickly risen to the need for Ram Mohan to be sidelined, but he—to his detractors' surprise—showed no sign of sullenness. That was not without reason. Ram Mohan had an alternate calling to fall back on, which he found equally, if not more, agreeable. Rather he was a trifle relieved. He could now get down to some serious research work with no distraction, though he had not given up on his chances in politics. His apparent stoicism was calculated to help him calmly assess the political ball game while engaged in an academically fulfilling pursuit. He would try, as was the idea, to finish his thesis by the time of the third general election. Before his trip to Rajasthan regarding his research, Ram Mohan went to Lucknow to meet Chaudhary Baran Singh, who after being cued in on the turn of events in Kanpur, rose and while gesturing for Ram Mohan to remain seated, left the room, and returned with a thick file in his hand with his middle finger stuck into it, marking some page. Opening the file, he handed it to Ram Mohan motioning him to read.

'You have tea while I dispose of some official work,' he said and went out of the room. Ram Mohan flipped through the file that contained papers generated through bureaucratic mesh in the run-up to the abolition of zamindari; then he turned to that which Chaudhary Sahab had pointed to him. It was a note written by the CM Sampoornanand, the scholarly, reflective leader, whose thinking had been informed early on by socialist ideology. But in that note he sounded leery of the proposed legislation—seeking to scrap the feudalistic institution called zamindari—the chief architect of which was Baran Singh, the revenue minister. The note, originally in Hindi, ran like this:

'*This* [legislation regarding zamindari abolition] *means assembling one more army of our opponents. We have managed to turn against us each such section of the populace, which hitherto has been in possession of education, property, social prestige and political clout. We must not forget that these are the people who have helped maintain the law and order in our society; the steps we have already taken, and the ones we propose to take, will definitely have a detrimental impact on the interests of the upper castes. And we must remember that these sections in general have put their back into our struggle, and riding on their shoulders we have come to power. But the measures our government has publicly stood by have either benefitted the landless or those with very little land. Subdued pique and frustration accumulated through centuries have led them to being cut off from the rest of us. These people* [the poor and the landless] *have been provided leadership only by outfits like Shoshit Sangh* [Association of the Exploited]. *Temperamentally these sections are sceptical about the Congress. No matter what benefits we extend to them they would not come to us.'*

Ram Mohan read the note several times over. He was bewildered by the line of argument taken by the CM, publicly known to be an intellectual, a man of integrity, a follower of Gandhi and Nehru, who had also written a book on Gandhi, extolling his commitment to the good of people, unmindful of the consequences. Like his hero Nehru, this author-cum-politician—and now CM—was said to be imbued with the ideals of socialism. But here in the confidential file, he was adumbrating his belief in power politics, in short term electoral gains, which meant adhering to constitutional values was absurd if it would not spell the prospect of corresponding electoral mileage.

Chaudhary Baran Singh had a frown on his face when he returned. Dressed in white homespun, a staple of political wardrobe, he sat down with a sigh in the chair across Ram Mohan, his dhoti looking dustier than his kurta; adjusting his Gandhi cap, he pulled the centre table aside to rest his feet on. Baran Singh was fair but had been tinged with red by the ruggedness of his political terrain; filling the space between his nose and upper lip was a thick but closely trimmed black moustache. Though slim built and of average stature, he looked taller than his height, because of his upright posture; and his flinty mien obliged people to be a little guarded while interacting with him. His dislike of sycophancy was legendary. But Ram Mohan maintained that nobody could remain immune to adulation. Some people tend to forget, he would say, that this human trait could don diverse garbs, that is, the success of a flatterer lay in the ability to tailor his approach to suit the palate of the praised.

'So what do you think of the views of our honourable chief minister?' asked Chaudhary Baran Singh with a wry grin and shaking his left leg lying across the right one on the table.

'Chaudhary Sahab, I began to consider being in active politics when a friend brought up the subject about a year ago; until then only two things would take up my time, literature and developmental work in my village, though it was obvious that politics would help the cause of Parsadpur a great deal—

'That's the name of your village,' said Baran Singh.

'Yes . . . The question that troubled me was: what would happen to my love of literature? Then all of a sudden the literary profile of our CM flashed through my mind, I made my decision . . . but here . . .' Ram Mohan waved towards the file, '. . . his advocacy of Brahmanism has shaken me a bit. What was all that big talk about moral principles and ethical values and egalitarian outlook underpinning the Congress agenda?'

'The real test of your idealism and intent comes only when you're in power and want to remain there,' said Baran Singh as he glanced at the quiet figure of his secretary waiting in the doorway. Ram Mohan tried to get up; Chaudhary Sahab signalled him to remain seated. 'I've told Savitri Ram Mohan will have lunch here . . .' Then to the secretary, 'If there are any urgent files, get them. I'll go to the office late . . .' He

stood up, took off his cap, tried to discipline an unruly strand
of hair before deftly arranging the cap back on his head using
both the hands.

There were hurried footsteps in the corridor outside and
then Baran Singh's cook looked in.

'Let's go and have food, Ram Mohan.'

Ram Mohan followed Baran Singh, flanked now by his
personal aides in the passage running between rooms on either
side; one of them was whispering into his ear. Just outside a door
Chaudhary Sahab stopped and flung some commands at them,
removed his chappals outside and entered the dining room. Ram
Mohan followed suit. Baran Singh was known for his simple
living, which reflected in the sparseness of his official house;
there was no dining table in the room. Instead, running parallel
to each other were two bamboo mats on the floor, with a strip
of a space left in between for keeping food-filled thalis. They sat
down on the mats, cross-legged, facing each other. Chaudhary
Sahab's wife and the cook could be seen in the kitchen.

'Savitri, you haven't met Ram Mohan.' She came out asking
the cook to get the food, which she had arranged in the thalis.
Ram Mohan greeted her with joined hands.

'He teaches at D.A.V. College in Kanpur. He's a Hindi
scholar, going to do his PhD in literature.' Then to Ram Mohan,
'I'm zero in literature. The only subjects that interested me
were economics and law. I'd started practicing law at Ghaziabad
courts and—'

'But you weren't cut out for that either,' Savitri Devi cut
in. Sitting on the farthest corner of the mat, she said to Ram
Mohan, 'He wouldn't fight the case of those he suspected to
be guilty.'

After they finished eating, Baran Singh led him to the
washbasin; then they were back in the drawing room. 'Even
while practicing law I was active in local politics and before

long got pushed into it full-time. I thought that through politics I could better serve the common man,' Baran Singh paused before going on, 'I'm a hardcore Gandhian and also Arya Samaji as you can guess from that picture there.' They both glanced at Swami Dayanand Saraswati's framed picture on one of the walls. 'But now I admire Gandhi ji more for his intentions than for what he actually achieved. He kept preaching against the sin of untouchability, but not much has changed on that front. Whatever little improvement we can boast of, that's due to Ambedkar's efforts.' He stopped to call his secretary and ask him to get the car ready.

'Chaudhary Sahab, a friend of mine says that but for Ambedkar's aggressive push for the question of social justice, it wouldn't have attained the status it eventually did on the Congress's agenda.'

'No doubt about that. All those freedom fighters were in a hurry to see the back of the British. People like Phule, Ambedkar, Periyar and others sang a tune that jarred with the classical ragas of these upper-caste leaders to whom the meaning of freedom was to capture the power to rule. They thought it was their right. While for Ambedkar and the like, the presence of the British provided the outcastes with a historical opportunity to give voice to their idea of freedom . . . freedom from the degradation and tyranny they suffered at the hands of internal forces.

'Chaudhary Sahab, you're a great well-wisher of the underdog, but going by the general impression, your electoral base consists mainly of the backward castes who are also against Harijans, just like upper castes.'

Baran Sigh sighed and said, 'these so-called backward castes are also very backward with respect to their presence and influence in the administrative structure of our government. Of course, they figure far above the Harijans in the societal setup and are powerful in their regions. Few Brahmans or Thakurs would dare use violence against them to score a point. Also, the aim of the abolition of zamindari was to distribute the land among the tiller, the tenant and the landless, but its chief beneficiaries happen to be these backward or middle castes, who are farmers mostly—'

'One of the reasons they were drawn to you was the part you played in the concerned legislation.'

'But to my dismay, the landless—all of whom are Harijans— got nothing out of it; their condition remains more or less unchanged. To soften the stark situation, some further reforms are needed. Our big leaders wax eloquent on what needs to be done but are at sea about how to go about it.'

'They seem as efficient at making policies for the common good as they are inefficient at acting on them.'

Chaudhary Sahab laughed and said, 'If my efforts had in any way impacted the lives of Harijans in UP, I'd also have their goodwill to count on; now I've no choice but to seek the support of the backward castes, because our electoral democracy doesn't allow us to rise above the caste considerations.' Chaudhary Sahab asked for water.

The man who brought water said the car was in the portico. Baran Singh put on his cap and asked Ram Mohan who had already got up, 'Where are you going? I'll drop you on the way.'

'I'll go to the station to catch the evening passenger. I wanted to meet the minister of primary education to thank him for helping our school for girls, but I don't have an appointment, and it's already getting late.'

'Dixit ji's not in town . . . He's one of the few colleagues on the Cabinet I really like. He's sensible and practical. I'll tell him about you.' He asked the guard to sit in the police Jeep; his secretary with some files got into the front. Baran Singh and

Ram Mohan took the back seat. The driver was told to take a detour and drop Ram Mohan at the railway station first; he gestured to the policemen in the Jeep ahead; one came running to be told of the changed route.

'But Chaudhary Sahab, Gandhi ji was against his son Devdas marrying his friend Rajaji's daughter because of their different castes, and Devdas as a result had to wait many years before Gandhi ji and Rajaji would agree to the alliance.'

'I am a Gandhian, which doesn't mean I have no issues with him. I do. The most fundamental of them is that he always took so long in correcting his skewed thinking. Leaders of his stature shouldn't take this long to recognize a daunting problem, a cruel injustice, such as this; they may take their time to think the problem over before finding ways to fight it. Take the example of Dayanand Saraswati. Right from the time he started out, he attacked the caste system and untouchability. Basing his arguments on the Vedas, he asserted that merit, not caste, should be the basis of one's position in society.'

'But some of his views also contributed to the communal situation; his Arya Samaj is now seen in the vanguard of consolidating mental blocks of mutual suspicion and hostility between Hindus and Muslims.'

Baran Singh turned his head to look at Ram Mohan and nodded, 'That's right, I guess. In his eagerness to prove the primacy of . . . no, not just the primacy but to prove that only the Vedas were the fount of all knowledge, Swami ji dragged Christianity and Islam through the mud. That was unnecessary. It diverted our attention from putting our own house in order to the pleasure of denigrating other peoples' credos. Even today our society is as caste-ridden as ever. Our democracy is hardening caste identities. As you hinted that I'm moving towards the distinction of being the leader of the backward castes, mostly

peasants, because some of my actions and demands are supposed
to have favoured them . . . Thanks to the direction our politics
has taken, it would also be unwise to shrug aside this support.
At the same time, I don't want to become politically dependent
on someone in Delhi and lose my voice. Politics of independent
India is pressuring people like me to court the backing of some
particular castes by making them view their interests in isolation
from others.'

'Chaudhary Sahab, some in the Congress are trying to find
a conflict between your ideas and party's policies. I see it in the
Congress committee's behaviour towards me in Kanpur. There
may be a conspiracy underway to discredit you.'

They had reached outside the station precincts. Just
ahead was the main entrance, crowding around which were
fruit vendors and beggars and a motley choice for means of
transport by way of tongas, ekkas, cycle-rickshaws. Usual din
and dirt pervaded the place. The policemen had got out of the
escort Jeep and were manning the immediate vicinity of the
minister's vehicle.

'They won't succeed,' said Baran Singh. 'Let them plan
and plot. The party has no leader who commands the kind of
support I do in western UP. The Congress has always been
rooted in the tradition of Brahminical machinations, the chief
reason Independence resulted in the country being taken over by
power-brokers . . . agents of partisanship and palm-greasing . . .
with casteism, communalism and corruption becoming the
defining features of our polity.'

Just as Ram Mohan was getting out Baran Singh held his
arm and said, 'You don't worry about these things. Go and
finish your PhD; I'd like you to be considered for an Assembly
seat in the next election.'

Ram Mohan started walking towards the entrance as people
gaped at him. On entering, his eyes fell on the billboard. Armed

with a rose and a smile, Pandit Nehru towered over the public toilet as before. Ram Mohan headed for the wall instead.

———————

To Kanti's surprise, Ram Mohan approved of her pursuing a six-month Lady Social Worker's course, a government-funded project started to provide training in basic healthcare for women. Those selected would be given scholarship to take care of their tuition and hostel fee. She had not expected him to agree, but she knew how he had been won over. It was Gayatri's intercession. During one of her visits to Lucknow, she had learnt about this course from Dixit ji whose ministry's initiative it was. She had seen Kanti's concern for girls and women needing help. Knowing her husband, Kanti was hesitant; Gayatri insisted; she told Baijnath, who then spoke to his daughter. 'You've to come to grips with this side of your husband's nature.' Kanti had already discussed it with her mother-in-law who had no objection but had asked her to take Ram Mohan's permission.

One day while serving him food, Kanti brought it up, haltingly, and before he could bellow his answer in the negative, Gayatri, who was there, spoke up, and mentioning that Kanti would not have to leave her teaching job, she set about explaining the benefits of the course; then dropping the name of Dixit ji, said, 'He says every eligible female should come forward and take advantage of the scheme.' The effect Gayatri's intervention had had on her husband took Kanti aback. His voice croaked and faltered as he tried to respond. Gayatri had caught him off guard. What made her think she could prevail? What was the source of her courage? It could well have been her closeness to Kanti whom she really cared about, but Ram Mohan could think of only one reason. He imputed it to her strength drawn from his weakness, his weakness for her. It lay in her subliminal

admission that she was sensible of his desire, which to Ram
Mohan, was like sighting an arbour of warmth in the woods of
coldness. She had made it possible for him to let her know of
his susceptibility to her; that he would defer to whatever she
thought he should do. He not only acceded to her wish but also
offered help in case of any problem.

However, his bowing to her intervention without demure
set Gayatri thinking, with a feeling of discomfort lurking through
her. It was a favour to her. She knew that. But after considering
the diminutive figure of Kanti standing beside her she faintly
shook her head, and pulling Nisha to her said, 'Didi, you start
preparing for this trip. Nisha and I will take care of things here
while you are away.' Kanti nodded, and seeing Sandhya tugging
at the hair of her grandmother who was shrieking, walked
briskly to them across the courtyard as Ram Mohan lingered
for a second to leisurely run a covetous eye on Gayatri. The
boldness of his gesture blasted a hole through Gayatri's cover of
doubt, leaving her unnerved, which to Ram Mohan revealed
the texture of their relationship, the possibility of which seemed
inescapable now. He had already thought out a plan to have her
person to himself.

* * *

Rooted to the spot, Gayatri was trying to regain her equanimity
when Kanti came and embraced her, and before she could sense
anything amiss Gayatri had composed herself; the twists and
turns of her life had given her crucial lessons on prudence. Her
experience of the past few years was enough to bring her round
to certain incapacity of men, the incapacity to contemplate a
woman outside her capacity to arouse them; before anything
else, she was destined to being measured in desirability. The
choice before a young woman in her predicament was not

between agreeing and disagreeing, but between less agreeable and disagreeable; relatively of course. Even this option was not available universally, Gayatri knew. So when stumbled over such a choice, Gayatri had managed to go in for the 'less agreeable' one. Otherwise the future of a high-caste widow would be stark, a future drained of colour and fun.

The choice Gayatri had had to make—the less agreeable one from her perspective—left Kanti aghast, who could not believe what was recounted to her after she had fished out the scrunched up khadi handkerchief from the outside pocket of the suitcase lent by Gayatri for her Narval sojourn. The alarm with which Gayatri had reacted to the discovery drew Kanti's attention back to what she held in her hand; she began to straighten it and noticed that the cause of its stiffness was some dried up sticky substance. Snot it certainly was not. Warily, Kanti sniffed at it; could not identify the smell. It was faint and funny but not unpleasant. Suddenly her eyes narrowed. She daintily lifted a strand of white hair with a flaccid curl from one of the wrinkles of the handkerchief; somewhat different in texture it did not look like belonging to somebody's head. She gave a quizzical look to Gayatri who had begun to silently cry. Kanti slid to her and clasped her to her bosom as Nisha who was playing with Sandhya watched her mother and Gayatri Masi in puzzlement. Wiping her eyes on her sari, Gayatri asked Nisha to take Sandhya to their Dadi.

'Didi, what I'm going to tell might shock you, but I request you to first listen and then decide whether I'm better or worse off than when—in the aftermath of my husband's death—I'd found myself in a situation so traumatic it had made me forget the pain of my loss; when everybody thought the tragedy had something to do with his marriage to me; once it was confirmed by the priest, it had seemed all over for me. If my Mama hadn't come in time, I might've ended my life, which would've solved the problem for both the families, the problem of how to deal with my widowhood. On the advice of a relative, my mother-in-law wanted me to be sent to Benaras to live with the likes of me.' Gayatri was mewling. Kanti put her arms around her and wiped Gayatri's face with her sari.

'I can't describe Didi what I had to go through during the weeks I was at my in-laws' house—'

'Please stop,' broke in Kanti, 'You don't have to relive that all over again.'

'No, I want you to know; it would make me feel better,' Gayatri said, mopping her face. 'My Mama, who'd gone back to look for a way to rescue me from the strait I was in, had yet to return when one day my mother-in-law came accompanied by this odious relation of theirs, who had spoken to some people in Benaras, who were in the business of making money through widows left in their clutches. My mother-in-law told me there was some rich man willing to look after me, that I'd be happy there. She whispered to me, "Don't tell anybody about the curse. You're fortunate to still be a virgin; that's why this man is so eager to take care of you; he's a middle-aged family man. He adores beautiful young widows and will treasure his bond with you like gold".'

'Oh my God,' burst out Kanti.

'I was too shocked to cry,' Gayatri continued. 'Certain that my consent to their plan was just a matter of time, they left. Luckily, a few days later my Mama returned to bring me back. They wouldn't listen to him. Everything had been arranged, they said; that for the sake of their son's salvation it was important his widow dedicated the rest of her life to the gods. This way I could also atone for my sins in the previous life, argued my mother-in-law. When his pleading didn't work, my Mama dropped Dixit ji's name, which put paid to their opposition.'

'What a nightmarish prospect it must've been,' said Kanti. 'I can't even think of you being in Benaras serving someone as his mistress. Is Dixit ji related to you?'

'Distantly. I didn't know of his existence before this. My Mama is socially and politically active; he knew him well; he took me along to Lucknow to meet him. That he knew such a powerful man I couldn't believe at first. However, when we got to his bungalow Dixit ji was hurrying away to some place, but when Mama pointed towards me, he stopped and met us in a small room next to where other visitors were seated. He was sympathetic and affectionate; it's owing to his kindness that I'm here today, leading a much better life than what my being a widow would've allowed. He said he'd think about my situation and do something to help.'

'He asked my Mama to come again the following week, and this time Dixit ji was ready with the solution to my problem, according to which I was to stay in Lucknow to do the primary teachers' training course before anything else. He organized everything from my admission to this course to my stay in Lucknow and so on. I've told you about these things before; today I'm going to share something that I won't dare tell even my mother or Mama. My only request to you Didi is that please don't get upset and calmly listen to what I'm going to relate. If you keep in mind that it was no less than hell that had awaited me earlier, you won't think I did anything wrong.' Kanti with a mixed expression of shock and curiosity placed her hand on Gayatri's head without saying anything.

'You know Dixit ji lives in a big ministerial bungalow with his family, while I was put up in his newly-bought house, named *Subhadra Kutir* after his late mother. I wasn't alone there. This woman by the name of Sughari stayed in that house and is still there; I lodge with her during my visits to Lucknow. She is from Dixit ji's native village; her family has been associated with him for decades; she's in her forties but looks younger and is also a widow. Her husband had died in a well-digging accident after about a month of their marriage. Dixit ji had brought her to Lucknow amid protests from the members of his extended family because she is Harijan. He was inspired by his friend Baran Singh, who has long employed a Harijan cook in his house. Sughari helped me settle down and kind of overwhelmed me with her affection; it was after a week or so that she explained it all to me. Her tone and expression was so matter-of-fact, it didn't come home to me at first; then I felt so tired I went to my room and fell asleep . . . When I woke up in the evening I found myself awash with a sense of utter meaninglessness. The world had once again turned so painfully alien. Even my own body . . . I was unable to relate to my own body; looked at my hands and feet as if they belonged to someone else. Shortly, Sughari came and said, "I've been waiting for you to wake up." She had brought tea.

"'When will you meet him then?" she asked me sweetly as she sat down on the floor . . . To tell the truth, it's only now that I realize how her plain manner while talking about such an intimate thing had helped me behave normally. She made it seem so ordinary one would feel foolish to be alarmed or agitated. She said, "I know what you must feel, but take my word for it, you'll curse yourself later for being unnecessarily scared." I told her about him being so old, almost my Dada's age, to which she said, "But he isn't your Dada. He's a man, a very good man at that. He's been dreaming about the moment you'd say yes. I wish you knew how concerned he feels about you, about your future. He has vowed to see that life never mistreats you again, even after he is no more. I've seen young widows being preyed on, called names and harassed no end. It's Dixit ji who I owe my physical safety and mental peace after my husband's death. At the start, I was also shocked but had to agree, as I had no choice. But the way he behaved and looked after me made me very happy with this relationship; it's been almost six to seven years since he last slept with me, but his caring attitude and affection has not diminished one bit. The problem is, he can't help feeling helpless at the sight of youth and beauty, but he never shirks his responsibility towards the person." That's how Sughari persuaded me to agree to meet him first and then decide.

"'At least, give him a chance to explain his point of view himself before saying yes or no,' she said brightly. Later, in the afternoon, she told me Dixit ji had cancelled all his other engagements for that evening and would come to see me; then quickly added "No, no . . . today he's coming to just talk." I was lying in bed when the knock came. I got up with a start as he pushed the door gently and entered. Wearing a smile, he looked at me and sat down in the only chair in the room asking me to do the same. Gingerly, I planted myself on the edge of the bed.

"'I have a granddaughter nearly the same age as you; we've found a boy for her; the wedding will take place next year; she's very sweet and I adore her. She's completed her secondary education," he paused. I was looking down nervously at my hands. He asked me to look at him and said, "Every true relation has a common basis in love, in affection; the degree may vary, but this feeling of affinity forms the substance needed to sustain any relationship. Now the question is how to distinguish my relation to my granddaughter from the one I propose to have with you . . . Clearly, the difference lies in form; even if my desire for you doesn't lead to physical union, the potentiality of it will always determine the features of our bond; that doesn't mean every expression of love in such a relationship has a physical orientation. No. Even when constant physical proximity eats away at the fangs of passion, the foundation of love remains the same; it's not undermined. A while ago someone I know

married a girl much younger than himself, leading to whispers
that his wife was young enough to be his daughter, which I
find absolute nonsense, this logic. Taking digs at this guy was
also a friend of mine. I asked him what he thought of someone
marrying a girl old or young enough to be his sister."

'I couldn't help smiling; that spurred him on, "And Gayatri,
you must know I'm not trying to make any deal here; I'll do
whatever I can to make your life comfortable. Whether you
allow this relation to take the form I desire or not is up to you.
You're free. My concern and affection for you will remain as
steady as ever; but you mustn't get muddled, haggling over
the morality and immorality of what I suggest; these things
matter only if we let society into it. Tell me, what's so ethical
about the severity to which girls like you are subjected in our
society? I don't subscribe to any morality that justifies cruelty
to ordinary beings in any way; however, one can't force the
general thinking to change overnight, can one? It's a slow and
gradual process and takes a hell of a lot of time to happen.
Individuals though don't have that kind of time. So those who
can afford must keep certain things to themselves. No one
in the world knows about my having had a physical relation
with Sughari; it was an absolutely private affair, concerning
just the two of us. No one else had any right to know of this.
I believe individuals are free to do as they please provided it
has no repercussions either for them or anybody else. That is,
if it's something that can fall foul of one's family or society
it must be done in complete secrecy. I don't have an iota of
scepticism about this. That's the reason I see no immorality in
my wish to have you, with your consent of course. I haven't
seen such a devastating blend of youth and beauty before. And
you have a right to decide what to do with it; given your
widowhood, you have two very obvious choices here. First,
you can let time slowly but surely unpick this great marvel of

irresistibility, which your body is, turning it into a withered copy of itself eventually . . . To think of it, what a waste it would be, absolutely meaningless. Second, acting generously you can allow me, an old man with fading physical fortune, one more go at experiencing what I describe as the most distilled form of pleasure a man can think of . . . " Didi, his behaviour was so sober that even listening to all this didn't unsettle me. On the contrary, I found myself relieved as he'd taken me out of myself.'

Kanti, who had been listening to Gayatri open-mouthed, said, 'Gayatri, I didn't know your Hindi was so good and you could talk so maturely and intelligently. I'm surprised I don't feel revolted at your story. I don't know why. Maybe it's the way you narrated it.'

'The credit for even this goes to Dixit ji, who inculcated in me the habit of reading; all those books you see there on that box,' she pointed to the tin trunk sitting against the wall, 'were given by him. I've also been keeping a diary; whatever I write I reread it several times and make changes to improve. The words and sentences I used today have come from my listening to Dixit ji and reading books, and since I also use them in writing they've become part of my linguistic know-how.'

'What was your response?'

'I didn't know what to say. He said I was free to take my time to decide; then what melted my heart was when he, just before stepping out, turned around and said, "Gayatri, if you're not comfortable and don't consider my wish worth even a thought, don't feel pressured to persuade yourself into it. Should you do that the beauty of my satisfaction will be stillborn; I might succumb to a momentary thrill in the blindness of passion. But the thing is, whether I'll be able to savour the afterglow, the fulcrum of any such relation for a person in the twilight of his life. If you don't feel up to it, nothing will change. I won't be any less solicitous on this account. You can carry on as usual. That I care for you isn't tied to my desire for you. However, I'd rather you didn't say no to the possibility of this union, which, as a tribute to my yearning, can be kept being put off until kingdom comes. That said, nobody could ever claim to be certain about the future contours of their emotional self, their feelings. I say this from experience." He didn't meet me for about two weeks after that; he did come to the house but only to enquire if everything was fine. It was Sughari who kept trying to convince me of what comfort and satisfaction a young woman experiences in a loving man's arms, especially if the man is much older.'

Kanti was silent as though in deep thought. Gayatri went to the other side of the roof terrace to relieve herself near the drain behind a charpoy standing on its side; when she returned Kanti was smiling.

'I wavered for more than a month; then one day I felt my heart going out to Dixit ji . . . I didn't say anything to Sughari. Yet the way she stole glances I knew I'd given myself away, and in the evening she came bounding into my room and hugged me. Feigning innocence, I asked her why she was so happy. She said, "Shall I inform him?" I tried to keep up the pretence but not for long. I asked her to wait, as I must get over the fear of what it entailed; she said there was nothing to fear. "He'll make you so comfortable, you'd regret delaying it." I capitulated. Dixit ji came the very next morning, and for the first time, he touched me by way of caressing my cheeks and lips. He looked sober and calm, but his excitement could not escape notice. "I can't wait to be with you tonight; it's going to be the apotheosis of my life of sensuous gratification. I'll be so very grateful to you for this kindness and understanding."

Kanti who had gone crimson, said, 'Oh God! Tell me how it all went when he returned for the kill that night.'

'Didi, I can't tell you how great it had all turned out, minus the pain of course,' she said, a sheepish grin entangled in her lips. 'He made me feel so special and important as if I was a queen. Would you believe he didn't finish it that night? He would take almost a week to complete the relationship.'

'What did he do all this while? My husband wouldn't even agree to wait another day; I was so much in pain but he would not listen. And when it happened I couldn't stifle my shriek, which must've been quite loud as a moment later I heard my mother-in-law's affected coughing. I was so sore the whole day that the thought of the following night was scary; but his father's rapidly worsening health kept him away. A day or two later, he died. I think that would've been the reason for his insistence during the first night, for it was almost a week before he could come to me again.'

'Dixit ji was all charm and tenderness,' Gayatri said. 'I was surprised that I let him undress me with the lights on. It was his solicitude that had torn down the walls of my bashfulness. He stared in wonder at my body. I was unable to foil his scrutiny . . .' Gayatri covered her face with her hands. Kanti was laughing. 'Then he started doing something I can't describe. Yet he was so normal and appreciative that I just let it be. Having relished what he called the treat meant for the most fortunate man on earth, he turned the lights off and spent some time cuddling, kissing and caressing me all over. He said he was thrilled no end by the dissimilitude between our bodies. He didn't mean the male and female thing. He was talking of the contrast between his leathery and sagging skin and my taut and firm flesh; this incongruity, he says, is the key to his inexhaustible appetite for me which keeps his "little friend" stirred up.'

'This shameless oldie of yours . . . I can't picture a wrinkly like him saying and doing all this . . . disgusting,' Kanti said, making faces.

Gayatri laughed, 'It's something any young person would find difficult to stomach; the idea was no less disconcerting to me at first, but Dixit ji's conduct eased my mind so much that in the end I helped him make a go of it, and in no time I began to feel at home with the thought of being in bed with him. This massive age-difference had no bearing on the way I looked at the equation. To me our relationship became as between two consenting adults with the world shut out of it; it concerned no one but the two of us. At the end of the day, what matters isn't the age of your partner Didi, but the way he treats you.'

'Okay, fine,' Kanti said, then pointing to the crumpled hankie, 'What's this to do with what you've told me? It belongs to Dixit ji as far as I can guess. He has somewhat curly hair, hasn't he?'

'Yes, this handkerchief is his, but whatever hair he's left on his head has no curls whatsoever,' said Gayatri, all smiles, piquing Kanti's curiosity. 'He calls it "coitus interruptus",' then she got into explaining in detail what the phrase meant and what that hankie had to do with it.

With her eyes opened wide Kanti stuttered, 'that's very good of him . . . it means he never leaves that thing inside you!'

'He's very careful.'

Kanti shook her head holding it in both hands.

* * *

With Kanti away in Narval, Gayatri was occupied attending to home and school. Kanti's sister had come over to help. On Baijnath's insistence, Sandhya and Deena had been left in the care of Kanti's mother in Ballamgaon. One of Kanti's two sisters-in-law had a two-year-old son and was still lactating. She was happily willing to suckle Deena while his mother was away. Nisha would look forward to Gayatri Masi's commands whereas

Nishant was happy to run errands for Chhote Baba who was happy with the way Gayatri handled the situation. Aided by Kanti's sister and Nisha, she managed things in school and at home, though a little sorry, she had had to cut down on her visits to Lucknow, but once Kanti Didi was back she would make it up to Dixit ji.

Though immersed in his research work Ram Mohan could not keep Gayatri out of his thoughts; he could not wait to be able to break the ice and make her comfortable with the idea of him being her lover; that done he could get on with his work with renewed ardour, luxuriating in the certitude of having her. No sooner was he done with things preparatory to his PhD project than he put his plan into action, the plan to set the scene for the forging of a liaison. He was at peace with the thought it would not happen at their first meeting. But it did, because of the pressure he would bring to bear on her.

I don't know if Kanti was back from Narval when Ram Mohan scheduled his meeting with Baran Singh in Lucknow, to accord with Gayatri's visit there. No matter how hard he tried to make it look like a happenstance, his furtive demeanour was not lost on her. His eyes when she had last seen him had foreboded this moment; rather than keep living under its shadow, she decided to confront it. So when he said he wanted her to see his new digs in Kanpur—from Parsadpur the easiest route to Lucknow was via Kanpur—she did not object and would respond torpidly when he pointed the landmarks out to her as they rode in a rickshaw from the station.

She was drinking water from the tap in the bathroom when he caressed her buttocks; she spun around and said, her mouth contorted, 'Shame on you, Jija ji.' He promptly apologized; then falling to pleading and reasoning, as she stood with tears in her eyes, he did not wait long to descend to supplication. Wiping her tears, she listened—restraining her rebuff—cognizant that her rejection would tell on Kanti Didi's peace of mind, let alone her own stay in Parsadpur becoming awkward. On top of that, his pathetic desperation and feverish entreaties, she found hard to handle. She reasoned it out in her mind: it was better to yield than feel crushed all the time beneath the mountain of his concupiscence.

* * *

Secure in his most erotic conquest, Ram Mohan threw himself into his work, rejuvenated. But soon it dawned on him that no way he could finish it by the time the next general election was due. He had to spend a lot of time in Rajasthan in search of material for his PhD. His labour and diligence were to result in unearthing not only substantial information on the poet-saint but also innumerable scattered pieces of his poetry. He knew it would be nearly impossible for him to get back to his research work if he left it mid-way to take part in the election. He went to seek the counsel of Chaudhary Sahab who reasoned, 'you are still young, and will get the opportunity later to have a shot at electoral politics. Coming into active politics will mean the end of your PhD dream; you'll be left with neither the drive nor the time to even entertain the idea of such an academic task.' The words of his political mentor, resonating with his own inclination, provided a great relief.

* * *

Once done with his research in the field, Ram Mohan got down to putting together his PhD thesis and would remain focused, barring the occasion when he took a break to enjoy the hoopla in political circles in the wake of the Congress sweeping the polls. Some attributed it to Nehru's charisma, while others held it was the result of disarray in the ranks of the opposition; the most interesting reason was given by none other than a State Congress minister himself, who at a private gathering in Kanpur, stated that his party leaders, though ideologically divided, were united against losing power; 'Many of us differ with Nehru on many things but we all are convinced of his magic,' which rang true even to the sceptic. It had got to be magic of some sort they would argue, or how could he have led his party to the throne third time in a row without so much as posing even a distant threat to the reigning poverty and distress in the country?

Still slaving away at his dissertation, Ram Mohan was struck by an idea so brilliant, which if incorporated, would lend an impressive dimension to his thesis. He was ecstatic. But then realized it could not just be inserted anywhere into his line of argument. He would have to make suitable but notable changes in whatever he had accomplished so far; a big ask. Caught in a dilemma, he found himself floundering. Right then, without any warning, rose from the depths of his being a tempest of desire for Gayatri, liberating him for the time being from the clutch of the poet-saint. Within an hour, he set off for Parsadpur, unaware that Gayatri had already gone to Lucknow. He made love to Kanti that night. Before heading back the following morning, he told her he would be going to Lucknow to meet Baran Singh and also Dixit ji, from whom he wanted a letter of recommendation to the education minister of Rajasthan, for a grant to enable the publication of the first collection of the verses by the Rajasthani poet-saint.

Kanti wondered a bit timidly if he could bring Gayatri back. 'If you're not too tied up in other things, I mean.' Albeit delighted Ram Mohan affected to ponder before saying, 'Which means I'll have to come to Parsadpur again,' but just as Kanti was about to respond, he hastened to agree, 'No problem; I'll do that . . . In point of fact, I also have to meet Gulab Singh and others to discuss something.' Kanti was pleased with his calm, sympathetic response.

* * *

After a couple of delicious couplings with Gayatri, Ram Mohan's mind cleared. The joy of being able to decide to rework the finished portions of his dissertation now surged through him.

Ram Mohan had scarcely got on with rewriting his dissertation when the warfare along the Sino-Indian border flared up. The argument over the legitimacy of the McMahon Line had been simmering between the two countries for years now. The gravity of the situation became public when the government decided to release the White Paper on the dispute, laying bare the contents of its years-long exchange with the Chinese government. With that, Nehru forfeited his option to settle the territorial question quietly with China, without popular sentiments being in the way.

After a spate of clashes on the border, he lost his nerve and wanted everybody on board. Sparks flew in Parliament. The Opposition laid into him accusing his government of having soft-peddled the Chinese intentions for so long, though the thing that had touched off the Chinese aggression was the sudden flight of the Dalai Lama to India. It was Tibet all the way that finally led to the Chinese action now, about three years later. The invasion hardly lasted a month. The Chinese withdrew to the pre-war positions as suddenly as they had penetrated into

India's 'disputed' territory; but Indian leadership was panicked into believing that after Tawang, China's next target would be Assam. Britain and America had already been requested to come to the rescue of 'non-aligned India', which had no answer to the modern Soviet weaponry used by China.

This short sudden war had left the country in a daze. Ram Mohan could not help his mind straying into the excitement generated by the war. After receiving word from Tiwari ji who was already in Lucknow, he too decided to go and learn how Chaudhary Baran Singh and his friends looked at the situation. Tiwari ji was staying in Dar-us-shifa, the favourite hangout of all kinds of politicos visiting Lucknow; this hotel-turned-hostel meant for members of Legislative Assembly, would at any given point be found overrun by their friends, acquaintances, supporters etc. Ram Mohan was fixed up with a place to sleep in a room allotted to one of Baran Singh's men; likewise an MLA known to Tiwari ji had put him up in his room. Ram Mohan took his friend along to meet Chaudhary Sahab who was not home; one of his assistants got him on the phone for Ram Mohan. They went back in the evening; the house was buzzing with activity. Chairs and sofas had been removed from the big drawing room to create more room for the visitors who all sat on the mattresses on the floor with bolsters thrown around. The focus of attention in the gathering was the politician from Delhi, a second term member of Parliament, addressed fondly as Saansad ji; he was great friends with Baran Singh. Ram Mohan was happy that Dixit ji and Shukla ji were there, for he hardly knew anybody else in the gathering. The topic of the discussion was the military thrashing China had given India at the front.

He and Tiwari ji squeezed themselves into whatever space was available beside Shukla ji. Baran Singh and Dixit ji sat together cross-legged across from Saansad ji who though a Congressman was not taken with Nehru's way of handling the boundary dispute; he seemed his own man in that he faulted the Opposition even more severely along with some Congress MPs, on their behaviour during the crisis. He said, 'The Opposition had already tied Nehru's hand and foot by pressuring him to divulge all the details of the territorial disagreements with China. Yet, I think Nehru ji should and could have stood his ground against this; this kind of capitulation doesn't flatter a man who swears by courage . . . And would you believe it, right in the thick of the mess some dolts in and outside Parliament bayed for an all-out war with China. These imbeciles, drunk with their imaginary heroism, clamoured for Indian troops' march into Tibet. Regardless of all this my view remains that it was the failure of our prime minister to recognize the gravity of the issue which snowballed into such a debilitating war for India.'

The way Dixit ji was fidgeting with his chin spoke of his reservations about what Saansad ji was saying. He spoke up, 'Pandit ji had all along been singing paeans to Sino-India friendship; he was the first in the world to recognize the People's Republic of China after the Communist revolution there. So who can doubt his bona fides as regards his friendly take on China? It was Pandit ji who helped end its exclusion from the international community; we all know the communist China had been turned into an outcaste by America and Britain. It was our PM who lent Chou En-lai a hand to get on an international platform.'

'You are referring to Afro-Asian conference in Bandung . . .' said Saansad ji.

'Yes, and who made such a strong pitch for a place for China in the security council?' exclaimed Dixit ji. 'Considering all its comradely gestures, how is one supposed to view China's invasion? Don't you think Saansad ji that to any neutral and sensible person it was an act of perfidy on China's part?' Surveying the nodding heads in the audience, Saansad ji smiled and said, 'When the situation had started heating up along the border, the PM fell back on these supposed favours to China. He was mouthing them like a tearful child even in his letters to the Chinese premier as well as in his discussions with people at home. He'd become extremely upset and unsettled by China's territorial claims, which caused him tremendous consternation; his statesman-like persona began to unravel in the heat of this emergency. If one—'

'That's because of the betrayal by someone long-regarded as a friend,' Dixit ji broke in. 'No wonder India was caught completely off guard. You don't guard against a possible war with a friend, do you? That's the reason most of our troops were watching over India's border with Pakistan when China decided to besmirch the concept of friendship. Any sensitive person would be shaken out of his wits by this kind of treachery.'

Saansad ji said, 'That's correct if you restrict yourself to India's vantage point. But the greatest challenge of great statesmen lies in their ability to find a balance between what is and what should be. They should be able to negotiate the tough patch that lies between the ideal and the achievable. On this boundary question, I'd say, Nehru ji was found wanting in profundity; he failed to appreciate China's sensitivity to Tibet. It's not as though he wasn't aware of the state of affairs there. China had reclaimed this region around the time India became a republic; later for a greater access to Tibet, it secretly built a road through Aksai Chin in Ladakh. India has a genuine claim to this area, no doubt. But truly speaking, it's practically of no use to us at all. It's barren and nothing grows there . . .

'In one of his letters to Chou En-lai, Nehru ji had also bewailed that China had never made such territorial claims until the British left . . . How ridiculous? You've all along been scathingly critical of the British imperialism; now you conveniently find McMahon Line perfectly legitimate. Let's leave that aside. What message to China had the PM intended to send by personally meeting Dalai Lama? Wasn't it enough to allow him political asylum and a suitable abode without much brouhaha? The PM could've used the occasion to demonstrate India's neutrality towards Tibet by not meeting Dalai Lama personally; this way he would've dissociated himself from the warm welcome Dalai Lama was given—to China's chagrin—in some quarters here . . . Then, and only then, his government's attempt to put it down to the freedom enjoyed by people in a democracy like India would've made sense. To aggravate the situation, there had also been the buzz that the Tibetan leader's hurried escape was planned and aided by the CIA.'

'But how can you connect the Dalai Lama thing with the boundary discord between the two countries?' said Baran Singh.

'I think India's rigid stance on Aksai Chin and Dalai Lama's unwillingness to listen to China and fleeing to India helped Chinese displeasure work up to this military conflict. It's not unlikely that China suspected India to be laughing up its sleeve at their Tibet-trouble; they might have thought it a good idea to gruffly confront us with our own territorial reality. There are important political elements here that stand for Tibet's independence. No denying that. Then there's the whole political class in India that roared in disbelief and anger on learning of China's road through that small plateau in Ladakh. All this screaming for the lost bald patch on India's head and the Dalai Lama–episode would have stung the Chinese into military action. However, it's clear they just wanted to jolt us out of our smugness by stressing the gravity of the border dispute through their raid. Or, there seems no point in their sudden withdrawal after making such swift inroads so deep into India.'

Dixit ji said, 'But does it befit a country as large as China to annex a small region in order to rule it and that too against the wishes of its people?'

'What about our own troubles roughly of the same nature with Naga territories, Kashmir, etcetera?' Saansad ji laughed, 'It's not that simple, Dixit ji. If I attempted to answer this, I would have to dwell on many more questions bound to pop up before we could hope to thrash out a reasonable explanation. However, any answer thus reached would only be relative and temporal, not final . . . which is the case with any answer to any question, I guess.' Noticing the gaping mouths, Saansad ji shuffled in his place and said, 'The point I seek to make is that there could be no absolute solution to any problem. For us, the best bet consists in our understanding a situation well before deciding on an option more desirable but relatively fair, more advantageous but feasible. Nothing can be truer of the task of handling international issues. It might sound blasphemous but since it's not a public meeting, I reckon I can say it.

'I wish the Indian leadership had shown the sagacity to seize with both hands the solution to this boundary quarrel hinted at by China! To put it plainly, India should have agreed to the swap implied in the Chinese suggestion. Chou En-lai had indicated that if India would let go of the area occupied by China in Kashmir, it was willing to drop its claim on the region known as North-East Frontier Agency and accept the McMahon Line. The beauty of this arrangement was that it would suit both the countries politically, geographically and strategically. But Nehru, by allowing the subject to become public, lost a great opportunity; because once the mob is involved, things most worthy of consideration beat a retreat.'

'The way the PM and our MPs were giving vent to their feelings had almost convinced me that they knew what they were talking about,' said Baran Singh. 'They sounded so sure of the ability of their forces to repulse Chinese moves on the border. As it turned out, our troops were blown helter-skelter by the Chinese storm.' Someone in the audience, chimed in loudly, 'Saansad ji, everyone is attacking Nehru ji. Where were these people before this spat with China began? No one had had the audacity to question his view on any national or international issues. Now that the lion lies hurt and weak and old, all the jackals and foxes are out to have a field day at his expense.'

Saansad ji grinned, 'Yes, but there did once exist a handful of mavericks who couldn't be his yes-men. Some of them like Ambedkar and Rajagopalachari had a much better grasp of the challenges the leaders of free India faced. Patel died before our Constitution could complete the first year of its birth. Ambedkar quit the Cabinet in a huff when Nehru ji dilly-dallied to get the Hindu Bill passed. He died a dejected man a few years later, while Rajaji, despaired of the PM's 'license-quota-permit raj', left the Congress to form his own party. Despite his vision and prescience, Rajaji could be no match for the inheritor of Mahatma's mass base. So, yes that's correct, most of the rest of the people could do nothing but to look up to Nehru ji. Yet the Chinese onslaught left him vulnerable, enabling his detractors, who had hitherto lain low, to train their guns at him. He cuts such a sorry figure now my heart goes out to him . . . which is natural because one tends to sympathize more with the powerful losing power than with the powerless.'

Turning to Baran Singh, he said, 'Yes, you're right. Listening to Nehru-regime, no one could have doubts as to our preparedness . . . To make up for the incapacity of our troops on the border, Indian mobs pounced on innocent Chinese living in Calcutta and Delhi. It was so bad that Japanese diplomats had to advertise on the windshield of their vehicles that they were not Chinese. Nehru and Menon both had had no idea of what shape their troops were in—so much so that they had the cheek to provoke the Chinese further by their "forward policy" . . . Having watched him for so long I can say that Nehru, though a kind-hearted, sincere and sensible man, has

never been a good judge of talent and aptitude; he always based
his assessment of people on their skill to make him convinced
of what he thought was good for the country. Krishna Menon
did it immaculately because of his good English, thanks to his
education at London School of Economics. His unqualified
love for the Soviet Union, comparable in intensity only with
his dislike for the US, was music to Pandit ji's ears. With his
thinking lodged in a straitjacket, he couldn't see things in
perspective; as minister of Defence, he was awfully reckless. He
tried to politicize the army through favouritism, treading in the
process on the toes of many an army official of proven calibre.
An impetuous man like Krishna Menon would, if allowed to
have his way, make conditions favourable for army rule. Isn't
there a couplet of Ghalib that says who needs bad luck if one
has a friend like you?'

Everybody laughed.

Baran Singh said, 'I agree with you, Saansad ji,' then a
little wonderingly, 'Listening to Nehru ji makes one believe he
knows in and out of everything. The letters he writes to chief
ministers explaining what needs to be done . . .But—'

'That's what he is good at really. He has no rival in articulating
the importance of what needs to be done; that's where he stops
before moving on in the same vein to other things, which await
the same fate. Not in the least does he seem bothered about the
evidence of any action on the ground. A beautiful delineation
of a problem in itself and the praise he receives for it are enough
to afford him the kind of elation identified with the actual
realization of one's goals. The conditions in the country remain
as heart-rending as ever. A very small section of people have
indeed benefited from his government's policies, but as far as
one can see, these policies have only succeeded in establishing
a regime of corruption, special interests, monopoly, nepotism
and so forth.'

'Saansad ji, why is it that your attitude to Pandit ji has become particularly harsh since the new Cabinet was sworn in after the second general election?' said Dixit ji. 'Is it not that you had expected to be on it?'

'What's wrong in that, Dixit ji? Yes, I did think I could do my bit to help realize the goals the country had set for itself. My claim to such a position was stronger than many others on the Cabinet; Nehru ji knew I'd alienated many people by insisting on things promised by our Constitution.'

'Saansad ji, everybody knows about your support to Ambedkar when he was quarrelling with Pandit ji over that bill. Once he resigned you tried to cozy up to the PM. You forget, however, that people for whom Nehru ji had great regard didn't like your self-righteous zeal for reforming and codifying the Hindu law. It alerted them and Nehru ji to the stubborn streak in you when you stood right behind Ambedkar.'

'Because I was still passionate about values implicit in our erstwhile national movement,' said Saansad ji. 'We, I and people like me, were so distressed when Nehru ji succumbed to the wishes of people opposed to Ambedkar and his reform bill.'

'That proves my point,' said Dixit ji, chuckling.

'Let's drop the matter right here or we would entangle ourselves in another long debate,' said Baran Singh and enquired loudly of someone if dinner was ready; then turning to people in the room, 'Please don't leave without having food.'

The dinner was arranged on the back lawn and consisted of puri, subzi and dahi. Ram Mohan had enjoyed the evening thoroughly. Baran Singh introduced them—Ram Mohan, Tiwari ji and Shukla ji—to Saansad ji, praising their efforts and abilities.

———————

Returning to Kanpur, Ram Mohan threw himself back into his work, and found that the changes he wanted to make to his half-finished thesis had become clear as day. He got on swiftly with them; thereafter his writing progressed lucidly. The first draft of his dissertation was ready the following year. However, he had to make one more visit to Rajasthan to confirm the accuracy of some of the sources and the names of places. The introduction was yet to be written; he'd left it until after the finalization of the main text. To make full use of this relative disengagement from politics, he was catching up with his literary friends. There were some who he knew would secretly be wishing for a sloppy outcome of his endeavour, the chief among whom would be Mishra; the man was held in terror for his erudition.

Now it was not just a PhD degree Ram Mohan had in mind. He wanted his thesis in prose so lambent it would make people jump and envious. He had taken his first draft to Sanehi ji, an eminent Hindi poet known for his sedulous treatment of each and every line he produced, whose observation that the rigour invested in the dissertation was shining through, gave Ram Mohan a lift. Following Sanehi ji's advice, he stepped away from the text for about a month. The discovery amazed him. The brief temporal distance endued him with the insight to spot the improvable points in it. By the time he was done with the revision a few more months had gone by. The final draft, to his amusement, seemed to have attained a character of its own. He could hardly recognize his struggle in it. The ideas and language were in such a dynamic alliance that each sentence and argument seemed to be spurring the next one.

No sooner had Ram Mohan been awarded the prestigious degree than he set about the process of getting his dissertation published. Dixit ji's good word had worked. Rajasthan government agreed to finance its publication, and shortly he was to start work on a collection of the poet-saint's verses.

THREE

Nishant came to bring Deena—who lay at the morgue of Safdarjung Hospital where the autopsy had taken place—back to Allahabad. I had arranged a dead-body ambulance in which Nishant accompanied Deena as I took Prayagraj Express later, and kept wondering if I should tell Ram Mohan uncle about Deena's preference, though he had left nothing in writing. It would have slipped his mind because whenever we happened to argue about the best way of dealing with human remains, his choice would be clear. In his view, graves had a kind of charm and served as poignant reminders of the 'final emptiness' without invoking fear. I still remember the way Deena had taken to the Christian cemetery in Mussoorie during our trip, ages ago. It had become his wont to pen his feelings whenever moved. On that occasion he described the atmosphere in the cemetery as redolent of romance and pathos, which bolstered the bond between the living and the dead.

Nishant had already reached Allahabad the previous night; people had yet to start trickling in when I arrived in the morning; some close relations and family friends had come the previous evening. My parents were also there. Many more were expected before the cremation took place. It was time I spoke to Ram Mohan uncle. I had hardly begun when he called out to Nishant, asking him to listen to what I was saying. After I finished, he said with Nishant nodding, 'If that's the case, I have no problem. We can give him a burial in Parsadpur.' His alacrity surprised me. But then he was never a stickler for ceremony. He suggested Nishant and I go to Parsadpur to meet Gulab Singh and see if a suitable place could be found there; when Vinod—a close friend of Deena's—arrived, he offered to take us there in his car. Vinod came from a business family. Deena and he had been classmates in Prayag Sangeet Samiti, the famous music school in Allahabad.

The development had turned the subdued and sombre conversations—taking place on the porch, in the lawn and the veranda, and inside the house—into a confused and noisy buzz. Some eyebrows were raised. But no one in his family was opposed to carrying out Deena's wish. We made it to Parsadpur in about five hours and got in touch with Badri—who was about to head for Allahabad; we all set off for Ballamgaon to meet Gulab Singh who had not kept well of late.

It was after twenty-six years that I had come to Parsadpur–Ballamgaon. My earliest memories of the area belonged to the time when Deena was sent back to Parsadpur after spending a month in Kanpur where he had gone along with her mother and Dadi who had to be put in hospital, where she would die. Kanti could not stay away for long from Parsadpur. It was difficult for Gayatri to cope with the tasks at school and home by herself. In a week she had to return, leaving Deena in Kanpur.

* * *

Ram Mohan's collection of the poet-saint's verses was ready for publication when the nation observed its fifteenth republic day, the day Hindi was to become the official language of India as decreed by the Constitution. He wanted to release it as a tribute to this momentous occasion, in the run-up to which the Hindi gentry had been rhapsodizing, for whom it signified real freedom from the English. With Urdu out of the way—thanks to Pakistan—Hindi seemed to have no challenge left; the time had also come for English to be shown the door. The place of pre-eminence now belonged to Hindi. There was some apprehension that south India might be a hurdle, but intoxicated with its strength the north was determined to steamroll any stink kicked up by other linguistic communities that had been allowed a grace period to learn Hindi. What had not been reckoned with was the intensity with which they would erupt when Hindi was formally imposed. At the time of the book-release event, the news of paroxysms of anger running riot in Tamil Nadu had already spread. No wonder that after token praise for Ram Mohan's effort, almost all the speakers responded savagely to non-Hindi regions opposing Hindi. One speaker went so far as to demand those opposed to Hindi should be thrown out of the country. The mood of the function became so volatile the audience was in no fit state to be sermonized, that too by someone looking like a Madrasi.

Mahavir Wilson taught history at Methodist High School, a very old English medium school in Kanpur. Originally Harijan, his parents had escaped into Christianity just before he was born. They hailed from the same village near Lucknow as the education minister Dixit ji, and were close to him. His father had retired from the army; it was during his posting in the south that he had decided to convert. Mahavir studied in various schools run for army men's children, and his father had inculcated him with a sense of earnestness to tame English. The importance of the language and knowledge gained through it was never in dispute for him, the father, who was deeply conscious of the emancipatory role it could play in an untouchable's life.

The possibility of Hindi's ascendance in free India had frightened him; it could set the stage for another long spell of despair for Harijans, the lowest of the low. He was thankful to the way south India rose against Hindi; listening on All India Radio to the news of the sudden upsurge in people's anger there, his eyes had moistened. Now there was a hope that English would be allowed to stay despite Prime Minister Shastri and his deputy Desai's attempts to the contrary. He was very happy at his son being one of the speakers at the book-release, the invitation for which came from Dixit ji who knew of Mahavir's interest in Kabir, another mutinous poet-saint.

Kabir had taken the young man's fancy after he had lit upon the *Songs of Kabir*, an English translation of some of his verses by Tagore. His further enquiries revealed how Kabir was conveniently kept outside the canon of Hindi literature because of his defiance of the dominant social, literary and linguistic norms. His tenor of voice could not be humbled to suit the central poetic tradition of Sanskrit and Hindi, which would spur Mahavir to delve a little further into his poetry. The speech he had planned for the function was to revolve around the question: why was such an unusual and interesting poet as Kabir given short shrift in Hindi literature? He felt a bit annoyed by his father's insistence that he talk some sense into Hindi chauvinists who would make up the gathering there. But on reaching the venue, Mahavir realized how right his father was. Two speakers who spoke before him had already set the tone for others to follow; given the mood at the event, the speech he had prepared would sound anomalous. No sooner was his name called than he pushed Kabir aside, deciding instead to give the audience a piece of his mind.

After touching on the Sufi tradition of poetry and Ram Mohan's work in its light, he dived into the controversy. Only to get his fingers burnt. Talking of his growing-up years in Madras

and his familiarity with Tamil—and how old and developed
the languages of the south were—he said that to expect people
in that region to adopt Hindi just like that, was preposterous.
For them, any language worth learning besides their mother
tongues could only be English, which gave access to a world
that otherwise would remain blocked to them. Acquiring a
good grasp of any language meant enormous sweat, so why
should they learn Hindi when it has nothing to offer except the
promise of communication with mostly 'ignorant' Hindi belt?
Would it not be better and fair that Hindi speakers should also
be taught English? Was it not our imperious hauteur to order
people in the south to learn Hindi or suffer the consequences?
Was it not an affront to their languages?

These were the arguments that charged Mahavir Wilson's
speech. The delay in the violent reaction was due to his
intermittent use of English words and sentences. Even that was
a bit too much given the prevailing anti-English atmosphere. As
he spoke, faint murmurs of displeasure going around the venue
could be made out; what proved to be the tipping point was his
contention that Hindi, compared to English, had little to impart
to non-Hindi speakers. Some in the audience stood up and
began to shout, 'Why don't you go to England to be with your
masters? You've displayed your true colours! The colour of your
skin represents the colour of your heart! Britishers have left their
spawn behind to betray the nation!' It all resulted in a melee.
Ram Mohan and Shukla ji were trying to calm the people down
while Dixit ji was dumbstruck at the turn of events. Mahavir
Wilson had left the mike and got off the stage. Not one to be
cowed, he tried to engage with the group that had converged
on the aisle. Provoked, Mahavir piled on his indignation; his
attempt to match them at invective incensed a man so much he
landed a smack on the side of his face. Stunned at first, Mahavir
hit out at him. That set all of them on him.

Dixit ji missed Baran Singh who, owing to some other engagement, could not come. Fearing for Wilson's life, he called to the policemen deployed at the venue because of him and Shukla ji—his junior in the ministry of education. Just as they were pulled apart, a man tore at Mahavir's shirt. Mahavir spat on his face; wiping the spittle with his sleeve, the man menaced Mahavir using insults as a policeman lodged himself between the two. Dixit ji wanted those men to be taken into custody but Shukla ji said, 'This Chamar-turned-Christian has brought it on himself. All present here are against what he said; he has insulted our national language. The situation can worsen if the police arrest these men.'

* * *

They scrambled over to Mahavir Wilson who stood tearfully beside the policemen, buttoning down the jacket to hide his ripped shirt. Putting his arm about him, Dixit ji said, 'Your view may sound reasonable Mahavir but this was not the occasion to voice it. People have become prickly. They've been awaiting the enthronement of Hindi. Now all these objections! You go home and rest.' Mahavir and some others touched his feet just as Dixit ji, nudged by Shukla ji, got into his waiting car. Now, having Shukla ji to themselves, Ram Mohan and Tiwari ji set to flattering him for his rise in politics, predicting his elevation to the Cabinet rank after the next Assembly election. Baijnath, Badri, Gulab Singh and his acolytes looked on; they had cycled down to Kanpur to behold Ram Mohan heaped with laurels but were disappointed at the way the event had wound up. Though opposed to his linguistic views, Ram Mohan was impressed by Wilson's English, and after Shukla ji drove away Ram Mohan put him in a cycle rickshaw; he wanted to take Gulab Singh, Badri and others to an eating joint nearby. It was getting dark but Wilson could still be seen sitting erect in the rickshaw as it crawled away; then they heard the shouting and saw some people running towards the rickshaw yelling insults. 'They must've been lying in wait', said Ram Mohan. 'Gulab Singh, let's beat the living daylights out of these louts.' They all made a dash as Mahavir Wilson had already received several blows. Gulab Singh stopped Ram Mohan and along with his two men fell on the thugs with lathis. Employing violence as starkly as a butcher—allowing no room for dickering—he had become adept in gaining control over situations apparently hazardous. He had long discovered this method to be immensely effective, which made even more powerful adversaries doubtful about their own strength.

It just took a few seconds for the attackers of Wilson to realize what they were up against. They fled, yelping. That was the beginning of the bonding between Ram Mohan and Mahavir Wilson.

The fifteenth year of India as a republic was quite eventful. After a large-scale disturbance and a few self-immolations against the imposition of Hindi, the centre backed out; the PM went on radio to assure people in south India of the status quo. The same day the Gujarat CM died in a plane crash somewhere around the Kutch-Sind border; PM Shastri claimed it was shot down by Pakistan; with its confidence topped up by its American arms and an India that had been demoralized at the hands of China, Pakistan had for some time been itching for war. It would have seen a big chance for itself to snatch Kashmir, but the fact that it was Shastri in the saddle—not Nehru, who had died the year before—blew up in its face. When it launched a fierce attack in Akhnoor sector of Jammu and Kashmir, Shastri gave the order to expand the war. India opened a new front and threatened to take Lahore, prompting the UN to intervene that led to a cessation of fighting.

This was also the year when Deena for the first time experienced first-hand the wrath of his father when he picked him up and threw him into a charpoy, shouting at Kanti, 'You have him spy on me . . . you spy on my . . .' What she had done was to ask Deena to inform his father that food was ready . . . I had better relate here the sequence of events leading up to Ram Mohan blowing his top: It was well past noon. Those who had come to see Ram Mohan had left; village life around this time would be markedly placid as the majority of people would be working in the fields; the ones remaining behind, mostly aged and elderly, would be lying down.

Despite signs of winter, there was still some mugginess in the air; to be under a thatch or a tree outside was much better than being inside. Right across from Ram Mohan's house, with a corrugated iron shade was this big chabootra, the right end of which was occupied by Madari Bapu who, old and blind, would seldom move out of his takht. He was a distant uncle of Ram Mohan's. Living nearby in the house adjoining Ram Mohan's was his son Kalla Prasad. He had five children the eldest of whom, Laxmikant alias Padhaiya—the one fond of studying, because in their family he was the first to have gone to primary school—stayed separately with his wife and son in a small house from across the other side of Ram Mohan's house. This house and the piece of land on which it stood also belonged to Ram Mohan. Kalla Prasad's second son Durgakant had joined the army as a soldier in the artillery. It was him being reported missing in Uri sector of Kashmir that had brought Ram Mohan to Parsadpur on a sudden visit.

Indian troops had repulsed a massive infiltration bid by
Pakistan in that very sector, and Durgakant being in one of the
platoons that had crossed the line of ceasefire in Uri to foil it,
was among those who had either lost their way or were captured
during the operation. To his parents who were in great distress,
Ram Mohan's optimism provided much relief; they were
worried about his very young wife; in fact, it had hardly been a
week after their wedding when the war broke out, and he had
had to report back to his unit at once. But it so happened that the
day after Ram Mohan came, news arrived that Durgakant was
safe albeit injured. Everybody's manner towards Ram Mohan
became more reverential, suggesting acknowledgement of his
part in the good news.

When Deena went outside looking for his father, he did
not find him. Sitting on his charpoy thumbing his rosary beads
was Chhote Baba, while across the cambered brick-lane lying as
usual on his takht on the covered chabootra was Madari Bapu.
Going back into the front room, the only one that had a roof
made of bricks and mortar, Deena ran up the small, narrow stair
leading to the roof and garret where Gayatri Masi stayed. She
had gone to Lucknow for a few days. Hopping around on the
roof were some sparrows whose incessant chirping would be
overlaid every now and then with the shrill cawing of a crow
perched on the parapet at the far end of the roof of Kalla Dada's
house, shaded by a big neem tree. The roofs of the two houses
were separated by the ridge running straight to the far end at
the back. Deena's arrival had pushed the birds away; when he
moved further, they took wing, plunging the setting into odd
quiet, to be stabbed at intervals by the squawk of the crow,
which as if ashamed of its sad presence, too flew away. Now
Deena could hear a faint voice behind the single brick wall in
the thatched structure over the stairs on Kalla Dada's roof; he
went over and stood close to his side of the wall straining to

listen in. It was his father. 'Not to worry, nothing will happen; there's no one in your house. Everybody is out in the fields. Even if somebody came up we would know well in time to avoid discovery . . . It'll give me such pleasure, and you won't lose anything.'

'Chacha, it's not proper,' said Durgakant's wife. 'It would be a sin . . .' Ram Mohan said, 'You haven't even known Durgakant properly . . . But you're fortunate that he'll be there now to spend the whole life with you. Everybody had given him up except you know who. I rushed here leaving everything aside to be of support to your family, and what I said has come true. Isn't it? And why do you think I asked everybody of your family to go out and work in the fields that lay neglected because of the shocking news? I knew that you being newly married wouldn't be allowed to work outside the house. Just think how wretched your life would be if my words hadn't been prophetic.' There was silence. He spoke again, 'Just let me have you once. Consider it an offering in gratitude for your husband being alive and safe. It's only a few drops that I want to drink from the ocean of your youthful charms. Just a touch of it and nothing will be amiss.' Everything was quiet for a few moments. 'Don't be so timorous and shy. I won't take off your sari, will just raise it . . . let me take these little pigeons out. Remove this veil.'

'No, I won't.'

Ram Mohan said, 'Don't torture me . . . Okay, keep your eyes closed while I kiss.' There followed a faint mixture of rustling, sighing, heavy breathing and whispers. Then there were more weird sounds. Deena got so scared his feet refused to budge; when he could move, he ran, rushed down the steps, went out and sat down a little breathless, on Chhote Baba's charpoy. Used to Babu ji's lordly nature, what he had heard made no sense. His father grovelling to a village woman,

younger than even Gayatri Masi! Whatever had happened to
his commanding voice! The voice he had just heard had an
unmistakable quiver and hurry in it.

Looking shrunk, Kanti did not know what to say to assuage
Ram Mohan's anger. All she could do was mumble it was
only about the meal being ready, though she sensed there was
something Ram Mohan wanted to hide. His anger spoke of
some male vulnerability. However, she would never learn what
it was that had so incensed him. Her efforts to cajole the truth
out of Deena proved futile; he was too discomfited to describe
something so bizarre.

Deena was still a toddler when his Dadi and Nani had died. He
had heard of people dying of sickness or old age. He had heard
of people dying unnaturally, say, in accidents or at the hands
of their enemies; yet the remoteness of such instances had kept
him emotionally sheltered. Gayatri Masi's sudden exit—a death
so close—tore down that shelter. Later he would experience the
same mortal pain at seeing Gabdu's severed head.

With the slenderness of her limbs besmeared by an insipid
thickness, Gayatri had not seemed herself for some time; now
she sat wrapped, rather bundled, like some agricultural produce
in a thick rough blood-soaked sheet under the neem tree by the
outer wall of Kalla Dada's house. The train had railroaded her
into pieces that had taken some time to collect. The discovery
of the foetus on the tracks however had left people agape. The
tragedy, doing a somersault, turned into relief for her well-
wishers, bringing consolation even to Kanti who had been
crying bitterly. There was no need to grieve as her departure
had saved her from merciless scandal. It made no sense to Deena
though. On waking up in the morning, he would feel afresh the

stab of her being gone. To think he would never set eyes on her again seemed so painfully unreal.

* * *

Badri and Gulab Singh took the noon train to Kanpur. A little staggered initially by the news, Ram Mohan regained his poise and informed Dixit ji through the collector's office before flying off to Parsadpur, which was lousy with idle talk. That she had been having a liaison in Lucknow was self-evident now. Earlier, when she was alive, one would catch people saying sotto voce that the purpose of her Lucknow sojourns was to meet her secret lover; that the guardianship, respectability and old age of Dixit ji only provided a cover for her whorish activities.

Wary of the controversy, Ram Mohan did not inform the police; he was waiting for Dixit ji. It was getting cold as the evening approached. The big dark patches on the bundle under the neem tree were black with flies; Padhaiya Bhaiya got it covered with a large open basket made of lentil twigs. Accompanied by Gayatri's mother and Mama, Dixit ji arrived a little after dark; there were security men with him; they had come in two Jeeps. Because of the badly rutted village track, his official ambassador car had to be left on the GT Road. Dixit ji and Gayatri's Mama were seated on the takht placed for them on the chabootra opposite Ram Mohan's house, while Madari Bapu, under his thick and grubby quilt, hardly visible, lay on his takht right next to them. The mother was led into the front room where Kanti and others were. No sooner had they come face to face than there was another burst of wailing; Kanti hugged her; they had never met before.

With Dixit ji and Gayatri's Mama agreeing, Ram Mohan gave instructions that a pyre be prepared in an open field, as he helped Dixit ji, who wanted to relieve himself, climb down the chabootra. A young man with a lantern held aloft walked ahead. Earlier it would not be easy to tell Dixit ji's age. No longer so. A trace of infirmity, a whiff of wobble, had become all too visible in his bearing. His career in politics had peaked; the last time when there had been a change of leadership in the state government, he had hoped to be handed the reins but could be no match for the one chosen, Sucheta Kriplani, the wife of a former Congress president who, once a close associate of Gandhi and Nehru, was running his own political outfit committed to socialist ideals. Following the let-down, Dixit ji would have found comfort in the thought of Gayatri, for soon after this, he had moaned that he did not want to achieve anything more in politics. He had said to Sughari, 'No political power can ever recompense for the absence of this pleasure. How many at my age can even dream of being conjoined with someone so young and alluring, who gives herself so lovingly and with such care and compassion.' No wonder Gayatri's death had taken a terrible toll on him.

As the basket was removed, there came an unmistakable hint of decomposing flesh; 'No need to open it,' said Dixit ji. 'Let's dispose of it as fast as possible.' Then taking Ram Mohan to one side, he said, 'Whatever could have forced her . . .? During the last two visits, now I recall, she didn't seem herself. She wouldn't say but I could sense she was concerned about her future . . . how she would manage her life after I was gone . . . You know how hard it is for a young widow to live, whose presence is considered inauspicious.' Ram Mohan did not know what to say. They had come back to the chabootra. It was cold. A pile of dry twigs and leaves were lit to build a fire. Seating Dixit ji and Chhote Baba on the charpoy near the fire, Ram Mohan followed Gayatri's mother, her Mama, Kanti and Baijnath into the front room of his house, while Badri, Gulab Singh, Kalla Dada squatted around the fire staying close to Dixit ji.

After discussing it with Baijnath, Gulab Singh and Badri, Ram Mohan had decided not to tell Dixit ji about the foetus. It would complicate his pain. He might even feel obliged to find the culprit. Yet, Gayatri's mother and Mama would feel better if told; Ram Mohan had Baijnath apprise Gayatri's mother and Mama of the truth. At first the mother began to curse the 'monster' as she called the unknown man; but shortly, after her brother and Baijnath calmed her down, she said, 'What else could she have done? There was no choice left for my daughter.' She stopped to wipe her face with a corner of her sari, 'While she was growing up, people wouldn't get tired of raving about her looks. Her mother-in-law was stunned when she had come to see Gayatri; she had fallen over herself to assure my daughter would be treated like a princess in their house. But it was this very beauty that proved her undoing. Their priest read a curse in it; if what that priest said is true, the monster behind my daughter's death will also die if not dead already.' Tears bubbled up again in her eyes; Kanti put an arm around her, while herself breaking out in tears.

* * *

Later Ram Mohan would share with Badri and Gulab Singh the reason why he had kept the cause of Gayatri's suicide from Dixit ji. 'She lived in my house, so I or someone close to me could have become prey to his misgiving; he wouldn't have aired it though, I'm sure. But it would in all probability have destroyed our relationship. A suspicion that can't be verified is often more disastrous than its confirmation.'

The cremation took place in a cleared sugarcane field. Covered with logs the bundle was set on fire without much ceremony; it had not totally burned when they left, leaving it in the care of some members of a Harijan family. Dixit ji had to return to Lucknow the same night; he left behind one Jeep to bring back Gayatri's mother and Mama who had stayed on to collect Gayatri's ashes to be consigned to the Ganges.

With Gayatri gone, Kanti's school lost its momentum. The marriage of Manno, her sister, only hastened its demise; Kanti had neither time nor will to continue with the enterprise. Nisha, Nishant and Sandhya were all living in Kanpur with their father. A few months ago, Nisha had brought even the two and half year old Mayank to live with them in the city. Deena stayed with their mother and Chhote Baba.

Deena was a great help to his mother when it came to tending their cattle, especially goats, and collecting mangos and Mahua during the season. His extraordinary love and compassion for animals had made people wonder; he had become known for this idiosyncrasy; was teased about it. His daring act to once save Gabdu from the jaws of his Mama had become a legend. Kanti usually had one or two buffalo cows, a portion of whose milk would be sold to fetch extra cash, the rest used for making ghee. Milk to be consumed at home would come from the two goats she kept; Chhote Baba and Deena both liked goat milk; it was easier for Kanti to manage them because of Deena's fondness for them. He would take them to graze. It allowed him to have fun while being with his goats, for Kanti was loath to see him waste his time just playing. If there was no work she would rather he sat at home and studied. Deena was an average sort of student except when it came to Hindi. No one in school could match up to his knowledge of it. He could handle texts considered out of bounds to children of his age. His teachers attributed his precocity in Hindi to his father, but his exposure to Ram Mohan's linguistic persona was very little. It was Gayatri Masi who'd helped him discover a wellspring of fun in the various storybooks that his Nana had given to Kanti. They were mostly fables, folktales and stories of mythological nature.

Now minding the goats and reading these stories was the chief source of amusement for Deena; other outdoor activities like playing with other children had stood curbed. He would have as much fun as possible while being out with his goats. One day there came this boy several years older than Deena offering to join him; he liked Deena. There were three nanny goats and about a month-old female kid to mind. She, the kid with a tender coat of russet, meant the world to Deena whom he had named Nanki, the tiny one. As they walked behind the goats, this boy kept talking non-stop. Deena was particularly attentive to Nanki as her mother and two others got busy eating grass growing around irrigation channels. 'Nothing will happen to her. You let her play. I'm here, don't worry,' the boy said taking in Deena's concern; holding his hand, he walked to the lone mango tree standing in the middle of a field.

It was getting warm. The winter had retreated without trace. The sun was high, and there was no clear pattern in the wind, either directionally or temperature-wise; it blew spasmodically, one moment hissing from one side, cool and pleasant, the next flurrying from other direction tepid and summery. Just as they sat down under the mango tree which being in bloom sent out a heady tang, Deena noticed an odd change in the boy's voice, suggesting a parched mouth; he kept running his tongue over the lips. Deena looked at him in perturbation.

'Deena, I want to talk to you about something; it's only between you and me,' the boy said. He took Deena's hand and put it on his crotch and kept it there aborting the latter's attempt to pull it free. 'What's the matter? It won't bite you,' whispered the boy. He then untied the cord of his drawers, using the free hand, and revealed his twitching big boney manhood. A contrast to innocuous little playthings Deena was used to seeing, it looked ghastly and menacing with no vestige of innocence that still clung to its owner's face. Deena looked around anxiously. In the distance to their left a man was busy ploughing his field; to their right, crawling along the dirt track towards Ballamgaon was a bullock cart, while further away a small herd of cows and buffalo cows were grazing. 'Don't worry, nobody can make out from this distance,' said the boy while getting Deena to wrap his small hand around the monster rising out of its shaggy base and move it up and down. Breathing in through the mouth, the boy made slurping noise; in no time his body stiffened; he quickly removed Deena's hand and let fly into the air a jet of something unfamiliar to the latter.

Wiping himself on his drawers, the boy grinned sheepishly but reassuringly. Deena had got scared by the way his body had convulsed as if in terrible pain. The boy began to talk about the approaching mango season as though nothing had happened; a few minutes later he said, 'Now that I've shown my thing, what will I see in return?' Taken aback Deena said, 'No, I won't show anything.' Right then his attention was drawn to Nanki's frantic but unavailing efforts to get to her mother's udder which was enveloped in a cloth bag with two long strings winding around her waist and tied at the top, a common practice to save milk for household consumption and keep kids from overfeeding. Deena ran to where Nanki was prodding the bag in search of milk, as her mother, having stopped nibbling weeds and tufts of grass on the sides of an irrigation ditch, stood serenely to feed her. Deena removed the bag letting Nanki suck at her mother's teats. Shortly he pulled her back, calling out to the boy to help him fasten the bag back. Now Nanki was bounding and leaping off the ground in delight, her muzzle still wet. Deena would often do this with the help of his friends. 'So how are you going to settle it, Deena?' said the boy again after they strolled back to the

tree. 'No, I won't do it. You took it out of your own accord.'
The boy said, 'But now that you've seen it, I must see yours.
If you don't, I'll tell your mother what you've done; she was
complaining the other day about not getting enough milk from
Nanki's mother . . . It's nothing . . . show it to me and that's
it,' the boy pressed on as Deena looked at him, then glancing
around Deena nervously untied the cord and slightly lowered
his drawers while the boy's lips and mouth went dry again. He
turned Deena's back towards him and leered at the bare bottom;
then Deena pulled away at once. 'What's the matter? I've seen
it. No need to blush. Let me enjoy it.'

'You said you just wanted to see. Now you've seen.' Deena
said angrily. The boy smiled and uncovered his erection again.
Even Deena would experience this change in his organ, which
gave a certain pleasure if touched and caressed, and whenever
playing *ghar-ghar* (house) he and other boys would become cows
to be milked by the girls who would insist on using the ends
of the strings in their drawers as teats, but Deena and others
demanded their little things be used for the purpose instead.
When the girls milked them this way, they would feel heavenly
and wanted nothing beyond that.

The episode had left Deena enlightened in some measure
about what it could be that kept older boys or men ailing one
way or the other, which had all been a mystery to him till
then. He now could pick out a leitmotif in all those apparently
disparate instances of men's conduct in relation to women and
young boys too.

Deena like other village kids had learnt early on that any
physical contact with Harijans was polluting; about the nature
of the pollution, he was at sea. The first time he overstepped

the mark was when he had drunk water from Danku's bucket, who had tried to head off this profanity, but all his entreaties were meaningless to Deena whose throat was so parched after a game of kabaddi that climbing onto the plinth of the well near his house, he had sated his thirst directly from Danku's bucket. He knew why Danku was fretful; if Chhote Baba found out, it would be he, not Deena, to blame.

But Baijnath, his Nana (maternal grandfather), being hostile to untouchability, was given to tirades against the practice, though his daughter's compulsions were not lost on him; he once even undertook the task of making Chhote Baba see the injustice, who laughed off his arguments. To silence the worshipper of Lord Ram, Baijnath had brought up the story of Shabri, a much quoted and celebrated part of Hindu lore, according to which Lord Ram while looking for his abducted wife Sita during his jungle exile comes across this low caste jujube-seller Shabri, a great devotee of his, who overwhelmed by her Lord's visit offers him jujubes but not before ensuring that none is sour. That she does by first tasting each herself, unconscious of rendering them impure. But Lord Ram, to the chagrin of his brother Laxman, eats them wearing a lofty smile.

Reminded of the story, Chhote Baba's eyes glistened. He said it only proved how far Lord Ram would go to acknowledge the devotion of his devotee; that he would make an exception in case of exceptional devoutness; that the importance of a gesture like this lay in it being just exception. To further clear Baijnath's mind of 'ignorance', he told him the story of Shambook who, despite being a low-caste, tries to seek salvation through ascetic self-mortification, a grave impropriety, a transgression, resulting in the death of a Brahman baby, a blot on Ram Rajya obviously. Thereafter, with the consent of his family guru Vashishtha, Lord Ram beheads Shambook with his sword, which brings the Brahman boy back to life.

Deena awaited his Nana's visits and clung to him during his stay. It was the first time he had heard the story of Shambook, which was not included in the popular simplified abridged version of Ramayana familiar to him. He never particularly liked Lord Ram whom he found a touch too stolid for his taste; the story of Shambook set the seal on his dislike of him, after which when he was asked to play the part of Lord Ram in the village Ramlila—there used to be enactments every year of various scenes from Ramayana in the run-up to Dussehra, the festival that marked the victory of good over bad—he refused, insisting instead on playing the part of Hanuman, the monkey-god.

* * *

To aspire to literacy and education for their offspring was not uncommon among Harijans; but those who would act on it, their number was negligible, making any such instance an oddity; thus the sight of these two puny boys from Kuriyan—a Harijan hamlet—treading towards the primary school near Dahiya would cause people to jest or curse at times for such a noxious trend. A rage would boil inside Deena.

One of them was Isuri, the son of the landless labourer who sometimes ploughed Ram Mohan's fields. Not allowed to sit with other children, they had to carry a tattered sack to sit on in the farthest corner of the classroom; and punishment for the breaking of any rules would be more severe and frequent in the case of these two, making them wary of catching undue attention of the teachers. Two of the teachers, including the headmaster, would scarcely let go of a chance to cane them. The third one treated all the children alike; as a matter of fact, he was a bit more attentive to the problems of these two, which was greeted with derision by his colleagues. Once Deena overheard a full-hearted argument between them; it was the day before

Independence Day; preparations were on at full throttle. They
were all busy. After cleaning their classrooms and bedaubing
the floors with dung, they were making paper flags, India's
tricolour. Deena along with a few other boys had been given a
space in the staffroom to work, while Isuri and the other Harijan
boy were outside under the peepul tree near the old mildewed
temple. Suddenly a couple of children scampered into the
staffroom to complain that Isuri had stepped onto the tricolour.
The headmaster was enraged. Picking up his rod he rushed out,
both of his colleagues treading on his heels. Deena and others
too followed.

A blubbering Isuri made an intrepid attempt at explanation;
that he had lost balance while trying to rise and could not help
stamping the flag. He had hardly finished when the headmaster's
rod felled him; Pandey, the third teacher, the sympathetic one,
bent over Isuri who was doubled over with pain, his hand on
one of the thighs where the rod had struck. The headmaster
said the boy was shamming. Pandey discovered the swelling, an
inceptive abscess—hard, red and warm to touch, yet to obtain a
mouth—which if touched softly gives a peculiarly nice sensation
but dreadfully painful in case of being hit. Helping Isuri to his
feet the third teacher asked the other boy from Kuriyan to take
him home. In the note where I found this incident described,
Deena writes, *'I still remember how feeble Isuri looked with his cheeks
caved in, the face streaked with tears and dirt'*.

Back in the staffroom, the headmaster and the other teacher,
the one that behaved like his sidekick, stood over Deena and
other boys who had resumed their task of making miniature
paper copies of the Indian tricolour; 'Make sure the colours do
not bleed into each other; all three should be neatly separate,'
said the headmaster, as Pandey watched with scowl.

'Why did you have to hit him so hard?' said he as soon as
the headmaster and the other teacher returned to their chairs.

'And why did you have to touch him,' barked the headmaster. 'Go take a bath; then we'll talk.'

Pandey quietly picked up his *gumchha* (a thin cotton towel) and made for the well across the mud street behind the school; they could see him through the window in the back wall.

'Swami Dayanand has been reborn, I'm afraid,' said the headmaster.

'No, he's a Gandhi-bhakt, Thakur Sahab,' said the other teacher.

'How many more divisions of the country do these Gandhi-bhakts want; aren't they content with one Pakistan?'

'He doesn't behave like a real Brahman.'

Turning his head to look out of the window the headmaster gazed at the bathing figure at the well and said, 'Have you noticed, the fellow is dark, darker than most Brahmans?'

'Yes . . . no . . . I've seen some of them even darker; but yes, it's not a normal thing.'

'It's not the darkness caused by the village life . . . by the sun. It has some innate quality to it,' the headmaster said with a smirk.

'It's no less weird than a fair-skinned outcaste. You must be familiar with this popular saying,

Kariyaa Bahman, gor Chamaar, Kanjaa Turuak, bhoor Rajput;
Sir kaa ganja hoy; Inse tab baat karo, Jab haath mein dandaa hoy.

(Dark-skinned Brahman, fair-skinned Chamar, a Turk with light-coloured eyes, a Rajput with brown-coloured ones, or any bald man for that matter—speak to them only when you have a stick in your hand.)'

'Yes, yes . . . I'm amazed by these sayings, simple yet insightful . . . He's coming.'

The dark-skinned Brahman entered the room with the wet gumchha over his shoulder; he went to the window to hang it on the iron bars. He manoeuvred his chair to face the headmaster.

'Thakur Sahab, where was the need to be so angry with the child? Your blow was so hard I could notice a welt right across where he has an abscess in the making. Can you imagine how terribly it hurt him?'

'How could I have known? I did feel bad about it . . . But let me ask you, how could you remain so calm after our national flag was trampled on?'

'Do you think the lad did it deliberately? His foot fell on it unwittingly. You know this.'

'Pandit ji, what I understand from this is that such an august symbol of our great nation can be dishonoured with impunity if we regard it as unintentional!'

'What logic is this, Thakur Sahab?'

'You just don't get it . . . One has to be extra careful when handling something like that, something that represents the country's pride and honour.'

'That is, anyone accused of a lax attitude to these symbols needs to be penalized regardless of them being a child or an adult! Is this your logic, Thakur Sahab?'

Turning to his other colleague, the headmaster said with an exaggerated tone of surprise, 'Whatever has happened to the famed Brahman intellect, Srivastava ji?'

'The darkness of my skin has also coloured my thinking, why Srivastava ji, isn't it so?' said Pandey.

Srivastava ji's job as a teacher in the primary school was yet to be regularized. His was the only Kayastha family in Ballamgaon.

'I myself am dark, Pandit ji. Why should I comment on your complexion?' said Srivastava ji with a twisted grin.

'You know the reason . . . Your being dark isn't viewed as weird; many Kayasthas are like that.'

'Enough is enough . . . Why have you two got stuck on the complexion of each other?' the headmaster said.

'Thakur Sahab, I feel a bit out of sorts that the child had to go back hurt and crying.'

'Can his being a child alter his status? An outcaste is an outcaste. How does it matter if he's a child or an adult? Tell me Pandit ji, was our freedom to result in this mire? I just can't stand the presence of these untouchables in the temple of goddess Saraswati.'

'What are you talking about? The Congress party of Gandhi ji dreamt of a new India, an India built in the light of new knowledge and sensibility . . . where all its citizens have equal rights.'

'The idea of this new India of which you seem so proud, represents nothing but foreign values running counter to our Indian ethos, and please don't drag Gandhi ji into it. He was all for a return to our traditional ways of life. The masses standing behind the Congress thought it was fighting for the retrieval of our cultural glory. I know of people close to the leaders of the freedom struggle; they were punctilious about caste rules, even while attending Congress conventions.'

'Headmaster Sahab, even a child can tell you Gandhi ji was against untouchability.'

'He wasn't an ordinary man, Pandit ji. These great and holy men are beyond the comprehension of us commoners. Gandhi ji was great enough to even pardon criminals and murderers. If he had remained alive for a bit after he was shot, he would've forgiven even Godse, his own killer. Who can doubt that? But can we even in our wildest imagination think of doing that? Look how his opposition to untouchability has created problems for the country. There's been much confusion and tension because of this . . . Great figures should be left alone.'

When Pandey tried to speak, the headmaster stopped him with the motion of his hand, 'There's no end to this discussion,

Pandit ji.' After a deliberate pause, 'No individual is greater than tradition.' They all turned their attention to Deena and other students who were through with their flag making.

* * *

The other boy from Kuriyan made it to school for Independence Day alone the next morning; Isuri had a fever. The tone in which Pandey responded to the news pushed the headmaster up the wall, 'Don't spoil today's proud occasion by harping on your love for him. Was this the objective of the freedom? That we change places with them; how can it be? It's like converting your footwear to headgear. If these outcastes agreed to adhere to their traditional position, they might have a claim on our pity. Not now when they want to compete with us, mocking us with their presence in Parliament and Assemblies and government jobs.'

They heard voices in the distance. Seeing Gulab Singh and his men, the headmaster sent Srivastava ji to escort them. Gulab Singh, the strongman of the area with Ram Mohan's political hand on his head, had been elected village chief of Ballamgaon and was invited to hoist the national flag at the school on the occasion of Independence Day. Having grown a little thick around the waist, he looked more imposing; his famous lathi had been ousted by a double-barrelled shotgun hung over the shoulder; his henchmen had also grown in number, four in total now. Deena avoided being caught by his eye during the flag hoisting ceremony; the ensuing attention would've embarrassed him. After the guests left, children were asked to form a crocodile for *Prabhat Pheri*.

As the march began, the children carrying paper tricolours broke into the song taught for the occasion, a famous patriotic song from an old Hindi film:

Where roost on every branch birds of gold,
Where truth, ahimsa, virtue are found untold,
That is my country, India.
That is my country, India,

The middle and tail-end of the two parallel columns of students
were being monitored by Pandey and Srivastava ji, each armed
with a long switch; the headmaster with the rod in his hand
marched at the front. The route was the same as before. The
first leg of the Prabhat Pheri had to pass a small *basti* (slum) of
swineherds on the right and a ditch running along the railway
on the left. This annual affair provided a kind of entertainment
to these pariahs, their children especially, who would be careful
to put the required distance between their polluting presence
and the crocodile bespangled with national flags. The day was
murky and sunless.

No sooner had they begun walking along the path skirting
this basti than the overcast sky set off making good its warning.
The headmaster swore as it began spitting; he shouted at his
junior colleagues to watch over their wards. The untouchable
adults hastened into their mud hovels; their children remained
outside capering and enjoying the rain-induced muddle that—
though all their pigs had been rounded up because of the Prabhat
Pheri—provided a sow with a breach, who, seeming at a loss
and a litter of piglets at her heel, headed towards the front of
the crocodile, which broke up like the moss on the surface of a
village pond. The headmaster's attempts to scare it away with his
rod while trying to hold his dhoti in place were in vain; the sow,
in the spatter and spray, could not see or hear the frantic figure
and kept on moving. Yelling insults at the outcastes, Srivastava ji
made a dash for the front of the procession. In the meantime, a
boy—the tallest among the untouchable children—managed to
drive the sow away, which the headmaster, having lost sight of

the gap between him and the pig, did not notice. He stepped
back in panic, teetered and fell to the ground. The tragicomic
scene—his feet up in the air, the dhoti flung back and the striped
drawers beneath revealed—made a joke of his authority; the
pariah children were unable to stop laughing when Srivastava
ji struck the rescuing boy on the naked back with his switch
leaving a weal visible even on such a grey day.

By and by Deena became more sensible of his father's growing
prominence; their peasant community was but a small part
of the population of the region dominated by upper castes,
some of whom still remembered with lingering bitterness how
cleverly Ram Mohan had talked the British administration into
changing the name of the railway station. As a young man,
he may have viewed it as a victory, a point of honour. In the
post-freedom scenario, the thought of achieving something like
that would be a foolhardy dream; Ram Mohan had accordingly
adapted himself to the new reality. While dealing with a high
caste personage, he would use arguments designed to humour;
he had already made inroads into the upper-caste consciousness
in the area, as he would try to be regarded as their well-wisher.
At the election for the posts of village chief, he had ensured
Gulab Singh's victory, which held no surprise as Gulab Singh
was Ram Mohan's friend. But his going all out to support a
Brahman candidate for the same position in another village—
where the real fight was between a Brahman and a Thakur
candidate—earned him some goodwill indeed; Ram Mohan's
intervention swung the balance in favour of the Brahman in an
otherwise nip and tuck contest. Though small in number, all
the Kurmi voters in that village listened to Ram Mohan; the
defeated camp's attempt to brand him as the agent of Brahmans

would not stick because of his close ties with Gulab Singh, a Thakur.

This was the tact and delicacy with which Ram Mohan endeavoured to win some upper caste friends, which gained in significance when he—as cued by Chaudhary Baran Singh— would be on the lookout for a constituency as an alternative to Fatehpur, affording Chaudhary Sahab some leeway. Though the fourth general election was a year off, the latter did not want to take chances. After the sudden demise of PM Shastri—who knew Chaudhary Sahab personally—things were somewhat fluid. Shastri ji would have had the final say in ticket distribution in UP, his own state, particularly so when he was riding the crest of public approval. His bold strategy had won a crucial war with Pakistan. But now if Fatehpur did not work out, Chaudhary Sahab would need the second option from Ram Mohan. To discuss the issue, Ram Mohan invited his political well-wishers for a meeting in Parsadpur; to the surprise of many, two notable members of the Brahman community too showed up. It was quite a gathering. The chabootra across from Ram Mohan's house did not have enough room, so it had to be the threshing ground where in addition to several charpoys, a big sheet of tarpaulin was spread out on the ground.

It was one of the two best short spells of weather separated by about one and half months of intense cold, whereas close at hand was Holi, one of the two biggest Hindu festivals, preparations for which were already underway; there was a variety of food items and snacks to be offered to the guests. The meeting was expected to go beyond the sunset; Badri and Gulab Singh had sent for some lanterns and a pressure lamp. Though Parsadpur had the distinction of being the first and the only electrified village in the province—Ram Mohan's glowing achievement in the sphere of village development—it would remain as unlit as other villages. At first, every four-five months the concerned substation would switch on the power to Parsadpur for a few minutes, generating a festive mood; children would beetle off up and down the lanes in great excitement while adults would drop everything to watch in amazement the light thrown by naked electric bulbs hanging from the poles. Neighbours would pour into wired-up houses including Deena's to savour the power-lit insides; such occasions however would become scarcer, so much so that people ceased to bother; the mere presence of electricity poles and wires was enough to mark off Parsadpur.

The idea of Ram Mohan contesting from his home constituency was endorsed by the two Brahman guests who assured the gathering of their support. Badri in his mild and hesitant manner suggested it should be an option only after the effort to secure Fatehpur had failed; Gulab Singh waxed sceptical about the upper castes' backing, drawing distrustful glances from the two Brahmans, while Tiwari ji with a wisp of a smile listened calmly; it was he who had planted the idea of Fatehpur as his parliamentary constituency in Ram Mohan's mind. Tiwari ji's measured tone quelled all the murmurings.

'We must understand it's not some family dispute we've gathered to sort out. Our concern is to find a suitable constituency, and in my blunt opinion any place other than Fatehpur would spell a certain defeat,' Tiwari ji paused before continuing, 'We all know Congress has the full support of three strong segments of the electorate, Brahmans, Harijans and Muslims; there're others too but not numerically significant. Being a Congress candidate would get Ram Mohan the votes of Muslims and Harijans anywhere. But . . .'

'What you're saying, Tiwari ji, is of critical importance and we should pay mind to it,' said Ram Mohan. 'So let's first get the lights working before it gets dark.' All the lanterns and the single pressure lamp were quickly lit; their light looked oddly sad as the sun, though out of sight, was yet to pull its luminous tresses out of the horizon. 'What I mean is that barring a few individuals, Brahmans won't support Ram Mohan. Even Muslims can't countervail the loss of Brahman votes here. On the other hand, Fatehpur not only has a strong Kurmi presence but also a big Muslim vote bank; then there're more Harijans there than here. In fact, fighting the election as an independent from Fatehpur is better than being a Congress candidate here. In Fatehpur, Ram Mohan would win laurels even in defeat. I mean he'd get his hands on so many votes that Congress would have to take note, which would brighten up his chances in future. They might offer him something else in the bargain.'

Tiwari ji's quick and clear analysis prompted hitherto quiet Mahavir Wilson to speak up, 'It's hard not to see Tiwari ji's point. Besides, all opposition leaders are busy drawing up their strategies; Shastri ji's death has given them hope; they must think that Nehru's daughter being the PM should be less of a problem for them. People's Union can be a good option before Brahmans if they don't find any Congress candidate worthy of their support. Losing this segment of votes in this constituency would mean losing the election.' It was Mahavir Wilson's first visit to Parsadpur; no one in the gathering, except Tiwari ji, Gulab Singh and Badri, knew he was an outcaste; he could easily pass for a Christian migrant from the south, whose confident manner and spontaneous use of English words would do away with the abjectness of his origins.

A stray cloud sailed across whatever brilliance was left after the sun fell below the horizon. So abrupt was the drop in the fading sunlight it wrenched a collective groan from the gathering. Deena and other children enjoyed these peppy occasions when so many people assembled around Ram Mohan. Unlike other children—for whom the freedom granted by such events was everything—Deena liked to watch the goings-on. The main thrill for him lay in his father's centrality in them. The arrival of dusk enabled Deena to move unseen and climb a mango tree for a better view; as he tried to straddle the limb closest to the ground; somebody helped him onto it from behind. It was Dallu, the big boy who had touched him up before; feeling a dart of uneasiness in his gut, Deena tried to ignore him but Dallu, undeterred, got behind him on the limb of the tree; Deena could feel it on his waist—the erection. Smouldering, he kept quiet. When Dallu attempted to dragoon him into touching his thing straining within the striped drawers, Deena jerked his hand away and said, 'If you don't leave me alone, I'll tell Gulab Chacha.' The threat put an end to Dallu's quest.

When the meeting got over, Deena set off for home, almost running; as he tried to squeeze through the disintegrating throng, Badri grabbed him by the arm. He introduced him to Mahavir Wilson, 'This is Ram Mohan's son Deena; he lives here with his mother.' Wilson put his hand over his head and asked Deena in which class he was studying; just before leaving to join Ram Mohan and others for food, Wilson enjoined him to study hard and become a scholar like his father. Deena would write in one of his notebooks: *Even in that passing encounter, I recognized something reassuring and pleasant in Mahavir Bhaiya.*

It was agreed in the meeting that Chaudhary Baran Singh should be brought into the equation; he might want to revisit his idea of an alternative Parliamentary constituency for Ram Mohan.

When Ram Mohan and Tiwari ji went to Lucknow, they found Chaudhary Sahab's earlier bounce missing. He was not so sure now of getting him the party's ticket for either of the constituencies; an unexpected suitor for Fatehpur had emerged out of nowhere. This man by the name of Udai Pratap Singh,

a Thakur from the landed gentry in Allahabad, was a product
of Oxford and Lincoln's Inn, which stood him in great stead.
Before long the word was out that Udai Pratap Singh would be
the Congress candidate from Fatehpur.

To confirm, Baran Singh contacted his sources in Delhi,
one of whom was part of the powerful Syndicate in the party
responsible for making her PM; the reason she had been preferred
was her supposed docility. Now she seemed to be moving to
turn the tables on these leaders who airily believed she would
do their bidding. Baran Singh said, 'Things in Delhi are so roiled
we don't know whose authority—the PM's or the Syndicate's—
will weigh more when it comes to ticket-distribution. But I'll
press with all my might for your candidature from Fatehpur.'
He sent Ram Mohan Delhi to meet some people. It was his
first visit to the national capital whose grandeur held him
spellbound, making him more determined than ever to get to
Parliament. He stayed with Saansad ji, an MP and Baran Singh's
closest friend; the same Saansad ji as had picked Nehru's China
policy to shreds in Lucknow several years before. During his
stay in Delhi, Ram Mohan met some central leaders known to
Baran Singh; Saansad ji arranged for him to meet Kapur who
was fast becoming a close confidant of Indira Gandhi. Dressed
in khadi kurta, waistcoat and churidar, the man came across as a
sartorial copy of Nehru. However, the meeting was just a brief
and polite conversation. He appreciated Ram Mohan's wish to
be fielded as Congress candidate in coming elections, promising
to do what he could to help.

Back in Saansad ji's place, Ram Mohan could scarcely
suppress his freshly stirred optimism; just as they settled down
to evening tea, he said, 'Kapur Sahab sounds quite sincere.
His stress on the need for honest, educated people in politics
is heartening.' Saansad ji brooded over his cup of tea for an
awkwardly long moment before raising it to his lips. Ram

Mohan waited. Placing the cup back on the saucer, he said, 'Let me bring you up to speed on the scene here.'

Ram Mohan straightened himself up. Saansad ji, who had impressed him in their first meeting by his take on China conflagration, began calmly, 'As you know, the party under Nehru ji had never bothered about his successor. There was no attempt on his part to groom someone for the big responsibility. It was unconscionable but conscious neglect. Why? I can think of only two reasons.' He stopped to ask the servant boy to remove the empty cups; he also enquired as to what was being prepared for dinner before going on, 'Nehru ji was more conscious of his own supposed greatness than the greatness of India's poverty and dereliction. He believed in great plans and symbols, seeing in them his own reflection. That there might be capable people to take his place would have been sacrilege to him; the allusion he had made to his being tired of the burden was nothing but to showcase his indispensability.' Saansad ji took a breath, 'The second reason based on my surmise is that he had had some inkling of his daughter leading the country one day.'

'But, Saansad ji, if what you say was correct, he would have made her a minister to start with.'

'No, it's more subtle than that . . . To make her minister would have had to be solely his decision, which would have rebelled against his conscience and integrity, but he would've been fine if she was chosen by the party. Hadn't he agreed to her being picked as Congress president while he was PM? I suspect he knew that in time Congress Parliamentary Party would have to fall back on the political legacy of which she, by birth, was the sole inheritor.'

'If Shastri ji hadn't died so soon . . . do you think she would still have a chance?'

'Even Nehru ji would not have envisaged it coming her way this soon. Yet, thanks to his not having any second in command, his death was bound to lead to a leadership crisis sooner or later. Be it Shastri or anybody else, no one could have fixed the problem for any reasonable length of time; only the anointment of his daughter would have the requisite strength to override diverse claims,' Saansad ji paused before resuming. 'There's no point in discussing all this now. Indira Gandhi has become PM, and people like me and Baran Singh need to take a fresh look at our politics . . . My word may sound discouraging but things seem to have ducked our earlier estimate . . .'

'How do you mean?'

'I'm saying you should be prepared for contesting from Fatehpur as an independent. Baran Singh and I have discussed it on the phone. He's doing whatever he can to have the party consider you for Fatehpur. If you want my honest opinion, chances are very slim.' Ram Mohan was not surprised at the blunt revelation. Chaudhary Sahab's idea of a second constituency had given him enough hints that with Shastri ji's death, his influence with Congress high command lay curtailed.

'But Shukla ji is upbeat about Indira Gandhi succeeding Shastri ji. When I asked him the reason, he just said we would come to know soon. Maybe he can help us! He's close to Chaudhary Sahab and has a soft corner for me. If Chaudhary Sahab could talk to him, he might be of some help.'

'Don't even mention this to Baran Singh,' said Saansad ji. 'We know what Shukla is so chuffed about. Indira Gandhi is forming a close circle of cronies around her, Kapur being one of them. I don't know if you know that Shukla ji's uncle— Umakant Shukla—who is in Rajya Sabha won her confidence when she was a minister under Shastri ji. Before leaving for Tashkent, Shastri ji had decided to send her to London as India's High Commissioner; he thought it would be hard for her to shake off the hangover of the Nehru years and her role in her father's political life . . .'

'Is that correct?' cried Ram Mohan.

'Yes . . . It was Umakant Shukla, who God knows how, got wind of this and told her; it's another matter she didn't have to do anything to forestall her banishment; but Tripathi proved his loyalty to Nehru family. In all likelihood, he would be made a minister soon.'

'All the more reason we should seek Shukla ji's help, don't you think?'

'Come on Ram Mohan, can't you see what I'm trying to say . . . Shukla is now on the other side of the fence, who may still be courteous and deferential to Baran Singh, but both know they no longer share the same political dynamics. Before Shastri ji's death, we thought the next change in the leadership in UP would bring Baran Singh to the helm; Shukla was so excited about it, about the prospects of being promoted to Cabinet rank. But now that his own uncle is in the coterie of the PM, he needs no one else. The uncle's happy with his Rajya Sabha membership and wants to remain in Delhi while Shukla's political aspirations lie in UP.'

'How would it impact the future of Chaudhary Sahab?' said Ram Mohan with a touch of despondency.

'Baran Singh is a self-made man who has worked his way through so much political garbage to the position he has today. Knowing him, I don't think he will be ready to compromise; he can't bring himself to truckle to the new Congress overlords. And those who think Nehru's daughter would remain pliable are in for a shock. She's taking stock of party politics in the Congress, and will soon have a fair crack of the whip. She has a different cast of mind from that of her father's. I remember how annoyed she was with Nehru ji when he dithered over dismissing an elected government in Kerala; early that year she had been made Congress president. She insisted that the law and order situation in Kerala gave Delhi grounds to use the article 356 against Namboodiripad's government. Nehru ji had to submit to the pressure . . . She won't let someone like Baran Singh become CM, someone with a mind of his own.'

The day after returning from Delhi, Ram Mohan took the first train to Lucknow. Chaudhary Sahab's residence was humming with activity, which given Chaudhary Sahab's political stake in the approaching elections did not catch him off guard. He paused to appraise the scene. To his right, two or three small groups of khadi-clad men stood on the front lawn having voluble discussions; up ahead around the porch, some people were talking in undertones. The supply of tea and snacks was non-stop. When he braced himself to partake of the heady political atmosphere, there was a melee in the veranda. Some important political personage was about to emerge out of the front door.

The short fat man was a senior member of the state cabinet who Ram Mohan did not know; he moved to one side of the passage as the minister holding one corner of his heavily starched white khadi dhoti proceeded towards the gate. Some people rushed to merge with the pack of the lackeys behind him. They all left amid the usual bustle associated with the departure or arrival of a person in power. Ram Mohan sighed with satisfaction; he did not let his interest in literature overpower the attraction of politics. His proximity to political figures had afforded him much influence. It was the possibility of a politician in him that had drawn people like Gulab Singh and Tiwari ji to him.

One of Chaudhary Sahab's aides received him warmly and had him seated in a room where other visitors sat talking ceaselessly. Anon he was escorted into the big room full of important people including several ministers and state party officials; sitting beside Baran Singh was Dixit ji who called to him. Ram Mohan touched their feet and sat down nearby while a smiling neighbour pushed a bolster towards him to lean on. They were brainstorming the options before Baran Singh in the light of political exigency thrown up by new political dynamics. The dominant view in the room was that Baran Singh should not do anything to give the party an excuse to sideline him before the polls. It would be better to wait. Maybe he was in error about the party's intent. He might after all be allowed to take up the reins of the Congress Legislature Party. He was the only Congress leader in UP to enjoy his own mass base, a fact the party high command would be hard put to ignore, but some of those present feared that this very fact might be hard for the party bosses to stomach, so Chaudhary Sahab had better warn the party leadership about his wish. Who knows, the final decision might turn out in his favour. However, the majority thought it more prudent to be patient until after the elections, for if the party learnt in advance of Chaudhary Sahab's political pursuit, it might decide against fielding his people in this election. At this point, those who knew of Ram Mohan's closeness to Baran Singh looked towards him. 'This time Ram Mohan shouldn't contest,' said Baran Singh as if in response to the unspoken question. He had discussed it with Saansad ji. But seeing Ram Mohan blanch, he was quick to add that the constituency he had in mind for him would in all probability go to Udai Pratap Singh whom Indira Gandhi consulted on international affairs; to avoid any misunderstanding with her at this juncture was highly advisable.

Ram Mohan waited as Chaudhary Sahab and Dixit ji stood on the veranda shaking hands with people taking leave; then they went back in, and just before entering his study, Baran

Singh bade his PA they were not to be disturbed. Settling into the chair behind the large study table, he motioned Dixit ji and Ram Mohan to the big couch to his right.

'Ram Mohan must be upset,' said he, addressing Dixit ji. 'I had no time to discuss with him before making that announcement . . . but I had to make it clear there was no imminent face-off between me and the party over ticket-distribution . . . You never know how your own people would cope with a possibility like this in such a politically charged climate. Any error of judgment would hand your detractors the opportunity to indulge in gossip at your expense.'

'Maybe you're right', said Dixit ji, and patting Ram Mohan, 'What are your plans now for this talented fellow?' Dixit ji and Baran Singh had always got along well as cabinet colleagues. Having twigged that CM's chair was not coming his way, Dixit had lost interest in active politics, and then Gayatri's death landed a crushing blow on whatever he thought was left as meaningful in his twilight years. It was Baran Singh who had first spotted his rapid decline. Unaware of the Gayatri factor, he had attributed it to the death of ambition. He had held long conversations with him and was able to dig him out of his sepulchral depths. Supplied with this new ambition—the ambition to install Baran Singh as CM—Dixit ji retrieved some of his former self.

'As a matter of fact, I do want Ram Mohan to stand in this election from Fatehpur . . .' said Baran Singh. 'That's what I want to discuss here.' He halted and rubbed his scalp under the cap, without removing it. Ram Mohan's mood lifted; he glanced at Dixit ji who said, 'As a rebel candidate?'

'No, we must be careful about that; it would be a godsend for the party to question my intentions,' said Baran Singh.

'Ram Mohan's closeness to you is known to all. To expect them to believe this doesn't have your blessing will be naive.'

'I know . . . Yet we can present it as a rebellion against me, not the party. I'll appeal to him to behave like a disciplined party soldier and withdraw in support of the official candidate.' Noticing Dixit ji's frown, he added, 'It can still be used against me, I know. Doubts will be raised about my loyalty to the present party dispensation because of my earlier equation with Late Shastri ji . . . Okay . . . suppose I fall in with every decision of the party! Where do you think it'll lead me . . . considering the atmosphere in the party under Indira?' Dixit ji and Ram Mohan listened as he continued, 'Just think of the predicament in which I might be caught if I don't show courage and forethought . . . while there's still time? I won't let my political career fall into the same drill as is the lot of every Congressman today. I just can't keep waving the party flag and wait for Delhi to take notice of my slavish obedience. We all know it was your chance, Dixit ji, to lead the government here when Sucheta Kriplani was dropped on us . . .And if I did nothing, that's what would happen . . . I'd land in your shoes. Now is the time to make a decision about our future options. I've little doubt that this woman . . . no, not the former CM; I'm talking of the PM . . . She'll find someone else to do her bidding here after the elections.'

'I agree,' said Dixit ji. 'So what's our next move?'

'Let's wait till we know how many seats has everyone got. This is the first general election under Indira Gandhi; the results will give us an idea of what people think of her. I don't expect any drastic change in general perception of the Congress; but I also think her performance would fall short of that of her father. Yes, Shastri ji would've swept the polls given his success against Pakistan and the measures he took to increase productivity in agriculture . . . Once I know . . .' then laughing, '. . . as if I don't know already . . . that they've found someone else for UP. Once it becomes official, I'll leave the party to tread my own path, free from Congress overlords. I want Ram Mohan to fight as an independent. We'll see how it plays out. It'll give him a chance to know about his support base.'

'Shouldn't some of your key men be put in the picture? It'll be such a critical moment! I think—'

'No, it's important we keep a clear head and be discreet about it for now. What's more, I'm still chewing it over. As of now I've shared it with only three people, you, Saansad ji and Ram Mohan. Let's keep it that way until after the elections. Because then I'd have some concrete grievance to ground my decision on.'

They ate lunch; then Ram Mohan was taken to the station. Baran Singh and Dixit ji had to go to the party office to attend the meeting called to work out a campaign plan to be sent to Delhi for approval. On the way Ram Mohan reflected on the import of what Chaudhary Sahab had said. Always looking at a situation from a rosy angle, he wrapped his mind around the fact that he was in confidence of a leader as important as Chaudhary Baran Singh.

––––––––––

As usual there were regular scenes of distress just outside the entrance of station precincts; but Ram Mohan was surprised at his sense of detachment; his curiously buoyant state produced, as it were, a filtered vision for him. Even after coming face to face with sickly beggars and skeletal rickshaw pullers, his heart did not cringe; his visit to Delhi and Chaudhary Sahab sharing confidences with him had done wonders. Later when he was to mention this to Mahavir Wilson, he, to his annoyance, would impart an irrelevant twist to it, attributing it to the workings of power. 'That's the impact they have on politicians, enabling them to enjoy power without compunction. The basic goodness of the Indian state for the leaders—from Nehru to the present crop—has lain in its Constitution, a proof of the idea of a liberal, democratic and equitable nation, which has blessed the leaders with the illusion of fulfilment of their duties. Indian national movement teemed with people in the grip of dreamy notions; one could accuse them of ingenuousness but not of insincerity; their words then had a sappy feel to them, leading their lesser countrymen to believe in the possibility of some tangible outcome after the freedom was won. Now those very words sound vacant . . . to a sensible ear. But the Congress is still good at employing them to its advantage.'

Mahavir Wilson's timing of this sort of declamation was to irk Ram Mohan; at other times, he could see sense in the young man's take on the dysfunctional Indian state. Now that Ram Mohan himself sought share of the Swaraj pie, he made a rather tetchy riposte. 'What you're saying Mahavir is no less rhetoric, that is, in order to redress dreadful injustices one doesn't have to be affected by them in a tear-jerking manner. When I said those derelicts didn't upset me this time the way they used to, I was alluding to the peculiar distance that seemed to have come between us—them and me. But I did notice them and thought I would share it with you, the feeling . . . somewhat complex I'd say. Remember, one can always handle a problem better by not allowing any useless emotion to undermine one's level-headedness.' Sensing he had touched Ram Mohan on the raw, Wilson aborted the topic.

* * *

Walking towards the station building, one more realization dawned on Ram Mohan. Now he could not think of his fellow teachers at D.A.V. College without the feeling of condescension; the gravity of issues occupying his mind had dwarfed the purportedly noble occupation of teaching. Musing on the triviality of their existence made him smirk. He was particularly irritated at the thought of Mishra seeking to display his erudition all the time. He sublimated it into pity for his bête noire, for his naivety. And perking up like a shot, he imagined the whole college talking of his plunge into active politics with awe, because of his audacity to venture out of the familiar terrain and into hazardous lands—the minefield of UP politics. Those who flourished in the world of learning were found diminished in the real world where their calling was little more than a symbol of weakness. Ram Mohan recalled with relish an instance when he had had to rescue Mishra—the poseur of learning—from a possible manhandling.

It was a Sunday afternoon, and Ram Mohan returning from somewhere had stopped to buy bananas from a roadside vendor near Naveen market. Just as he was about to climb back into the rickshaw, his attention was caught by a rough and loud voice on the other side of the street; seeing Mishra being shouted at, he crossed the road at a canter. Ram Mohan had a personality, which did not blend in with the general run of people. His face that radiated profundity in a literary gathering could be like thunder if the occasion warranted; his eyes and words articulating pure menace. He could frighten the life out of a lout.

The uncouth man having bullied Mishra into silence was now pushing him away, asking him to make a run for it. Some passersby had stopped to enjoy the scene. Nobody saw Ram Mohan arriving, and removing one of his shoes. When it caught the man on the side of his face, everybody caught their breath. 'Beat it fast if you don't want your legs and arms broken,' said Ram Mohan to the man who then without so much as saying a word left, nursing his face, looking disoriented; while Ram Mohan helped a mousy looking Mishra climb into the rickshaw waiting—the confusion about who had hailed it first, the man or Mishra, was the cause of the quarrel.

That practitioners of a rhetorically venerated vocation like teaching could not face up to the reality on the ground, Ram Mohan had long known.

———————

Thinking of his political prospects, he became so sanguine that even the beckoning of the public urinal to his far left seemed pleasant. The ever-present option of the wall was there. Yet he decided to check out the officially designated place first, where serving as urinal now was this new enclosure adjoining the old one that lay abandoned with its crumbling walls. He took a tentative peek inside. The state of the bowels of the new structure was no different from what he remembered of his earlier experience—he was taking a train after a long gap as travelling by bus suited him better—which, when contrasted with the newness of its surrounding walls, looked even worse. As he headed for the wall, his eyes fell on the billboard looming over the toilet. He gazed at the beauty of the smiling face of Indira Gandhi. She had pushed her late father into the background, into the left-hand corner at the top, the other corner adorned by Mahatma Gandhi, both smiling. Ram Mohan was smiling too, thinking how solely she embodied the Gandhi–Nehru legacy, a legacy that would remain much touted, though she did not owe her surname to the Mahatma but to Firoz Gandhi, the man she had married. But the phrase would be used to kind of suggest that she, besides being the daughter of Nehru, was also a descendant of Mahatma Gandhi.

* * *

Soon the word got out that Ram Mohan was going to stand in the coming Parliamentary election. People in Parsadpur and his well-wishers in other villages counted the days until he was due for his next visit after Diwali. Finally, when he disembarked from the shuttle that ran between Kanpur and Fatehpur, a gratifying sight was to greet his eyes. The crowd gathered to meet him at Parsadpur station that late afternoon was larger than usual, a telling validation of his decision. He was surprised to see Padhaiya, Kalla Dada's eldest son, who avoided his village assemblies to emphasize his independence. He had a temper and was the first in his family to start living separately. The small house he had built for his family stood on the plot gifted by Ram Mohan. Padhaiya could be quite endearing when it came to cracking jokes or pulling somebody's leg. Deena and other children would watch with delight when Padhaiya stood his little daughter on the palm of his right hand and moved about skilfully, holding her steady like an acrobat at a circus. Yet the same Padhaiya Bhaiya, given the slightest reason, would lunge at his scrawny wife and pound her within an inch of her life.

The big chabootra across from Ram Mohan's house was swarming with people. Chhote Baba sitting in his charpoy was responding to greetings as best he could amid a babble of voices, trying at the same time with whatever vision his eyes could muster to get the hang of the composition of the crowd; while Madari Bapu—who would usually lay sightless and quiet on his takht—was stirred to life by the cheerful flurry around him, inviting people to sit on the takht beside him. Ram Mohan's weekly visits were the only source of vivifying his existence, which otherwise was dark and dismal, but even he knew that today's excitement was in a different league.

———————

The task Ram Mohan had on his hands now was to raise enough funds to provide for his election campaign, a challenge indeed,

because those with deep pockets did not consider independents
worth more than a pittance. Ram Mohan had already approached
one such person through a former Congress party worker in
Kanpur; he—the big bellied businessman—had said, 'It's not my
standard practice to entertain party-less candidates. All kinds of
people join the fray without the remotest chance of getting in.
But now that you've come, I won't let you leave empty-handed.
Consider it my tribute to your education and teaching profession.'
It was chickenfeed, what Ram Mohan had got from him.

Baran Singh and Dixit ji each made a personal contribution.
Ram Mohan made Kanti part with some of the gold jewellery
she had got from her late mother-in-law. Badri, Baijnath,
Gulab Singh and others worked on people in Ballamgaon and
Parsadpur with good results; even those two Brahmans who
had attended the big meeting that was called to discuss Ram
Mohan's constituency, came up with a token sum as a goodwill
gesture. Being a big landowner Tiwari ji—it was he after all
who had identified in Ram Mohan the makings of a successful
politician—put up a large amount enough to rent three Jeeps
for the campaign. He would brook no reservations about his
friend's victory, basing the assertion on his knowledge of the
caste equation in Fatehpur where Kurmis comprised a sizeable
block, which could not return him to Parliament on its own but
to make up for this, he pointed out a fact hitherto overlooked.
He said, 'Ordinarily Kurmi voters remain lukewarm about
voting, because of their lack of stake in the politics. They have
grudgingly been voting for the Congress. But of late, they've
started showing interest in Baran Singh. He is with the Congress
but word of Ram Mohan's closeness to him can be spread,
which will be in addition to Ram Mohan himself being Kurmi.
This combination will bring out Kurmis, Yadavs and other
backwards in hordes to support him. Their voting en block will
make all the difference . . .'

Badri who had been squirming to voice his query said, 'But Tiwari ji, even after Ram Mohan secures all the votes of our caste what makes you think that will be sufficient?'

'I didn't say it will be sufficient . . . but it'll form a strong foundation. There are other factors behind my optimism. Ram Mohan's opponent will in all probability be Udai Pratap Singh, a Thakur, and in Fatehpur as everywhere else there has been an old rivalry between Brahmans and Thakurs. Some of Brahman votes can go to the candidate backed by People's Union, which does not bode well for the Congress candidate, particularly when there is Ram Mohan who has a strong presence of an entire caste standing behind him. Then there is this other important section in Fatehpur. Muslims are hardcore supporters of the Congress, but given Ram Mohan's knowledge of Urdu and his oratory I wouldn't be surprised if some of them decide to vote for him. The only wholesale support the Congress can bank on is that of Harijans and Thakurs. And mind you, Shastri ji's death coupled with Indira Gandhi's inexperience, which led to bitter squabbles in the party, has eroded Congress's traditional strength.'

Tiwari ji's confidence—his working himself into victory mode—took hold of Ram Mohan who had been thinking only in terms of the strong showing at the polls to make the Congress leadership take notice. Yet the notion of seeking votes in the name of caste made him feel a bit uneasy. He said, 'Tiwari ji, you know I'm against these caste divisions that put talent and ability out of the reckoning. I wonder if I could try and convince the people that it's in their best interest to make me their MP . . . that I'm better equipped to deal with the problems ailing their lives.'

'I wish you were right, Ram Mohan. You might be taken in when people listen to your words with rapt attention, but no sooner do you leave than they let out a sigh, "What a pity a person like him is Kurmi." I know their cast of mind. Just the other day an acquaintance of mine who teaches at a higher secondary school in Fatehpur was telling me exactly the same thing. He said "These intellectual footmen of the British empire with no grasp of the genius of the structure of Hindu society have caused unthinkable damage . . . Now that the foreign rule has ended, all of us who champion the Hindu way of life should unite to restore its former sanctity, in a different guise maybe, given the fact that some irreversible changes have been inflicted." I am saying we should not entertain any notion of winning the upper caste support. That'll be a waste of time.'

'That's all very well Tiwari ji, but I can't invoke the issue of caste affinity while campaigning. That'll be embarrassing.'

'You don't do it . . . Others will do it, and later your visits to Kurmi areas should make it sink in'. Ram Mohan left it at that. Tiwari ji at any rate was more knowledgeable about the prevalent voting patterns in Fatehpur.

'We'd better set up an election office in Fatehpur straight away,' Tiwari ji said. 'We should delegate some workers forthwith to the task of caste mobilization . . .' Adding after a pause, 'I have a relative in Fatehpur who I'm sure will allow an unused portion of his big house to be turned into an office space for our purpose.' In no time, there emerged a group of workers composed of men from Parsadpur and Ballamgaon, with Badri and another fellow in charge but under the overall leadership of Tiwari ji who said they would soon leave for Fatehpur and have a meeting at their would-be election office, to discuss all aspects of the gruelling effort and get a sense of how the land lay before them. Everybody agreed. Ram Mohan asked Kanti to start putting aside whatever cash their crops could bring in the next couple of months. He would need money all the time during this period.

* * *

Unaware of what exactly the pother was about, Deena could sense his father was up to something big. He became the leader of a band of boys that went around the village with a new-found sense of self-importance. But then it all changed. One day, on coming back from school, what Mithila—Kalla Dada's youngest daughter—told him tore into his innards. A numbing sense of alienation washed through him as she hastily reminded him that Nanki was still with them. They both hugged Nanki who bleated softly making Deena's eyes brim with tears. Mithila was also wiping her eyes when Kalla Dada, on his way to the well with two iron buckets and a coiled rope slung over his shoulder, seeing them cuddling the little goat, called him goatherd, the name he had given him, and told Mithila to take some gur and water to her Baba, that is Madari Bapu, who enjoyed it between the meals. Deena and Mithila exchanged looks. It was Madari Bapu who had set off the bomb of the possibility of Nanki's cruel end. These were the times when meat-eaters were few and far between in rural areas. Madari Bapu was one of them but would not easily get the opportunity to satisfy his meat-deprived palate.

Aware of Kanti's disquiet over Nanki's stunted growth, Madari Bapu, on learning about his visit, had invited the butcher of Ballamgaon for a chat; the latter would make the rounds of nearby villages looking for goats on sale. His profession unbeknownst to her, Mithila, as asked by her Baba, had brought Nanki to him, thinking the man loved goats in the way that she and Deena did. Poking Nanki here and there, he gave an idea about how much flesh she could produce, which left her in no doubt as to the purpose of their conversation. What Madari Bapu wanted out of the deal was a portion of Nanki's flesh, cooked.

After that, Mithila would not let Nanki out of sight till Deena's return. The only person who could protect Nanki was Chhote Baba; he told him about the butcher and extracted assurance that Nanki would not be taken away from him. When asked, Madari Bapu told Chhote Baba of Kanti's frustration with Nanki taking so long to grow big; then he mentioned the butcher willing to pay more than what a goat this small would fetch in the market. Chhote Baba tried to coax Deena into letting go of Nanki, promising to get a better goat for him, but Deena's howling forced him to give in for the moment; later Madari Bapu and he concurred there was no need to pay mind to children's fancies. A week or two went by. Then one day, Deena, walking back from school, saw Mithila running towards him, shrieking; what she said between sobs and breathlessness paralysed him; coming to his senses, he felt his heart and entrails wrenched at. No sound issued from his mouth. Just before he exploded into a run, his horror-stricken face had wrung another fit of crying from Mithila who ran after him. On entering Nanki's shed, he plunged into the deserted corner groping in the gloom desperately, as if his hands would find what his eyes could not. That she was gone sank in as he sat there grasping the bare stump to which she was tethered in the night; her little droppings lying about drew a gush of tears from him. Meanwhile, Kanti reached there and brought him out holding his hand; when her attempts to placate him failed, she blurted that Nanki had been sold to make him concentrate on his textbooks. He also got a rebuke from Chhote Baba for whiling away his time with goats and suchlike.

Some boys who had followed the butcher to the edge of Parsadpur told him how Nanki kept resisting while being dragged by the ear. They also claimed to have seen tears in her eyes. Later that evening the butcher's son came with a small aluminium box and heated it upon a makeshift hearth; then Mithila, as asked, brought chapattis from the house. Deena stood close watching Madari Bapu dip his fingers into that beat-up vessel and lick them with naked relish; Deena could not stop conjuring up the image of Nanki, small and tender, pinned down by the butcher with a knife in his hand. He said with tears in his eyes to Mithila that Nanki might have thought him to be complicit in her excruciating end.

The day following, Deena collected Nanki's droppings, sobbing and mumbling her name. The little earthen jar containing the tiny dry lumps was to be found by Kalla Dada who would buy Ram Mohan's house a couple of years later. The memory of Nanki would for Deena be a leitmotif of man's easy cruelty towards fellow animals on earth.

The filing of Ram Mohan's nomination papers turned out to be quite an event. The effort to stir their potential key support base yielded astonishing results. Tiwari ji's unfaltering emphasis on a feeling of caste solidarity had worked, though Ram Mohan had yet to accede to the fact that things like education, honesty, ability, intent, etc. meant little to the electorate. He wondered how a country awakened by the cries of freedom, a country that held people like Gandhi and Nehru in such high esteem could behave in this manner. Tiwari ji had endorsed Mahavir Wilson's view that Nehru, for a crucial part of his rule, had his head in the clouds. The country delivered to him 'at the stroke of midnight' was largely a product of his wishful thinking, a fantasy.

The mass of people that showed up for the occasion overwhelmed everybody's reckoning, lending a bounce to Tiwari ji's bearing, who oversaw the event of Ram Mohan being taken to file his papers in a procession amid slogan-shouting. It was such a good show that the rival camp had to sit up and consider. The possibility of Kurmis being turned into a formidable vote bank was not lost on Udai Pratap Singh, the Congress candidate, who made an unscheduled trip to Delhi to tip Mrs Gandhi off about Baran Singh's machinations. Baran Singh issued a statement rubbishing the charge that he was behind the rebel candidates. Indira Gandhi at the time had her own problems. The powerful group of party seniors called Syndicate had turned hostile—its members having second thoughts about her being allowed to continue as PM—and were waiting to see how things stood after the fourth general election. In the meantime, she was working closely with her supporters within the Congress to stymie any plot to bring her down. Shukla ji's uncle in Delhi had become part of the group known as her 'kitchen cabinet'.

When somebody wondered if Shukla ji could help tackle Udai Pratap Singh's insinuation, Baran Singh was quick to take offence. Despite his long association with Congress he had lost none of his wilfulness; he had also been critical of the increasing centrality of sycophancy in Indian polity, and Shukla ji and his uncle would often come under his sarcastic gaze. He would sooner quit the party than compromise his political persona that set him apart in the wheeling and dealing world of politics. Though there was no bad blood between them, he had distanced himself from Shukla ji, which also suited the latter. Yet they could run into each other without feeling awkward. Aiding this mutual understanding was the sneaking awareness that with Indira Gandhi's emergence, Baran Singh's future in the Congress hung in balance. Shukla ji had said to Dixit ji, 'You were denied the chieftaincy of the state twice, which you handled with dignity, but Chaudhary Sahab is too bumptious to settle for anyone other than him being the CM. He's his own man. It's unlikely he would get a chance, and the buzz is he is set on a showdown as soon as the process of government formation in UP begins next month . . . I see little possibility of any reconciliation. He has ventured too far.' This helped Baran Singh to be rid of any doubt he might have had about the question of his departure from the Congress. He could not pin his hopes on Indira Gandhi's trouble with the party's old guards who had made her PM, hoping she would be more manipulable than Desai, the other contender. They were regretting their choice now. She knew that, and going by hints from Delhi, was psyching herself up for any challenge mounted to her leadership after the elections.

'Letting the dynastic genie out the Syndicate has got all of us in a deep hole.' This off-the-cuff remark by Baran Singh on her taking on the mantle of Prime Minister had seemed uncalled for at the time. Some had ascribed it to his frustration as he was thrown off balance by Shastri ji's sudden death. Time, however, would bear him out.

Baran Singh became focused on what he thought he should do. In consultation with his close aides, he began to devise a strategy that could help his loyalists return to the state Legislature; a few of them were given a Congress ticket. Among the rebels who had his blessings, the only one standing for Parliament was Ram Mohan; about his chances Chaudhary Sahab had no illusions, but he did not think the exercise was in vain. It would demonstrate his growing political clout in north India. As it is the middle peasants in some Hindi states had begun to flock to him.

To sending his message to the party, Fatehpur was the key. A substantial part of its electorate, if mobilized, would come to Ram Mohan, making Indira Gandhi realize her folly. She might be obliged to review her opinion of Baran Singh, given his strength on the ground; and who knows, voters of Fatehpur might unite against the anglicized, foreign-returned and aristocratic Udai Pratap Singh whose defeat would vindicate Baran Singh who had pitched for Ram Mohan being fielded from

Fatehpur. Come to think of it, it was not pure fantasy. Fatehpur
had done that before. In the previous general election, a small-
time local leader contesting independently had brought off a
stupefying upset against Keskar, a politician of national stature,
held in high regard by Nehru. This local politico had made a
shrill pitch against Nehru's man, calling him an outlander—that
Delhi had to be taught a lesson for ignoring the local sentiment;
that these new emperors of the country could not be allowed to
take the proud people of Fatehpur for granted.

* * *

To keep Ram Mohan abreast of his post-poll strategy, Baran
Singh sent one of his reliable men to Parsadpur to brief him.
Parsadpur, because it had no territorial connection with either
Fatehpur or Lucknow, for if meeting was disclosed, it would
become grist to the mill of his opponents in the party. Baran
Singh's message made Ram Mohan's day. A break from their
exacting campaign schedule was more than appetizing. Leaving
Badri in charge of managing the canvassing for a day, Ram
Mohan, Tiwari ji and Gulab Singh went to Parsadpur. Baran
Singh's man spelled out all the possible post-poll moves to which
Chaudhary Sahab might resort, depending on the politics of the
day, but he would not agree to anything less than the office of
chief minister this time, and given his precarious standing in
the party a hurt and weak Congress would be to his advantage,
hence all the more important that all his men in the fray left
nothing to chance to prove Chaudhary Sahab's strength. Ram
Mohan's showing should be such, the man stressed, that even
his defeat was seen as a victory. And if Fatehpur decided to
repeat a Keskar, Ram Mohan would be Chaudhary Sahab's man
in Delhi. The messenger dropped hints that their leader would
stop at nothing to capture the throne in Lucknow this time; that

they should all be prepared for a war like situation. The meeting put paid to whatever fears Ram Mohan and his friends might have had of the uncertainty the election results could throw up. They had been having this discussion on the chabootra. Madari Bapu lay on his takht nearby. The winter had all but faded. Just as they were to start back their mood turned sour. It was Padhaiya Bhaiya who had been hovering around to suggest through his manner he did not think much of the topic under discussion, which Ram Mohan and other had sensed; when they rose Padhaiya Bhaiya said, addressing the small crowd standing at a distance of a few yards, 'Have you ever seen so much effort being made to achieve nothing but defeat?' Piqued, Baran Singh's man looked at Ram Mohan, as Tiwari ji, exchanging a quick glance with Gulab Singh, said the young man was related to Ram Mohan and had a worthless egotistic vein. The man said, 'I know his kind. They're terribly jealous of anyone among them growing beyond their imagination; they may not be a direct threat to you; yet they should not be ignored. They have illusions about their own importance. They want to touch the sky but have no idea of the ground they stand on. Their behaviour seems harmless because they can't effect any change in their own or anybody else's reality. But you can't let it be. There may be others, more capable and hard-headed, who might take their cue from a person like this relation of yours,' then adding hurriedly, 'I'm not saying there will be anyone in this region able to outflank Ram Mohan as yet.' He glanced towards Padhaiya Bhaiya who stood smirking at the entrance of his father Kalla Dada's house. 'My point is there could be others smart enough to become a nuisance . . . with the potential to draw you into the task of subduing them, a distraction one can do without . . . You must make this pathetic case, this young man, understand the futility of his frustration. Rather, he should beg you for your patronage.' Expressing regrets for his distant nephew's behaviour,

Ram Mohan agreed with Chaudhary Sahab's man and said, 'I see the significance of your point. I'll take steps to check such acts of defiance before they become a menace.'

After the Jeep carrying the visitor left, Ram Mohan said, 'Let me talk to this stupid man.' They all quickly walked to Kalla Dada's house. The number of people waiting for Ram Mohan there had increased, all keen to hear about the election campaign; a tumult of murmur swept through the crowd as he approached; those sitting scrambled to their feet. Padhaiya Bhaiya had left, again a gesture to convey his independence of Ram Mohan. Gulab Singh sent for him. His man who had found him at his oil mill returned and whispered Padhaiya Bhaiya's words into Gulab Singh's ear, 'I'm not like your Thakur, the bootlicker. Whoever wants to see me should come here.' Gulab Singh looked at Ram Mohan who shrugged and said, 'I leave it to you. Do whatever needs to be done.' Gulab Singh sent his men, three of them, to bring him, 'Don't say a word to him. Let your well-seasoned lathis do the talking.'

Deena, who had up till then been watching from a distance, rushed in to tell his mother how black a temper Gulab Chacha was in; that Padhaiya Bhaiya was going to be killed. Kanti, busy doing the dishes, told him not to use such sinister words. She rose and ran towards the staircase with Deena at her heels. On the roof terrace, they secured a suitable place behind the parapet, obtaining a clear view of the goings-on in front of Kalla Dada's house. Gulab Singh was in his element, spewing whatever frightening phrases he could summon, making Kalla Dada realize how dangerous a situation his son had got himself into. He went up to Ram Mohan who sat on the chabootra, talking to Madari Bapu. 'I've had enough. Padhaiya can no more be allowed to misbehave like this.' Kalla Dada said, 'I don't know who he thinks he is. He must think you would ignore his madness. You happen to be his Chacha after all.'

'Kalla Bhaiya, you had better stay out of it. If not reined in now he can't be kept from turning into a real nasty character . . . Look at his crazed notion! He thinks I'm his rival here, in Parsadpur. At other times, I would take no notice, but this is the limit; he has no idea of the seriousness of the battle I'm engaged in. He just pours scorn on whoever is trying to contribute to my election effort . . . The way he behaved in front of Chaudhary Sahab's man, it's high time he knew it's not on . . . You don't understand Kalla Bhaiya. Others might get infected with the same bug if he remains untreated. I suggest you go inside and ignore his screams.' Right then a ruckus rose from the dirt track next to Kalla Dada's house that made him leave and go inside.

A big throng watched Padhaiya Bhaiya driven forward by the three men, the dexterous shoves of whose lathis were meant to hurt less than to convey the gravity of the intent. And Padhaiya Bhaiya, no matter how serious a trouble he was in, was able to keep up appearances; his body language was that of a man caught unawares by his adversaries; every poke from behind into his person drew nothing more than a look of annoyance, showing no hint of submission; just then Gulab Singh bellowed at his men to stop as he walked up to them. The set of his jaw was enough to sound the alarm; without so much as a word to Padhaiya Bhaiya he ordered the threesome to hit him on his legs till he fell to the ground. That threw a sheet of silence over the spectators. The raw deliberateness of Gulab Singh's command brought home the impotence of Padhaiya Bhaiya's posture. It was plain he had miscalculated. Of having used up Ram Mohan's forbearance, he had had no inkling. Disbelief was all his eyes could express when the first of the many blows landed on him. Trying to fend off the next one he got struck on his right arm. Gulab Singh yelled at his men cautioning them against injuring his hands that he would need to crawl after his legs were put out of action. Padhaiya Bhaiya got hold of one of the lathis but had to release as a torrent of cracks rained down on him everywhere below the waist. A mixture of pain and panic, he slumped to his knees. Gulab Singh directed he be pinned to the ground so the blows aimed at immobilizing his legs could not be disturbed; after that two of the men held his arms and feet as he lay face down, while the third one with full swing of his lathi clouted him on the calves and thighs repeatedly. Padhaiya Bhaiya's screams having reached their highest decibel levels were ebbing away. He was conscious but his legs seemed to have lost connection to him. His groans sounded out of tune with the lathi on song.

Once sure he could not stand up, Gulab Singh had the clubbing stopped. His trouser legs below the knees had turned from white to red. Now, according to Gulab Singh's plan, he was to drag himself to where Ram Mohan sat with Tiwari ji and others. 'If he fails to comply, smash his arms, make mincemeat of them as well,' thundered Gulab Singh. The man trying to wipe bloodstains from the base of his lathi with a handful of grass came and stood over the sprawled figure. Padhaiya Bhaiya began to crawl, and never stopped wincing all the way to Ram Mohan who sat not far from Madari Bapu. They all paused as Padhaiya Bhaiya approached. He had to be pulled onto the chabootra. Ram Mohan recited a Sanskrit verse that spoke of the necessity of the wicked being treated wickedly.

Brutally humbled, abjectly shorn of his pretensions, it was impossible to associate Padhaiya Bhaiya with his vanity anymore. When told to place his forehead at Ram Mohan's feet his alacrity to obey was startling, given the miserable shape he was in. Putting his hand on his head, Ram Mohan pardoned him and proceeded to give a discourse on the rudiments of good conduct for anyone interested in a fruitful existence, but had to discontinue in the middle as Padhaiya Bhaiya was attracting swarms of flies and was in terrible pain. Ram Mohan instructed he be taken to his house; to Kalla Dada he said, 'Have the wounds washed before applying any herbal medicine.' The gathering broke up as Ram Mohan rose announcing he must get back to Fatehpur.

When he went to meet Kanti and Deena before leaving, both of Padhaiya Bhaiya's children were there in the house, the son being a little older than Deena while the daughter a little younger. They had not been allowed to go out and see their father. In fact, they did not know of the beating. Their mother had just left to look after her husband. Kanti was in the small dark storeroom next to the cooking corner looking for something she could give the children to eat while Deena lay awake in a charpoy. On hearing Ram Mohan, she hastened out. He asked why Deena was in bed. She did not tell him the real reason and gave instead the excuse of stomach ache. Seeing Padhaiya Bhaiya on the ground with two men holding his hand and feet, he had felt a rush of nausea, and as soon as the third man's lathi had begun to rise and fall, drawing dreadful screams from Padhaiya Bhaiya, Deena had dropped to the terrace floor. Kanti had quickly helped him downstairs and put him in bed.

'Don't give him anything other than watery khichari tonight,' Ram Mohan said, sitting down beside him. He ran his hand over his head, then to Deena's delight, he unclasped his new fountain pen, the colour of oyster shell, from his shirt pocket and gave it to him; he also took out some change and handed a coin of fifty paise each to Padhaiya Bhaiya's children.

After the result of Fatehpur was announced, Udai Pratap Singh came to meet Ram Mohan. Everybody was floored by the gesture. But Udai Pratap Singh knew he was not just being gracious. Towards the end of the campaign, the fight had gone down to the wire. His confidence had been rocked. The tumult and excitement generated by Ram Mohan in certain important pockets of the constituency had been demoralizing to the Congress workers. Udai Pratap Singh had seen for himself the growing disdain of Kurmi voters for the Congress. At one of the meetings he had tried to rouse people against the opposition by invoking the injury that his leader Indira Gandhi had sustained during the election campaign in Orissa, when one of the stones thrown had fractured her nose. He had also referred to one of her speeches given in Raebareli her constituency, not far from Fatehpur, where she had fired up the audience by saying that instead of a few individuals his family was comprised of billions of Indians. In response, Udai Pratap Singh had had a number of raw and hard guavas hurled towards him. A few of them had hit some members of his campaign party. He had truly been given a scare. His defeat would have been a big letdown to Indira Gandhi who had had to fight for every single ticket for her men during the selection of candidates, the majority of whom were hand-picked by the Syndicate. That's why this victory for him was more than just a victory; his relief was the relief of the man pulled back from the brink.

On the other hand, the winner having come over to pay tribute was gratifying to Ram Mohan; it also gave a lift to his supporters who realized that even their defeat had a dimension of triumph to it. It was not a defeat that could question the basis of the ambition of their candidate; it had only revealed his political brawn. He was to learn later in Lucknow that among the losers he had got the highest number of votes in UP. After thanking his campaign managers, he along with Tiwari ji, Badri and Gulab Singh, headed for Parsadpur; to spend the night there and then, refreshed, make for Lucknow the following morning.

He could not wait to know how Chaudhary Sahab was faring in the fresh round of political bargaining.

Learning about his arrival the whole of Parsadpur and many from Ballamgaon converged outside his house. Tiwari ji presented a brief narrative of some interesting aspects of their campaign, stressing that their beloved man was destined to go places in politics. He capped his tale with Udai Pratap Singh's unexpected visit. The villagers were thrilled that Ram Mohan had given the heebie-jeebies to the winner, the man close to Indira Gandhi. Deena and his mother watched through the chinks of the front door. Moments before leaving, he went to see Padhaiya Bhaiya who, though unable to get up, was recovering; Ram Mohan expressed his relief that his bones were left intact, looking admiringly at Gulab Singh who said, 'I'd kept a watchful eye on my men to ensure they were not tempted into causing any critical injury.' Turning to Padhaiya Bhaiya, Ram Mohan said, 'All defeats and all victories are not the same. Sometimes a defeat signals the light and promise, and a victory the dark and gloom. I have lost this election, but we have achieved something in the process.' There were tears in Padhaiya Bhaiya's eyes. Ram Mohan bent and placed his hand on the side of his face. 'Jealousy and egoism at your age will only wear you down. Take a fresh look at the world and move ahead.'

* * *

Only Ram Mohan and Tiwari ji went to Lucknow. Gulab Singh and Badri had to deal with pending work on the home front. Mahavir Wilson—who had no stomach for the transitory nature of realpolitik—had hardly been in Fatehpur when a sympathetic Ram Mohan had sent him back. This aside, Ram Mohan and Tiwari ji themselves were not aware of the shape of things to come in Lucknow. Their concern, first and foremost, was to be put wise to how Chaudhary Sahab was placed in the new equation; they did however know the Congress had been given a warning by the electorate. As to its political implications in terms of Baran Singh's chances of heading the new state government, they had no idea.

In Lucknow, the first thing they did was to contact Dixit ji on the phone, who asked them to go to Subhadra Kutir and stay put till they hear from him. This house, in contrast to his official bungalow, was removed from the political arena; this is where Gayatri had lived before Parsadpur and would stay during her monthly visits afterwards. Sughari, the caretaker of the house, was still there, about whom Ram Mohan had heard from Gayatri. What he did not know was that she was Mahavir Wilson's long-widowed *Bua* (father's sister). 'I'll shift to Kanpur to live with my brother and nephew after Dixit ji is gone,' said Sughari while serving them food.

Dixit ji had yet to get back to them. Ram Mohan was on tenterhooks. He called Baran Singh's residence and spoke to one of his personal assistants. Dixit ji was on his way, he was told. He asked Sughari to make tea; then Dixit ji arrived and took them into the most secluded room of the house, asking Sughari to bring tea there. Ram Mohan and Tiwari ji could not wait to hear about the post-election developments. Reclining against a bolster on the bed, he began to fill them in. They drew their chairs up close as his voice, an old man's voice, had long lost its ring. 'Let me first congratulate you, Ram Mohan, on your excellent showing. To be honest, Baran and I were a little worried. He would wonder if asking you to fight independently had been the right thing. All his men who could not get party ticket for Parliament, so-called rebels, have lost, but none looks as good in defeat as you do. Now Baran rues that if he had had you stand for Assembly, you would have won.'

'What now . . . is there any chance of Chaudhary Sahab getting CM's chair?' said Ram Mohan.

'Let me put you in the picture . . . The opposition as you know has been resurgent in these elections all over the country; the picture that has emerged leaves one in no doubt that if polls were to be held again with the opposition coming together, Congress would be licked. It's lost almost half the states. Its majority in the Lok Sabha stands drastically reduced . . . Our main concern now is UP as Congress in all likelihood will form government here, but given its negligible majority its survival would hang by a thread. What remains to be seen is who will head the government. Baran Singh received a trunk call from Saansad ji this morning . . . He is keeping watch on how things unfold in Delhi.

'What concerns us is that the poor electoral showing of the Congress has ironically strengthened Indira Gandhi. She had a limited say in running the party; was largely kept out of the process of ticket distribution, so the blame for this loss is being laid on the old guards under whom the party's image has taken a hit . . . What's more, the Syndicate has been decimated. Its most visible faces have lost. Her camp's calling them "sweet defeats".'

'It'll help her take a grip on the party . . . That's what you mean!'

'You can say that again,' said Dixit ji. 'But we hear Desai is at it again. He won't let go of his ambition just yet, though he knows if it comes to a contest in Congress Parliament Party his chances are pitifully dim. According to Saansad ji, some sort of deal is in the works . . . to clear the way for smooth government formation in Delhi. Gupta has become very active there.'

C.B. Gupta had been UP CM before Sucheta Kriplani replaced him. He was among those who'd had to stand down to serve the party organization.'

'He wants to come back to UP again . . . That's what you're saying? Hasn't he been looking up to the Syndicate all these years?' said Ram Mohan.

'Yes, that's why he is busy currying favour with Mrs Gandhi, and has put his shoulder to the wheel of her being unanimously picked as PM; D.P. Mishra, the tallest Congress leader in Madhya Pradesh, her close confidant, he's trying to cajole Desai into not acting like a spoilsport . . . But the question who will take reins in Congress states will be taken up only after they have a government in place in Delhi.'

'Is there any chance that Indira ji reviews her thinking on UP and see a strong ally in Chaudhary Sahab?' said Tiwari ji. 'In that case she might offer him the top post here . . . As a gesture of magnanimity.'

'Given the way things stand, we cannot afford to be under any such illusion. After discussing the existing scenario, Baran and I have realized that henceforth he has to employ his own resources to further his career. If some people shift their loyalty from the Syndicate to Indira Gandhi, her coterie would view it as a coup for itself . . . but it is unlikely that Baran Singh will be welcome there. His independence and ambition have threatening implications for her.' Dixit ji paused before going on, 'I think there's no need to keep this from you now. Saansad ji, in fact, met Indira to sound her out about the prospects of Baran Singh's association with her, which she seems to have dismissed. However, she would like to have Saansad ji back in the Congress . . . That's the impression he got from the meeting.'

'What should be our strategy now?' said Tiwari ji. 'As far as I can see the whole party is going to fall into her lap.'

'We've decided not to make a play for CM's job. We're going to sit quiet and watch. No matter who becomes the CM here, Baran will be on the Cabinet. No doubt about that.

Nobody can ignore the fact that we have enough MLAs to topple the government at will.'

'Will Chaudhary Sahab be willing to go that far?' said Ram Mohan.

'That's what will happen when the time comes. Why don't you stay in Lucknow for some more time. Have you resumed your teaching duties?'

'No, I'm still on leave.'

'Then you had better hang around . . . as long as the situation remains fluid, and Baran would like to discuss his future plans with his close people after the Congress has announced the name of its new chief minister.'

Saansad ji kept Baran Singh up to date with developments in Delhi. Soon all furious guesswork was laid to rest by a call from Delhi at an unearthly hour. To accommodate Desai's vanity, Mrs Gandhi had offered him the position of deputy PM with finance portfolio, and he had agreed, giving up his insistence on Home Ministry. However, the most relevant part of the Delhi drama for Lucknow was that Gupta's spirited contribution to mission Desai would be rewarded with Uttar Pradesh; he had managed to ingratiate himself with her.

Less than a week after Indira Gandhi was sworn in Delhi, Gupta took office in UP as CM for the second time. Baran Singh's calm unruffled manner on the occasion caused many to scratch their head; nothing to give him away, no suggestion of any turmoil, nothing. Rather, he had a pleasant expression on his face as he rose and walked towards the rostrum to be sworn in as cabinet minister, looking like a man whose dilemma and doubt had been resolved. Dixit ji had opted out of being considered for another stint as a minister, citing old age. Hours after taking charge of his ministry Baran Singh went into a huddle with his loyalists at his residence, and they all broadly agreed with his assessment of the political scene, though one of them, an MLA, wondered if it was the right time for such a big step. Baran Singh said he had thought it through. The way people had voted in these elections carried a message for politicians with gumption and dynamism, who could take up the task of moulding people's growing anger at the Congress into a future mandate against it.

Ram Mohan had hardly been in Kanpur a fortnight when Dixit ji called. The week following Baran Singh would quit the Congress. Ram Mohan rushed one of his students who came from Fatehpur to Tiwari ji's village; they—Ram Mohan and Tiwari ji—reached Lucknow a day before the big event. Watching the proceedings of the Legislative Assembly from public gallery they sensed word had not got out yet. There was no sign of turbulence. Just when the house was settling down to the day's agenda, Baran Singh rose, and speaking over the normal hum of voices, informed the speaker of his decision; before the latter could gather his wits and grasp the thrust of Baran Singh's statement he had crossed the floor followed by a dozen of his loyal MLAs. A moment later the house turned into a hive of hubbub.

Gupta government had fallen. Outside the Assembly, Baran Singh announced he was willing to wait out the President's Rule likely to be imposed if no group emerged to have enough MLAs to claim the throne. He was willing to face fresh election if necessary. Only his core group knew it was just the gimmick, the fresh election bit, which, as expected, produced the desired effect. All political players opposed to Congress queued up to parley with Baran Singh as none of them wanted to be put through the grind of the polls again so soon.

The two major non-Congress parties in the state, though ideologically poles apart, contacted Baran Singh, promising their support and urging him to round up other MLAs, independents and those from smaller outfits, to reach the magic figure. Baran Singh had anticipated this. He was ready for the number game. People's Congress was the name he gave to his group that had broken away from the Congress, which—this hastily floated outfit, insignificant in size—was to be the heart of the coalition of creeds as diverse as Hindu nationalism, capitalism, socialism, communism and agrarianism. Their hostility to the Congress was the glue. Baran Singh's house was buzzing with his supporters and coalition partners and journalists. It was only to sleep at night that Ram Mohan and Tiwari ji would go to Subhadra Kutir. In the early stages of negotiations, Baran Singh had agreed to People's Union's offer of support from outside, which would allow him to fill his Cabinet with his own men. He had hinted at Ram Mohan's inclusion. Tiwari ji felt exhilarated. The truth of his prognosis on Ram Mohan's political future seemed to be knocking on the door.

That was not to be. With its largest coalition partner sitting outside the government—with no skin in the game—was a big problem for Chaudhary Sahab. People's Union on the other hand was averse to being part of a dispensation that also had communists in it, but Baran Singh's blunt refusal forced its leadership to rethink. In the meantime, he explained to Ram Mohan and others the reason for the sudden change in his stance. 'After first saying yes, I pondered over their offer only to discover a hint of patronage in it. People's Union is only second to the Congress in terms of its size in the Assembly, whereas my People's Congress has no more than a dozen MLAs, and yes, the way I see the situation, this number can increase many times over in the next election. The reason I'm keen to form government in UP is just that. I want to give the people a taste of governance they haven't known before . . . If I accepted the outside support of People's Union, it would pat itself on the back for all the good work that I do; if something went wrong, it would have the option of pulling the plug on me. This arrangement doesn't sound good. Besides, a government thus put together would have a built-in instability, keeping part of my mind needlessly occupied,' he looked at Ram Mohan and others before continuing, 'Earlier I thought that in the absence of People's Union from my government I could make minister even those of my men who either lost or didn't contest at all. But now, being the largest constituent of our United Legislator Party, People's Union would fill quite a few places on the Cabinet; then there're others in the coalition who would have to be accommodated . . . I have no hesitation in admitting to my admiration for people like Ram Mohan whose respect, love and support I'm fortunate to have. I need not spell out here the constraints coalition politics places on one. At the same time, none of you should have the slightest doubt that you will be handling important departments in my next government. For now I expect you all, especially you Ram Mohan, to meet me regularly and help me with your suggestions.'

Ram Mohan and Tiwari ji stayed on in Lucknow for a few more days after the swearing-in of United Legislator Party's government. Dixit ji who had not joined his friend's Cabinet had a long conversation with Ram Mohan and Tiwari ji before they left. He, as asked by Baran Singh, had to identify constituencies in the state where in the event of mid-term poll, People's Congress could have a chance to win. He also asked Ram Mohan and Tiwari ji to make a list of such seats in their areas.

FOUR

We found Gulab Singh on the front chabootra of his house with his grandson sitting beside him on a big takht. A few young men armed with guns occupied the charpoys nearby. Though old and long retired, there were no signs of diminution of his awe-inspiring personality of yesteryears; the white moustache and the furrows dug into the face and neck by the plough of time served only to testify to his enduring presence in the realm of violence. Mistaking Vinod and me for government officials posted to the area, he made an attempt to get up. Nishant stopped him. In the meantime, a few chairs were brought out and placed in front of Gulab Singh. He did not recognize me at first but when told of my father, he even recalled my name, surprising everybody. He had seen me as a child before we had taken up residence in Kanpur. The reason the name Kartik had clung to his memory lay in a lively discussion sparked by it during one of Ram Mohan's visits to Parsadpur in those days.

When asked if I knew the meaning of my name, I could not answer out of diffidence. My father said I had been named after the Hindu month of my birth, only to be chided for his ignorance of the other and more resonant reference. Ram Mohan Uncle had then gone on to explain the significance

of my name in Hindu mythology. 'Kartik is another name of
Kartikeya, the son of Shankar and Parvati.' Deena used to get
irritated by Indian penchant for the meaning of people's names;
children would constantly be subjected to this enquiry. He
suspected that people thought the meaning of a person's name
had to do something with their intrinsic character, like in a
certain social milieu people tend to be christened underscoring
some physical or mental characteristic. The same way as
someone with a physical deformity or handicap would be given
a name suitably describing their misfortune.

Gulab Singh agreed to Deena being given a burial in
his ancestral place in deference to his wish. Next, he fell to
lamenting his 'mindless deed' before asking Badri to discuss
with others and decide on a suitable piece of land for the
purpose. As they left, Gulab Singh told one of his men to
get tea and something to eat; shortly Deena's only surviving
Mama—Kripal—came to meet us; being unwell he was unable
to travel to Allahabad. However, Rajvansh, Deena's favourite
cousin, had already left. I came across Rajvansh quite a few
times while sifting through the notes of my late friend, who
it seemed had relied on Rajvansh for many such episodes as
he would have thought of using in his book, the book—the
first one of the supposed trilogy—that I am writing now.
Rajvansh has indeed emerged out of Deena's VIP suitcase as
a good source.

Just as we finished tea, Badri returned with an apologetic
look and said, 'If it was a natural death, there would have been
no issue . . . But if that's what Doctor Sahab and you want,
there should be no problem. Everybody in Parsadpur is sad to
hear about the tragedy. They all remember Deena as a child
cuddling his goats.' The thought of someone buried in their
vicinity, especially someone who took his own life, would be
disconcerting to people and might give birth to a restless spirit,

putting people under the dread of visitation. Before Gulab Singh could respond, Nishant spoke out, 'Never mind. There's no compulsion as Deena left no word about how he would prefer his remains to be dealt with.'

* * *

While Badri went to pack a change of clothes—he was travelling with us to Allahabad—someone was assigned to take us to places associated with our childhood. The sites and landmarks once clearly distinguishable had either disappeared or dwindled to a trace. Much had been added randomly to what I recalled of the physical setting of the area. Nearly all groves were gone, so had many independent trees; the threshing ground had been turned into fields. All the wells had long gone dry. The one next to Deena's erstwhile family house had fallen into ruin, wearing a forlorn dusty look.

The reddish-brown building of Parsadpur railway station, once so neat and alluring and haunting, with so much greenery around it, could now only be seen up close and had been turned nondescript by small brick structures that had grown all over. Even the once expansive vista on the other side of the railway track had been replaced by a confusion of human habitation. The site of Dahiya, the big pond that at one time looked so forbidding to children, was reduced to a shallow depression covered in weed, with no hint of water. The peepul tree on the edge of the compound of Deena's school still stood tall, but despite its reassuring and imposing presence I could not help noticing something missing of its former beauty. The foliage of the great tree no longer had its erstwhile shine. The old temple nearby presented no better picture either; the claws of time had left it scuffed; the pinnacle on its dome was torn, and thick on the ground were other telltale signs of ruin. From where we stood, the main school building could not be seen; obstructing the view was this addition to it by way of a classroom, which had shot up exactly where the open-air class used to be held. This space had also acted as the prayer ground. I found in Deena's notes the mention of his last day in that village school, particularly of how the seriousness of prayer time had suddenly given way to hilarity:

The exams for class five those days were held at the district level under the aegis of the District Primary Board. It was the last day for at least those of us who after passing the exam would bid goodbye to this school, and as a special favour to our headmaster and Srivastava ji the Deputy Inspector of Schools had come to give his blessing to the class five students who were soon to sit the district board exam. His help had once been critical to the regularization of Srivastava ji's position.

On the prayer ground, we stood in separate files, class-wise. Isuri and the other boy from the Harijan hamlet were as usual standing apart, at one side. After the deputy inspector of schools finished speaking, we all—as briefed—clapped loudly. But there was a slight delay on the part of these two in joining the applause as Isuri was whispering something to the other boy. This did not escape Thakur Sahab, the headmaster, who with an angry stare and his feared rod in hand advanced on them, causing a sudden silence; a moment later, as if by magic, the tense atmosphere dissolved into a light-hearted one as Srivastava ji and the deputy inspector of schools broke into laughter and were joined by all, barring Pandey, the dark-skinned Brahman. Thakur Sahab, who had lost his outraged look, was laughing heartily.

Isuri and his friend both had pissed in their dusty drawers before he could even reach them.

While Deena was away in another village for the board exam, Chhote Baba fell ill; by the time he returned, his condition had become worse. He needed constant attention. His diarrhoea refused to defer to the greatness of Ayurvedic medicine. To maintain a façade of treatment, the famous Vaidyaji of Ballamgaon would visit him regularly, while Kanti would be kept occupied changing his sheets and clothes. Deena would recite Chhote Baba the verses from the simplified version of Lord Ram's story. Ram Mohan was busy in Kanpur, his teaching responsibilities at D.A.V. College having resumed. From time to time, he had to make trips to Lucknow.

Every day Chhote Baba asked about him, expressing his longing to see his dear nephew one last time before slipping out of this world. It made Kanti cry. Then on sensing the futility of his wish, Chhote Baba's affection for Ram Mohan morphed into bitter resentment; at the same time he was overwhelmed by Kanti's care and attention, and one day with Kalla Dada's help, he unstrung from his sacred thread an old key. Kanti understood and brought his old trunk to him. He gestured to Kalla Dada who unlocked the trunk and fished out of its contents the cloth pouch that contained two gold coins and five one hundred rupee notes. Tears rolled down Chhote Baba's hollow cheeks as he thrust the pouch into Kanti's reluctant hands. Two days later in the small hours, he drew his last breath. To get the news to Ram Mohan, Badri and Raja Ram had the stationmaster of Parsadpur telephone Kanpur station requesting them to call Ram Mohan's residence.

When Kanti had woken Deena up, he could not grasp the sense of the grave liveliness of that morning. A weird alertness of all those familiar persons outside the house tricked him into thinking the world had been awake while he slept. Then he noticed Chhote Baba missing from his bed. Only the ever-present heaviness of reek vouched for his existence. Kanti—pointing to the figure shrouded in white cloth, lying in semi-darkness on the floor—said, 'Your Chhote Baba—'and burst out sobbing.

By the time Ram Mohan came on the scene, riding his Rajdoot motorcycle, a bier had been thrown together. He went into the front room to have a last glimpse of the man whose love for his nephew could have put a father's love for his son to shame. Coming out, he broke the funereal atmosphere by bantering with Kalla Dada, asking how scary the idea of death was to him, and going on to talk light-heartedly of those who made an issue of someone dying, he—as Chhote Baba's stiff body was being fastened to the bier—told them how the great Urdu poet Ghalib viewed death. 'When a close friend of his was taking long to recover from his second wife's death, Ghalib wrote him rather jocularly that weep he must if he himself would not die.'

Some of those present were impressed, but Badri said, 'That's fine. Nobody can question the therapeutic power of looking at death this way. Yet who can escape the grief from the departure of someone from one's life? The fact that one can never see them for the rest of one's life is hard to bear.' Ram Mohan looked at him and said, 'Badri, don't be so serious. I know what you are saying, but when something is beyond your control, the sensible thing would be to get over it, the sooner the better.' Presently they embarked upon the ten-kilometre-long journey to the Ganges. Deena walked behind the sole ox-cart carrying Chhote Baba, and could not help tearing up as they walked past places he used to visit with him. He clung to the company of Rajvansh, his cousin. He was missing his Nana Baijnath who had not been well lately. They passed several villages on the way. The landscape remained more or less the same during most of the journey, but the suggestions of the Ganges were visible much before they came in sight of it. Deena was amazed at this reach of the great river, conspicuous in the pleasantness of the atmosphere, in the absence of dust, in the increasing presence of sand, in the crops different from the ones familiar to him. It was the first time Deena was seeing such a big river; the mere thought of getting caught in such a vast body of swift waters gave him the shivers. On one side of the bank was this area earmarked for cremation. He could see a couple of burning pyres. The daylight had turned the leaping flames into wraiths, hard to pick out if it were not for the dark smoke fumbling at them, then there was this extinguished smoking pyre with some men converged on it, one sprinkling Ganges water on the debris to cool it. Rajvansh told him they were looking for what was left of the body, and shortly a big blackened lump was lifted out along with some smaller ones, bundled up and taken to be consigned to the holy river.

Two pariahs associated with the business of cremation tried in vain to make Ram Mohan revise his decision to let the Ganges take care of Chhote Baba. He had little patience with things done merely in the belief of something. They, four at a time, took turns in carrying Chhote Baba on their shoulders to the marge of the mother Ganges; Gulab Singh and one of his men, the strongest of the group who could swim, stepped into the water and began to push the floating bier towards the main current. It was neck-deep where they left Chhote Baba bobbing up and down, and waded back to the bank; then Badri spotted the bier floating back to the edge a little ahead down the stream. This time they took it as far away from the bank as possible and had to swim a little on their way back.

Kanti thought Ram Mohan would not know of Chhote Baba's largess to her. Yet the first thing he did after returning from the cremation was to ask her to show him what his Chacha had left for him; got irritated when she played at not getting what he was talking about. 'Look, I've no time to indulge in soft-soaping you. There was an important class today that I had to cancel;

tomorrow I have to go to Lucknow. So don't try my patience and stop pandering to your ever-alive greed.'

'Chacha gave those things to me. You can ask Kalla Dada; it was he who had opened the trunk and—'

'Who else would I learn it from? You wouldn't have told me . . . And what do you mean he gave them to you, the money and the gold coins? Who is in charge here? If you want to become the family's provider, then I'll withdraw. You take care of everything.'

'When did I say that? You're the head of the family. I only feel it's better to have some money and valuables put by.'

'Then you had better follow what I say. I'm responsible for all of you, so leave every decision to me. Whatever I manage to achieve socially or politically is meant to benefit our family, our children. I know what to do and when. Now go and get them. I am trying to secure a bright future for all of us.'

Kanti went and brought Chhote Baba's pouch. Ram Mohan took it and said, 'Soon, you and Deena will move to Kanpur . . . Get down to winding things down here. Once my political career takes off, there will be no looking back for us.'

Ram Mohan rode his Rajdoot back to Kanpur the same day.

Kanti had not anticipated this. Irrespective of Chhote Baba's tantrums, she had hoped he would live long enough to enable her to train Deena in managing the family's property in Parsadpur. She knew her husband would not have the cheek to dispose of their fields and trees so long as Chhote Baba was around. Besides, moving to Kanpur meant ceding whatever independence she enjoyed in day-to-day affairs. In Kanpur, she would be left with no room to manoeuvre. Nisha had told her that with Babu ji at home, the only thing for them to do was to live in constant dread, the fear that he would find some excuse to create a scene. The last time Nisha was in Parsadpur she had seemed a bit lost, distant; with a hint of tension in her bearing, as if something was on her mind. Kanti had pressed but she would not open up. So the only thing that could persuade Kanti to let go of Parsadpur was her concern for Nisha and Sandhya. The boys she was not so worried about. And now with Chhote Baba's death, much earlier than expected, there was no choice left. If Deena was old enough, she would not mind him taking charge of their agrarian interests; any movable or immovable assets of the family were to be treasured and looked after. The key words to define her disposition were thrift and diligence.

When Ram Mohan sold their house to Kalla Dada, she felt numb with despair. Now she feared for their other ancestral assets in Parsadpur—trees and fields, indeed a big piece of land near the station—but the immediate danger to their survival was averted by a political development that would keep Ram Mohan preoccupied for some time to come.

* * *

Dixit ji had called twice before Ram Mohan's return to Kanpur. He booked a trunk call and spoke to Dixit ji and arrived at Subhadra Kutir a few hours later. Soon, a girl brought tea. He sat in one of the chairs as she, a little nervously, put the tray on the table and began to make tea; he picked a biscuit watching her. Barely eighteen or so, she was incredibly dark, the blue border of her sari giving a cerulean hue to her skin, a smoother version of which was hard to imagine; though plebian at first glance, a close look would reveal some indistinct but delectable details of her face. When she handed him tea, their eyes met— scarlet traceries dulling the whites of her eyes—and before she could lower them, he was impaled.

She was the granddaughter of Baran Singh's Harijan cook. Her parents had died when she was just a child. It was some accident. Her grandparents had brought her to live with them in the servant quarters at the rear of Chaudhary Sahab's bungalow, but when her Dadi too had passed, it had become too fraught for the old man to have her on his hands alone. Learning of his travails, Dixit ji had offered to employ her as domestic help under the overall supervision of Sughari, the senior caretaker. He could not have asked for more, the grandfather. His mind thus set at ease, he could now retire and go back to his village to spend his remaining days with the families of his youngest son and nephews. Dixit ji's offer promised his granddaughter a better life than in village, and what's more, Dixit ji had also assured him of finding a groom for her.

Just as Ram Mohan was leaving to meet Dixit ji, Sughari gave him an impish look. She had sensed his sudden ache, though there was no hint of shock or disgust in her manner, enabling Ram Mohan to grin and leave in a pleasant mood; with grounds for hope. He would wait for an opportunity to engage Sughari in a heart-to-heart.

He took a rickshaw to Dixit ji's official residence that he, though no more a minister, could retain for some time on a nominal rent. When Ram Mohan got there, Dixit ji was all set to leave. The plains of UP had of late been under the assault of a heat wave; temperature was at its peak. Not many people were about that afternoon. Defying the raging sun, the security personnel stood to attention as Dixit ji's car entered the CM's bungalow. People respectfully stepped aside as Dixit ji and Ram Mohan made their way to the main door; they were shown into the room where Baran Singh was immersed in conversation with two of his close confidants. The new arrivals joined in the confab. No single minister was there. Chaudhary Sahab wanted to first consult those of his loyal associates who were not in his government. After usual pleasantries, they fell quiet as though weighed down with some vague angst. None seemed willing to speak until fully seized of the matter, which as they understood, might lead to some sort of political crisis. Baran Singh sat absently, his gaze fixed on his lap. Then raising his head and surveying the room, he said, 'My government can fall soon.' Nobody, not even Dixit ji, had any inkling of something this serious. 'Are you joking?' said Dixit ji.

'What do you make of the announcement of the United Socialist Party? It's been in the papers.'

'What announcement?' said Dixit ji and then, 'You mean that stunt? Do you really think they're crazy enough to attempt that?'

The PM was to shortly visit Benaras to preside over the annual meeting of Indian Science Congress. In the meantime, the local unit of the United Socialist Party, a crucial component of Chaudhary Baran Singh's government, had decided to 'take Mrs Gandhi in custody' and make her stand trial in a people's court. Baran Singh said, 'Crazy! That's a mild way to describe them.'

'Chaudhary Sahab, it might just be a ploy to seek public attention,' said Ram Mohan.

'I hope it's that. For if they're serious and under the impression that I'd let that happen, they are living in a fool's paradise.'

'Don't they know the administration has to be extra vigilant during PM's visit? It's incumbent on the CM to see the event passes off peacefully,' said another participant.

'These people have little patience with things that don't suit their agenda . . . My government depends on their support, so they think I would be willing to ignore my duties for their sake.'

'Do you want me to speak to them?' said Dixit ji.

'I've spoken to Raj Narayan. He says nothing has been finalized yet. Their party leaders are still discussing the idea. What I learnt from Raj Narayan is that the socialists are excited about it and expect me to cooperate.'

'What kind of cooperation, Chaudhary Sahab?' said Ram Mohan.

'That they'll only tell me if they decide to go ahead with the plan. I hope better sense prevails, and they don't put at risk the survival of the first ever non-Congress government in UP.'

The one person who sat quiet all this while, said, 'Chaudhary Sahab, assuming the socialists don't back away—'

'That would put my abilities as an administrator to test. I can't shirk from acting decisively if it comes to that; I'll take whatever action needed to keep the situation under control.'

Dixit ji said, 'In that case I doubt if the socialists will continue to back your government.'

'I've thought about this. But I won't let anybody get under my feet while I try to discharge my duties. If these people withdraw their support, so be it.'

No one, not even his close associates on the Cabinet knew about this threat. Though piqued at the development, Ram Mohan felt awash with a deep sense of satisfaction. To be made privy to a matter as explosive as that was past his expectation. On their way back, Dixit ji confirmed that Baran Singh saw in him qualities that most of his key men lacked.

———

After a word with Sughari alone, Dixit ji left. Ram Mohan had changed into a lungi and a vest when the girl came with a glass of water. He saw her and felt despoiled of the good feeling he had enjoyed till then. With an aching urge, he looked her over as she bent to set the glass on the table, then turned and walked out of the room, seeming embarrassed at her body broken out in unwieldy protrusions. Presently, Sughari entered carrying tea and snacks. He said, 'I want to relax with a little chat, Sughari. Go get yourself a cup.' She went and came back with a glass of tea and lowered herself to the floor against the wall. 'Dixit ji has burdened you with an additional responsibility . . . A girl as young as that on your hands. You have to be vigilant all the time.'

'True,' she said. 'She's at an age when—'

'She's most vulnerable . . . vulnerable to being inveigled into what can cause problems for Dixit ji,' broke in Ram Mohan.

'I don't let her go out alone. Now Dixit ji has more time to spare us. When he was minister, it would sometimes be weeks before he could find time to visit.'

'Though kind and well-meaning, Dixit ji is an old man. Has anything been thought about her future?'

'She has been living in Lucknow since childhood and has studied up to class five. Her Dada does not want to marry her off to some villager. She's not used to rural life.'

'But it'll be difficult to find her a groom in the city.'

'Yes. Most of the Harijans in the city clean sewage and remove excreta from toilets. There should be some with government jobs, but then her colour might repel them. Wheat-like or fair skin is rare among Harijans . . . but rarer still is to find someone cursed with the blackness of her skin.'

'I can't vouch for others but to me, she is very attractive,' said Ram Mohan, faintly nervous; but was relieved to see her smile.

'Yes, I know. I could make out from your face when you asked about her before leaving for Chaudhary Sahab's.'

'What do you make of this attraction?'

'Nothing much to make of it . . . It's an illness common to men, nearly all of them.'

'At first I thought I needed to be watchful, you being Mahavir's Bua . . . Now I realize you're incredibly sensible and practical.'

'But it's better to curb the longing for something beyond reach.'

Vexed, he said, 'What happens if Dixit ji fails to find a boy for her? Will she be sent to her grandfather in the village?

'She has nothing to worry as long as Dixit ji's around. God forbid if anything happens to him, she can come with me to Kanpur. My brother will have no problem with that. He has a retirement pension from the army, and Mahavir is also earning. She can be a lot of help in the house there. That said, Dixit ji will never leave her in the lurch. She'll receive sufficient money from him to take care of her personal expenses for a long time to come. Then, as you know my brother and nephew lay so much stress on education, I don't think she would remain uneducated while living in their house. As far as I can see, she will get along all right . . . Of course, a woman's life cannot be without its usual difficulties and pitfalls. But at least Malti—her name is Malti—will be saved from the hell which is the lot of the poor, unprotected women.'

'That's all very good. What about her other needs in case she remains unmarried? Do you realize the seriousness of a lapse on her part? What about unsavoury innuendos bound to come her way if she remains single?'

'She won't be living in a village or some country town. In Kanpur, few people know about our family or relations. Also, the society is not so morally exacting with regard to us untouchables. There's no place lower than where we already are . . . After moving to Kanpur, we will become Christian. My brother says things are going to get better.' She paused and continued, 'We might find someone willing to marry Malti . . .'

'Marriage isn't the only way out . . . There's another way . . . She can be in a relationship not sanctified by rituals but reliable. An alliance of this nature is most workable and durable when the man is much older than the woman.'

Sughari chuckled. 'What kind of logic is this?'

'I'm not saying this for a laugh, Sughari. It's very pragmatic. Young men are liable to stray because they have time on their side. For a senior man on the other hand, such union with a younger woman is elixir of life. It's not just physical for him, but also emotional because it fills him with a sense of achievement, which is like a tonic for his flagging physical self. Imagine the value of this relation to an old man! He would cherish it with gratitude.'

'I know why you're saying all this. I suggest you forget about Malti for now. As long as Dixit ji is around, she will live in this house. You might, if in luck, succeed in your wish after we have shifted to Kanpur . . . But you're married and have children. How would you be able to support and maintain a lifestyle like that? I know you're not that rich.'

'With Chaudhary Sahab's hand on my head, I'll soon get to some position of consequence; then I would stay mostly in Lucknow. A visit once or twice a week to Kanpur would be enough. Malti can stay in my official residence here and take charge of cooking and other household things. She would have the same role as you have here in Dixit ji's house. People would find little to read into it other than the obvious. Anyway, who would think that a man of my station could have anything to do with her, physically? The colour of her skin is such . . . It's a curse. To me though it's a boon, providing protection from malicious gossip.'

'Is there nothing on your mind but her? I could not have guessed you were so amorous. You clap eyes on someone as black as Malti and come up with a plan to make her your mistress . . . It is not that simple. But if there is ever any sign of its possibility, I'll tell you.'

'I didn't say I wanted it to happen tomorrow . . . It was just to let you know. I'm willing to wait.'

'That's better', said Sughari as she rose, picked the tray and went out of the room. He slid back to the pillow and leaned on it. Something that had burst into his head as a wild wish, a fantasy, had come within the realm of possibility. What a moment of catharsis it had been, his talking with Sughari. His passion for Malti had changed into tingling expectancy.

When he failed to talk United Socialist Party out of their 'foolish' agenda, Baran Singh made up his mind. It was time to show— for the benefit of friends and foes alike—the strain of steel in his character. The day before the annual meeting of Indian Science Congress, he put in prison many a USP legislator including Raj Narayan who was an MP at the time.

Accompanying Indira Gandhi to Benaras, Baran Singh learnt that the USP's local unit was going ahead with its plan to stage a demonstration. He gave orders for any such attempt to be met with force. During the PM's speech, the demonstrators made a bid to get inside the venue. The police had to resort to lathi charge. Many people were injured, some gravely. The United Socialist Party was raving mad. Its leaders after they were set free announced the withdrawal of support to Baran Singh government. The next session of the Assembly was a few months off. They met the governor demanding that a special session be called and Baran Singh be asked to prove his majority on the floor. All players went into a huddle followed by hectic parleys between various political outfits. Given the composition of the Legislature, no other coalition was possible, unless of course the socialists and the Congress joined hands, which was unlikely. Baran Singh decided to sit out the tumult. Once it became clear that no alternate coalition was on the horizon, the socialists began to clamour for the dissolution of the Assembly. As the inevitability of midterm poll dawned, Baran Singh knew he would have to advance the floating of his own outfit. He looked to buy time.

The Congress too was wary of a fresh election so soon. Baran Singh contacted Shukla ji who was now among the top leaders of the state Congress; he assured him of cooperation. Ram Mohan was sent to Delhi. Baran Singh had alerted Saansad ji, and Ram Mohan was to explain to him the political course on which Chaudhary Sahab had set his mind. Finally, Saansad ji and Shukla ji's uncle convinced Indira Gandhi of how useful the proposed manoeuvre was to the Congress. Ram Mohan came back, elated; but there was something else, something upsetting, of which Ram Mohan had to make Chaudhary Sahab cognizant. He could not bring himself to spoil his mood right then and decided to talk to Dixit ji, who had already left the CM's bungalow, complaining of a headache, and Ram Mohan, instead of staying the night at the CM's bungalow, went to Subhadra Kutir, where he could set eyes on the 'black rose' as well as chat with Sughari.

* * *

It was already dark. Sughari was taking unusually long to answer the door. As he stood waiting, there blew a pleasant zephyr, bringing relief from the humidity. He looked up. The sky was growing overcast. He knocked again, a little harder this time. A moment later, he heard the door being unbolted; after a pause, it started moving on its hinges, a couple of inches at first, making it evident the visitor had chosen a wrong moment. Sughari, a bit surprised, looked kind of relieved that it was Ram Mohan. Without a word, she took the bedroll from him, which he had had to bring to use on the train to Delhi. Holding his small suitcase, he followed her into the room where he had been put up previously.

Setting his luggage down against the wall, she strode back to close the door, and then turning to him, flashed a smile. He sat down at the edge of the bed and took off his shoes when Sughari moved closer. Her words made him stand up. He could never have assumed Dixit ji's presence at Subhadra Kutir at that hour. She said he was tired of the constant bother at his residence; had come to unwind and repose in peace, free from having to talk politics or meet visitors. Sughari left to apprise Dixit ji of Ram Mohan; he might be wondering about the unexpected visitor. Hearing footsteps, Ram Mohan hoped it was Malti. It was Sughari again, wanting to know if she should give him something to eat; Ram Mohan declined; he had eaten at Chaudhary Sahab's. 'Dixit ji wants you to take rest; he will talk to you in the morning.' Before she could close the door behind her, he asked about Malti. She smiled and said she was kneading the old man's legs.

Ram Mohan hit the sack. He must have slept soundly because when Sughari woke him, he felt rested; then, noticing her terror-stricken face so close to his face, he sat up wide awake. Putting on his glasses, he saw Sughari gesticulating to make up for the incoherence issuing from her mouth. It was nearly six by the clock on the front wall. He jumped out of bed; placed his hands on her shoulders as she gulped for breath; then she rushed out, ran back along the narrow corridor with him close behind and plunged into the room at the end of it. What confronted Ram Mohan, who had braced himself for the worst, did not strike home at first. It was a picture, contrived as it were, to underscore the limits of his imagination. Both of them were in a state of nature. A supine Malti had most of her body hidden beneath Dixit ji's. Weeping quietly, she made no attempt to wriggle out from under the inert figure, for Sughari who had hastened into the room after hearing the shriek had told her not to move—fearing it might compound the problem given Dixit ji's decrepit state—until she was back. The situation was straight from hell, and Sughari could not stop being thankful for the timely presence of Ram Mohan. The very thought of having it entirely on her hands chilled her blood.

He stood transfixed for a second before sizing up the scene before him. The setting bore no sign of coercion or trauma. The two chairs sitting against the wall to the left side of the bed contained their clothes. One held Dixit ji's vest, lungi and drawers, forming a small mound, the other Malti's petticoat, blouse and sari, carefully folded and neatly placed on one another. Nothing to suggest rush or impetuousness. It had been thought out in advance, and they were proceeding nicely just before being frozen in their tracks by an unforeseen calamity. Ram Mohan, gazing at the spectacle, thought how odd to associate the form sprawled over Malti with the way it appeared in public. The elegance of Dixit ji's person, his fine dress sense, his impeccable manners . . . The reality in view now—the extent of devastation inflicted on his frame by age—was shocking. The flesh on Dixit ji's faded body had melted at places, leaving the skin horribly shrivelled; the part that came across as most unsightly was the rear. Whatever loose flesh remained in that part now dropped away from the parting like a pair of panniers.

Ram Mohan felt Dixit ji's pulse. Sughari, who had stopped crying, held her breath, nodding to Malti in a gesture of solace and assurance. Though weak, the pulse was there. 'He's passed out.' Signalling to Sughari to give him a hand, he lifted Dixit ji's torso a little; as Malti moved out, he got an eyeful of her throbbing voluptuousness. Covering herself with a sheet, she bounded to her clothes in the chair. That even a circumstance like this could not arrest his passionate imaginings surprised Ram Mohan; catching Sughari's pleading look, he laid Dixit ji gently on the other, less crumpled side, of the bed. Then they noticed bloodstains on the pink bed-sheet. Peering closely, Ram Mohan spotted dried smudges on the septuagenarian's member, which shrunken to the limit, lay nestled in the flaccid white pubes. He looked at Sughari who said she would talk to him later. First they had to race Dixit ji to hospital, and inform his family. He told her to cover the stains on the bed with a pillow or something and wipe the dried blood from his private parts. Hurrying towards the door, he said, 'Put clothes on Dixit ji.'

The weather was pleasant. It had drizzled the previous night. There was hardly any traffic at this hour. Knowing he had to get help immediately, Ram Mohan—taking long strides—walked to the nearest police post about a hundred yards away. Standing just outside with an aluminium mug in his hand, a constable was blowing his nose; Ram Mohan dashed past him—escaping narrowly a flying piece of mucus—and into the shanty like structure where the sub-inspector was snoozing in his chair as a glass of tea covered with a saucer holding two biscuits sat on the table in front of him. The constable who had come trotting behind Ram Mohan was kept from yelling by his khadi outfit and an unusually confident gait. The sub-inspector opened his mouth before opening his eyes, but before he could let out expletives, Ram Mohan shouted, 'Get up'. The officer, wide awake, hastened to his feet; after told of the urgency, he straddled his motorcycle and sped off; the dumbfounded constable slunk to a stool in the corner and sat down. An earnest but calm Ram Mohan began to pace up and down outside. Soon the sub-inspector returned piloting a police Jeep; Ram Mohan got on beside the driver. A policeman was on the way to the main hospital to get an ambulance but the sub-inspector feared it might take time. They had to get Dixit ji to hospital at once.

A big name in state politics, Dixit ji was also known as a close friend of the CM. No government official in their senses could have had the nerve to treat the matter offhandedly. The senior police officials of the city had been informed, who in turn notified the CM as well as Dixit ji's family. The hospital compound was reverberating with a quiet rush thanks to the presence of so many VIPs, including Baran Singh himself and his security detail. Nobody took notice as the police Jeep drew up in the portico. It was only after the police inspector got cracking that the waiting throng became alive to the arrival of Dixit ji. Sughari accompanied the comatose figure carried off on a stretcher.

The entire hospital was abuzz with speculative murmurs as to the emergency. It had to be something big and serious. The sudden advent of the CM and his predecessor Gupta along with several ministers and other VIPs this early in the day was no simple matter. A big room close to the main lobby was made available to Baran Singh and his troupe—all sat in a circle talking gravely, surrounded by government officials and doctors. Baran Singh motioned for everybody to be quiet as Ram Mohan walked up to describe the entire sequence. 'I was surprised to find Dixit ji in Subhadra Kutir. Sughari said he had come to relax in peace, without being disturbed by constant telephone calls and visitors. When told of my arrival, he sent word that he would have breakfast with me in the morning. Feeling tired, I went off to sleep only to be roused by a hysterical Sughari early in the morning.' He had hardly finished recounting how he managed to secure help when trooped in Dixit ji's family members who had been waiting outside the room where Dixit ji was being examined by a team of doctors.

Dixit ji had suffered a stroke and was in a coma.

A senior doctor came to brief the CM on his condition. Whether his friend would pull through or not was hard to say. Chaudhary Sahab held the doctor's elbow and led him aside. 'Dixit ji is in a terribly bad shape,' the doctor whispered. Some of Dixit ji's family burst into tears. Baran Singh comforted them, and after a brief visit to Dixit ji's room, he and other VIPs left. Ram Mohan had to meet Chaudhary Sahab before heading back to Kanpur, and with Dixit ji all but gone he would have to tell Chaudhary Sahab about Saansad ji's future plan all by himself. First, he needed Sughari to tell him the complete story.

The police Jeep dropped them back. Sughari went straight into Dixit ji's room—which had been spruced up by Malti—and slumped to the floor, tears gushing into her eyes; she began muttering about Dixit ji's kindness, generosity and other noteworthy attributes of his nature, as Ram Mohan, flopping into one of the chairs, mopped his brow and neck with his khadi handkerchief. When Malti offered him a glass of water, he picked his glasses from his lap and put them on and pinched her cheeks facetiously, affecting affection; he asked her to have Sughari also drink some water. Malti sat down beside her and cajoled her into taking a few sips. Sughari wiped her face using a corner of her sari as Ram Mohan addressed her, 'I'm not trying to make light of how you must feel. I know. My feelings are no different. The presence of Dixit ji in my life has been no less important . . . He had long deserved to be chief minister and felt cast down when he was passed over twice. Then a few years ago, he realized there was no reason for him to continue in politics . . . but who can ignore the role Dixit ji played in energizing Chaudhary Sahab's campaign for the top job . . .' Sughari latched onto Ram Mohan's words. He went on, 'When my wife started a school for girls in our village, it was Dixit ji who helped us out. He had also sent Gayatri, and no words can do justice to what she meant to us . . . We should be proud of Dixit ji . . . and Sughari I must commend you for the way you have served him all these years, with sincerity and devotion.' He stopped, as if weighing his words. 'How many men at his age are so fortunate as to be afforded the opportunity of physical love . . . That too with a girl as young as Malti? I cannot mask my envy of him.'

Sughari looked at Malti who went red as a beetroot and left the room. 'Which proved so costly eventually,' said Sughari, shaking her head.

'He's quite old, seventy-seven, isn't it? Let's not blame it on what he was doing. I consider him lucky. To pass out while enjoying something like that is an apt tribute to his ardour.' She looked relieved. He continued, 'I had no inkling of anything of the sort. To associate something like this with him would have been beyond me.'

'He would say nothing could be more private than this union . . .' said Sughari. '. . . and those not involved, had no business to be in the know. It was something sacrosanct, talking about which with anyone other than one's partner was to demean its beauty. Men who use force or stratagems or lies to get a woman into bed are the greatest enemies of the idea of lovemaking. He was very clear about this. For instance, even if Malti had not agreed, he would have kept supporting her like nothing had happened.'

Ram Mohan said, after a long pause, 'One more thing Sughari—' and was pulled up short by a rethink perhaps of what he was going to say. He straightened himself up. 'Now that I'm in the know of this facet of Dixit ji's life, could you tell me if there was anything like this between him and Gayatri?'

'No . . . not at all. One of the reasons he had sent her to Parsadpur was that with her being around he could not think of anything like this. Her presence at Subhadra Kutir would have shut the door on the possibility of this bliss. I mean going to bed with a girl like Malti.'

While Dixit ji was still comatose, Gupta, the former CM and leader of Opposition, sought an audience with the Governor. USP's withdrawal of support to Baran Singh government had roiled the political waters in UP; with no party in a position to give a stable regime, midterm poll seemed the only recourse, which barring the socialists, nobody wanted because the current term of Legislative Assembly was hardly a few months old. There were whispers that Baran Singh and the Congress had reached an understanding. Finally, Gupta's statement after meeting the Governor gave a quietus to the speculation about the fall of the government. It also scotched the threat of dissolution of the House any time soon, as Gupta had conveyed to the Governor that the Congress, the largest party in the Assembly, wasn't keen on a special session. 'Chaudhary Baran Singh can be asked to prove his strength on the floor of the House once the Assembly is in session a few months from now. What's the rush? Let him run a minority government until then . . .'

The socialists were livid. Raj Narayan accused Baran Singh of being hand in glove with the Congress. 'To retain the CM's chair for a few months more . . . Chaudhary has become a pawn in the Congress's campaign for the recapture of Lucknow. But we won't sit quiet. Our party will put this period to good use. Our workers will fan out across the state, marshalling people against this subterfuge, the conspiratorial alliance between Gupta and Baran Singh. Soon we will hold a big rally in Lucknow.' But before the socialists could make good this pronouncement, Dixit ji died, handing Baran Singh an occasion to drown out their threat. He declared three days of state mourning. Dixit ji was built up to be one of the foremost figures from UP.

The entire city came to a halt as the serpentine procession made its way amid slogan-shouting to the cremation ground. Baran Singh's strategy worked; on top of that, the issue on which the USP was banking lacked the punch to rouse people; many of its own supporters did not appreciate the urgency of the stand the party had taken. In the meantime, Baran Singh—to expedite his plan to form his own party—called a meeting of his loyalists in and outside the government; he began with remembering, Dixit ji, 'I can't tell how terribly I miss my dear friend today. As some of you know, it was he who had first spoken about the need for a party of our own, and the idea was bolstered by his analysis of the votes polled by various parties and independents in the last election. Now is the moment we act on it.'

Many questions came up for discussion. The one that took the longest to resolve was that of naming the new outfit. The People's Congress—the name of his faction in the coalition— Chaudhary Sahab rejected outright. He wanted something fresh, something with no trace of Congress; finally they settled for Indian Revolutionary Party (IRP). 'I want the groundwork for the party to be laid before we go public,' said Baran Singh. He assigned the task to some of his ablest men. The actual formation of the IRP would come only after Baran Singh's resignation as CM. Ram Mohan was tasked with preparing a draft discussing what warranted the IRP.

Ram Mohan along with Tiwari ji hung back after the meeting. He wanted a word with Chaudhary Sahab alone. 'We'll talk over dinner,' Baran Singh said before going to his home office to dispose of some files. Ram Mohan and Tiwari ji were debating the prospects of the new party when Savitri Devi showed up, followed by a help with a tea-tray. Motioning them to remain seated, she took a seat close by and started making tea for them. They looked overwhelmed. Smiling sadly, she began to talk about Dixit ji . . . how suddenly it all happened; Ram Mohan and Tiwari ji changed their expression to go with her look of solemnity. She talked about how much Chaudhary Sahab had come to count on Dixit ji; and before taking leave, she enquired if they would be staying the night. When Ram Mohan said they would go to Subhadra Kutir as he had his luggage and some books lying there, she said, 'Tell her . . . I forget her name,' she tried to recall when Ram Mohan helped. 'Yes, Sughari . . . Tell her not to worry. I think she already knows . . . Dixit ji's son was here yesterday, the one who teaches at the university; he's got a house on the campus, and after vacating the official bungalow, the whole family is going to live with him, which means they won't need Subhadra Kutir for now. He said Sughari could continue to be the caretaker, until of course she goes to Kanpur to live with her father . . .'

'It's her brother,' Ram Mohan corrected her.

'Fine, whatever . . . My worry is Malti. I think she will have to move back in here. I wonder how we are going to deal with the situation. She is the granddaughter of someone who had been in Chaudhary Sahab's service since his student-days . . . You know with a girl of her age how watchful one has to be all the time. There is an unending stream of visitors here . . . all kinds of people lounge around every day, not to mention our staff members. There's so much to occupy my mind . . . and how disconcerting it would be if some nasty character managed to wheedle her into something unseemly, leaving a blot on Chaudhary Sahab's prestige.'

'I think you should not be exercised about it anymore . . .' said Ram Mohan, '. . . for as far as I know she too will be going to Kanpur.'

Staring at him for a second, Savitri Devi said, 'It makes no sense. Why should anybody concern themselves with someone

who is not their responsibility, unless of course it can be of some
advantage to them? Naturally, all kinds of dreadful thoughts
come to your mind, particularly so if the person involved is a
young girl, let alone a Harijan.'

'No, it's not like that at all,' said Ram Mohan; then looking
at Tiwari ji, 'We know Sughari's nephew Mahavir Wilson. It
was Dixit ji who had introduced him to me. We are very close
now. He teaches history in a premier English-medium school in
Kanpur, and wants to become a lecturer at some degree college
eventually. Both he and his father are progressive and kind-
hearted people and know firsthand what it means to be Harijan.
They will make something of her . . . What I'm saying is that she
is fortunate to get an opportunity like this. She might in time be
able to lead a life mostly denied to people of her ilk.'

Savitri Devi said, 'Your words, Ram Mohan, are reassuring.
I hope what you are saying turns out true.'

Then, Chaudhary Sahab was heard outside the door; a
moment later he emerged wearing a tired smile. They rose. He
gestured them to sit. 'From the previous regime, I inherited a
huge backlog of files, a mountain of them; today I dealt with the
last of the heap. I don't know what Gupta had been up to all the
time he was in office!'

'Chaudhary Sahab, most Congress CMs today owe the
crown not to their ability but to their sycophancy. Matters of
governance matter little to them, these Congress loungers.'

Savitri Devi got up saying she had to go and check what was
happening in the kitchen.

'So, Ram Mohan, what is it you wanted to talk about?'

'It has to do with Saansad ji, Chaudhary Sahab. I first
wanted to discuss it with Dixit ji, which was not to be. He
had this fatal stroke almost the same day as I returned from
Delhi—' Ram Mohan stopped as Baran Singh leaned back in
his chair with the hands clasped against the chin. Ram Mohan

had his attention. 'Saansad ji might respond to the feelers put out by PM's coterie. He was not specific but I could sense his bitterness about not getting a chance to serve on the Union cabinet. This when he has always been so vocal in Parliament . . . He said, "My case parallels Chaudhary Sahab's own, whose claim to the reins of the state was ignored by the party high command." That was the reason he followed you out of the Congress. Now he thinks the ongoing turmoil in the Congress has compelled Indira ji to right a wrong. Kapur told him she was all set to throw down the gauntlet to the old bats of the party, so she wants a 'true' Congressman like Saansad ji to return and join battle with the elements intent on subverting the political legacy of her father . . . In other words, he would take the offer to become part of her Cabinet. He also noted that your priority was UP whereas he had to look for something in Delhi . . . But I—'

'Why did he need a messenger or indulge in hedging? He has known me for so many years . . . He could have told me himself, over the phone. I would have understood. He wants to return to the Congress, fine . . . Why should he stick with me if—'

'But Chaudhary Sahab,' broke in Tiwari ji, 'I hear Saansad ji was instrumental in getting the Congress to help foil the Socialists' bid to topple your government.'

'Chaudhary Sahab knows that,' said Ram Mohan. 'I had gone there especially for that purpose,' then to Baran Singh, 'Yes, Saansad ji is embarrassed about it, but he views your friendship above politics.' Before Baran Singh could respond, Savitri Devi came. Food was ready. They rose. Pretending he had something in his eye, Baran Singh took out his handkerchief to wipe the moistness off.

Once in Kanpur, Ram Mohan launched into catching up with his teaching work for the year. Mishra had taken some of his classes. With no time to be thorough, he would give the students an outline of every important topic and the names of books where they could find the relevant detail. This was the best he could do for he did not know when he might have to visit Lucknow again. Indeed a week or so later, on reading in the paper that Indira Gandhi might go in for an expansion of her Cabinet, with Saansad ji's name among the three hopefuls, he went to meet Chaudhary Sahab.

The news was largely true, a little inaccuracy being in the detail. Saansad ji would not get Cabinet rank as reported but the position of a minister of state with independent charge. Not a bad deal, considering he had not been minister before. Yes, he had called from Delhi the previous night, seeking his friend's best wishes. The gesture, Ram Mohan could see, had had a mollifying effect on Chaudhary Sahab; he looked happy for Saansad ji who was going to get his long-denied due.

Unable to resist the urge to see Sughari and Malti, Ram Mohan went to Subhadra Kutir, and noted the change in Malti who sat down unselfconsciously beside Sughari; when their eyes met, she seemed in no haste to drop her gaze. As Sughari sent her to get tea, he asked if Malti knew of his ache. 'No . . . If she knew she would not come before you let alone make eye contact.' He let his jaw fall. Sughari laughed and said his presence in the house that day was what probably led her to feel a kind of affinity for him. The memory of that nightmarish moment still made them catch their breath. 'I shudder to think how we would have coped without you.'

'I would have left for Kanpur after meeting Chaudhary Sahab, but the temptation to see you both proved too strong.'

'My brother was here, wanting to know when I would be shifting to Kanpur. Then, this poor old man, Malti's Dada, came

all the way from his village to know if he had to take her back
in his care. He was grieving for her dead parents again, saying
he did not know what lay in store for her. Baran Singh's wife
eased his mind. He came back and had a long chat with me; I
told him about my brother and nephew, and of their consent to
Malti living with us in Kanpur . . .' She stopped as Malti came
back in with tea. She put the tray on the table before resuming
her place beside Sughari on the floor.

Smiling at her, she continued, 'Yes, her Dada did not insist
on taking her back, convinced she was in safe hands.'

'Once your brother and nephew take her in their hands, she
would be able to take care of herself before long. Then I'm also
in Kanpur . . . But Malti can help matters in her own way, isn't
it?' This last bit he said a bit waggishly.

'Of course, she can; she won't flinch if necessary.'

Looking somewhat lost, Malti smiled shyly.

'She already owes me,' said Ram Mohan.

'No doubt you were our rescuer that day, and Malti respects
you for that.'

'Respects me?' said Ram Mohan with a put-on perturbation.

'What's so surprising in that? She also respected Dixit ji,
and it was out of respect that she acceded to my request on his
behalf. She sensed it would not be long before he exited this
world. Giving him a few moments of what he desired so much
was perfectly in order.'

Flushed, Malti tried to get up. Sughari foiled the attempt
and carried on, 'It was an act of kindness on her part. Or it
would be outrageous to expect a girl of her age to bring herself
to have that kind of an interest in a man as old as Dixit ji. It had
to be on compassionate grounds.'

'Which means,' said Ram Mohan, 'she would not remain
cussed if there came a moment genuine enough to warrant her
kindness—'

Before he could finish, Malti—giving the older woman the slip—rose and went out of the room. They laughed. Ram Mohan too got up. Walking down the passage towards the main door, he murmured, 'Sughari, take pity on me, use your persuasive skills to steer her thoughts . . .'

Sughari asked him to have patience.

* * *

As he sat in the Hindi faculty room, the next day Ram Mohan realized he had been neglectful of his literary life lately; the fear of having to cede to Mishra or others the position he had come to occupy among his colleagues and the literati of the city seized his mind like a flash. No one, not even the erudite Mishra— his rival, also a friend now—could match his flamboyance in hawking their wares, literary or otherwise. Come to think of it, he could sense something in the air, some stirring in people's perception of his priorities. He recalled the last faculty meeting soon after he had joined back, when everybody had something good to say about his political venture—his remarkable performance in Fatehpur and his closeness to political bigwigs of the state. But when it would come to discussing topics of academic importance, he might not have been there. The head of the department would mostly turn to Mishra for advice, even on things previously considered Ram Mohan's strong suit.

A wilful attempt to slight him would not have troubled him. Being always game for a good fight, he could have enjoyed it. He could have enjoyed finding ways to pay the departmental head back for the brushing off. No, that was not the case. They, the whole department, thought he had found his true vocation in politics, allowing them to lead the field here. Ram Mohan could not afford to let this impression gain ground; he had yet to achieve a well-defined position in politics. Even in

political circles, his reputation was that of a Hindi scholar who
dabbled in politics. Further, he was disinclined to compromise
his place in the august sphere of letters that had always been
a Brahman domain, punctuated now and then by individuals
from other upper castes. He was the only one from his caste
who had burgled this burg. He recalled the occasion—the first
of its kind in his academic life—when he had outshone all other
speakers at a function in his college. In his speech he had called
India the Mount Everest of civilizations, the envy of the world.
'The greatness of thought, the magnificence of culture and the
resplendence of linguistic tradition are what set our country
apart, rather a sublime synthesis of the three.' It had been a
stirring oration, causing the Governor—the chief guest at the
function—to hail Ram Mohan as one of the foremost exponents
of Indian cultural tradition he had come across.

No, he would not let go of his hard-earned reputation of
a literary scholar, just like that. There were still a few months
before Chaudhary Sahab launched his political front; by putting
this interlude to good use, he could reinforce his presence in
the arena of Hindi letters. He had had this long-standing wish
to write in verse a slim volume, discussing the power of poetry
and proving its supremacy over other arts. More, his renown
as an academic lay inter alia in being a lover of poetry with a
considerable grip on Sanskrit aesthetics, poetics and prosody.
But it was too arduous an enterprise to be finished in the time
available, so he decided to consider the suggestion once made
by his publisher who was keen on a book on Hindi language—a
book that could serve as a basic text for BA students in Kanpur
University—in which Ram Mohan had shown little interest at
the time. The subject was a bit prosaic for his taste. But now that
he did not have time for composing a book in verse on poetry as
a genre, the idea made a lot more sense. To be able to elucidate
the mechanism of Hindi language would give his rivals a taste

of his scholarly breadth. Thanks to his knowledge of English, he could seek help from works available on Language.

Forthwith he phoned his publisher who visited him the same day, gleeful at the prospect of a book he knew was vastly marketable. He offered to provide him with a place in his office to work without being disturbed. Ram Mohan sent for Mahavir Wilson who had a friend teaching English at the prestigious Christ Church College known to have a well-stocked library; the two books he thus obtained, discussed in detail 'human language as a phenomenon', with lucid introductions packed with insightful arguments—unheard of in Hindi circles—whose employment in his book would put his fellow Hindi scholars in their place.

In the meantime, he stayed in touch with Lucknow. Twice he had sent Tiwari ji there to learn of things that would not make it to the papers. A few months later—when he had already finished three chapters and was deep in writing—Savitri Devi called and handed the phone to Chaudhary Sahab who had during his recent trip to Delhi been argued by a dissident Congress MP into advancing the formal launch of Indian Revolutionary Party. Ram Mohan had to put off finishing his book; the publisher did not object, who knew how proficient Ram Mohan was in writing fast. Besides, without his political heft, it was difficult to have the book awarded the status of a textbook by the concerned committee of Kanpur University.

To canvas support for his new political venture, Baran Singh had been going out to various parts of UP almost every other week. In a few days, he was due in Kanpur from where he would travel to Fatehpur where Ram Mohan was to organize his meeting with some influential people of the area. He got himself and his Parsadpur band stationed in Fatehpur three days ahead of Chaudhary Sahab's visit. Tiwari ji's relative was more than happy to put them up in his house. It was only when the district magistrate and the police chief dropped in to meet Ram Mohan that the enormity of the occasion dawned on their host. For anyone to have a visit from these two most powerful officials of the district would be a matter of pride and honour. It would also send a message that the person thus visited was not to be messed with.

The officials were directed by Lucknow to keep Ram Mohan in the loop of the arrangements being made for the CM to meet his core supporters at the Circuit House. Ram Mohan had two days in which to do all the necessary work to make the meeting a success. He was provided a Jeep to move around. The following morning, he and Tiwari ji went to Dhata, fifty kilometers east of Fatehpur, which was part of the city's Assembly seat. Full of dirt lanes and paths, Dhata was nothing but a straggling village with a distant air of small ramshackle country town; known for its shops and a big weekly bazaar dealing in agricultural produce, it served as a commercial centre for all villages in its vicinity. To Ram Mohan, however, the importance of Dhata and the area around it lay in its demographics. The largest chunk of its electorate was made up of Kurmis, which if voted en block had enough strength to secure a win for anyone standing for the Assembly from Fatehpur city.

On reaching Dhata, they went straight to the house of the man whose support had got Ram Mohan thousands of votes in his last Parliamentary bid. Pratap Singh—the biggest landowner in Dhata also a Kurmi—was the most influential man in that part of the district. He had been the village chief for several years, and whenever he would quit, the post would go to his hand-picked man. Ram Mohan and Tiwari ji were received by his old father as Pratap Singh had gone to the village square. A lad was rushed to inform him. Two important-looking men dressed in khadi arriving in a Jeep presented an awesome sight to ordinary villagers; soon, in the distance, Pratap Singh was seen, almost breaking into a trot, followed by a group of men and boys. A well-known figure in the region, Ram Mohan's impressive showing in the last election had left few in doubt as to a great political career in the making. Pratap Singh had not experienced an occasion as imposing as being face to face with Baran Singh and no sooner had Ram Mohan and Tiwari ji taken their leave than he called a meeting of prominent people of Dhata to announce that the CM wanted to meet him and he would also be taking some people along to Fatehpur.

Ram Mohan and his men managed to put together an impressive show before Baran Singh that day. Some of those present vindicated Ram Mohan's trust when they spoke assertively while assuring Baran Singh of their support to IRP. Some also expressed their wish to see their leader Ram Mohan in a position befitting his stature as a backward caste leader and a man of letters. The Chief Minister's audience consisted largely of people from Parsadpur, Ballamgaon and Dhata. Pratap Singh had got a truckload of people to Fatehpur. The room in the Circuit House where the meeting took place was filled to capacity. A large number had to stand outside. Their day however was made when Baran Singh came out along with everybody else to address them briefly; just before winding up, he held Ram Mohan's arm and said, addressing the audience, 'I must compliment you on your sagacity, your choice . . . Yes, this is your man. I've known him for quite some time and can say without an iota of doubt that currently no one else from the farmer community can represent its interests better . . . I ask you not to sit quiet until you have sent him to the Assembly. We would soon have midterm poll; if I succeed in forming the next government, Ram Mohan will serve on my Cabinet. Take my word for it.'

* * *

After about a week, Baran Singh announced in Lucknow the formation of the Indian Revolutionary Party, which according to the general tenor of the speeches made on the occasion, was a new revolution. Speaking last, Baran Singh set forth his vision of the time when long-neglected peasantry would get a fair shake. He spelled out issues at the top of his party's agenda, focusing particularly on corruption and communalism for which he blamed the Congress and the People's Union. He called them enemies of the people. The severity of his utterances left many in the gathering staggered. No matter how precariously he held on to it, his chieftaincy of the state owed much to these two parties, one way or the other. While the People's Union was the main coalition partner in his government, the Congress had helped it tackle the socialists' threat to topple it. These two had their own reasons to support him. Even so, he was the main beneficiary of the arrangement.

Baran Singh's harangue set off another round of clamour for his resignation. That surprised no one. This time the Congress, rather its middle ranking commanders, were making the hullabaloo, but not without their leadership's go-ahead. The People's Union was not that vociferous. It tried to laugh off the CM's comments but it did stress it was time Chaudhary bowed out. The Socialist Party on the other hand merely reiterated its demand for a special session of the house for Baran Singh to seek a vote of confidence, but now the socialists attacked the Congress and the People's Union more than they did Baran Singh, calling them opportunists with no qualms, whereas Baran Singh—responding to the ruckus his speech had ignited—said,

'I won't resign . . . why should I? Assembly session is just over a fortnight off . . . I'll submit myself to the authority of the house then.' Next, pressing home the point, he added, 'I stand by what I said about my two chief opponents, which was calculated to define how my politics were different from theirs.' That led to a fresh bout of slanging match.

———————

The day before the Assembly session was to begin, Baran Singh put in his papers, leaving the Opposition—which was ready for a showdown in the House—to tear its hair, looking like a knot of halfwits. With Baran Singh and the Congress in favour of midterm poll, no other party could get to the magic figure. Baran Singh was keen to continue as caretaker CM, but Congress— loath to forgo the advantage of having the bureaucracy and the police under its thumb during the election—got the state placed under President's Rule.

Uttar Pradesh was one of the four north Indian states where the collapse of non-Congress coalition governments occasioned midterm poll. Ram Mohan had no time to lose. He postponed Kanti and Deena's move to Kanpur until a more suitable time. He was to contest Fatehpur Assembly seat of which Dhata was a major part. Election time brought about the feel of carnival in the countryside. Days leading up to the polling day were never dull. People would talk non-stop about the parties and their chances and the castes associated with them. This was also the time when many an unsavoury anecdote from the past of the candidates would be revisited, mostly for amusement, as the personal probity of a candidate mattered little to people. They enjoyed various canvassing methods, and children would watch the outsides of all standing structures, brick or mud, being covered with slogans, names, election symbols and so on; they would collect lurid posters, flyers, flags, badges, imprinted with usual election or party stuff and compare their stockpiles.

Ram Mohan could not visit Parsadpur during the campaign in Fatehpur, but whenever somebody came, Kanti, like others, would feast on the stories from the poll front. IRP was—to her delight—making waves in many parts of the state, giving rise to the impression that many of its candidates would win. Baran Singh had addressed a well-attended public meeting in Fatehpur and was scheduled to visit Dhata before the canvassing ended. Ram Mohan's speeches had fired his prospective electorate with tremendous fervour. There was nothing to suggest anything other than his victory. Pratap Singh and his men were bent on ensuring that Dhata stands emphatically behind Ram Mohan. As the polling day neared, Kurmis in the constituency became gripped by the idea of one of their own in the Assembly.

About eighty percent of the electorate in Dhata region was Kurmi. The rest—comprising Brahmans and Harijans, also some Thakurs—were inflexible in their support to the Congress. When somebody during the meeting of Ram Mohan's key associates in Fatehpur city had asked Pratap Singh if he could get some of the Harijans in his area to vote for the IRP, he had laughed. 'It's no use trying to wean Brahmans or the Harijans from the Congress, so let's not . . .' Before he could finish, Mahavir Wilson who had come to share in the excitement had cut in, 'For Brahmans, the sole—if somewhat hidden—rationale behind the struggle against British Raj had been to establish Brahman Raj, and Ambedkar's defeat in his battle against Gandhi for separate electorates had left the Harijans with no option but to dance to the Congress's tune. Heaven only knows how long they would have to bear this cross.'

'No point in your carping about something with no bearing on the issue we are discussing.' This was Tiwari ji, after which there was a momentary silence before Pratap Singh had said he would not leave it at that and would do something to minimize the impact of the Harijan support to the Congress in Dhata.

Congress had taken overly long to pick its candidate for Fatehpur City, reason for which in local political circles was imputed to Ram Mohan who in the last Parliamentary election had unnerved Udai Pratap Singh, the then Congress candidate, and the region that had made it possible for Ram Mohan to poll the highest number of votes amongst the defeated candidates had been none other than Dhata. Fatehpur proper, no doubt, was full of Congress's traditional voters, predominantly Muslims and Brahmans; then there were Harijans scattered across the constituency. Yet the fear of Dhata was hard to take out of the mind of the Congress leadership in UP.

All this logic was turned on its head after the suspense over who the Congress would field from this dicey seat was broken. That Liyaqat Argali would be in the race few would have known. What had swung the balance in his favour was a hypothesis used by Shukla ji to lethal effect, and beaten to it by a political novice like Liyaqat Argali, a prominent Congress ticket seeker poured out his frustration to Tiwari ji, who knew him, 'This motherfucker Shukla made it a point of honour to get the party to field this minion of his; the scum who I hear procures young randis for his master. Shukla also got his wily uncle in Delhi to weigh in. My name had been cleared, but Shukla forced the party to replace me with his pimp, arguing that the combination of Ram Mohan and the IRP bodes ill for the Congress unless it puts up a Muslim candidate. His thesis being that Ram Mohan might also get some Muslim votes this time because of the perception that Baran Singh refused to bow to the People's Union when his government depended on its support. Only a Muslim from the Congress could remove the threat of Muslims voting for the IRP.' The disclosure made Tiwari ji seethe. He had not thought Shukla ji could be so keen to make things difficult for Ram Mohan. There was no hope now, he thought, for his friend of getting any Muslim votes.

———————

Ram Mohan's campaign proceeded largely as planned except that they had given up on Muslims who were fired up by the candidature of Liyaqat Argali; the day he and Shukla ji arrived, the city Congress committee took out a procession through the city. In the meantime, Ram Mohan held a meeting of his key campaigners to explain what points needed to be emphasized whilst votes were sought. Tiwari ji shunning his usual calm demeanour, let out a war cry, 'Forget about Muslims, Brahmans and Harijans. Don't waste time trying to reason with them; they might listen to you out of politeness but vote they will for the Congress. Nevertheless, it's a battle we can and must win,' then gesturing towards Pratap Singh, 'The lion of Dhata is with us. Leave that part of the constituency to him; the rest of us should make the rounds of other areas, and please mark what I'm saying . . . Each and every vote that we can get is critical; every effort has to be made to see that no favourable ballots remain uncast.' Stopping to catch his breath, he glanced at Pratap Singh and said, 'Barring Dhata, nowhere else are we in a position to attempt capturing booths.'

'I have thought of a better and safer alternative to booth-capturing,' said Pratap Singh. 'I am not questioning the virtue of the stuffing of ballot boxes with favourable votes, but it is easier and most effective when it is done for the Congress, because then the administration cooperates by either delaying or not taking action. It can still be successful in far-flung villages even for non-Congress candidates because word would get to the authorities only after it's too late . . . No doubt this method is far superior to any other since it fetches you all the votes from

a particular area. But without suitable conditions, it is very hard
to pull it off and in my—'

'That's called daylight robbery; personally, I am against
anything that undermines my integrity, my principles, my
honesty,' said Ram Mohan. 'The chief reason for my being in
politics is that I want to set an example of how constructively
the power thus obtained can be put into service, if one has vision
and strength of purpose.'

'That's all very well,' said Tiwari ji, 'but do you think all
these things . . . your integrity, principles, honesty, are of much
significance if forced to remain within the confines of the Hindi
department of D.A.V. College? Your intent becomes relevant
only after you have bagged the desired position. You yourself
had to employ somewhat dishonest means to land this teaching
job. Tell me, if you had not thought of that trick, would you
have got it?'

Tiwari ji turned to Pratap Singh without waiting for Ram
Mohan's reply as though his unease had been sorted out. 'Pratap
Singh ji you were talking about some alternative!'

'It's not exactly an alternative . . . It cannot be as effective
as booth-capturing. Yet, given that it can be exercised rather
quietly, without drawing much attention, it makes up for being
less productive in terms of ballots, and is widely popular across
many states, this method. If some people cannot be persuaded
to vote for us they should, if possible, be kept from voting at all.
Thus we can deprive Liyaqat Argali of votes which otherwise
are certainly his . . . I intend to keep the Harijans in my area
inside their homes on the polling day. They will be warned
against venturing out. My men will keep a vigil.'

'What if local Congress leaders get wind, and start howling?'
asked Gulab Singh.

'First, Congress activists in Dhata are not so strong as to take
up cudgels on behalf of Harijans, and second, these Harijans

who have to live there, would avoid any run-in with me. My goodwill means more to them in Dhata than fighting for the right to vote.'

'Fantastic,' said Tiwari ji before surveying the people in the room. 'What a good job it is that we have Pratap Singh to take care of such a big and key part of our constituency . . . That does not mean we can let our hair down in the slightest. We must make certain not a single pocket of our prospective voters is left untapped . . . Scattered on the outskirts of Fatehpur town are a few villages which some of us need to visit and rope in those willing to be involved in the campaign.'

Pratap Singh said, 'Has anybody here met Deep Narayan yet?'

This man, an elderly fellow, a Kurmi, was influential in the villages to which Tiwari ji referred; he had been the head of his village panchayat for three consecutive years before his son came to grace that chair. In the previous Parliamentary election, he had refused to leave Congress and was associated with Udai Pratap Singh's campaign. He could not countenance that someone of his own caste, and younger than him, could think of taking on the Congress as an independent. Later during electioneering, Deep Narayan was heard haranguing, 'Who does he think he is? Look at his impetuosity! What made this man think that he just had to announce his candidature for all Kurmis to line up to vote for him, not to mention that he is an outsider and belongs to Kanpur. Am I a fool to have been endeavouring to draw Congress's attention to the strength of our caste? Why can't we have some patience and try and convince the party leadership of our lasting loyalty? Just think of the political avenues that will be open to us if we manage to prevail on the Congress to regard Kurmis as one of its tried and true supporters. But people like Ram Mohan are out to wreck the whole effort.'

Tiwari ji said, 'Oh, yes we have to approach him. Though he mocked our ambition in the last election, we might find him amenable now that the situation has changed. The Congress is out of power in UP for the first time after Independence; Baran Singh's emergence as undisputed peasant leader is going to hurt the Congress most. Lohia's passing has thrown the Socialist Party into disarray. The situation looks ripe for the IRP to make an impact.'

'I have met Deep Narayan twice,' said Pratap Singh, 'on both occasions accidentally. The first time when he had come to Dhata, canvassing support for Udai Pratap Singh. He had smiled, yet I could sense he had not liked my being introduced as someone who commanded so many votes in Dhata. Maybe because he knew I had already generated a wave in Ram Mohan's favour.'

'And the second time?' asked Ram Mohan.

'That was during Baran Singh's visit here. Deep Narayan came with some people and wanted me to help him meet Baran Singh. I looked for you but then there was a melee as Chaudhary Sahab was leaving; so Deep Narayan could not meet him.'

'Which means,' said Tiwari ji, 'he can be persuaded to join us this time.'

Pratap Singh said, 'Yes, perhaps! This man, I'd say, is a little complicated; not easy to deal with. But yes, I think he would appreciate if we pay him a visit . . .'

The very next day Ram Mohan and some of his supporters went to see Deep Narayan who received them gaily and appeared happy at the consideration shown by Ram Mohan, who he once thought was too overbearing. Deep Narayan assured them of his support but said he would join the IRP only after meeting Baran Singh. Ram Mohan promised he would personally accompany him to Lucknow.

Dhata region was bubbling over with enthusiasm in the run-up to the polling day; even amongst Yadavs the mood was electric; they were fast becoming the cornerstone of Baran Singh's electoral base in UP.

* * *

The mood in Ram Mohan's election office was buoyant. Some members of his core campaign team entertained the gathering by relating their experiences during the electioneering. Pratap Singh recounted how successfully he had prevented the Harijans in Dhata from casting their ballots.

The polling day in Fatehpur remained relatively peaceful; incidents of violent conflicts and murders were less than in the previous election. Ram Mohan and Tiwari ji hardly moved out of their election office that day. There was no shortage of favourable tidings from areas thick with their voters; going by various accounts, Kurmis and Yadavs came out in hordes to vote. Tiwari ji was in no doubt as to the outcome. Cutting in however on the triumphal mood, Ram Mohan said, 'Hold your horses, please! Some restraint here is in order . . . Votes have yet to be counted; we should wait till the counting is over and done with.' His words did not chime with his face which had victory written all over it; there was a moment's silence before the room exploded into peals of laughter.

When the ballot count began a day or two later, Ram Mohan stayed neck and neck with Liyaqat Argali till only a few thousand votes remained to be tallied up; as the counting entered the final round, the word on the street was that Ram Mohan had won, which soon turned into the buzz that on directions from above the vote was being rigged in favour of Liyaqat Argali. But when counting of the votes from Deep Narayan's area got underway, Pratap Singh ordered his men to get some garlands, telling all to get ready for victory procession. Gulab Singh and Badri got down to gathering their people who had come from Parsadpur and Ballamgaon, while Tiwari ji asked some young men to go and look for Deep Narayan who had not been sighted since the polling day. It was past midnight when the news that Deep Narayan was seen roistering in Liyaqat Argali's office on the other side of the town came as a blow.

The final result was announced in the wee hours. Liyaqat Argali won the Fatehpur City Assembly seat by a margin of just over two hundred votes. All fervour in Ram Mohan's camp collapsed like froth. Pratap Singh burst into vitriol against Deep Narayan accusing him of treachery of the worst kind; Tiwari ji said, shaking his head, 'He did not have to lead us up the garden path like this. We could have understood his practical unease about supporting us. It's all so obvious now. I mean the reason for—'

'It is nothing but jealousy turned outright malice,' said Pratap Singh.

'Yes, but as far as I can see the reason he chose to deceive us in this fashion has more to do with his own ambition than anything else.'

'What? Wouldn't Doctor Sahab help him fulfil his ambition, whatever it is, if he had honestly supported us?'

'No, Pratap Singh ji, it's a bit more complex. If we had won this seat, it would become nonsensical for anyone else of Kurmi stock to entertain the wish to be a candidate from here, unless of course Ram Mohan decided not to stand for the Assembly again.'

'Okay, I know what you mean,' said Pratap Singh. 'But I doubt it still. Do you really think this was the reason why

Deep Narayan backstabbed us?' Without waiting for Tiwari ji's response, he carried on, 'Can this man be so thick as to imagine himself to be sitting in the Assembly anytime soon? First, how can he forget he was a mere village headman a while ago? The amount of support he boasts would be no more than one-tenth of what I command in Dhata. Second, if he really fantasizes about contesting this seat, it can only be on the basis of being Kurmi . . . and who among Kurmis can even dream of fighting an election from this seat without the backing of Dhata!' Pratap Singh had all eyes fixed on him. He hung back for a second and cleared his throat, 'Let me put this to you, Tiwari ji. Who to your mind would be the most suitable candidate for this constituency after Doctor Sahab? I mean from among all the probable Kurmi claimants.'

'You, Pratap Singh ji,' replied Tiwari ji as an instant reflex. 'If not Ram Mohan, there is nobody else I can think of except you.'

Ram Mohan and others nodded.

Pratap Singh said, 'I know Doctor Sahab's main interest is in Parliament . . . in Delhi. This election was forced, so to speak, on him by the changed circumstances.'

'Even Chaudhary Baran Singh would,' said Tiwari ji, 'prefer to send Ram Mohan to Parliament, because after losing his most trusted voice in Delhi to the Congress, he needs someone equally capable to fill the void left by Saansad ji's exit.'

'I know that and thought I would in time speak to Doctor Sahab about it. But that moment has not come yet. It won't come till we have sent him to Delhi, which is our immediate battle now. My ambition for Lucknow can wait; rather my passage into politics can take place only under the leadership of Doctor Sahab in whose strength lies our strength; he has the ability to negotiate the rough terrain of politics and lead us to our deserved place in it.' Pratap Singh stopped and looked at

Tiwari ji, 'Despite being a Brahman, Tiwari ji supports us . . . because our caste is blessed with someone like Doctor Sahab. That's why. On the other hand, we have in our ranks a character like Deep Narayan who is so consumed with jealousy that he wouldn't hesitate to throw away a chance like this. I don't agree with Tiwari ji that he wants to keep this constituency safe for himself. He should look at his stature in the mirror first . . . He knows very well that as long as Pratap Singh is around, he had better forget about becoming MLA . . . He forgets there are ways to tackle him and put a stop to this balderdash.' Pratap Singh, as he declaimed, had no notion of the impact he was making on those present; the mood of despondency brought about by the loss had lifted somewhat. His words sounded like the approaching footfalls of a new, robust dawn in the midst of gloom. The sudden but palpably refreshed atmosphere in the room struck him as he halted to take a breather. Flustered at what was his own doing, he failed to pick up where he had left off. It fell to Tiwari ji to bring them all back to the here and now.

'What really pains me is the margin of the defeat . . . so narrow . . . excruciatingly hard to swallow . . . A little more effort, a little more foresight, a little more sense of urgency might perhaps have seen us through. I have been assailed by this thought since yesterday.'

Ram Mohan grinned at him.

A ghost of a smile flickered on Tiwari ji's lips in embarrassment. He knew of his friend's disgust with bemoaning. Ram Mohan was used to chiding people for dwelling on things that could have been done better; he would urge them to focus on what lay ahead and to take steps to prevent further setbacks. I will quote Deena here: *Babu ji's optimism bordered on pathology. His aversion to taking stock or looking back would often lead him to act in the same way as before.*

'I admit this is all delusion,' exclaimed Tiwari ji and looked unsure as to how to give voice to his sense of regret and despair and perplexity. He surveyed the expectant faces; he looked back at Ram Mohan and met with an amused expression on his face. 'That's what the benefit of hindsight does to one,' Tiwari ji said in self-deprecation.

'I know how you must feel Tiwari ji,' said Ram Mohan. 'Victory and defeat seem so definitive and polar opposite that their being separated by merely two hundred votes sounds outrageous. I can appreciate how senseless it all must appear to you. But you know something? The margin of victory or defeat is not of much importance to me. I don't view it this way. What's important to me is the person you triumph over or lose to. Not by how many votes. No, certainly not. It's your rival first and last—in success and failure both—that should be the cause of your discomfiture or self-esteem.'

Tiwari ji and others looked intrigued.

'You're defined to a degree by the personality of your opponent,' he continued. 'In other words, the fact of having to compete with Liyaqat Argali for a place in the Assembly is more frustrating to me, to my sense of reasonableness, than the nonsensical margin of votes dividing my defeat from his victory . . . which is nothing compared to what actually sets me as a man apart from him, this bootlicker of someone like Shukla ji, this illiterate philistine oaf,' Ram Mohan paused, his face flaming. 'Even his routing would have failed to ease my unease.'

'I think, we've talked it over before, haven't we?' said Tiwari ji. 'You yourself have had first-hand experience of one such situation when you sought a career in teaching . . . and without that tactic of yours, you would not have got your foot in the door. And now again—'

Struck dumb for an instant, Ram Mohan said, 'I know, but the thing is, Tiwari ji, I don't want to be reminded all the time how near I came to victory, which is really hard to bear, because in such a close contest the pain experienced by the loser is more profound than what the winner feels in terms of joy. Therefore, I've long taught myself never to stand merely gazing at an adversity but move on. No point in fretting about something past retrieval. The day I realized this, was the day I empowered myself. It gave me strength . . . strength to withstand the knock and brace myself for another challenge.'

Spoken majestically using his impeccable Hindi diction Ram Mohan's words swept over his audience like a wave, leaving them submerged in silence. Relishing it, he went on, in a somewhat jocular vein now, 'There's another reason for my raising the issue again, which in fact allows me a more meaningful way of dealing with my predicament . . . There's a larger, more substantial and solemn question to be considered: what does ignominy actually mean in a political fray like this? And when faced by a turd like Argali one can be neither proud of winning nor ashamed of losing. One would be giving off that smell either way.'

Some in the room sniggered, but no one spoke. They all sat on the mattresses that covered the entire floor of the room— Ram Mohan was flanked by Tiwari ji and Badri, with Gulab Singh and Pratap Singh right across him. 'My idealistic hot air is of little value or purpose here . . . I know. It might have sounded better if we had won. But I downplay a disappointment like this to enable myself to put it behind me . . . Okay, I need to get to Lucknow. Counting at some places is still on. And IRP seems to be doing well . . . according to what I heard last.' He turned to the man with the transistor, 'Let me know when the news comes on.'

He told Badri and his team to stay on in Fatehpur till all bills and other pending things were settled. He and Tiwari ji had to stop at Kanpur before heading for Lucknow. Gulab Singh and others would go back to Parsadpur or Ballamgaon. Ram Mohan was effusive in his praise for Pratap Singh's doughty efforts, and gushed as he thanked Tiwari ji's relation who had made available his place to act as their office for free. Overcome with emotion, both had tears in their eyes. Ram Mohan loved the way his words worked on people.

IRP won close to a hundred seats. Baran Singh would have comfortably formed government had his former partners also done well. The Socialists lay battered, while People's Union barely managed to reach halfway to where it had stood previously; there was a marked reduction in the number of independents this time. The IRP's remarkable growth made the headlines in the papers. Some called attention to the irony that Baran Singh's success had largely been at the expense of his former allies.

The midterm poll was supposed to mark the end of the Congress dominance in UP, but it managed to secure a majority—howsoever wafer-thin—over all its opponents combined. Gupta made it to the helm again. Opposition leaders called on Baran Singh, assuring him of their support if Gupta government fell, meaning he should engineer defections from the Congress. Baran Singh told Ram Mohan how sorely he missed Dixit ji who being in no race himself would be better placed to tap discontent within the ruling party. In the meantime, a senior leader of the right-wing People's Union told the press that non-Congress parties were working on a plan to bring down Gupta government; when asked about the veracity of the claim, Baran Singh said, 'Plan or no plan, the Congress government in UP hangs by a hair. It doesn't inspire much confidence in its stability.' He however asked his loyalists not to take what they have heard at face value, and that he saw no reason why the Congress government in UP would not complete its term. 'Still, I won't be surprised if the ongoing strife in the Congress lead its two factions to a showdown; when that happens, there would be political bedlam here in Lucknow, to which we must prove equal.'

The IRP being the largest group on Opposition benches, Baran Singh was set to become leader of Opposition. His spirits were up. He suggested Ram Mohan concentrate on his duties in Kanpur for now, as things were likely to remain quiet for some time. Disengaged from electoral battleground, Ram Mohan was staggered by all the work awaiting him in Kanpur: the unfinished book on Hindi, making up for his absence from teaching, all the reading to be done to catch up with Mishra and others, filling himself in on literary and social gossip, devising a plan to get to savour the fragrance of the 'black rose', etc. Also, he had to have Kanti and Deena join the rest of the family in Kanpur.

Before being taken up with things pending in Kanpur, he visited Parsadpur where Badri and Gulab Singh organized a gathering for him to address. Badri talked about the betrayal that robbed Ram Mohan of a certain victory. Gulab Singh roared with venom in his tone that people like Deep Narayan deserved to be spat on in public and beaten to a pulp. 'If he was from this area, I would have had his tongue pulled out.'

Ram Mohan addressed the gathering in his usual confident, optimistic and inspiring manner. 'I want to remember how many people supported me, not how many votes I fell short of. If we believe in our cause, these reversals are meant to smooth our path, provided we don't allow ourselves to be led astray. If I had ever doubted the achievability of my aims, I wouldn't be where I am today. Sometimes we fail to realize our objective, but that does not mean we're back at drawing board, definitely not. We still get somewhere if not exactly to the desired destination. Our story does not remain the same,' he paused for his words to sink in. 'If Chaudhary Sahab were to become chief minister again . . . where would I be?' he stopped with a smile on his face. 'I'd still be made a minister.' The statement kicked up a din in the audience. Ram Mohan raised his hand and said, 'He would find a way to accommodate me.' He then set forth what he—in the meantime—intended to pursue aside from his scholarly goals. 'I'm going to donate the land I own near the railway station to the cause of secondary education in this area, and help raise funds for a suitable school building; I'll have an asphalt strip laid to connect our village to the GT Road. I'll also bring a post office and a primary health centre to Parsadpur.'

The news of Ram Mohan giving away another portion of his ancestral property put Kanti off. She did not keep her annoyance from him. She reminded him of Padhaiya Bhaiya, the earlier beneficiary of his generosity, who should have sought a place among Ram Mohan's lieutenants, but he sought instead to insult him and defy his authority. Ram Mohan called him a fool. 'He isn't worthy of notice. If anything, he needs to be pitied. Such an ass he is! I don't know how he got this insane notion into his head that he can be in competition with me for influence in Parsadpur.' In a voice tinged with sarcasm, he wondered what happened to Kanti's vaunted interest in education. She refrained from arguing further and wound up by muttering there were many in Ballamgaon who had more properties, to which Ram Mohan said, 'You should ask your father if I have done the right thing or not.'

She asked him to go see him, her father, part of whose body was incapacitated now. 'I must rush back; I have some pressing matters in Kanpur to attend to . . . My visit to Ballamgaon would achieve nothing except delaying my departure by another couple of hours . . . Oh yes, you and Deena, would move to Kanpur before long.' He called to Deena who was lurking behind a door and said he should get ready to go to school in the city. Kanti got him a glass of water, which he drank and went out. Badri, Gulab Singh and others were waiting to walk him to his Rajdoot, the motorbike. Two boys had just finished cleaning it.

Allahabad–Kanpur passenger train brought Kanti and Deena to Kanpur in the heat of the day as summer had begun raging through north India. Their rickshaw moved very slowly—the thin man in a grimy vest and drawers had to stand on its pedals, pressing down hard by turns on each of them, putting his entire weight behind the effort. Plying the road leading away from the station was a confusion of vehicles—cars and Jeeps, trucks and buses, motorcycles and scooters, rickshaws and bicycles, horse-drawn conveyances, hand-carts and buffalo-drawn carriers. Then there were pedestrians—the lowest in the street hierarchy—who kept straying into the path of variously moving traffic; had to be constantly shooed out of the way. Buildings on either side of the street with no space in between presented a picture of muddy mishmash; occupying the ground floors of which were shops dealing in hardware; the floors above housed either traders' families or cheap hotels. Pasted everywhere on the walls, doors, pillars, around electric poles and so on were film posters and broadsheets of all sizes, advertising all kinds of panaceas. A ceaseless racket pervaded the atmosphere. Then, they heard the crackling of a loudspeaker behind them. A man sitting on a rickshaw was announcing gravely the death of the President of India, Zakir Husain. Nobody at that point could have imagined the impact this event was going to have on national politics. It would also fling Baran Singh's way a chance to rule the state again.

From the station to the Parade crossing on Mall Road, the entire route had a peculiar dreariness about it. Deena could not wait to get past this crossing and into the chic Naveen Market; from there to their neighbourhood opposite McRobert Hospital in Civil Lines, the whole area was spic and span; bungalows and houses swathed in greenery were set back from tree-lined roads; some could be glimpsed through overhanging foliage.

As their rickshaw turned right rounding the small triangular park, there came into sight Hudson School; forking left a bit, one could enter its premises through the low green gate; Deena could see from their moving rickshaw a portion of the wide winding tarmac inside. The school wall ran parallel for some time to the street, on the other side of which was the green iron fence of McRobert Hospital.

The sun was hot. There were few people in view. As their rickshaw carried on along the path between Zaheer Sahab's house on the left and the grassless park with henna bush on the right, Deena saw Mrs Zaheer from above their low boundary wall. Standing on the veranda, she was gesturing and saying something to the gardener working among the plants. In the adjoining and a much smaller house, lived Bhatnagar Sahab, the man with the largest family in the neighbourhood. When they turned right, away from Bhatnagar Sahab's house, Kanti told the rickshawallah to stop under the drum-stick tree close to a rather unremarkable door on the right-hand side of the house; she wanted to avoid the front veranda a few paces ahead that led straight into Ram Mohan's room—the big room which he shared with Nishant—where he entertained visitors too. Nisha and Sandhya used the side door that opened into the small inner courtyard. Right across from there, on the far side, was a small patch of brush.

Ram Mohan was at his publisher's, working on his book on Hindi. It was during his absence that Nisha and Sandhya could look out the two windows in their room. The one—though partially hidden behind a bougainvillea outside—afforded a good view of the circular wide track around the henna hedge and of a section of the front boundary wall of the compound, while the side window took in the scene as far as the houses of Zaheer Sahab and Bhatnagar Sahab. It was from this side window that Nisha saw Kanti and Deena getting off the rickshaw. Shouting to Sandhya and Mayank, she ran out and hugged Kanti. Nishant too made an appearance as Sevak Lal took their luggage inside.

In two months when schools reopen after the summer vacation, Nisha and Nishant would be in class twelve, while Sandhya would move from Hudson School to M.G. Girls Inter College, Nisha's college. Mayank was to remain in Hudson for three more years; Deena was to be admitted to Nishant's school, B.N.S.D. Inter College. They all went to the big room to sit under the ceiling fan for some time; in their room, Nisha and Sandhya had only a table fan that was more noisy than effective. She asked Sandhya to keep listening for their father's motorcycle, for if caught together they would be in trouble. Deena found the anxiety odd. He remembered how aggrieved he used to feel at Kanti's restrictions, but the way Nisha Didi expressed her fear—the fear of being caught together—reeked of something nasty. Even Kanti—though aware of her husband's suspicious nature and his animus against women's presence anywhere near men in public—had no idea of his being opposed to even brothers and sisters sitting together and talking. Then, Nisha's look—inscrutable rather disturbed, that she had worn during one of her visits to Parsadpur—flashed through her mind. Kanti made a mental note to talk to her later, alone.

Deena stood diffidently behind Kanti who was in a chair close to the big takht on the left where Nisha and Sandhya sat. Nishant who occupied the other chair would get up now and then to go out onto the veranda for any sign of Babu ji—

that's how they addressed their father—as the usual hour of his return approached. Pulling him towards her, Nisha asked Deena where he wanted to stay, with them in their room or with Nishant Bhaiya in their father's room. 'With you,' said he eagerly, overcoming his shyness. Nisha laughed and hugged him, looking at Mayank whose face lit up.

It was Nishant who with his keen sense of hearing first picked the shallow sluggish cracking of the Rajdoot in the distance. Nodding, Nisha stood up, gesturing them to get a move on. Kanti and Sandhya followed as Deena found in this sudden breaking up of their assembly something eerie. Why couldn't they—the brothers, sisters and their mother—have kept on sitting together? What could be their father's objection? This sudden change in the atmosphere unsettled him; disorientating him further was the speed with which Nishant Bhaiya left his chair and shifted to the takht and grabbing a book, became in the twinkling of an eye, a cross-legged figure of concentration. Deena's long-fostered notion of the warmth and freedom of their city abode was giving way to a sense of desolation.

The sisters' room had a large bed made up of two takhts placed against the rear wall less than a couple of feet above which was the window with the bougainvillea outside. Nisha sat there holding the window curtain slightly aside; seeing the Rajdoot she quickly left the window. Sandhya was already seated at the dressing cum study table by the door on the left, with her back to the revolving bookshelf that stood in the right-hand corner across the door and which Nisha started dusting. Both these pieces of furniture in this room and a collapsible wooden table along with two chairs and a wooden cupboard used by Ram Mohan in the big room belonged to the British era. Kanti had opened her trunk and was rummaging around, as Deena learnt his first lesson that their father must not find anybody talking or doing anything other than household chores or studying; then it occurred to him that Mayank had remained unperturbed by the approaching Rajdoot. He had not even bothered to leave the big room with them.

Shortly Ram Mohan walked into their room holding Mayank's hand; having already changed, he now was in a lungi and vest. He said he would not have lunch; the publisher had treated him to pooris and sweets. The air in the room was heavy with the smell of sweat; the table fan was not enough; Kanti went and stood by Ram Mohan to fan him with a hand fan. He had not been to Parsadpur for over two weeks; she gave him the latest from there. 'I'll soon resume my visits to Parsadpur,' he said before beginning to instruct Kanti to take control of the household work and ensure his orders are carried out without question. 'There'll be visitors, mostly unannounced, some of them important; they should be served tea and snacks promptly. From time to time, we will also have overnight guests . . . And your relations have to be discouraged from coming over. Our children are at a stage when they should not be wasting time entertaining these good-for-nothing fellows.' Looking around, he saw Deena standing in the corner by the side window. 'Come here, Dinkar.' Deena with his heart pounding did as told. 'This is not Parsadpur; you'll have to learn some manners and look neat. Go and see yourself in the mirror,' then gesturing at Mayank, 'Do you see how your younger brother looks? You too have to get that rustic expression off your face and become like him. In a couple of months, you'll start going to school, the same as Nishant, so you had better get used to spending more time with him.' He turned to Kanti again, 'I'm against my children going out and mixing with other kids in the locality. You will have to be watchful in my absence; and don't ever fail to report any instance of indiscipline on this score. I don't want them to get into bad company of which there is no dearth here. This Bhatnagar guy is the nastiest of the lot. He is thoroughly corrupt and is known to take bribes to help students get admission to the third-rate school he teaches in.

'His wife is a degree college lecturer while he is content with teaching at a mere higher secondary school. How disgraceful! And they shamelessly allow their children including girls to move freely in and out of the house; their daughters do not even hesitate to interact with the male visitors and are so frank with their brothers' friends. One of their sons, what's his name . . . yes, Randeep, his disposition seems that of a rogue. They've no fear of their father whose presence or absence does not make one jot of a difference. Rather perversely, there's more gaiety in their house when Bhatnagar and his wife are around. He often sits in their front yard in the evening and watches contentedly as his children frolic about. Disgusting!

'Zaheer Sahab's family appears dignified and seemly at first glance, but soon they betray their airs and graces. They seem to take pride in everything about them—their fair complexion, the fact that they are modern and send their children to English-medium school, that they have a car, that the wife teaches English at M.G. Girls Inter College, that they live in the best house in this neighbourhood, which has a front lawn and a vegetable patch at the back . . . No doubt, their children are more disciplined than Bhatnagar's and far less cacophonous. But they also come out to play in the evening and are friends with Bhatnagar's children; their daughter . . . what's her name?' he asks Nisha who tells him. 'Yes, Saba, she can often be seen perambulating with one of Bhatnagar's daughters; they're the same age, I guess . . . The problem is that Bhatnagar with his eight children can cater to any age group of youngsters in terms of vile friendship.'

In view of the new arrivals, Ram Mohan needed to reiterate the rules to be observed in his house. It made Deena emotionally estranged from his new surroundings; the excitement that had surged in him since they had left Parsadpur that morning was dissipated. In the midst of this fearful and suffocating atmosphere at his new home, he drew some comfort from Mayank's immunity. When he asked Nisha Didi how come Babu ji was so fond of him, she said, 'Once when Babu ji was about to start his Rajdoot to go somewhere, Mayank who had just been brought to Kanpur yelled in his village accent that he would also come with him. Babu ji looked back and found Mayank standing outside the door. I got scared and tried to take him back, but to my astonishment Babu ji stopped me and walked back as Mayank stood his ground, smiling. Babu ji picked him up and asked him to repeat what he had just said. Mayank mouthed his wish again in the same rustic tone; Babu ji taught him then and there how to say it in correct Hindi. He set him down asking me to put some decent clothes on him, and finally we saw him leave with Babu ji, sitting astride the motorcycle, in front of him. It was something we could not have dreamt of till then.'

Later, Deena would reminisce in one of his notebooks: *It was a moment of great revelation to everyone in the family and probably to Babu ji himself, who had long given the impression that children were more or less a drag on the prospects of an enterprising man; the best way to deal with the nuisance was to keep them on a tight leash. However, the boundless love and affection that he came to lavish on one of us caused my mother and others to revise their perception of him. It had a redemptive aspect to it, his attitude to Mayank; but for that, we would have remained innocent of our father's mostly unrealized capacity for love.*

During the course of the summer, Deena tried to orient himself as best he could in his new abode, the hallmark of which were two disparate ways of being. Babu ji's presence in the house meant an atmosphere charged with fear, when everybody barring

Mayank would sit apart doing their work, and the moment he went somewhere the house would start breathing again. Such a turn-around it would be! All of them would get together and talk and talk and talk. They could turn on the radio and listen to film songs or whatever other programmes were being aired. If it was late afternoon, they would either go out onto the front veranda or step out through the side door from the inner courtyard to survey the scene outside. Given his myopia and slow grasp of things, Sevak Lal could not notice much and was hardly any threat. Often, he would not know what his master really wanted to know. Yet once in a while his tattling would help ignite Babu ji's fearsome temper.

To taste the real freedom, they would have to wait for Babu ji to be out of town. How delicious those occasions were, the most longed-for, the real thing! They could go to Naveen Market or to the movies if they had money, visit friends and also play or spend time outside the house. Their neighbours could sense the reason, to which they sometimes alluded in jest, but they were sympathetic to their plight.

Soon, Deena became attached to his sisters and Mayank, and would cling to their company all the time, if possible; as for Nishant, Ram Mohan's method had not been in vain. He had grown away from the rest of the family, emotionally, failing to be part of the special bond forged between the four of them— Nisha, Sandhya, Deena and Mayank. Nisha was the leader and philosopher of the group. In school too she had her following and was known to do things with aplomb. Conscious of her appeal, she tended to repeatedly relate instances of her being praised by her teachers or friends for something or the other; it was she who had the courage to speak to Babu ji if there was anything to be asked of him, provided he was in a good mood. She seemed to have some kind of leverage with him, the extent of which though was limited and depended on his whim.

Deena remembered the day when he and Kanti were taken by surprise by Nisha Didi's visit to Parsadpur; she had brought a carton of overripe apricots and plums, the fruits Deena had never seen before and had heard in amazement about her trip to Nainital and Bhuwali; that Nisha Didi had been to a place full of trees laden with those fruits had added something special to her image in Deena's mind. He felt proud of her when she narrated how she had pulled it off.

In school, she was a member of the National Cadet Corps—a voluntary body under the aegis of India's armed forces—that had organized a training camp in those hills for the volunteers from girls' schools. Despaired of permission from Babu ji, she had informed the teacher-in-charge of her inability to go; when probed she, nearly in tears, had divulged the reason. The teacher, a friend of Mrs Zaheer's, knew they were neighbours. She consoled Nisha. The very next day Mrs Zaheer floored Ram Mohan with her first-ever visit to their house. Sitting on one of those cheap sofas, the middle of each of which was faded and frayed, she radiated class and elegance set off further by the general shabbiness of the room along with the static figure of Nishant concentrating on his book.

Soon Ram Mohan had sent for Nisha. It was one of those rare cases in which their father had had to make an exception; otherwise as I have hinted earlier the big room remained out of bounds to the females of the family when he was around. Mrs Zaheer's intercession had done wonders for Nisha's cause, and before taking her leave, she had wished her all the best for the trip, giving her a gentle hug. It was such a heady surprise for Nisha who had already made up her mind to not even broach it to Babu ji, who though sometimes receptive to her other small requests, would not have agreed to this one. He might have further tightened the noose of restrictions around their necks.

It was Nisha who every once in a while would communicate to Babu ji about their wish to go out—to the cinema or the market—and six out of ten times he would accede and also give some money. Sandhya and Deena looked up to Nisha. Nishant seemed his own man. Nisha felt disquieted at Nishant's behaviour that verged on impertinence to the emotional authority she enjoyed over her other siblings.

Now a bit about the influence, however limited, that Nisha had over Ram Mohan. How come she was the only one who could at all—though not always—answer him back! Her retorts would betray a note of odium as if she had found him out. Ram Mohan generally ignored this toxicity in Nisha's tone, but whenever it looked like an attempt at extortion, he would beat her up. One day within a week of their arrival in Kanpur, Deena stumbled across their mother and Nisha Didi talking in whispers. Kanti sent him out. Deena ran to Sandhya Didi who had also been driven out of the room and was in the kitchen. Mayank had gone with their father to the publisher's. Scared of Babu ji, Sandhya always appeared meek and reticent; was patronized, so to say, by Nisha who would be at the forefront of dealing with him. Nisha had no doubt as to her own intelligence vis-à-vis her other siblings and was particularly protective of Sandhya. Deena and Mayank however looked forward to being alone with Sandhya Didi; they knew how quietly smart she was and would marvel at her storytelling and drawing abilities. Also, she was the most studious among them. It was Ram Mohan's terror at home that made her purposely avoid attention by merging into the background, her docile low-key existence serving as camouflage.

As to why Nisha Didi was crying while their mother looked distressed, Sandhya had nothing to share with Deena, but she feared a scene on their father's return. She had heard just before stepping out of the room their mother's angry words, 'He'll have to explain himself.' How bizarre these words had sounded! That Babu ji could ever be answerable to their mother for anything was beyond Sandhya, who having a premonition of him flaring up at any such insolence, looked frightened, while the looming unpleasantness flung Deena's innards into turmoil. However, when Ram Mohan returned in the afternoon the spectre of the dreaded development failed to fully materialize, that is, it lacked in its nastiness for which Sandhya and Deena had psyched themselves up. As soon as Babu ji's siesta was over, an agitated Kanti had sent Mayank to him with a folded piece of paper. Shortly, he came. All of them—Nisha, Sandhya, Deena and Mayank—had waited edgily in the kitchen while their mother was trying to stand up to Babu ji in their room. Then, in the absence of the expected thunder, Nisha crept out and stood by the door listening to the exchange inside. Babu ji's tone was atypically subdued and mild.

Confronted with what Nisha had told their mother, he took recourse to a normal male's susceptibility to a certain temptation, a fiercely potent one. 'However, it presents no threat to a stable marriage. There are so many men who, unbeknownst to their families, have these secret dalliances and those who don't that's because they can't. They don't get the opportunity. But if you make an issue out of it the entire family will have to suffer the consequences of your indiscretion.' That had silenced Kanti. Nisha stole back into the kitchen as Ram Mohan rose to leave a sombre Kanti.

* * *

Whatever relief allowed occasionally from an otherwise perpetually fraught atmosphere in their house was chiefly thanks to Nisha. These little favours from Babu ji were the result of either his feelings of contrition or a sense of fear. At the first hint of Babu ji being in a good mood, she would use her so-called influence with him to obtain a few moments of relief and joy for the family. One day their father returned late in the evening carrying a bunch of bananas. Deena could not wait for his share of them. It was seldom they would get a chance to enjoy fruits. Ram Mohan looked pleased as he ordered everyone to come into the inner courtyard and told them about the completion of his book; then his eyes fell on Deena who, perched on the edge of the one of the two charpoys, was busy scraping with his teeth the underside of the peels of the banana he had eaten. Ram Mohan laughed and asked him to come near him. With one arm around Mayank who sat on his lap, he hugged Deena with the other and made him sit beside him, while dishing out sallies that made them laugh.

For Nisha, it was an opportune moment to bring to his attention the fact of their food lacking in proper nutrition. She mentioned Bournvita and Horlicks, the two popular health-drinks. He took out his wallet and gave her the money to buy one bottle or tin of any of these powdery substances for each of them. They all beamed at her, except Nishant who though happy did not want to show it. Then Nisha braced herself to revive the issue considered long closed. She and Nishant had once endeavoured to persuade Babu ji to put Mayank in an English-medium school, which apart from lending lustre to the family's social image, would do a world of good to Mayank's future. The difference between the English-knowing and the non-English–knowing was something that could not be covered up. It would show screamingly all over—in taste, style, manner, outlook and so forth. How they all stood in awe of Zaheer Sahab's family, Banerjee Sahab, his wife and Mahavir Bhaiya who all knew the language well! Two of her classmates, who had had their elementary education through English stood out in the class, and Nisha, in their company, had developed a flair for using some English words while talking, but she could not produce a sentence in the language. She had no idea of English syntax. Yet, according to her friends, who too were handcuffed to Hindi, Nisha could pass for someone who knew English. What a compliment, Nisha had thought!

There was one more reason that they wished for Mayank to study in an English-medium school. His being set free from the confines of Hindi would help the not-so-fortunate of the family too. First, it would ease the atmosphere heavy with Hindi. Second, they, as Nisha and Sandhya had discussed many times, would start learning English afresh with Mayank, reading his textbooks. 'Mayank can still get admission to the Methodist School,' said Nisha rather gingerly. Ram Mohan was used to petitions popping when he held court with them. He looked at Nisha. Then glancing at everybody else, said, 'Look, this is not a bottle of Horlicks or a movie . . . You must know the implications of your demand before making it . . . Hudson School is the ideal school for this locality. Not only because it's close but also because it's a Hindi–medium school, run by this American woman, Ms Lillian Wallace, a Christian missionary who hardly knows any Hindi herself but knows about its greatness and also that English has no prospects in today's India. On the other hand, Hindi's golden era is about to dawn, when it would rule over the length and breadth of the country. When all its bitter opponents, south Indians and others, all of them, would have no choice but to prostrate themselves before its might, the might of Hindi.

'It's curtains for English in India. Even Ms Wallace knows that . . . Or you think you are more intelligent than she is? You know, Mahavir and his father are on very good terms with her, because of their faith maybe. Though not a practising Christian, Mahavir believes in his religion's concept of service and is appreciative of Christian missionaries' work; he and his father have been trying to brainwash Ms Wallace into replacing Hindi with English as medium of instruction at Hudson School. Their efforts have failed. English like any other language can be acquired on one's own. One doesn't have to go to an English-medium school for that . . .'

Catching on to the need of not letting his hair down, Deena soon got in the swing of the constrictions of life under Babu ji. In the beginning, Nisha and Sandhya had told him to be vigilant; that Babu ji must not catch him doing anything other than sitting at one place quietly. That's why they would become alert as soon as Babu ji was expected home, and before he could park his Rajdoot, everybody was at their appointed spot, Nishant on the takht in the big room concentrating on his book, Nisha, Sandhya and now their mother and Deena too, in the only other room of the house. Except Mayank—whose state was the only constant—they all oscillated between ease and anxiety. Deena initially had had no idea how exacting Babu ji was in terms of behavioural norms for them. He had to find this out the hard way one evening.

Too curious to ignore the racket raised by children outside, he had sneaked out and stood watching them playing; could not notice Babu ji—who had just returned from somewhere—walking towards him. 'What are you doing here?' That Babu ji was angry, he could sense, but to what extent had dawned on him only after receiving a stinging slap, so unexpected he could not move a limb. Kanti too was rebuked for his offence. Later he figured that Babu ji would not be explicit about his idiosyncratic understanding of certain things; one had to infer what was expected of them from his overall demeanour. Even his casual remarks could provide clue to things not said in so many words. You were supposed to be able to read between the lines, or you would have to risk learning the way Deena did that day.

Nisha had consoled Deena caressing his cheek as Mayank looked on, a picture of sympathy. She told him that freedom allowed by Babu ji's absence was to be used discreetly; that they could enjoy themselves more freely only when he was out of town; then she herself ensured they spend some good time together. Otherwise the best thing to do was to watch the children playing outside, sitting at the window like they, the sisters, did; and this way Deena came to know about most of the children and other people in the neighbourhood. Sandhya would point them out one by one to him telling him their names.

Then there was Ambika, the gardener, materializing every late afternoon with his rose-fitted watering-can to sprinkle water on the dirt track around the henna bushes. He started right across their window, so they were the first to experience the delicious smell of the freshly wet soil; after Ambika's departure, there emerged the spruce figure of Bade Babu, who dressed in a kurta and a dhoti tied in Bengali fashion, would set about his daily brisk walk, his face wearing a stern, set expression and a stick held firmly in his right hand. He would brook no nonsense. Deena and Sandhya at the window laughed at the suddenness with which his appearance put the lid on the ruckus kicked up by the children and the way it was restored once he left. Sometimes a dapper Mr Banerjee along with his wife would also show up but only after his father-in-law was done with his brisk walk, for unlike him, Mr and Mrs Banerjee preferred a leisurely stroll. Some of these dramatis personae had their funny little quirks identified by Nisha and Sandhya, which now amused Deena too. Bade Babu, as he walked along the

main boundary wall at the far end, would stop twice to climb
one by one onto the two low stone benches, a few paces apart
against the wall, and would spend a minute standing on each,
looking over the wall at the road with its sparse traffic and at the
fenced-off McRobert Hospital right across, with its huge lawns
and swathes of flower beds throughout the green expanse. He
did this without fail. Mr Banerjee on the other hand was so
given to talking that he would stop moving and would need
to be nudged off and on by his wife. Among the children
Anjum—Zaheer Sahab's son—had this odd tic in the face,
which he flashed with such regularity that Sandhya and Deena
could guess its next coming. Deena envied all those fortunate
to be out at the sunset, as most of the day the view from the
window remained of desolation; few, barring the children from
the servant quarters, came out in the glaring summer sun. The
stillness of that hour would only be disturbed by an occasional
whoosh of wind. Deena marvelled at the way the advent of
evening transformed the setting outside, changing the feel of
the atmosphere entirely. How he yearned to be part of it! The
window was not enough.

His closeness to Mayank was a great relief, which sometimes
allowed Deena to drink, in howsoever tiny amounts, from his
brother's cup overflowing with their father's love. Babu ji would
often fold Mayank in his arms kissing and cuddling and uttering
names he had given him; if he happened to be nearby some of
this affectionate attention would also come Deena's way. He
was now required to knead Babu ji's legs and arms once or
twice a day, and the presence of Mayank made these occasions
enjoyable. Sitting astride his large belly, he would have Babu ji
tell them stories. The hero of these adventures was Mayank and
Deena his loyal aide.

Most of the summer holidays Ram Mohan was kept tied up by his publisher. Except for two overnight visits to Parsadpur and one to Lucknow, he remained in Kanpur, leaving his children vexed, who could hardly go out during this period. Nisha took them once to a movie, Deena's first, and twice to Naveen Market. They had thought that once he was done proofreading, Babu ji would spend some time in Lucknow and Parsadpur; might also go to Delhi to enjoy the hospitality of Saansad ji who was a Union minister now. Their plans were wrecked by the vile publisher, who overjoyed at Ram Mohan's book, *Hindi Language—Part One*, wheedled him into commencing work on Part Two. The second part of the book was for BA final year students, and both volumes were bound to take off commercially; a large number of students studying for an arts degree opted for Hindi, the reason for which was the perception that though a scoring subject it did not require much effort.

* * *

Soon, with the start of new academic year the hectic process of admission to schools and colleges got underway. Deena had mixed feelings about going to this new school B.N.S.D. Inter College, the best-known Hindi-medium higher secondary school in Kanpur. He was both excited and nervous. B.N.S.D. Inter College stood just off the main, the most famous, road of the city. Deena found its two-storey building grand. It had a big quadrangle with two paved paths running across each other, and in the centre sat a concrete circle with a flagpole rising out of its heart. Between these paths, lay several small rectangular grounds where students played kabaddi during lunch-break.

Though low on many comforts of their station, Ram Mohan's family enjoyed one privilege not many could boast—a telephone connection. Despite being a senior official at the Kanpur Electricity Supply Authority, Zaheer Sahab had managed a connection after a wait of five long years coupled with no end of pleading. Bhatnagar was still awaiting it. But all the neighbours were gobsmacked when Ram Mohan had got the damn thing within a month. It was none other than Saansad ji, Union minister for communications, who had personally seen to it. Ram Mohan would often declaim it was better to cut down on one's food if necessary than not have this magical device at one's place.

Even among those who had this device, Ram Mohan had a distinction, a certain cachet, for if it developed a snag, a regular occurrence, your phone could remain out of order for weeks on end, sometimes months. Once when an exasperated Zaheer Sahab went to the telephone office to lodge a complaint, his sullen look caused sniggers among the staff as he waited outside the cabin of an official. His earnest agitated mien stood in comic contrast to the languid nonchalant air in that office. Finally when he got to narrate his woes to the man in the cabin, he was flustered to find himself thrown in the dock. The man sitting behind the table piled with hillocks of files, laughed at his 'unrealistic' grievance and said he should be proud of having a telephone at all; even if it was not working, his status as one of the chosen few did not change. Sooner or later, it would be put right, but he should not expect the telephone department to respond in the manner a doctor should to the sick. When a startled Zaheer Sahab had reminded him of the tens of thousands of people recruited with the exclusive purpose of manning the system, the official with an edge to his voice said the State's purpose was more in the nature of providing employment than satisfying the luxurious needs of individuals like him.

However, with the telephone office aware of Ram Mohan's connections—that he was close to the minister himself—his telephone would, if ever out of kilter, be fixed in no time, which was also the cause of some relief to Kanti and the children, for there were occasions when on receiving a call, Ram Mohan would have to go out mostly in town somewhere but sometimes out of town too, chiefly Lucknow. And the call rather a trunk call he got that day was from Delhi. He held the line as asked. Shortly, Saansad ji came on the other side. Nishant who as usual was concentrating on his book became alert, latching on to every syllable he uttered, and could detect a note of excitement in Babu ji's voice. No sooner had he got off the phone than Nishant was ordered to gather everybody in the big room. He had something good to share.

He told them Saansad ji was going to be in Kanpur coming week to lay the foundation stone of the new telephone exchange, and while in the city, he wanted to discuss with him an ominous stir in the national political firmament, which though still within speculative domain, had the potential of leading to something profound. If what Saansad ji suspected came to pass, Lucknow too would feel the impact. Baran Singh, according to Saansad ji, was keeping a close watch. 'It may eventually lead me to a position from where there will be no looking back,' said Ram Mohan warmly and to Kanti, 'Be prepared. We may have to move to Lucknow soon, into a big bungalow.' Kanti though pleased said let that time come first. Ram Mohan said he had no doubt as to a wonderful life awaiting them. They all believed in his future achievements in politics. Nisha and Nishant in particular dreamt of a time when he, because of his position, would be rushed off his feet, affording them not only a sense of security but also freedom from his tyranny.

Ram Mohan asked them to gear up for the likely visit of a Union minister to their house. Because of its sensitive nature,

Saansad ji would prefer to discuss the issue in private, the issue he had mentioned on the phone. Ram Mohan would have Tiwari ji present to help him make sense of what Saansad ji seemed so keen to impart. Ram Mohan sent for Tiwari ji whose son Sukesh—one of his younger ones—was doing a BA at D.A.V. College, staying in the hostel. He was used to being sent on such errands.

Tiwari ji reached Kanpur well in time and was with Ram Mohan at the station when Saansad ji got off the overnight train from Delhi. Some local Congress workers scrambled to garland him as a posse of policemen looked on. Saansad ji acknowledged the two friends as he was led out of the station, and before stepping inside the Ambassador car with red beacon, had a quick word with them.

Ram Mohan told Kanti Saansad ji would come in the evening. Nisha prepared a list of things, and Nishant was off to the market at once. Ram Mohan and Tiwari ji went out somewhere, while Nisha and Sandhya got down to cleaning and tidying up the big room. In the late afternoon, according to the plan, Tiwari ji went to the Circuit House to accompany Saansad ji back. The sky was a little overcast when Saansad ji descended with his boisterous ministerial retinue, taking the locality famed for its serenity by storm. Several Ambassadors fitted with red or blue lights escorted by a couple of police vehicles filled the entire length of the approach road to Ram Mohan's house. The unusual hubbub stirred all the neighbours to come out onto their veranda or front yard. Though aware of Ram Mohan's association with Baran Singh, they had no idea he could be so close to someone on Indira Gandhi's Cabinet at the Centre. They viewed Ram Mohan as a martinet and strait-laced at home, located a notch or two lower in the modern pecking order than them whose outlook was 'liberal'. Their naivety now lay in a mangled heap. They could only marvel at the import of a successful politician having your back. Their inconsequential existence took on certain poignancy as they watched the scene before them.

Ram Mohan and Tiwari ji led Saansad ji into the spruced up big room. The rest of his entourage stayed outside near their vehicles, chatting. Nishant would make sure they were served tea and snacks. Saansad ji while settling down on one of the sofas looked around and sighed as if in preparation for a long conversation, but before saying anything, he laughed languorously, straightening his long kurta over the knees. Perched on the edge of the takht at the far end, Nishant was alert to anything Babu ji might command. Saansad ji asked him his name and after a brief small-talk, he was silent for a second and said, 'It might sound too early Ram Mohan, but I have a feeling that Indira ji sees in Dr Zakir Husain's death the opportunity to gain control of the party and remove any future threat to her premiership.'

Ram Mohan and Tiwari ji beamed with interest.

'I don't know what local party workers here make of it,' Saansad ji continued, 'but Delhi has been agog with implications of the way the PM asserted herself at the Congress Working Committee meeting in Bangalore the other day. She wanted her flunky Jagjivan Ram to be the Congress candidate for India's presidency, knowing full well the Syndicate is considering Reddy for—'

'The speaker of the current Lok Sabha?' said Ram Mohan.

'Yes, Sanjiva Reddy . . . When her proposal was given the thumbs down she felt affronted; the very next day Vice-President Giri who had been acting President since Dr Husain's demise, entered the fray. She is bent on undercutting the Syndicate and won't let go of this chance. After Bangalore, she had a confab with her close aides, Haksar in particular . . . who is rumoured to enjoy some special kind of intimacy with her. He was close to Krishna Menon and like him is a closet Communist.'

'Doesn't she take the Cabinet, the ministers, into her confidence?' asked Tiwari ji.

'She does but only her favourite ones. I'm also considered her man but I'm never called for the meetings she holds with her trusted lieutenants. I suspect she hasn't got over my former closeness to Baran Singh . . . That's an aside. What I'm saying is that there seems to be something serious cooking, because just before I left Delhi, Kapur told me we should be prepared to ignore the official party nominee for President and support Giri instead; that she would soon make her stand clear to the Congress MPs and MLAs.'

'I don't understand why she should be itching for an unnecessary clash with the Syndicate. This might rebound on her, don't you think?'

'I asked myself the same question when I first learnt of it. But she is convinced Congress rightfully belongs to her family, that all its senior office-bearers can hold their positions only at her pleasure. The present Congress bosses, the Syndicate, she sees as usurpers. She cannot allow this. She has to remove once and for all the impression they might still have of her being pusillanimous. The time is right for her to deliver the final blow to their formal authority . . . Kapur thinks they have brought it on themselves; she won't have Reddy as country's President, in whom she sees as a threat to her chair.'

'How can President be a threat to Prime Minister?' said Tiwari ji.

'Political uncertainty in New Delhi can invest a bold President with decisive authority . . . You forget her long-standing feud with Desai, her deputy and finance minister. He hasn't forsworn his desire for PM's chair . . . If he's tempted to take another crack at the top job, her job, with the Syndicate's support of course . . . then the President would have the power to arbitrate; he can favour either of the claimants . . . With

Reddy in the President House nobody but Desai would be the chosen one.'

'You think the situation can take a drastic turn like this!'

'The way I read Kapur, it seems a certainty. She would try not only to give Desai a crushing thump but capture the party too, turning it into her own fiefdom. Didn't she announce in Bangalore, to the utter vexation of her critics in the party, her intention to nationalize banks and resort to some other socialistic measures? She's listening to these so-called Young Turks in the Congress, who want her to embrace socialism unreservedly. Their leader, this young bearded fellow Chandrashekhar, has earned himself a name for putting hard questions to his own government . . . Advised by Haksar to use him and his cohorts in her fight against the Syndicate, she's now openly dared the likes of Desai and the party's top brass.'

'The development has something for us to take note of . . .?' said Tiwari ji.

'Yes, because she seems set to fight . . . fight to the finish . . . There's no hint of posturing in her manner . . . And Lucknow might not survive the storm in New Delhi, in which case there's no one other than Baran Singh who can take advantage of it . . . of this turmoil in the Congress. In my view you should spend a little more time in Lucknow these days. Baran Singh I'm sure has his eyes fixed on the situation as it unfolds.'

'Let me see if I follow you correctly Saansad ji, said Ram Mohan. 'You mean there might emerge a situation in UP as a result of what's happening in Delhi, which can help reinstate Chaudhary Sahab's primacy here.'

'Yes, he might become CM again.'

Ram Mohan and Tiwari ji exchanged glances as Saansad ji took some sips at his tea in quick succession.

Tiwari ji sighed, 'How I wish we had won the Assembly election!'

'That would've made it easier,' said Saansad ji, then looking at Ram Mohan, 'Still, if the opportunity comes, Baran Singh can accommodate you with a place in his government. Later he can help you become an MLC.'

'That means I put everything aside and head for Lucknow.'

'There's one thing you must bear in mind . . . If Baran Singh does get a chance to rule the state again you wouldn't know how long he'll last . . . No party or coalition is in a position to ensure a stable government in UP. This fluidity would remain until my party sorts itself out, and the opposition doesn't have the stamina to fight it out with the Congress. What I suggest is that you be flexible enough for Baran Singh to find you something else if not a ministerial position. He can appoint you to one of the other important although non-political posts.'

'Such posts are usually meant for non-political persons or for those who have reached the fag end of their political life . . . My absence from active politics at this stage can make my return rather difficult.'

Saansad ji laughed, 'I reckon it's still a bit premature to bother about these details. You just wait and stay in touch with Baran Singh and see what transpires. Even people like me in the Congress who are not part of Indira ji's inner circle don't know what lies ahead. Let's hope whatever happens, happens to benefit us and does not put our political interests on line. Being circumspect is the name of the game.'

No sooner had Ram Mohan seen Saansad ji off than he gathered the whole family in the big room, and his words began to conjure up delightful images of a life close at hand. They listened, bewitched. According to him he would soon have enough power to fix each of them up with a secure and happy future. He then let his friend hold forth about all the benefits accruing from his being a minister. Tiwari ji, in his measured tone and distinctive manner, with deliberateness, began by putting flesh on the quintessence of his friend's 'incomparable' personality. Tiwari ji's animated words gripped them all. Only Kanti looked restrained, but those who knew her also knew the poker face she presented on these occasions meant only to hide her true feelings. Familiar with this device of hers to attract attention, Ram Mohan would not stop having funny digs at her 'pretentious' solemnity till she too became cheerful. For them the moment was also significant in that the temporary moratorium put on his out-of-town trips by his book would now end. The prospect of his visits to Lucknow, also to Delhi maybe, held the kind of appeal they had not known before, which on the one hand meant he would soon enter the realm of real power—sealing a sparkling future for them—and promise the immediacy of freedom on the other. Yes, the very next day Ram Mohan informed his publisher he would have to defer his work on the book for the time being. The same evening, he and Tiwari ji got on a bus to Lucknow.

The whole house was now echoing with footfalls and chatter. Nisha's jingling laughter could be heard everywhere. She had a luminous voice. Her friends in school would not get tired of admiring it; one of her teachers thought the quality of her voice was the same as that of Lata Mangeshkar. Nisha never missed a chance to mention the compliment. Sometimes she had to produce a laugh on demand, which now had become her second nature, the business of laughter.

Nisha and Nishant would follow the news from Delhi. The banner headline the next day in the Hindi daily related closely to what Saansad ji, Babu ji and Tiwari ji had discussed. Indira Gandhi had divested her deputy Desai of finance portfolio, and the manner she chose to flaunt her prerogative as PM had left the leaders associated with the Syndicate flustered. It was the presage of something more and something bigger to come. Her logic was that Desai, a votary of private enterprise, was in the way of her plan to consolidate and expand the public sector.

* * *

A couple of days later, Ram Mohan returned, plunging the house back into its fearful and gloomy mode, but this time his return was only to herald a longer phase of freedom for them as he was to leave for Delhi shortly, where he would watch out for anything of importance to Baran Singh who was in contact with those state Congress leaders who were sympathetic to the faction opposed to Indira Gandhi. Lucknow and Delhi were rife with speculation. Desai had in a fit of pique resigned. Things were heating up in the presidential campaign.

Suffused with a quiet excitement, everybody looked eager to contribute to the preparation for his Delhi trip. Sandhya who resented being made to wash their father's heavy khadi clothes offered to do the same happily; as soon as they dried off, Nishant took them with a spring in his step to their dhobi in Parmat for ironing. With Sevak Lal gone to visit his village, Kanti's hands were full. Nisha and Sandhya helped her in the kitchen. In short, they were full of warmth for him. Nisha, Sandhya and Deena watched the scene out of their window as Babu ji cuddled Mayank while the IRP worker who had come to drop him to the station stood smiling. Nishant put the suitcase and bedroll in the back of the Jeep. The moment it left, Nisha left the window and ran to the big room tailed by Sandhya and Deena. Picking up the paper, she began scouring the page that told of movies showing at the city cinemas. Nishant was getting ready to go out somewhere, perhaps to meet some friend; all his friends were his schoolmates. He cultivated no friendships in the neighbourhood, which given Babu ji's restrictions, were hard to maintain.

So plans for seeing a movie or two and visiting friends were made. Deena felt heavenly. Ram Mohan in all probability was going to be away at least for a week. They also talked about his landing some plum political position; the thought only enhanced the beauty of their present freedom. They would try to understand the developments in Delhi by listening to the news on AIR and reading the Hindi paper thoroughly. It was just the day after Ram Mohan left that Nisha was reading the paper to everyone else sitting in the drawing room in the late afternoon when Mahavir Wilson made a surprise appearance. But he looked more surprised than they. Going by the silence, he thought Doctor Sahab was home. In fact, all regular visitors could tell before entering, if the master of the house was home or not.

They all beamed at him, their Mahavir Bhaiya, for whom they felt a special affinity, whose visits were looked forward to, especially when Babu ji was away. Gesturing at the paper in Nisha's hands, he said he did not know they were so keen on reading the paper, much less the front page, and said they should keep it up; then picking up the *National Herald* lying next to Nisha on the sofa, he advised them to read it as well, for reading the English paper was an effective way of improving one's English, and waving it, he stressed laughingly that this paper should in particular be read more for its language than content. Nisha and Nishant both presented a look of curiosity. He explained, '*National Herald* was started in Lucknow by Nehru almost thirty years ago with the aim of indulging his ideas of secularism, socialism and the Non-Aligned Movement, a movement which for all practical purposes seeks the consolidation of all anti-American and anti-British forces in the world. Run at a loss, its only purpose now as before is to sing from the same song sheet as the Congress, which funds it.'

Sometimes they did not know what Mahavir Bhaiya was trying to say, but that would not diminish their interest in his words one bit. It was always a joy to listen to him. Nishant told him about Saansad ji's visit of which he already knew. He said, rather jovially, that all the turmoil within the Congress today might pave the way for something good for Doctor Sahab. Their eyes twinkled with gaiety. Nisha wondered whether Babu ji would join the Congress. The question surprised Mahavir Wilson. He said, 'Why, what makes you think so? Did Doctor Sahab mention anything like that?'

Nishant spoke up, 'No, there was nothing like that in their conversation. They only talked about the problem in the Congress; that it might prove advantageous to Chaudhary Baran Singh.'

'That's what I think,' said Mahavir. 'The row in the Congress over who should be its Presidential nominee is heading for a crisis. From the way Mrs Gandhi forced Desai to resign makes it plain she wants to settle it once and for all. She accuses him of not having executed her government's programmes, which doesn't make sense, because Desai agreed to her economic proposals in the Bangalore meeting. She admits as much . . . then why all this ranting and raving now? Word has it she has designs on the party, which she thinks belongs to her and nobody else! There's also the buzz that Congress is moving towards a split . . .! Desai while talking to a journalist stormed, "It's she who is angling for that. Or why can't she recount just one instance when I tried to stall on her government's decisions. All these allegations are nothing but attempts at obfuscation." I learnt this not from the *National Herald* but from the BBC—'

'Isn't it odd, I mean . . . her behaviour,' said Nisha, intrigued.

Mahavir laughed and said, 'Those involved in a power struggle don't say openly what they really want. They act in a manner that seems politically correct and reasonable, because to look nakedly ambitious is uncouth. So they prevaricate. Yet people know what it is that they are after . . . Unlike small children, they need to wrap their greed up in the rhetoric of fairness, logic, decency and so on.'

Nisha said, 'Mahavir Bhaiya, I still don't get how the problem in the Congress would help Chaudhary Baran Singh and Babu ji.'

Before he could answer, Kanti arrived. He stood up to greet her, as she in a chiding tone said, 'Nisha, would you people just go on talking or offer Mahavir some tea and biscuits?' Nisha, a bit abashed, rose but Mahavir asked her to sit and let him first answer her question. Kanti who was still standing said, 'No problem, I'll make tea,' then turning to him, 'These children can't have enough of your company. Then they all noticed Sandhya quietly reading from the Hindi paper to Deena and Mayank, the mesmerizing story of Apollo 11 moon landing mission and Neil Armstrong being the first man to set foot on the moon.

'Nisha, if this crisis in the Congress worsens, it might lead to the party being rent asunder which in all likelihood would produce an earthquake in Lucknow. I'm not talking about other states . . . but nobody should be surprised if Gupta's government in UP falls. And who knows, Baran Singh may become CM again; his party after all is the largest amongst the non-Congress ones. If that happens . . . then your father will be part of his government.'

Ram Mohan was away for six days. No other occasion, however joyous, could compare with the gaiety of his being out of town. Deena had never had such a good time before. During this glorious interlude, he saw one movie and went to Naveen

Market several times and was treated to some delicious snacks there. For the first time in life, he saw a bakery. The experience was delectable. The fresh crispy aroma took his breath away, reminding him of the contrast—the unsavouriness of cloying heavy smell of an indigenous sweetmeat shop. They also went to M.G. Girls Inter College to see Nisha Didi playing basketball, a game she loved the most. Ram Mohan did not approve of her being into sports and athletics, so much so that when she was recently offered to captain the college basketball team, she had to decline, for every time there was a match she would have to seek his permission, which he rarely granted. Mostly she could play only in the matches that took place when he was not in town.

During this period, Deena was free to step outside in the evening and watch children play. One day when he and Mayank stood a few paces away from Zaheer Sahab's house gazing over its low boundary wall at Saba and her friends frolicking on the lawn, Mrs Zaheer who sat in a rocking chair on the veranda, reading a book, saw them. She called to her daughter and said something. Saba glanced in their direction, then walked to the wall on her side and motioned for them to come inside. Taken aback, they looked towards Nisha and Sandhya who were chatting nearby with Bhatnagar Sahab's two daughters; they had seen Saba gesturing to Deena and Mayank. Giggling, Nisha told them to go. After walking Deena and Mayank to her mother, Saba went back to join her friends on the lawn. Mrs Zaheer made Mayank sit on her lap as Deena stood by them. She asked about their mother and schools and friends. Deena was in visible awe. She rose from the rocking chair and seated them both in it, and went inside the house. A moment later, she handed them each some ice cream in a tennis ball-shaped container. Deena was fascinated by both the container and its contents. It was the first time he ate something so delicious. Mrs Zaheer said they could come whenever they want, and called her son Anjum who was going to join other boys playing football outside, and introduced them. He asked them gaily why they did not come out to play.

They came back overwhelmed, Deena in particular, who had never seen such a clean, well-kept house, smelling enticingly fresh; and Anjum and Saba looking so tidy yet so relaxed. When they emerged outside, Nisha called them. Bhatnagar Sahab's daughters wanted to meet Deena. They all stood in their front courtyard, and through the open main door Deena caught a glimpse inside the house, which was the opposite of the way Zaheers kept their home. Later when he pointed it out, the contrast, Nisha said Bhatnagar Sahab's house was small and bore all the hallmarks of a place struggling to hold a large family. It was crowded, cluttered and clamorous. Plus Bhatnagars lacked the polish and elegance of Zaheers and were rather carefree, happy-go-lucky sort of people. 'But Bhatnagar siblings don't live in mortal fear of their father like us,' Nisha stressed. 'They enjoy the freedom we can only dream of.'

During these occasions, they also longed for visitors whom Babu ji resented; who comprised relations chiefly on their mother's side, and who knew the dynamics that no matter how put out Ram Mohan must feel at their visits, their company was immensely desirable to his children. Their cousin Rajvansh who was studying in Kanpur came when he learnt of his Delhi visit, but Kanti sent him to Ballamgaon to bring his Dada—Kanti's father—to Kanpur. She had been concerned for his health. Rajvansh returned the next day, accompanying Baijnath who had slowed down after the stroke; he had also aged except in his eyes that looked as lively as ever. His arrival brought joy to the children. They were never tired of the stories he told them from his World War past. He would enjoin Nisha and Sandhya to study hard so they could fend off the world inimical to women's aspirations, the world where despite his best efforts, Kanti, their mother, had ended up. His disquiet was palpable when he learnt of Ram Mohan's opposition to Nisha's enthusiasm for sports.

Kanti had helped her father bathe and was buttoning up his shirt when Nisha informed that Babu ji was back and was paying the rickshawallah; Rajvansh who was chatting with Nishant in the big room scuttled into the other side of the house, collected his books of Hindi pulp fiction and shot out of the side door held open by Nisha. Rajvansh was adept at beating these hasty retreats. When told about Baijnath's arrival, Ram Mohan went to the inner courtyard where the former sat on a charpoy; after enquiring how things were in Ballamgaon, he advised him against making these trips for the sake of his health. Kanti simmered with helplessness. Nisha, Sandhya and Deena felt angry and ashamed. Later after breakfast, Ram Mohan came into their room and sent for Kanti. She listened silently as he said, 'It must have been your idea.'

'I was missing my father and wanted to see him.' He smirked and said, 'I used to make fun of it but now I see the wisdom of the tradition that forbids parents from visiting their married daughters.'

'My father is old and not well. Is it a crime if I want to look after him for a while? Did I not tend to your parents and Uncle?'

'What about his sons, your brothers . . . Can't they take care of their father? When did our society put the burden of the old and sick parents on their daughters?' Kanti was crying. 'You're a drama queen! Cut it out.' Between her sobs Kanti mumbled, 'I'll send him back to Ballamgaon tomorrow.' With a look of annoyance, Ram Mohan quoted one of his favourite Sanskrit sayings, 'Of woman's wiles, even gods are ignorant.'

Shooting a glance at Nisha and Sandhya who sat at their table by the door, he strode out and bumped into Mayank in the corridor. Holding his hand, he walked back to the big room where Nishant was concentrating on his book. He told him to empty his suitcase out and give the dirty clothes for washing. Settling on his takht, he placed Mayank on his lap and began cuddling and rocking him to and fro while mouthing one by one all the adoring names he had given him. Nisha and Sandhya were relieved the argument fell short of what they were dreading, for whenever their mother answered Babu ji back she would get thrashed. Sometimes she seemed intent on looking exactly for that. Her belligerence on these occasions made no sense to them; Nisha would admonish her for provoking him, knowing full well what would follow. Yet there were times when nothing stopped him from charging at you right away because your offence called for swift retribution.

Deena who had witnessed these scenes several times since his arrival was still hiding in the toilet, trying to invoke God for coming to their rescue, when Sandhya asked him to come out. He opened the door and his eyes fell on their Nana who, sitting in the charpoy under the shed adjacent to the kitchen, was eating something out of a bowl placed uncertainly on his lap. Deena began to cry. Why could their Nana not stay with them? Deena was unable to fathom his father's strange outlook. Also, Babu ji's presence at home would make him lose his bearings. He frowned on Deena's proximity to Nisha and Sandhya Didi. There was something sordid about Babu ji's glances when he found Deena hovering in their vicinity; and before long, he would find some pretext to give Deena a tongue-lashing. With Babu ji home, Deena did not know where to take his person.

———

After Ram Mohan left for Lucknow, Kanti wanted to delay sending her father back, but Baijnath said no. He did not want his daughter to suffer on his account. Nishant accompanied him to Ballamgaon and returned the same day; so did Ram Mohan from Lucknow the day after that. He seemed on a high and made everybody's day by announcing he had to go back to Lucknow again in a day or two. He told Kanti to get his clothes ready for a slightly longish trip this time; when Nisha asked about his recent Delhi trip, he asked her to gather everybody in the big room. There was nothing concrete to talk about but he was sure of something important afoot. He said the scene in Lucknow was more interesting where the political circles were abuzz with hypotheses of varied connotations. Baran Singh was busy identifying the Congress MLAs loyal to the Syndicate and those supporting Indira Gandhi, and held his cards close to his chest. He would say nothing with any measure of certainty on the desired and awaited breaking up of the Congress, though he did predict that Mrs Gandhi's coterie would not let up till it had taken its fight with her opponents in the party to its logical end. The control of the party had to be ceded to her before long. Yet her true intent would come to light only during and after the Presidential election. Chaudhary Baran Singh had then quipped, 'What the guru did to the father's international policy, the disciple is doing to the daughter's economic one.' Ram Mohan explained that Krishna Menon was great friends with Nehru ji while Haksar who had served under Menon in Indian High Commission in London, was now in charge of Mrs Gandhi's secretariat. Both romanced with communist ideology.

Before being off to Lucknow, Ram Mohan tried to soft-soap a sullen Kanti. 'I know how bad you must feel about my objection to your father coming here! I've nothing against him. But why encourage people to scoff at him. It's ridiculous he should go to his daughter's place rather than being in the care of his sons! And at this old age, he should refrain from travelling outside Ballamgaon.' Kanti said nothing but could not keep from breaking out in tears. He said there was no point talking to her. Snivelling, she said her father was not well. He said, 'That's why I don't want him to exhaust himself needlessly. He's in no condition to travel.'

Ram Mohan had not returned from Lucknow when Rajvansh came with the news that Baijnath, his Dada, was very ill and would not respond to the treatment of the local herbalist. Kanti left along with Rajvansh the same day. The thought of her father's loneliness distressed her. Her Bade Bhaiya, Rajvansh's father, would have little time, energy or patience to spare to their father's illness. He was wrapped up in work related to his fields and crops, while Kripal Bhaiya could not be much of a help as he was soft and slothful and poor. He could talk intelligently but hard physical work was not his bag. Kanti and Rajvansh brought Baijnath to Kanpur's Hallet Hospital. He was in a bad shape. Leaving Rajvansh with him in the hospital, Kanti rushed home to pick up some clothes and utensils, and told Nisha to tell Babu ji on his return of their Nana's critical condition; that she expected him to come to the hospital as soon as he could. The next day after school Nisha, Sandhya and Deena rode a rickshaw to the hospital. It was their first visit ever to a big medical centre like Hallet Hospital. Right from the entrance various spectacles of misery stormed their vision, making them reel. Just outside, two bodies lay on either side of the gate, both shrouded—one in white and tied to a bier, and the other in a grubby checked sheet. Several women sat around the white one, wailing, as two men stood nearby apparently grappling with the question of how to transport their dead home, while sprawled on the dirty pavement was the other body, sitting beside which was a boy in his early teens, looking bewildered.

Holding the hands of Sandhya and Deena, Nisha tried to quickly pick her way through sickly traffic along the road leading to the portico, yet the sight of the gravely ill or injured being helped either in or out was unavoidable. Nisha found out from the enquiry counter about the ward they were looking for; inside the hospital the picture was that of a settled chaos. Over the general hubbub could be heard the constant groans of patients lying or hunched up here and there along the corridors, waiting to be allotted a bed. Then there was irritated loudness of the nurses trying to get the pestering relatives of the sick off their back.

When they located the said general ward, Nisha was the first to see the diminutive figure of their mother in the distance; they started down the passage flanked by two rows of beds. Pleased to see them, Kanti smiled feebly. Their Nana, half asleep, looked much weaker than when they had seen him recently. He was in no condition to acknowledge them. Right then, a sudden yawl drew their attention. Kanti walked to the source a few paces away, where a woman, bent over the head of a bed, was weeping hysterically. Shortly a young man, probably their son, came back with a doctor who after examining the patient said something, which drew another cry of grief from the woman. Kanti put her hand on the woman's shoulder, said a few consoling words and came back. 'It's a regular thing here. Someone or the other dies every day,' she said; then added that these frequent deaths also meant relief to some—those waiting for a bed. Kanti now knew about all the neighbouring patients, variously suffering from heart and kidney and liver problems. There was one afflicted with cholera, and another had hernia. Some in the ward had been injured in a variety of accidents. I found amongst Deena's papers, a detailed note describing this hospital visit, but I will make do with just the way he ended it: *All healthy persons are alike; each unhealthy person is unhealthy in their own way.* He also mentions about reading Anna Karenina.

Baijnath needed constant attention; Kanti being the sole attendant was run off her feet. Rajvansh had left. There was no chance of anybody else coming to relieve or assist her, but there was not even a semblance of protest on her part about being weighed down by a responsibility incommensurate with her physical and financial means. The mere thought of being unable to care for her father when he was so alone and fading away was excruciating. Even if Ram Mohan were to order her to leave him to his fate, she would defy him. Looking at the sleeping figure, she said tearfully to the children, 'He wanted me to study and make something of myself, and would also try to persuade others to have their daughters educated. Indeed, there were some willing to act on his advice but it was not easy in those days. There used to be hardly any schools for girls. Many thought he was off his head. His purpose of taking up this job at the district court here in Kanpur after retirement was largely for my sake, so I could go to school. Your Manno Masi was just a baby then. Bade Bhaiya had already joined the army. Kripal Bhaiya and I went to school here, but I was more interested in studying than him. Your Nana encouraged me all the time. Then and even now, all good things in life would be reserved for boys and men; I remember how sisters would watch their brothers being treated to delicious food. My father felt tormented.' Sobbing loudly, she said, 'Despite his small salary, he would bring Jalebi, my favourite sweetmeat soaked in warm milk, every now and then . . . ' They were all crying now. Nisha slid her arm around their mother who noticed through her tears that people from around other beds were looking towards them. Then some visitor on the far side of the ward said something about the weather getting cloudy outside. Visiting hours were not over but Kanti asked them to get a move on as it might start raining. Outside a pleasant breeze greeted them—a complete contrast to the atmosphere inside, but that did not lift their mood. Sandhya and Deena looked up at Nisha who walked in silence, opening her mouth only to hail a rickshaw outside the gate.

Babu ji arrived the same evening, a day earlier than expected, and was surprised on learning about Baijnath's condition with Kanti in attendance, but did not say much. He looked happy and told them about his long conversations with Chaudhary Sahab. 'Gupta,' he said, 'is confused. He does not know where to look for succour in case the Congress party breaks into two. His government cannot survive the split, and neither of the factions would be in a position to claim majority. Considered close to the Syndicate, Gupta was one of those instrumental in bringing about an understanding between Indira ji and Desai, who was subsequently made deputy PM. She had acknowledged his help by not objecting to his becoming CM again. Now he is undecided about whom to hook up with if it comes to that—Indira or Desai. Either way, he won't have the required numbers in the Assembly. That's why he invited Chaudhary Sahab to his chamber for a cup of tea.

'He said he wanted to have a friendly chat about the ongoing crisis in his party; Chaudhary Sahab told him the Congress was well on its way to a split. It was just a matter of time. Gupta agreed. Then he tried to sound Chaudhary Sahab out about how he would respond to a situation like that, if it did arise after all, which alerted Chaudhary Sahab to the real reason for Gupta's sudden desire for a 'friendly chat'. Chaudhary Sahab has over ninety MLAs in his pocket. In a scenario like this, Gupta said, he could offer Chaudhary Sahab the position of deputy CM plus several ministries for his men; this way they would provide political stability in the state. Chaudhary Sahab thanked him and agreed it was a good idea, but said he would cross that bridge when he came to it. Later, laughing at Gupta's condescension, he said, "I wonder if he's gone soft in the head. Or what could have made such an experienced man imagine I might be talked into something like that when I myself could force either of the two prospective groups of the Congress to help me form government?"

'There were five of us in the room that evening with him when he related this episode. I waited if anybody else had something to say. They all looked perplexed. I looked at Chaudhary Sahab who said, "Can you enlighten us on what may really have prompted Gupta to put his cards on the table before me?" I said, "Chaudhary Sahab, when he touched on the question of political stability, I'm sure his intent was to underline that you might not last long if you insist on heading the government yourself with the support of either of the two Congress factions, whereas with your help, his government would complete its full term; you can use this period to expand your support base".' Ram Mohan laughed and continued, 'Chaudhary Sahab looked askance at me—he was feigning of course—and said, "I don't know Ram Mohan what Gupta exactly had in mind, but you do want me to cooperate with him!" He was just winding me up and conceded that I was close to the mark.' Ram Mohan paused. 'But I did indulge in over-interpretation of what Gupta might have been thinking.'

Nisha looked withdrawn, which was unusual. She and Nishant had begun to enjoy the complexity of a political issue or situation. Ram Mohan asked her what the matter was. She glumly said their Nana was in a bad state and their mother was alone in the hospital with him. That he should visit him. This irked him. He said he had many other demands on his time, adding that their Nana's own family had abandoned him, leaving him dependent on his daughter. He paused and said, 'I have to visit someone at the Hallet Hospital anyway; I would look him up too.'

Three days later, Kanti telephoned from the hospital. She was crying. Ram Mohan sent Nishant to go find Rajvansh who lived with some relation of his, not far from his college. When not in college he would be home, reading popular Hindi fiction; he would sooner finish a novel than attend classes. Rajvansh set off at once to get his father and uncle; they reached Kanpur the same day. It was dark by the time Baijnath could be taken to the cremation ground on the Ganges. Nishant had gone to the cremation. Distraught and embittered, Kanti said, 'It's very painful . . . that my father was left to cope alone in his declining years. Much more than his death . . . Death is better than being reduced to a burden to your family . . . Your father beating me is nothing compared to what I felt when he visited the hospital and left without caring to see my father. I was in the corridor outside the ward talking to a nurse when I saw him holding Mayank's hand, coming down the path from the main gate. I rushed back thinking they were coming to meet us. But he had come to visit someone else and soon left even as I kept waiting.'

'He had said he would be visiting the hospital,' said Nisha. She asked Mayank, whom Babu ji had taken to his publishers, from where they went to the hospital. Mayank did not know where they were going. He remembered the name of the 'Auntie' though, whose father was in hospital. She was one of Ram Mohan's PhD students and had come to their house a couple of times with her father.

———————

When V. V. Giri was declared elected President of India, Ram Mohan and Tiwari ji were in Lucknow. It was Indira Gandhi's personal victory over her rivals in the party. In the run-up to the election, things had been in the political whirl.

Suspicious of her intent, the Congress president had, in a grave miscalculation, contacted the right-wing People's Union and some former Congress stalwarts, asking them for their second-preference votes to Reddy after their own candidate was out of the race in the first round. The PM faction accused him of entering into a conspiracy with the rival parties to help elect Reddy as President so he could help install Desai as PM. Despite signing Reddy's nomination papers Mrs Gandhi had not only refused to issue a party whip to its MPs and members of state assemblies but also appealed for a vote of conscience. Clearly V.V. Giri was her choice as President, not Reddy, the official candidate of the party.

Nervous of the fall-out of a now roaring factional war in his party, Gupta rang up Baran Singh who was evasive, saying he would consult his MLAs and party colleagues before making a decision. Ram Mohan and Tiwari ji were excited. According to Chaudhary Sahab, Gupta's desperation showed what was coming, a clear sign of which was the show-cause notice the party president had served to the PM, asking her to explain her anti-party manoeuvres; then within a week—before she could respond—Congress Working Committee withdrew the notice. The Committee also marked off the functional domains of the party chief and PM. Thus the Congress—to the opposition's dismay—managed to avert the crisis. Not in Baran Singh's view. He said the measure was cosmetic and would not work. Gupta pooh-poohed the remark; a day or two later he had Baran Singh over to his residence and told him that Giri's victory was not because of Indira Gandhi's hold on Congress MPs and MLAs; more than two-third of them had stuck by Reddy, the official candidate. Giri could scrape through, thanks only to the support of some regional parties and the Communists to the delight of whom she had nationalized banks and had some other programmes on her agenda befitting their ideology. Baran Singh brushed the statistics aside, saying it was of no moment because Indira Gandhi had after all emerged stronger from the face-off. 'And Gupta ji, the next time she decides to push ahead with something like that, many of those who voted for Reddy would fall in line with her. Take my word for it.'

With no issue at hand to quarrel over, the two factions of the Congress went in for a break, putting a halt to hectic politicking and infighting. Not only had Indira Gandhi got the better of the rival camp but was also rid of the threats embodied by Desai and Reddy to her continuance in power. Ram Mohan was crestfallen at the sudden lull in politics. But then as was his propensity, he saw in it yet another opportunity to catch up on his reading, teaching and writing. His comings and goings thus stopped, the familiar jittery atmosphere returned to his household, and the time spent in school became a blessing to his children once again, Mayank being the sole exception.

Deena had made some friends in his class and began to enjoy the new environment. Introduced to English, he had learnt the alphabet and was happy to be taught sentences like 'This is a cat' 'That is a rat' or more of the same, but ran out of steam when things began to get a little complicated. In Hindi, he was the most fluent in the class, but English—unlike many in his class who had studied English as a subject from grade one onwards—became his scourge, and one day when they were being randomly asked to read aloud from their textbook, he had sat petrified in one of the front rows. When the teacher's eye fell on him, he had to stand up holding the book in his trembly hands, unable to move past 'this' and 'that' and mute before the words like 'bread' and 'door' and 'wall'. There were sniggers. From then on, he sought refuge at the back of the class during the English lesson. Anon he would begin to cut classes.

Ram Mohan had reverted to his old routine. In the morning, he would walk to D.A.V. College to take classes and after post-lunch rest at home would ride the Rajdoot to his publisher's office. He wanted to add a few chapters to the second part of *Hindi Language* before politics beckoned again. His busy schedule brought some relief to the family. They could spend some time together and visit the neighbourhood children. Nisha was especially thankful. She could stay on in school after her classes to play basketball; they had a match coming up against a rival college; their sports teacher had asked them to practise hard. These fixtures would usually be slated for Sundays, but with Babu ji in town, it was hard for her to evade his notice. Hence, every such occasion warranted his permission which would be refused or granted depending on his mood, that is Nisha could not be certain of her participation till the last—a cause for consternation to her sports teacher and teammates. But this time she was hopeful of Babu ji's nod. He seemed in a jollier mood than usual. His book was shaping up splendidly. That Baran Singh might come to power soon would not leave his thoughts. Nisha got his consent to the Sunday match.

Though they won, it was a close-run match. Nisha finished as the second-highest scorer from her side. These matches and other sporting events received wide coverage in the local Hindi newspapers. She would preserve all the clippings carrying her name or picture in action. On Monday, coming back from school, Nisha and Sandhya found their mother crying; Babu ji had either beaten her or said something hurtful before going off to the publisher's. Kanti told Nisha he had become tetchy after reading the news of their match in the paper. 'Now I know why Nisha is so keen on these matches! And you encourage her to draw attention, men's attention! I have caught her smiling at Zaheer Sahab and that loafer, Bhatnagar's son Randeep. Left to your own devices, it would not be long before this place becomes a whorehouse. Tell Nisha to stay away from these matches. Her school seems to be full of women and girls of loose morals . . . Or why would they employ a man to coach girls?' This time the sports reporter had referred to their coach who besides praising his team made a special mention of the girl scoring the highest number of baskets and of Nisha for her tremendous effort when she cleverly shot the decisive basket just before the whistle was blown.

Nisha's performance and her last-minute basket clinching a victory in a match that had all but ended in a draw, had been on everyone's lips on Monday. She had returned from school very happy, unaware of the turn of events at home. Now both Nisha and Sandhya sat sunk in gloom and dread, listening to their mother. But when he returned in the evening, to their surprise, Babu ji did not bring it up. Maybe because he was on the phone for a long time, discussing politics with someone. There were hints emanating from New Delhi as to something terrible brewing afresh in the Congress. Excited, Ram Mohan said to the person on the other side that Chaudhary Sahab was right about the crisis in the Congress being far from over. Once off the phone, he said aloud for the benefit of Nishant who was concentrating on his book that he should start taking extra classes before being forced to be in Lucknow again. Nishant did not lift his head from the book.

Nisha had yet to get over what Babu ji had said to their mother and his decree forbidding her from playing any more matches. At first, she had felt embarrassed at her friends' reaction to her father being so old-fashioned as to be against her taking part in extra-curricular activities, but in time, her friends as well as her teachers had, instead of sneering, begun to look at her situation with sympathy. However, that day— the day after her father's caustic comments—something else, something outrageous, awaited Nisha at school. One of Nisha's close friends Shinju Dalmia whispered to her that she needed to tell her something, something freakish; her voice carrying an undertone of disbelief. Nisha thought it would be an interesting piece of gossip for which her friend was known to have a nose. Shinju came from one of the elite business families in Kanpur and was the only student in their school who came in a chauffeur-driven Ambassador. It was she who had first made overtures to Nisha. Now they were close friends. Nisha had also been to her house once when Shinju had—during one of Ram Mohan's absences—sent the car to pick her up. Nisha had taken Mayank along. On coming back, Mayank had told Sandhya and Deena what a big fabulous house it was, and how the lush green lawn running around it could be seen from every room; then Nisha had told them about Shinju's affectionate parents. They could not help but take note of how other parents treated their children.

When they met at break, Shinju took her to a secluded spot. Nisha went crimson as Shinju narrated what their old housemaid confided to her mother. The young woman who had recently started coming to Nisha's house to sweep and mop the floor was related to Shinju's housemaid and was married, with a three-year-old child. She usually came around noon when all of them were away at school, which was also the time when Ram Mohan returned from his college. He would have lunch and some rest before going out again. One day, he had got back to find the woman mopping the floor in the big room as Sevak Lal sat on the front veranda keeping an eye. After sending him on an errand, Ram Mohan had got into a conversation with her while affecting to read the paper, asking about her family. The next day she had received praise for the tasks she did from him; how all that physical work had kept her fit and her waist small even after she had had a child, and suchlike. He had given her two rupees to buy something for her baby.

Two days later, Ram Mohan had told her in a honeyed voice how seductive she looked. She blushed and kept quiet, not knowing what to say to such an important and educated man. With his words and style kept charmingly decent, he had managed to winkle out her thoughts on the matter. She had diffidently mumbled something about it being wrong, mentioning also the presence of Kanti and Sevak Lal, upon which he had assured her that he would ensure nobody ever got wind of their peccadillo; then, in another attempt to foil him, she had mumbled her fear of getting a bun in the oven, which he had swept aside, claiming he had had a vasectomy.

Shinju to her shell-shocked friend said, 'Your father promised her financial help in return . . . Though we have several servants in our house, my mother offered to hire her because she is fond of our old maid who is her aunt. The only trouble is that her husband works at Lal-Imli woollen factory and they live in Parmat which is close to his work and closer to the houses where she goes to work, including yours. Our place is a bit too far for her to walk to and fro every day, especially when she has a child to look after. Let's see what happens . . . My mother has told her aunt that your father won't do anything rash that would soil his reputation.'

'Did your mother say anything about me?'

'No. According to her, there is no dearth of such people whose behaviour causes unnecessary pain to their families. In fact, she was asking about you. She thinks you're intelligent, and yes, your voice, your diction and your sharp features have made an impression on her. No, this thing about your father has not affected her opinion about you. Not in the least.'

Kanti was not surprised. She said it was clear why their father wanted her, the cleaning woman, to come around noon or early afternoon. His pretext had been that in the morning she was in the way of the children getting ready for school. Ignoring Nisha's plea, Kanti asked the woman to start coming in the morning again. A furious Ram Mohan roared how she dared interfere with his decision! Kanti said she did not like the floors being swept while she was in the kitchen cooking. There was dust all over. 'You nasty woman, in this house I'm the one who makes and enforces rules. Everybody has to fall in line. I know what's good or bad for my family. If you were allowed any leeway, this house would in no time become like Bhatnagar's.' Kanti seethed, could not check her reaction, 'I don't know why you have got so upset about such a trifle!' Enraged at the insinuation, Ram Mohan lunged at her. A trembling Deena rushed into the toilet to pray to God for help, while Mayank went to the big room where Nishant sat in silence with a book in his hands, trying to make out the gravity of the situation behind the wall separating him from the other side of the house. Sandhya stood cowering into a corner as Nisha tried to protect their mother from Babu ji's blows, receiving some of them herself in the process. Kanti kept crying and uttering, 'Beat me, beat me as much as you want.'

After this, Ram Mohan did not mention the subject again. The rancour resulting from it seemed to make him lose his appetite for the woman. The beating however left Kanti aching all over for some time. The pain she felt now and then in one of her shoulder blades would be sharp. One day as she was squeezing the water out of the clothes she had just washed, Ram Mohan who had come for a bath, heard her groan in pain. He asked her to consult Vaidya ji, the famous Ayurvedic doctor of the area. She went to see him later in the day, taking Deena along.

Deena had been to Parmat a few times before. Located by the Ganges, it was a residential-cum-commercial neighbourhood, a warren of narrow lanes and passages. It also had several compounds with two or three-storey-high buildings containing tiny living quarters, in one of which had once lodged Baijnath with Kanti and her brother Kripal. Noisy, congested, densely populated, bestrewed with filth and open drains, Parmat was the image of contrast to the area of Civil Lines where they lived. Nishant had first taken him to Parmat to show him the place where their father's clothes were brought for ironing. One side of that cramped lane was lined with the houses of dhobis; running along the wall on the other side was a gutter full of black muck. While waiting for their clothes to be ironed they had had to move aside with difficulty every time someone would pass by. It was late morning, and on seeing a woman trudging along the lane towards them from the opposite direction, carrying two buckets full of something, Nishant motioned to Deena to get out of her way. Flustered by the urgency in Nishant's manner, he—in a hurry to move up—had tripped over, almost falling, but the woman with her heavy load had lost her balance, dropping one of the buckets right before them. Appalled, Nishant had slapped Deena. A commotion had erupted around the woman as the contents of her bucket poured out into the middle of the lane forming a thick gooey tawny splotch. The stench was unbearable. Deena had never seen it before, human faeces carried in buckets. People were cursing the woman as she hurriedly tried to put the produce of the dry latrines back into the bucket using her hands.

It was Deena's first visit to Vaidya ji's clinic-cum-house that sat off the main road and accessed by a short flight of stairs over a gutter. The patients, some of them children and their minders, sat on the wooden benches placed around the takht where Vaidya ji would sit; according to the woman beside whom Kanti had sat down, he was going to be late. She did not know why. It was odd. Vaidya ji was never behind time unless it was an emergency. Kanti made Deena who stood beside her to sit in her place and crossed to the back of the clinic to the wooden cubicle lined with narrow shelves filled with small tin canisters and bottles containing herbal medicines. The man who gave medicines to the sick according to Vaidya ji's prescriptions knew Kanti. He said she had better come the next day, confiding that Vaidya ji had taken his ailing son to the doctor's and might be long. Before leaving, Kanti took Deena to the basement to show him the small workshop where various herbs and roots were crushed into powder and mixed as per the traditional recipe. Furred with soot, the place was dingy. The sole naked bulb, hanging from the ceiling by a wire that was blackened with flies' faeces, looked distraught; the cloying odour from a cauldron placed over a large coal stove in one corner was hard to stand. Kanti told him that is how sugar was turned into honey. One of the men working there gave a phial filled with the honey thus made to Deena.

Rains were long gone; left in the air was no trace of humidity. The azure sky and crisp cool air had become the norm; nights were getting nippy. It was arguably the most agreeable time of the year, especially for the young, because within a space of about three weeks, it brought them two festivals, Dussehra and Diwali; Ram Mohan's absence on such occasions was the most desirable thing for his children, making them cross their fingers, and seven out of ten times, as if in answer to their prayers, Ram Mohan would travel out of town, being always due to attend one literary function or the other around these festival holidays. If nowhere else, then it was Parsadpur, which never ceased to beckon.

Dussehra had come and gone without Ram Mohan going anywhere, as the publisher wanted him to make full use of the quiet in politics and finish the book. So he kept at it. Moreover, to his children's distress, he now spent more time at home, reading the material on linguistics; would go to the publisher's only in the late afternoon to do the actual writing. Diwali being still a couple of weeks away, they were hunting desperately for the elusive sign of their father's travel plans. Nisha would ask Nishant everyday about Babu ji dropping any hint to the effect. One evening, the telephone rang. It was none other than Chaudhary Sahab to whom Nishant, who had answered the call, listened displaying whatever capacity he had for deference. Gulping for air, he responded mainly in monosyllables, and started breathing freely only after Baran Singh hung up.

The following morning, Ram Mohan left for Lucknow with a big suitcase, suspecting his trip to be long. His joviality the previous evening had filled everybody with much hope. He had laughed and said soon they would have a lot to look forward to; that caused them to be back with a bang to their daily fix of political news through radio and newspaper. People in the neighbourhood viewed their interest in politics as weird if not morbid. Few teenagers would pick up a newspaper for anything other than stories of sports and crime and films. This habit of theirs was broadcast in the locality by Bhatnagar Sahab's two daughters who had once dropped in for a chat with Nisha and Sandhya while Ram Mohan was out of town, and were shocked to find them discussing politics and referring to the likes of Indira Gandhi, Desai, Baran Singh, Saansad ji, Gupta and even Nijalingappa, the Congress president. Bhatnagar Sahab had imputed this to their father not letting them mix with other children and take part in things more appropriate to their age. He had no idea that only in Ram Mohan's success in politics lay the promise of his family's emancipation.

Nisha and Nishant got a buzz out of reading in the paper that the knives were out again in the Congress. Mrs Gandhi had accused in the opening salvo the party president of plans

to boot some of her loyalists out of the Congress Working
Committee (CWC), a charge termed baseless by Nijalingappa;
then, she demanded that the scheduled CWC meeting and party
conference be advanced. The rival faction condemned her for
pursuing an anti-party agenda. Things were heating up in Delhi.
Then one day they heard on the news that Indira Gandhi would
boycott the CWC meeting and hold a separate one, consisting
of her followers. Nisha suggested a visit to Mahavir Bhaiya's
place the next day, a Sunday. Nishant opted out saying he had
to meet a friend.

Mahavir Wilson lived in a decent locality not far from their
school, M.G. Girls Inter College. It was not a big house but
looked neat and friendly like Mahavir Bhaiya himself. As their
rickshaw turned down the quiet lane they could see his father,
Mr Wilson, sitting in a chair on their tiny front lawn bordered
by a short hedge, engrossed in the *National Herald*, his face
hidden behind it. He looked up only when the small wicket gate
was pushed open. Rising from the chair he exclaimed, 'What
a pleasant surprise!' He hugged them one by one, complaining
they were coming after such a long time. Together they went
inside. Mahavir Bhaiya's mother who had seen them from the
kitchen window came rushing with a broad, welcoming grin
on her face; Mr Wilson left after they all were seated in the
drawing room, saying he had some new family members for
them to meet. Mrs Wilson said Mahavir was getting a shave and
would soon join them. She enquired about their mother, saying
they should have brought her along. 'I hear Doctor Sahab has
gone to Lucknow. She could have come.' Among people close
to Ram Mohan, his restrictive rules at home were common
knowledge; they also knew he did not take kindly to anyone
casting doubt on his idea of discipline. Mahavir Wilson had once
said to them, 'I disapprove of Doctor Sahab's tyrant-like attitude
at home . . . But if I try to make him see the unreasonableness

of his behaviour, I would risk my closeness to him, depriving us
of the interactions we have now and then . . . '

Nisha was watching a chirpy Mrs Wilson. She and Sandhya
would marvel at her confident manner while conversing. Born
an outcaste and in poverty, she had never gone to school, but
after her marriage to an army person—also an outcaste—her
world had changed. Mr Wilson had taken it on himself to teach
her English at home, at least enough to read and understand;
a long exposure to life in army cantonments had helped her
to also pick up some spoken English, an ability she would not
hesitate to demonstrate off and on. Nisha and Sandhya were
hard put, rather found it surrealistic, to imagine that Wilson
Auntie had grown up in a place not different from Kuriyan, the
Harijan basti near Parsadpur.

Mr Wilson came back with his sister and Malti, and made
introductions. Nisha had heard of Sughari in connection with
Gayatri Masi; that how both the women, suffering at the
hands of their fate, had bonded together. About their common
benefactor, Nisha was to learn much later; only after getting
hold of Gayatri Masi's diary and reading her touching account
of Dixit ji's decency. Malti however was a stranger to them. As
they stared at her peculiar inky blackness, Mr Wilson recounted
how she came to be living with his family. 'I reckon you all
know Dixit ji, your father's late friend; he deserved to be CM
but was done out of it by this crafty Gupta, our present CM,
who was also behind Indira Gandhi's dislike of Baran Singh,
which—'

'Well, according to our Doctor Sahab,' interrupted his son,
'Baran Singh had incurred Indira Gandhi's animus long before
that . . . when at a party conference he had dared question her
father's proposal regarding some big agricultural reform.'

'I was talking about Dixit ji to whom we owe a lot,' pointing
towards Sughari, Mr Wilson continued, 'He gave shelter to my

sister after an untimely death of her husband . . . and the way
he rescued Gayatri from a dreadful life after her husband was
killed in a fire accident . . . albeit her life finally ended in tragic
circumstances as we all know, but Dixit ji had done all he could
to help.'

Sughari said with a faint smile, 'Gayatri took a very wrong
step. She betrayed Dixit ji and also me. She should have just
come to Lucknow,' wiping a tear from her eye, she said to Nisha,
'She had nothing but praise for your mother; during her visits
to Subhadra Kutir in Lucknow, she would prattle away about
Parsadpur. And Deena! She doted on him.' Looking abashed,
Deena avoided her gaze. Mr Wilson said, 'This is not the
occasion to make everybody sad by invoking these memories,'
and turning to Nisha, said, 'I hear you all wanted Mayank to be
shifted to Methodist High School . . . '

'Yes, Uncle, very much. But Babu ji's attitude is so rigid.
He thinks education through English is just a passing fad, and
people who send their children to these schools have no more
than a superficial understanding of things. He also says if we
really want to learn English nothing can stand in our way—'

'Yes, that's right but—'

'But Uncle, how can one refuse to see the obvious? You
stand any two students, one from Methodist and the other from
B.N.S.D., side by side, and see. A villager can tell them apart . . .
Even Babu ji's manner becomes more sophisticated when he's
talking to Mahavir Bhaiya.'

'Personally, I'm for English being the medium of instruction,'
said Mr Wilson. 'In Mahavir's case, I had no doubt as to which
language he should focus on. Yet I can't say for sure your father
is completely wrong. Maybe Hindi in time would manage to
topple English from its dominant position . . . But you should
not waste time lamenting what's not in your hand. Your father at
least acknowledges the value of English and would support your

endeavour in this regard. If you all try to learn it by yourself, I mean. You must all be reading English as one of your subjects though, surely . . .? And by the way—'

Nisha looked downcast as Mahavir Bhaiya cut in, 'Papa, I don't know why, but in Doctor Sahab's house, rules are abnormally harsh for the children. They cannot mingle freely even with each other if he's home, much less with any visitor, including myself.' Mr Wilson kept looking at his son before saying, 'Whatever could be the reason? I'm intrigued. This doesn't dovetail with his personality, he who in his interaction with others is so lively and generous . . .!' Sughari and Malti gazed at each other; Mr Wilson went on, 'He visited us about a couple of months ago to meet Sughari who used to be his hostess at Subhadra Kutir during his Lucknow trips. He was all charm . . . so jolly and full of fun . . . Difficult to imagine he can be so hard on his children. He was concerned for Malti and offered to help her in whatever way possible. Our house isn't that big so he suggested safe and good lodgings for Sughari and Malti in Parmat. I appreciated his kind thought but would not have my sister living separately in the same city. That we had kind of adopted Malti, I told him. It's quite natural for a father of two girls.' Nisha noticed a faint change of expression on Sughari's face, but then it was gone. 'By the way I must tell you,' continued Mr Wilson, 'Malti is learning English these days. Mahavir is the teacher. He sits with her for at least one hour daily. We once took her to Hudson School; Miss Wallace was happy to meet her. She promised that after she had become literate, the school would consider her for a job at its girls' boarding house . . . My point is, if she who comes from a poor and illiterate background can try for a better future then surely you can find a way to tackle any difficulty related to learning English. There's no comparison between her and your social circumstances.'

'But Uncle, now she's much better placed,' said Nisha. 'A lot of our attention is spent on how not to give Babu ji a chance to lose his temper. When he goes out of town, we put everything aside and try to make the most of the brief period of freedom.'

'Well, I can understand that. The young need their space and are entitled to their share of independence to do things consistent with their age and interest. Still, when things are as awkward as you tell me they are in your house, then you should also be willing to forgo things normal in other circumstances and devote instead whatever time and opportunity you get to what is crucial to your independence in the long run.'

'Papa, it's a big ask for people in their teens,' said Mahavir.

'It's not easy . . . It's not easy for even grown-ups to recognize the true worth of a compromise like this. But there is no other way. And aren't adverse conditions supposed to oblige people to think beyond their years?'

Mahavir chortled and said, 'Yes, but the atmosphere in their home has only helped them understand politics . . . the way it's played in Lucknow and Delhi. Not many of us can match them in that domain.'

Nisha said, feigning anger, 'Mahavir Bhaiya, you know well why we are so interested in politics . . . Once Babu ji becomes a minister or MP, it would be easier for us to act on Uncle's suggestion, utilizing our time in a more mature manner, for he would become too busy to be able to terrorize us into acting like statues at home.'

'I know . . . I know. I was just kidding.'

Nisha said, turning to Mr Wilson, 'Our chief purpose of coming today is to know what Mahavir Bhaiya thinks of the political moves of Indira Gandhi, because if the Congress fails to hold together then Baran Singh might become CM again.' Mr Wilson shot a glance at his son and rising said they should look at Mahavir's new study.

They were at Mahavir Wilson's place till late afternoon, had lunch and left only after tea and snacks. On the way back, Nisha and Sandhya shared their thoughts about the Wilsons' way of life, the cool relaxed atmosphere of their house. They would compare the freedom enjoyed by members of such households with the prison-like environment of their own. Nisha said, 'Wilson Uncle and Mahavir Bhaiya think that Babu ji is just a strict disciplinarian . . . over-concerned for his children wasting time on tittle-tattle, or getting into bad company. I wonder about their reaction if they were to come to know about Babu ji's suspicious and dirty mind.' Nisha also observed with some satisfaction how Wilson Uncle's family made even her and Deena's skin look fair, and were drawn into a discussion about Malti's peculiar blackness. But Deena—sitting squashed between his sisters in the rickshaw, with Mayank now looking too big for Nisha's lap—was stuck on Nisha Didi's remark about Babu ji being of 'suspicious and dirty mind'. How one's mind could be dirty was not clear to him.

On reaching back home, they found Nishant showing something to Sevak Lal and their mother—the reason he was so keen on meeting this friend of his. It was a flick knife known as Rampuri, after Rampur, a provincial town, where its manufacturing was a cottage industry. They all crowded around Nishant as he demonstrated over and over how the squeezing of a tiny brass lever made a large menacing blade leap out from its handle. Widely used by rogues, Nishant boasted about it being the most popular murder weapon in UP towns.

Indira Gandhi's mind was made up. That's what Saansad ji had told Ram Mohan. She would not relent in her fight against her decriers in the Congress. She wanted to run both the party and the country, without let or hindrance. Saansad ji was right. All attempts at making peace between the two groups came a cropper. A renowned editor of a national daily, sympathetic to the Congress, coaxed her and Nijalingappa to meet and thrash out a settlement, but she would not soften towards the latter; anon the CWC expelled her from the party, but by then, she had secured the support of the majority of the party MPs. Her faction at its meeting dismissed Nijalingappa as party president and picked one of her flunkies to head the new entity. Thus the Congress, the grand old party, formally split into two with Indira Gandhi in total control of the much larger group.

All eyes were on Congress-ruled states. Her next step would be to oust the chief ministers close to the former Congress bosses. Ram Mohan and Tiwari ji were at Baran Singh's place in Lucknow, when Shukla ji called on him. The relation between the two had now been limited to that of formal politeness during chance meetings. Shukla ji hugged Ram Mohan and Tiwari ji, saying he was meeting them after a long time. For about an hour he and Baran Singh talked alone. Shukla ji, Chaudhary Sahab told them later had had a message from Delhi, from his uncle who along with Indira's other lieutenants wanted the IRP to help her group to drum up a majority in UP Assembly after the overthrowing of Gupta government. The number of ministries or the kind of portfolios he desired in return could be discussed later. Baran Singh asked for some time to think, but he would hold firm to his decision not to lend support to either of the Congress factions, especially the one led by Indira Gandhi.

What Saansad ji had told Ram Mohan, corresponded with Chaudhary Sahab's own assessment of her politics—her autocratic approach to it. 'If I were Baran Singh, I wouldn't even think of it,' Saansad ji had cried. 'His sense of independence would run afoul of Indira ji's notion of her authority.' Baran Singh knew Saansad ji, who was not interested in messy provincial politics, had no axe to grind here. Delhi had always been his sole destination. Even when he was in the IRP he had wanted his friend to manage electoral politics—something too chaotic and banal to suit his disposition—and be the party chief or CM or whatever. Saansad ji was more comfortable in front of an informed audience and happy to work under any leader with a mass base.

Gupta in the meantime was busy making rounds of Delhi. His desperation was obvious. His past cooperation with the Congress Syndicate was proving difficult to shrug off; now with some help from Shukla ji's uncle, he was trying to dispel her coterie's doubts about his loyalty. He reminded them of the support he had once lent to the efforts required to prevail on Desai not to contend with Indira ji for the leadership of Congress Parliamentary Party. All these endeavours could only buy him a little time. The fall of his government in UP was inevitable, because once he jumped ship, the other faction of the once unified Congress would withdraw support from him. He knew that, and also that in UP, the old Congress had no future. But Indira Congress had.

Ram Mohan was in Kanpur when he heard on the AIR of Gupta's resignation. It was without warning. It had taken Indira Gandhi about three months after the great split to decide against his continuation as CM. She, it later transpired, had waited for her old enemies i.e. Gupta's old friends, to bring him down to help prove his claim that he was through with them. Nothing of the sort occurred. Gupta made a dash for Delhi but failed to get an audience with her. Shukla ji's uncle told him it was all over; the party had conveyed its decision to the Governor. He returned with no option but to put in his papers. Presently, Ram Mohan—whose book had finished and was in the press— came to Lucknow and found it plunged in unprecedented political excitement. All IRP MLAs had descended on Baran

Singh's residence, filling up its front, side and back lawns. With their offer of support some independents had also come, who while talking to journalists had so many good things to say about Chaudhary Sahab, who was in a closed-door meeting with Indira Gandhi's emissary from Delhi—Shukla ji's uncle—who had taken the same overnight train to Lucknow as Gupta after his failed Delhi-trip.

It was noontime. With winter on its last legs, the weather had become pleasantly warm. Tea and snacks were being served to everyone. The mood of Chaudhary Sahab's bungalow was decidedly upbeat. Ram Mohan went straight in to meet Savitri Devi, who was in the inner courtyard surrounded by a clutch of people. She signalled him to go into the dining room and presently joined him and called to the cook in the kitchen to get Ram Mohan tea and something to eat. 'Things have moved fast,' she said. 'Umakant Shukla is here with an offer from Delhi.' Ram Mohan's eyes glittered with anticipation. 'No, no, Indira ji wants the IRP to support the Congress government in UP,' added Savitri Devi hurriedly as if to arrest Ram Mohan's racing thoughts. 'But Chaudhary Sahab has declined, asking them instead to help form his government which they are welcome to join.'

'What about the other faction, the old Congress? What are they planning to do?'

'There's so much confusion in the group. Most of its members, according to Chaudhary Sahab, will end up knocking at the door of Indira Congress on bended knees. On top of that, the group's strength in terms of numbers is less than that of Indira Congress.'

'What's her response to Chaudhary Sahab's proposal?'

'Umakant ji is constantly on the phone with Delhi; he and Chaudhary Sahab are in the study. Nobody else is there. Let's see what happens.'

At length Indira Gandhi came around. Baran Singh was asked to meet the Governor with the letter of support from her party leader in Lucknow. She also made it plain her party would not be part of his government, which—conveyed in a 'take it or leave it' manner—left Chaudhary Sahab with no choice. Though aware she would not stick for long with the arrangement—that the rug would be pulled from under him whenever it suited her—he acceded. The same afternoon Baran Singh met the Governor and was invited to form government. The news drew flocks of politicians, supporters, friends and many others to his bungalow. Even the Ambassadors ferrying VIPs had to inch their way through the throng. Those with no red beacons were stopped at the entrance of the lane. Security personnel deployed at and around the residence of the CM designate got into the swing of ensuring order, for even the main road had now become edged with four and two wheelers.

Ram Mohan touched Chaudhary Sahab's feet. He embraced him, saying their patience and optimism had paid off. He wanted to take Ram Mohan out of the crowded drawing room, into some other place, to have a quiet word but was prevented by the arrival of Umakant Shukla and some state leaders of Indira Congress, who he took into the study from where they emerged after an hour, only to leave together for the Governor's house. Baran Singh was carrying the first list of his men to be sworn in as ministers under him. In the meantime, Tiwari ji too arrived, beaming. It was late at night when Baran Singh could meet them alone for some time. The list submitted to the Governor earlier in the day contained only eleven names apart from Baran Singh's. There would be a second and probably a third round too of swearing-in to complete his Cabinet. Ram Mohan's absence from among the probables surprised Tiwari ji, who asked specifically about his friend's fate. Chaudhary Sahab said Ram Mohan was one of his closest confidants; he could wait and need not worry. He would try to induct him as a minister a little later, 'When I expand my Cabinet . . . '

What made Tiwari ji wary was the way Chaudhary Sahab referred to Ram Mohan's loss in the last election, bemoaning that how a couple of hundred more votes for his party in the Fatehpur City seat would have made things so much easier for him. The allusion as understood by Tiwari ji was to the effect that making someone defeated at the polls a minister, entailed problems, more so when he had never been an MP or MLA before. The hint was substantiated by what Baran Singh had to say next. 'Ram Mohan would be on the top of my list if I were not dependent on Indira Gandhi. That I don't have a majority of my own also gives a mistaken sense of importance to the MLAs of my own party; mistaken because most of them would have lost fighting on any other party's ticket. Yet given the fluid situation and frenetic attempts all around at defections and horse-trading—with bundles of hard cash and ministerial prospects being dangled before MLAs—no wonder if some of my men find the bait irresistible.'

It was not hard to understand Chaudhary Sahab's concern. Even people like Shukla ji and his uncle, though supporting Baran Singh, would not let go of a chance for Indira Congress to rustle up a majority of its own. Tiwari ji asked if Ram Mohan could be sent to the Legislative Council in order to be a minister. Chaudhary Sahab said that was the only option, but it would be foolish to rush it. He would have to first take stock of this relationship with Indira Gandhi, born out of political exigency, and see how it plays out. 'Because,' Baran Singh said, 'her chief aim is to get her party in power here and thwart the emergence of any serious contender.' He then said that promoting Ram Mohan's political career was his responsibility. They should not bother. In the meantime, Ram Mohan along with other close aides should help him with matters pertaining to governance! Baran Singh said, 'It's not the right time for any of us to be anxious about our individual interests. We should address ourselves to what concerns us most now. For instance, how we plan to consolidate the gains made by the IRP . . . UP being ruled by a non-Congress party is an affront to Indira's inheritance. Not just UP but all the states as a matter of fact. She can't stomach the audacity of others to develop their own political base. She wants to be the paramount leader of the country and everybody else at her beck and call. Look how she's been indulging in populist measures. Over a week ago, her Bank Nationalization Act was annulled by the Supreme Court on grounds of it being unconstitutional; a few days later she got it issued afresh, through an ordinance signed by the President.'

'But Chaudhary Sahab, this move indeed has proved popular with the common man and endeared her to the masses who think the rich have been delivered a hurtful blow,' said Ram Mohan.

'That's true,' said Tiwari ji. 'The papers had reports and pictures of people celebrating in the streets in Delhi when the measure was first pronounced.'

'Crowds that had gathered in front of her house to cheer her and express their solidarity were told it was just the beginning,' said Baran Singh. 'This woman can't put up with people like me, people who have some standing with the public. To support the IRP in UP now is part of her long-term strategy, part of her plot to finish her old Congress colleagues and demolish me politically. After all I'm the first to have broken the stranglehold of the Congress, its monopoly, on this state. So we must view our being at the helm here as an opportunity to expand our support base . . . We don't know when she decides on her next move. Whenever she thinks the situation is in her favour, we will be shown the door . . . But then she might overestimate her strength, because my focus as CM would not be merely on matters of governance this time. I would also be looking to enlist support from other groups, the other Congress faction in the main.'

'It might then be difficult for you to include Ram Mohan on your Cabinet. At least not during this stint of yours, I mean,' said Tiwari ji with a sigh.

'No . . . whenever I see a chance he would join my government. Meanwhile, as and when Ram Mohan can take time out from his teaching and scholarly pursuits I'd like him to work for the party, addressing district-level public meetings organized by our local party workers in UP as well as in Haryana where the IRP is getting good response.' Ram Mohan's face lit up. The reaffirmation of Chaudhary Sahab's faith in him was enough to make up for any disappointment.

———————

To Ram Mohan's family, it came as a jolt of distress. They were not prepared for this denouement. Even the local Hindi paper had listed his name among those likely to join Baran Singh's Cabinet. But Ram Mohan's optimism and the reason for his omission restored their confidence. That he was charged with addressing meetings not only in UP but also in another state addressed the children's anxiety, who hoped to see him preoccupied; this would keep him away for a few days a month, if not more, affording them the vaunted freedom albeit in smaller amounts than if he was made a minister.

As to their Babu ji getting his due sooner or later, they harboured no doubt. Yet it was not enough to deflect the gaze of the ogre that loomed up as soon as the excitement in Lucknow had subsided, the ogre of their annual exams. Nisha and Nishant had to sit the twelfth board exam. Nisha loathed the idea of being tested on her ability to learn by rote, but that was not entirely the reason for her inability to get serious about exams, because if her efforts offered the possibility of her talent—her voice and locution—being applauded outside home, she could memorize a text of any length. This she had demonstrated twice when she had taken part in debating contests; written in Ram Mohan's glistering Hindi, she had rendered the scripts flawlessly, leaving few in doubt about her being the winner on both the occasions, though the second time, she had had to be content with the second prize. The girl declared the winner was said to be a relation of one of the three judges.

That she could prepare for exams in this manner had proved a non sequitur. She had given it her best shot but the motivation and energy would be missing. To commit to memory the answers to probable questions during exams was a common practice among students, but no sooner would she bring herself to sit hunched over a textbook than Babu ji would seize hold of her thoughts. Shinju Dalmia's account and Gayatri Masi's diary, though disturbing in their own way, seemed nothing beside what she had come upon once. Nisha was in class nine when on one occasion during a game of Kho-Kho Sandhya had a fall and hurt her arm; Nisha was asked to take her home. They had the spare key to the house as Sevak Lal was away in his village and Nishant had been sent on an errand to Parsadpur; Mayank had gone with him. Nisha and Sandhya were surprised to see the Rajdoot parked up ahead near the front veranda. It was only eleven o'clock. Babu ji was supposed to be in his college! Leaving Sandhya behind at the side door, Nisha made for the front door, the door to the big room, which was closed but wasn't bolted from the inside. Gently she pushed it. It took her a second to see the naked figures clearly. The girl looked quite young whom Babu ji, lying on top, was kissing furiously. Panicked, Nisha closed the door and ran back to Sandhya. Moments after the girl's departure—she had her dupatta around the face—Babu ji walked up to the side door and sent Sandhya inside; then holding Nisha's hands implored her to forgive him and forget about what she had seen. Since then, Nisha would tell Kanti, she had had trouble studying and would feel more at ease in school—in the company of her friends and teachers—than at home.

Nisha decided, as a face-saving measure, to skip her board exam this time. She got Kanti on her side, arguing it was better to skip than fail. Ram Mohan showed his displeasure and tried to reason with her, saying she should not think in terms of success or failure alone; the experience would come in handy when she sat the exam next year. But Nisha insisted and he agreed. Nishant, though not good at studies, usually managed to clear his exams. Sandhya as usual had been studying for her class nine exam, whereas Deena after his miserable performance in the half-yearly exam had emerged as one of the weakest students in his class. Two subjects, English and Mathematics, especially the former, became his bête noire. He had always been drawn to reading stories—ever since he had learnt to read Hindi—now it was something of an obsession. Even the school textbooks, the ones with some kind of a narrative—like those of Hindi and History or of Civics and Geography—he would read avidly, but with no anxiety to do well in the exam. Now the ghastly event being round the corner terrified him, knowing he would not even get a promotion to the next class much less the pass mark.

How else could it be described if not as divine intervention that saved Deena from an exercise in disgrace! After a horrible performance in the Civics exam, he was walking back home in the early afternoon alongside a friend whose exam had gone well. When they turned off the main road their attention was drawn to this roadside magician who, standing against the backdrop of the high wall of the Lal Imli Mill, was playing a brass flute and a drum at the same time as his young assistant shouted something or the other. Deena and his friend joined the spectators gathered around the two. Anon the man put down both the instruments and began some magic tricks and acts of jugglery, talking non-stop, and a bit later the magician, while moving around, started throwing questions one after another at his little partner who replied mechanically, without batting an eyelid. That was just the lead-in to their main performance, the flagship act.

The sight of the boy lying inert covered in a dusty check sheet, evocative of death, unsettled Deena, who with a sense of foreboding watched the man who was still flinging questions at his sidekick who was answering them as before, from under the shroud, his voice muffled. In the meantime, the man's words, assuming severity and a hint of menace, flashed with urgency. The dagger he had taken out from his large grubby bag was held threateningly. Deena implored his friend to leave. Some others in the crowd shifted in their places, looking to decamp. 'Don't make a move for God's sake! Everybody stay rooted to the ground!' the man screamed. Next, he dashed to the supine figure, and crouching on his haunches slid his hand under the shroud and drove the dagger into the boy's breast, wrenching a drawn-out grisly shriek. All held their breath. The knife seemed tearing at the boy's chest under the sheet. Deena stared at the macabre scene as the magician revealed his blood-drenched hands, clutching a chunk of flesh. The crowd gave a gasp of horror. 'What you see is the heart of this poor child,' the magician yelled. The boy flailing beneath the sheet turned Deena's stomach. The man cried, 'Please give generously if you care about this boy's heart being restored.' The people dipped into their pockets. With one hand gripping the heart and the other holding an aluminium bowl, the magician began to move along the ring. Soon, he replaced the heart and yanked the sheet; the boy rose sleepily as if nothing had happened, drawing a loud applause.

When Deena got back home, Kanti looked at his face in alarm and touched his forehead. He had a fever. Nobody asked how his exam went. Ram Mohan was not home. Telling him to lie down she asked Nisha to keep wiping his forehead with a wet cloth. Later he was taken to Vaidya ji in Parmat, whose herbal powders taken with honey he relished. His temperature had come down but he had also vomited once; Kanti was concerned about his next exam; Deena was delighted at his illness, a godsend, probably a result of the magician and his ghoulish act. The next day Deena ran no temperature, but he made a fuss about feeling weak; to make it look authentic he stage-managed his own fall while getting out of bed. Ram Mohan allowed him to drop out of the remaining exams, saying tenderly, 'He'll do better next year.' Thus Nisha and Deena both managed to avoid the painful process, let alone the embarrassment the results would have caused. Deena's relief from the exams was to be heightened soon.

One day when Ram Mohan was in Lucknow, Sukesh—Tiwari ji's son—dropped by. They all sat in the big room, listening to his exploits during his BA final exams that had just finished. 'I always pass my exams without preparation,' he claimed. It was not that it required no effort. It did. But it was a different kind of effort. He would go through the question papers of the past several years, making a guess at the questions likely to be asked; then one by one copy the answers onto neatly cut strips of paper. 'Once done, I forget about the exams and enjoy life as usual,' he boasted. Deena decided he could do that too.

* * *

Released from the tyranny of his textbooks, Deena now had kind of carte blanche to read whatever he liked. And stories, all kinds of them, were what he liked most. To Ram Mohan, anything not in verse was not serious literature, so the books of fiction at home belonged mostly to Kanpur University's syllabus of Hindi literature; Deena had read all of them, novels and collection of short stories, the Mahabharata—rather its shortened version—versified in simple Hindi, gifted to Ram Mohan by the author. Deena would read them over and over. And that summer, he chanced upon something new and riveting material.

In addition to newspapers, Ram Mohan subscribed to two Hindi weeklies, *Dharmayug* and *Saptahik Hindustan*—both reputable publications—that contained reports and articles about current affairs and cultural issues; the fictional pieces they published were too melancholy for Deena's taste. So without so much as flipping through their pages he would go straight to the page meant for children. Every week, if Ram Mohan was not home, these weeklies caused a scramble amongst them as each child in the house wanted to make a grab, though often it was either Nisha or Nishant who succeeded in getting to read them first. Now with everybody else busy with their exams, apart from him and Nisha, he had one of the weeklies to himself as soon as they were delivered. After reading its childrens' page, he—while turning its pages listlessly—came across this article about the long tradition of banditry in and around the ravines and forests associated with the river Chambal, which meanders through parts of central India before flowing into Yamuna.

What caught his attention first were the pictures accompanying the article, of some rather foreboding men, moustached variously, holding firearms, dressed as policemen. These were some of the old and contemporary dacoits of Chambal who called themselves rebels and who, as they claimed, were forced to take up arms by the unjust circumstances rife in their region. This particular article discussed how about a few years earlier many of them had been persuaded to surrender by this great disciple of Gandhi, Vinoba Bhave, who was all for bringing about a change of heart in the souls gone off the rails. Deena became hooked on these accounts of dacoits of Chambal, the power they wielded in their areas, the terror they evoked in their enemies, of their old and latest escapades. He now avidly awaited anything about them in the two weeklies or the newspapers; he and Mayank would cut their pictures and paste them on a notebook, making an album, and he could recount these legends fervidly to anybody willing to listen, astonishing them by his ability to mention even the minor, lesser-known figures of Chambal. He would separate the 'good' dacoits from the 'bad' ones and admire the former.

While Baran Singh was CM, Ram Mohan decided to get some development work done in Parsadpur. He was clear about three things first—a post office, a primary health centre and most of all an asphalt road, connecting Parsadpur as well as some other villages to the Grand Trunk Road. Ram Mohan spent a week in Parsadpur, holding meetings, visiting nearby villages, getting a charge from people's response to what he was up to. He had long chats with Badri and Gulab Singh and others; made people guffaw at his hilarious remarks. But the day before he was to leave, his euphoric sojourn was smudged by Padhaiya Bhaiya's gratuitous behaviour. Ram Mohan had drafted a letter to be sent to Lucknow—making out a case, a mere formality though, for the link road—which he had asked Badri to read to the people gathered on the chabootra opposite his former house, where now he would stay as Kalla Dada's guest, in the front room, the only concrete portion of the house, the room where Chhote Baba had lain sick before dying.

As Badri finished, there was an abrupt silence, which, unaware of its coming, Padhaiya Bhaiya, perched on the edge at the far end, had filled inadvertently. His words that what else could a failed politico do except write these pleading letters, prolonged the hush. Beset by unease people were saved by the timely response from Gulab Singh by way of his heavy village shoe that swam over the people and fell into the path beyond the chabootra, missing its target, of course. Padhaiya Bhaiya and his two friends bolted, making some of those present, laugh. For Gulab Singh, it was no laughing matter. He ordered his men to catch them while Ram Mohan sat quietly with a smirk on his face. Badri—conscious of Gulab Singh's rage—tried to cool him off. A little later Padhaiya Bhaiya and his friends after having received a few light blows of lathi were lying in front of them. They were not hurt much. His two friends were let off with some more beating and a warning. Kalla Dada watched helplessly as his son was kept pressed to the ground with two lathis digging into his ribs. He had heard what Padhaiya Bhaiya had said.

'Cut off his tongue,' bawled Gulab Singh. One of his men produced a knife from somewhere under his kurta, and got ready, asking his associates to hold him tight. Kalla Dada began to plead with Ram Mohan; those nervous of the development began to leave. Children were shooed away; some of the older ones lingered. Ram Mohan said to Kalla Dada, 'Did I say anything to result in this? Padhaiya said what he had to say; Gulab Singh is doing what he has to do . . . Let me tell you Kalla Bhaiya, this son of yours will one day make you wish you had let me handle him.' He gestured to Gulab Singh but not before the man with the knife had made a cut on Padhaiya Bhaiya's cheek; the blood oozing from it became difficult to distinguish from the mud that coated him; it had been raining earlier in the day.

* * *

In Kanpur, Ram Mohan's children made the most of his week-long absence. Nishant would mostly hang about with his friends, making an impression on them with the Rampuri; Nisha, Sandhya, Deena and Mayank went to the pictures once, and visited Naveen Market twice. They would also chat every evening with Bhatnagar Sahab's daughters, interrupted sometimes by Randeep Bhaiya, whom they thought was funny. Once, Saba—Zaheer Sahab's daughter—took them to their house where they sat for close to an hour, soaking up the pleasant and friendly ambience of the place, sighing as always at the thought of how their own home could not be like that. Mrs Zaheer treated them to ice cream and talked graciously about Nisha's impressive presence at school, and Zaheer Sahab who sat in his rocking chair on the other side of their drawing room lowered the paper he was reading and said, 'I hear Nisha has multiple talents.' 'That's right,' said Mrs Zaheer, 'She is a good athlete, excels at basketball, one of the two best in the school team. She's a pretty good debater as well.'

They had also got Mahavir Bhaiya to bring Sughari and Malti to their house for a day. Kanti was keen to meet them. Sevak Lal would not betray them to Babu ji, they were sure; he seemed to have lost interest in giving them away, which combined with the efforts of Nisha and others to keep him in good humour, had served them well. No, it could not have been Sevak Lal. Then how had Babu ji learnt of this transgression of theirs! Mahavir Bhaiya would later tell them that his Bua, Sughari, had let it slip while Ram Mohan paid them a visit after returning from Parsadpur.

The moment Babu ji entered the big room that day in the evening Nishant could smell out trouble. That look of solemnity that he had, was the look they all had come to fear. Nishant sat stock-still on the takht, head bent, eyes fixed on the book in his hands, tense and taut to the degree that his limbs ached.

When Babu ji asked him to get a glass of water—in a tone sounding only an audible extension of the look on his face—he felt relieved. Nisha and Sandhya could guess Babu ji's mood from Nishant's face when he came to their side of the house. Nisha's questioning gesture was in vain. He without so much as a glance hurried back with the glass of water in his hand, and anon, as they feared, Babu ji emerged into their room and sat down in the chair vacated hurriedly by Sandhya, who then was asked to take Mayank out of the room, after which he called out to Kanti who was in the kitchen. Deena had already shut himself in the toilet. 'Either you don't understand or ignore what I say,' he said to her when she entered.

'What happened?' said Kanti, cringing.

'You didn't tell me that Sughari and Malti came when I was away.'

'I had never met his Bua . . .'

'Okay . . . never mind . . . But what about you sending Nisha and others to their place before that, while I was in Delhi or Lucknow . . .

'I don't know why you're trying to make an issue—'

Ram Mohan reached out and struck her across the face. 'What do you know about them . . . Sughari and Malti?'

Kanti was sobbing and did not reply. Nisha said, smouldering, 'They both are very nice, and Malti is keen to get some education. Mahavir Bhaiya teaches her English at home.'

'You seem to be warming to Mahavir!' shouted Ram Mohan. 'I know what happens in this house in my absence.' He looked uncertain for a moment and then went on, 'Both the women are of loose morals. I have heard things said about them in Lucknow.'

Nisha could not hold back. 'Look who's talking!' There was a limit to the leverage she had with him, the limit she just crossed by mentioning the unmentionable, keeping quiet about which was what precisely had given her that leverage.

Ram Mohan leapt to his feet, lunged towards Nisha, grabbed hold of her hair and started pummelling her, his foul vocabulary in full flow. Springing across, Kanti pulled on his shirt's collar with all the strength her small frame possessed, screaming. The two upper buttons of his shirt snapped. Letting go of Nisha, he punched Kanti, knocking her down, and kicked her as she lay on the ground, accusing her at the top of his voice of being the mastermind of all this; that her mean, womanly nature, was taking its toll on the children's behaviour and their perception of him, painting him as the villain of the piece. Scared for her mother, Nisha shrieked in desperation that she would tell everybody what she had witnessed. Ram Mohan turned around and smacked her on the side of her head and yelled that he knew what she was up to these days, referring insinuatingly to Mahavir Wilson and the sports coach at Nisha's school. Her face contorted with disgust. Ram Mohan left. He came back a few minutes later to talk to Kanti alone, and told her he would not tolerate anyone threatening to cast a shadow on his public image, on the reputation he had built through years. Kanti must talk some sense into Nisha.

For four days Nisha could not go to school. She had contusions across one side of the face, also a black eye, while Kanti's old pain in one of the shoulder blades became worse; she was also hurt somewhere in the ribs. Their bodies remained sore for some days. They had been to Parmat already and were applying Vaidya ji's herbal ointment.

Baran Singh had barely been eight months in office when Indira Gandhi withdrew support. She wanted to run the state from

Delhi through the Governor. The day AIR broke the news Ram Mohan and Tiwari ji rushed to Lucknow. Baran Singh, out on a spree of meetings with various Congress leaders, was also in touch with people in Delhi, including Saansad ji. Having enough MLAs on his side to prove his majority on the floor of the House, he petitioned the Governor, though knowing it was useless as the latter was nothing but a stooge of Indira Gandhi, and she knew it was in order that Baran Singh was given an opportunity to prove his strength. But that's what she feared, for he had the support of the rival faction of the Congress, which would give him the requisite number. Then Saansad ji told him she might dissolve the current Lok Sabha and go in for midterm poll to take advantage of the enthusiasm her recent statist steps had generated among the masses. To have President's Rule in UP would help her party during the polls. However, Baran Singh, as a last resort, wrote to Indira Gandhi—reminding her of the Benaras episode and his tough stand as CM against his own coalition partners who had planned to hold her to ransom when she had gone there to attend the inaugural session of the international science conference; that he had had to pay the price for that principled stance—but in vain. She foisted President's Rule on the state, which was also a message to prospective defectors from other parties, interested in greener pastures; a message that their future lay only with Indira Congress. The strategy worked. Her group garnered enough numbers—within a month of the state being placed under President's Rule—to form government. She promptly appointed one T.N. Singh, a family loyalist, as CM, a man with no membership of either of the Houses of Assembly.

With Baran Singh out of power and no elections in sight, politics had come to a standstill for Ram Mohan—a state of affairs that made Tiwari ji particularly resentful. He was pissed off with Baran Singh who, according to him, could have done something more for his friend during his second stint. Though he would not say so to her face, he had refused to buy into Savitri Devi's argument that Chaudhary Sahab would have included Ram Mohan on his Cabinet after showing his strength in the Legislature, which was denied by Indira Gandhi's puppet-Governor. 'It was only to wheedle us into keeping our faith in her husband,' said Tiwari ji. 'We should start looking at other options.'

'It's time we did that,' said Ram Mohan gleefully. Tiwari ji had voiced what he himself had been thinking for a while.

There were only two people in the Congress with whom Ram Mohan could discuss his possible course of action. Though Shukla ji was no longer that friendly—particularly after he had brought Liyaqat Argali to Fatehpur to fight against him in the last Assembly poll—a rapprochement could well be brought about with him. Yet the idea of Shukla ji being his mentor was rather unpalatable to Ram Mohan; especially when he had a much better choice in the person of Saansad ji who was not only well-educated, an intellectual, but was fond of Ram Mohan; albeit Shukla ji was a bigger name in state politics, and his uncle was closer to Mrs Gandhi than Saansad ji. But Ram Mohan would always prefer Parliament to Assembly. He and Tiwari ji decided to go to Delhi to discuss the matter with Saansad ji.

Ram Mohan knew how everybody else in his family felt. The gloom in the house was hard to miss. One evening, they were all asked to assemble in the big room for one of those jolly interactions he would have with them, when the brothers and sisters and the mother, and even Sevak Lal—they all could sit together before him, an occasion that never failed to perk them up. He began by asking Kanti rather teasingly if she was ready to set up house in Delhi. Struggling to maintain her dejected mood, she said they could not move to Lucknow when Chaudhary Sahab was the CM and how Delhi could be a possibility now.

Ram Mohan said, 'Perhaps it all happened for our own good. Even if I had become a minister, we would have had to move back to Kanpur in a few months after Chaudhary Sahab was forced out . . . Nothing's happening in Lucknow now. Assembly polls are still far off; how good or bad Chaudhary Sahab will fare in them is anybody's guess. But chances of his becoming CM again are slim, almost negligible, as Indira Congress seems in ascendency across the country. I guess it's time I looked to other possible ways of furthering my chances in this game, the game of politics. In a week, Tiwari ji and I are going to Delhi to meet Saansad ji. Maybe there is . . .' The sudden call of the man who delivered their bread interrupted him. It was already dark. They could see through the open front door of the big room the silhouette of the man and his bicycle with a large wooden box tied to the carrier over the back wheel. Deena touched Mayank's elbow; Mayank in turn mouthed his desire for a fruit bun. Babu ji laughed and told Nishant to get everybody a bun. Mayank and Deena went with him. The delicious aroma along with the loaf of bread being sawed at made their mouth water.

Giving a glimpse of another political possibility, Ram Mohan lifted their mood. Cast down as they had been by Baran Singh's ousting, the thought of Saansad ji being in power was quite warming. That Babu ji would soon be leaving for Delhi doubled their delight; Nisha's especially, for in her school—after the long spell of heat, humidity and the rains—sports activity was in full swing. She had been participating in practice sessions off and on, in tune with Babu ji's travels out of town. The inter-school basketball tournament was about to take off. With Babu ji gone for a few days she would be able to play at least in some of the practice matches to be held before the tournament. And Ram Mohan left for Delhi sooner than expected. The day after he had told them about other alternatives, Tiwari ji came. They were off the next day.

They had hoped he would be away at least a week. But he was back in less than four days. He had had a long and fruitful meeting with Saansad ji, who after chewing over the question, had spelt out his view, which made perfect sense, freeing Ram Mohan from the clutches of ambivalence over his next course of action. In the evening, Ram Mohan gathered everybody in the big room and let Tiwari ji have the floor; after clearing his throat, he paused and began with his usual deliberateness, 'At the end of the day our association with Chaudhary Sahab has been of little political significance. Yes, if we had won the last Assembly election, Doctor Sahab would've got a Cabinet position, no doubt. But that loss was hardly a loss. If anything, it proved our electoral strength which Chaudhary Sahab had acknowledged yet failed to give Doctor Sahab his due. The way things stand the fate of the IRP looks uncertain. On the other hand, there seems no looking back for Indira Gandhi; she is now in absolute command of things . . . In light of all this, our trip to Delhi was very productive. Saansad ji has suggested a neat script that we should follow. Technically, we won't leave Chaudhary Sahab for now. Indira ji will go in for midterm poll soon, very soon, of which Saansad ji is sure. And Doctor Sahab will contest against her man Udai Pratap Singh again. If we win, Saansad ji would arrange for Doctor Sahab to meet Indira Gandhi, after which he would join the Congress . . . If we lose, the script would remain more or less the same, that is, there might not be a meeting with her before joining the Congress but Saansad ji would tell her about Doctor Sahab's strong support base in Fatehpur. We would have polled enough votes to back the argument. Saansad ji would then make a pitch for Doctor Sahab to be sent to Rajya Sabha, the Upper House of Parliament.'

'Now you know I wasn't kidding,' said Ram Mohan to Kanti, laughing. 'So make ready for a life in Delhi soon, maybe in a year or two.' The former buoyancy returned to Ram

Mohan's household. Kanti told Nisha it was the right time to ask permission for playing in the first match of their basketball tournament, beginning two days later. The next day, shortly after Tiwari ji left, she got Babu ji's nod. The match—their first—they won comfortably with Nisha scoring the highest number of baskets from her side. After reading her name in the local paper, Ram Mohan warned her against playing anymore. Crushed, Nisha begged for being allowed to play at least till the tournament was over. Kanti's intervention brought her a cutting rebuke from him; he blamed her for the way Nisha was developing and said she was more interested in wining these silly matches than passing her exams; the thrill of being praised by male spectators and that male coach was too precious for her to let go of.

Nisha had no choice but to inform their sports teacher of her unavailability for the remaining matches. The teacher gaped at her in disbelief. With no one else to take Nisha's place, they were as good as out of the tournament. She took Nisha along to meet Mrs Zaheer who as if thinking aloud said that for her to approach Nisha's father yet again with another request was not right. Earlier he had acceded but might not be so amenable this time and might see it as an undue interference in his family matters. However, Mrs Zaheer suggested a better way, namely to make the request rather official. She and the sports teacher went to see the principal who after being apprised of the situation agreed to write to Nisha's father. She dictated the letter right then and there, and a school peon was dispatched to deliver it.

Mrs Agha, the principal, came from an elite Muslim background and had spent some time in England as a young girl with her family. Her letter in English talked of Nisha's talent, of how critical her presence in the school's basketball team was and that their school's reputation could be at stake. Its civilized voice, polite phrases and overall tone, acknowledging

his—Dr Ram Mohan's—authority, made him read the letter
twice before he read it to all of them, explaining in Hindi
how beautifully drafted it was. That letter won the day for
Nisha. Later, when the tournament ended—which M.G. Girls
Inter College lost after reaching the final—there was a small
function organized by their sports department, where the effort
of the basketball team was lauded. Some of the performances,
especially of Nisha's, were mentioned glowingly by the sports
teacher, the coach and Mrs Agha herself. Later Mrs Zaheer
said to her, 'I wonder how your father, who is so funny and
lively, and appears very liberal and large-hearted whenever he
drops around for a chat and a cup of tea, can be so repressive
at home!' Nisha was taken aback at the revelation. Not by
what Mrs Zaheer had to say about him, but by the fact that
he visited them at all. It was not easy to picture him sitting
in their house, having tea and a hearty conversation, an utter
oddity to her. There could be no greater mismatch between the
two lifestyles. It did not surprise Kanti who said in a deadpan
manner that attractive women could alter their Babu ji into an
entity unknown to his own family.

About a month after Ram Mohan and Tiwari ji's return from
Delhi, the Lok Sabha was dissolved and general election was
announced, proving Saansad ji's prognosis right. Caught on
the hop, the opposition parties cried foul and called for the
installation of a national government. General election under
Mrs Gandhi's minority government was bad news for them.
Her government remained heedless of the demand as well as
of some other questions regarding incomplete voters' lists or
the Election Commission lacking enough supporting staff, etc.
Instead, she launched herself into a two-month-long campaign,

trotting tirelessly around the country, addressing innumerable meetings, with the entire administrative machinery waiting on her hand and foot.

Ram Mohan and Tiwari ji went to Lucknow to meet Chaudhary Sahab. To keep him in the dark about their plan to run for Parliament from Fatehpur would have been scurrilous. Saansad ji had also asked them to seek his blessings. Baran Singh was shocked. He thought Ram Mohan should direct his energies to the Assembly seat he had come so close to winning. Other than that, he wanted to groom Ram Mohan for something else, some key position in his party at the state level, an idea he had kept to himself, waiting for a suitable moment to announce it. He asked Ram Mohan to have patience and leave the question of his political aspiration to him; that in the end, he would not be disappointed. But patience was never Ram Mohan's forte. Ram Mohan and Tiwari ji listened to Baran Singh with no remonstrance or interjection.

All the main opposition parties came together against Indira Gandhi. Ram Mohan did another trip to Delhi, and as suggested by Saansad ji wrote to Desai, the leader of whatever remained of the old Congress, who in his response acknowledged Ram Mohan's impressive showing in Fatehpur earlier twice and made it clear that anyone able to give Indira Gandhi's men a run for their money was welcome; that the grand alliance under his leadership would support even independents if they were up to it. Ram Mohan pitched into making preparations for the battle. He, with Tiwari ji at his side, held a meeting of his former lieutenants in Fatehpur; this time they also won Deep Narayan over, the man whose betrayal had cost him the Assembly election; the assurance that Ram Mohan was no longer keen on state Legislature had done the trick. Yet the bargain could not have been struck without the active cooperation of Pratap Singh who promised to support Deep Narayan in his poll outing in the future; in return the latter would help him get elected as their area's Block Head, a post for which only village headmen could vote. Things were looking so good that Tiwari ji in the very first meeting of the campaign team declared, 'However small a margin, we will win this time.'

FIVE

Just before leaving Parsadpur/Ballamgaon Nishant had Gulab Singh speak to Babu ji on his cell phone. 'People here are reluctant . . . to have Deena buried in their midst . . . He took his own life . . . you know what I mean . . . ' It did not surprise Ram Mohan, who told Nishant they would hold the cremation that day itself. 'Give me a ring when you cross Fatehpur; we'll start making arrangements . . . and come directly to the cremation ground. We'll be waiting.' A little over two hours later we were passing by Fatehpur; Nishant called his father, and soon after hanging up, he gestured towards a building—old and decrepit—on the left, as we drove along the GT Road going through the city. 'That's where Babu ji's election office was; it was the first time I took part in the campaign. It was the fifth general election—a midterm poll—and Babu ji's third outing.'

'You were all of eighteen then,' said Badri as Nishant went on to tell us stories from that campaign, with the former pitching in.

* * *

To be able to prove his worth to Indira Congress, it was crucial that Ram Mohan performed well in this election. Just as the campaign picked up steam, a terrorist act against India threatened to escalate into something serious between India and Pakistan. The hijacking of the Indian Airlines Fokker Friendship airplane by the militant outfit Al Fatah sent New Delhi into turmoil. The hijackers—received like heroes in Lahore by Pakistani authorities—threatened to kill all the thirty-two people aboard if India failed to release their thirty-six guerrilla brethren held in Kashmir. India's rejection of the demand gave a scare to Ram Mohan and Tiwari ji. If the terrorists made good their threat the election might become the first casualty of the ensuing bellicosity between the two countries. To their relief, however, nothing of the sort happened. All the passengers and the crew were allowed to go before the hijackers blew up the plane.

The electoral battle for Parliament was back on track, and 'Remove Indira' was the slogan taken up big-time by the opposition. Coined by Raj Narayan—the socialist and a staunch follower of the late Congress-baiter Lohia—the slogan was to boomerang on the opposition. Her leftist coterie replaced 'Indira' with 'Poverty' and got their own slogan 'Remove Poverty', which she would mouth all the time, 'They say "Remove Indira", I say "Remove Poverty"', as if the effort to rid India of poverty was the same as the effort to unseat her, but the masses bought into the allure of the phrase, the charm of its abstraction and sentimentality. Indira Gandhi swept back to power with a two-thirds majority in Lok Sabha. The parties that had formed the Grand Alliance against her were decimated. Though he lost to Udai Pratap Singh again, Ram Mohan improved on his earlier performance—a remarkable feat in view of the 'Indira Wave' sweeping across north India—and polled again the highest numbers of votes amongst the losers in UP.

Saansad ji himself won from Allahabad, his old bastion, by a landslide. A while later when Ram Mohan and Tiwari ji went to Delhi, Saansad ji had already discussed his case with Mrs Gandhi, who had listened to what he had to say about the Hindi scholar's electoral exploits, his power of oratory. She had shown interest without promising anything; had asked Saansad ji to remind her of him once the crisis in the neighbourhood subsided. But the crisis—namely the rapidly worsening relations between the Pakistani mainland and its other part called East Pakistan which lay on the other side of India—would not subside. Till that point Ram Mohan was not heedful of the calamitous situation developing on India's western and eastern side; with his political fate linked to its resolution—also for fear of appearing insular if caught in the midst of a discussion on the subject—he began to follow the issue closely, remembering how about a decade earlier a confab involving Saansad ji, Chaudhary Sahab, Dixit ji and others in Lucknow, had revealed to him his ignorance about the complexity of the quarrel between India and China over the border, resulting in that war.

He made an effort to have a clear idea of whatever was happening in Pakistan and how it affected India. India had, after the hijacking episode, banned Pakistani airplanes from its airspace, denying it the shortest route by air to its eastern part, which forced Pakistani aircrafts to make a long detour as the situation deteriorated further. The crisis was the result of West Pakistan having long treated its Bengali-speaking part, the eastern wing, in the worst possible manner. Exploited to the hilt by West Pakistan—where people were taller, fairer and spoke Urdu and Punjabi—East Pakistan was looked down upon, because of their language, skin colour and smaller build. Though larger in numbers, these Bengali Muslims were allowed no place in the country's army, economy, polity, and bureaucracy; and that—the searing sense of being wronged— had found its utterance in a people's movement in East Pakistan. The campaign that had begun with the demand for democracy and autonomy, had after being brutally subdued, been recast as freedom movement. In an attempt to bring the situation under control, General Yahiya Khan had, just a few months before, called an election, and contrary to what he and his cronies were expecting, Sheikh Mujib's Awami League secured a majority in Pakistan's National Assembly, winning almost all the seats in East Pakistan. Pakistan People's Party of Bhutto and Islamic parties in West Pakistan were dead set against Sheikh Mujib forming government. Denied to lead the country despite having a majority, the latter launched a civil disobedience movement, which—about a month after Ram Mohan had met Saansad ji in Delhi—was met with Yahiya Khan imposing martial law there. Sheikh Mujib was arrested; his party banned. Thus began Pakistan army's diabolically vicious dance in East Pakistan, the dance of savagery and barbarism against Bengali Muslims and Hindus. The atrocities—large-scale rapes and the massacre of civilians bordering on genocide—resulted in tens of thousands of refugees—Bengali Muslims, Hindus, Christians, Buddhists— streaming across the border into India every day.

The police and paramilitary units of East Pakistan, most of them, had rebelled. A number of Awami League leaders giving Pakistan army a slip had based themselves in Calcutta and formed with India's help a formidable outfit called the Liberation Army to wage a ferocious guerrilla war. Worried at the events next door, and with no solution in sight, Indira Gandhi proposed a motion in Parliament, expressing India's 'solidarity with the people of East Bengal.' The motion, calling for 'immediate cessation of the use of force and the massacre of defenceless people,' sought to pledge India's support to the beleaguered Bengali people. When Ram Mohan visited Delhi again, Saansad ji asked him to sit tight as nothing could be done regarding his Rajya Sabha thing for now. They would have to wait it out. His effort and patience would not go waste, he assured him.

About Saansad ji's assurance, he told everybody at home and explained how their tryst with Delhi was now tied to the

resolution of the problem confronting the country. What lit up
their faces was the fact that Saansad ji had already spoken to
Indira Gandhi about Babu ji; then to their delight, Ram Mohan
announced they would all go to watch a movie. Their results
had just been declared. Nisha had finally passed her twelfth
board with a third division; Nishant who had failed the previous
year got through too. Sandhya was third among the top eight in
Kanpur district, and her help and supervision had led to Mayank
faring well in his class in Hudson School. Deena had been
promoted to class seven thanks largely to the cheating method
taught by Sukesh, Tiwari ji's son.

No other form of entertainment, nothing whatsoever,
could even distantly resemble the pleasure that Hindi films
gave Deena. No sooner did the big screen in a cinema hall
come to life than he would cease to be conscious of anything
else around him; so when the hero in the movie they were
watching descended on the villain's den to rescue the heroine
in distress, Deena jumped up and screamed with excitement
and was brought back to reality by a slap from Babu ji. His
craze for movies was growing exponentially. In his and other
schools, there were students who would bunk off regularly to
go to the movies. What a great way, he thought, of indulging
one's passion with nobody at home getting wind of it!

Months slipped by with no sign of the situation easing off in
East Pakistan. Refugees from "Bangladesh" swamped the Indian
states abutting that part of Pakistan. Indira Gandhi had travelled
to Calcutta to visit some of the innumerable camps that had
cropped up all around the city. There was too much to stomach,
the sheer scale of suffering. 'She returned to Delhi upset, fuming
at Pakistan,' Saansad ji had told Ram Mohan who had gone to

meet him in Allahabad when he was visiting his hometown-cum-Parliamentary constituency. There had been a significant development in his case. According to Kapur, Indira ji had handed the chit given by Saansad ji to her PA, instructing him to place it before her after she was through with Pakistan. Ram Mohan's brief introduction along with his electoral record was what that piece of paper carried. 'That was thoughtful of her, which convinced me of what Kapur and others had been telling me; that she values my association more than I thought,' said Saansad ji, sitting on the front veranda of his house in Allahabad.

'But, Saansad ji, as things stand . . . I mean she has so much on her plate, it doesn't seem—'

'Oh come on, don't be a spoilsport! I can say with a fair amount of certainty that your Rajya Sabha membership is just a matter of time. The present crisis is going to be over soon. Just keep it to yourself . . . what I'm going to share with you . . . a piece of inside information,' Saansad ji stopped to cough as Ram Mohan waited eagerly.

'India can't sustain the present situation for long, the influx of refugees and what not. To look after these many people, variously damaged people, whose number has risen to almost a crore is beyond the means of a poor country like ours. Indira ji is about to go on a tour of western countries along with the two of her Kashmiri gang to internationalize the issue; to stress that this can no longer be viewed as merely an internal problem of Pakistan . . . How India alone is supposed to deal with such a huge drain on its limited resources. It's the responsibility of the world community to ensure the speedy return of normality in East Pakistan to enable the refugees to go back.

'Over two months ago, India signed a peace and friendship treaty with the Soviet Union during Andrei Gromyko's visit, which she followed with her own trip to Moscow a month later. She met Brezhnev and Kosygin and returned with an assurance that if need be Soviet Union would help India militarily. To be ready for a rapid military action she had already asked the army. If it were not for the weather—the monsoon, that makes all the small and big rivers in East Pakistan go berserk—she would not have waited even this long. The way things stand, the outbreak of war between India and Pakistan is a strong probability . . . If you ask me, Ram Mohan, it's a certainty come December, because by then, according to our army chief, the threat of China coming to its ally's aid will have been reduced drastically because of heavy snow blocking most of the routes up there.'

'What about America? A month before Gromyko, Kissinger had come, and you told me that in the event of war between India and Pakistan we should not expect help from his country . . . that is what Kissinger told Indira ji, which can also mean that America might lend a hand to Pakistan. Don't you think? In that event, who knows for how long Pakistan can hold India off!'

'Obviously, with India's increasing closeness to the Soviet Union, Pakistan has become America's natural ally. More so after Pakistan helped America and China to break the ice, paving the way for reconciliation between the two hostile, communist and capitalist countries. And who has been Pakistan's main supplier of arms? America! But you don't worry, India will crush Pakistan with little hitch. The possibility of America's active intervention has been undermined by our friendship treaty with the Soviet Union. So the days of this morass are numbered, and as soon as things stabilize, I'll broach your case to the PM again.'

Now Ram Mohan became ever more absorbed in whatever appeared in the papers or news broadcasts on radio about the ongoing Indo-Pak quarrel. Indira Gandhi had returned from her tour. Except for America and its allies, most other nations were sympathetic to what she had had to say. Just as she was set to order military action against Pakistan, India was saved from being the one to start the war as Pakistan, in a surprise move, tried to steal a march, carrying out air-raids on various military airfields in western India. It was past midnight when Indira Gandhi went on air to tell the nation about the 'full-scale war launched by Pakistan' and about India's resolve to give the aggressor a pasting. The so-called Bangladesh Liberation War was well under way.

All through the period of hostilities, there was a carnival atmosphere in the city to be tinged with fear every time an air-raid siren went off during the night, which however, gave an exciting edge to the convivial mood as people would hasten to switch the lights off. Full of beans, they speculated about India's treatment of Pakistan after the victory, about which everybody agreed. Newspapers and magazines would not tire of describing the way Indian troops were thrashing the enemy forces; and Gnats, India's small fighter aircrafts, making short work of Pakistani Sabre Jets, supplied by America. Deena would, in a state of excitement, read all the accounts of the war appearing in *Dharmyug* and *Sapatahik Hindustan* and explain to Mayank how India was making mincemeat of Pakistan. The mood in Ram Mohan's household was electric. Tiwari ji was also in Kanpur. Mahavir Wilson dropped in almost daily, sometimes accompanied by his father; every afternoon there would be a small gathering of friends to discuss India's awesome showing in the ongoing conflict. Kanti, Nisha, Sandhya were kept on their toes by constant demand for tea and refreshments. Most of his friends and acquaintances now knew Ram Mohan's nomination to the Rajya Sabha was a done deal; that not long after the conflict was over he would make his debut in Parliament. His closeness to Saansad ji was no secret.

Hardly a fortnight into the conflict, India won a conclusive victory. Pakistani troops in Bangladesh—ninety-three thousand in total—were forced to surrender. There was an explosion of pictures of the occasion, the moment of glory, in the papers.

The euphoria swept through the country, erasing memories of the shaming at the hands of China about a decade earlier. Indira Gandhi was called Durga, the goddess—the slayer of evil-doers. A week later Ram Mohan got a call from Saansad ji who told him about how busy New Delhi was, dealing with the delicate post-war issues. 'The decision on your matter might get deferred a little, but as to its certainty you should have no doubt.' That was not the main purpose of the call. The developmental project in and around Parsadpur sanctioned during Baran Singh's regime was being held back by the Congress government, and Saansad ji, whose help Ram Mohan had sought, was—as it turned out—not on good terms with T.N. Singh who had suspected him to be behind the petition filed in the Supreme Court, challenging his appointment as CM on the grounds that he was not a member of the Assembly at the time of the nomination. But months before the war, Indira Gandhi had replaced him with another flunkey of hers. This man, the new CM who, with a round sandalwood paste mark on the forehead, his crown flaunting a big *choti*—the lock of hair kept in a knot—looked more like a Hindu priest than a politician. Every morning he spent hours performing puja. To this man, Kamlapati Tripathi, Saansad ji had spoken about the asphalt road linking Parsadpur and other villages to the Grand Trunk Road. Now Ram Mohan was to meet the state PWD minister who was seized of the matter. Saansad ji's call in the main was about that. But even that was a sign of things getting better, something for Ram Mohan to feel happy about.

———————

Mitra family, the landlords, had for some time been talking about moving back to Calcutta, their ancestral city, but now because of Bade Babu's indifferent health, they were in a hurry to dispose of their property, except for a small portion as Mr and Mrs Banerjee were to stay back because of their jobs. All their tenants were informed—Ram Mohan, Zaheer Sahab and Bhatnagar Sahab. With the rental laws skewed towards tenants, few would dare buy a property thus occupied. To get it vacated needed financial or muscle power, or if one had time and patience and could afford a lawyer, there was this third option, the option of a court battle, the battle of attrition, that could go on and on for years on end. Sometimes the buyer of such a property would choose the legal way only to wear the tenant down, forcing them to have the case settled out of court, or vice versa as the tenant could also use the same tactic. In many cases, the owners were obliged to sell their property to the tenant for peanuts.

Pressed for time, Mitras were more than willing to close a deal with their tenants. Ram Mohan was more than happy to oblige Bade Babu, his landlord, and bought the portion of the big bungalow he had been renting—in addition to some land in front and on the side, and a room that had a bath and latrine attached—for a great deal less than what the property was worth in the open market. Zaheer Sahab, who was about to be transferred to some other city, declined the offer. To forgo a chance like this was not easy for Bhatnagar Sahab, the chance to own the place where he had lived for so many years. He dawdled before saying no to the offer. True to his nature, he was laughingly frank about it, about the fact that the job of teaching at this inter-college was his sole source of income, and the family he had to look after was large. Things would have been easier a year or so before, before the untimely death of Mrs Bhatnagar who had been a teacher in the D.G. College, a sister institute of D.A.V. College. Being the only girls' degree college in the vicinity, Nisha was also a student here, doing BA. Mrs Bhatnagar's death had left her family with only one salary that of her husband's, who unlike Ram Mohan had no other assets to count on. Bhatnagar Sahab told Bade Babu he had no cash to spare and that he was free to find some other buyer. One more reason Bhatnagar Sahab thought better of it was that a close relation of his was building some flats on one of the many pieces of land he owned in the city; he had offered that once ready Bhatnagar Sahab could move into one of them and live there for free as long as he wished. Ram Mohan was thankful they would soon leave their neighbourhood. But it was not to be soon. They would continue to live there for close to two years to the chagrin of the new owner, a goldsmith.

The thought of Zaheer Sahab's departure made Ram Mohan a trifle put out. 'They're affable and courteous, if a bit reserved, and have a quiet liveliness about them, unlike Bhatnagars who are a crowd—loud and cacophonous. What kind of a man is he, this Bhatnagar? It doesn't matter to his children if he's home or not. They carry on uninhibited. He even joins them when they scream and guffaw. What vile people!' Afterwards, Kanti muttered to Nisha he was upset because of Mrs Zaheer whose company he was going to miss.

What a shock it was to Deena and his siblings! The idyllic setting, their immediate surroundings, which they had come to take for granted, was being taken apart, but their grief at the unravelling seemed a joke compared to the enthusiasm of those bringing about the change. Despaired at not getting possession of the property he had just acquired, any time soon, the goldsmith—Bhatnagar Sahab's new landlord—was adding one more floor to it. Zaheer Sahab had left. Their place was being altered to accommodate two families—the families of Goyal brothers, the new owners—and the most visible change was that the house became invisible from the lane. A high, jail-like thing, had replaced the erstwhile low boundary wall. Deena recalled seeing Mrs Zaheer standing on the veranda while their rickshaw had moved along that wall when he and his mother had come to live in Kanpur. And coming up fast was a businessman's two-storey house on the plot he had bought, which comprised most of what had served as children's playground where Bade Babu and Mr and Mrs Banerjee used to take a stroll round the henna hedges along the wide dirt path on which during summers, Ambika—the gardener—sprinkled water. This whole portion in front of Ram Mohan's house—the dirt path, the henna bushes, and the main boundary wall beyond them—could be seen from the window of the room of Kanti, Nisha and Sandhya. Soon all this would become a memory. The part behind Ram Mohan's property—the part where Bade Babu had lived—was the new abode of Khatri Sahab, a senior clerk in the Kanpur branch of Reserve Bank of India. Though variously employed and of different castes, the fact common to these new arrivals was that they had come from the old parts of the city, and the men, the family heads—barring the goldsmith of course—had had their college degrees of one type or the other. Yet there was little that was 'educated' about them. Not in the sense the Zaheers, the Bhatnagars, the Banerjees, the Mitras or Ram Mohan sounded educated.

Ram Mohan's house ceased to offer any outside view up ahead. The entire open space in front, including the henna hedges and other things—was gone. The only consolation for them—Kanti, Nisha and Sandhya—was that they still could see the visitors from the tall side-window that looked out on to the path leading from the entrance by way of an iron gate in the corner on the farthest side of their property. Ram Mohan had got the gate installed after the purchase and demarcation of the property. He initially frowned on the Khatri household. They were as noisy and loud as Bhatnagars, if not more, and minus of course the latter's taste and sophistication. Ram Mohan's main worry was on account of the three teenage Khatri girls, all pretty

and in various stages of bloom, and the boy Rammu in his mid-
teens; while Khatri Sahab's youngest child was just a few months
older than Mayank. Then Nisha learnt from one of the Khatri
girls that Babu ji had already dropped in on them—twice within
a week of their moving into their new house—something he
had kept to himself, but soon it became a regular thing in the
evening. Now Nishant knew where to find him in case of
any telephone call or visitor. The task fell mostly to Deena's
lot; on every such occasion he would find him in a hilarious
mood, laughing and making everybody else laugh, and—after
hearing his mother and Nisha talk about Babu ji's fondness for
Mrs Khatri—he could also sense, whenever he went there to
call him, that Babu ji's funny talk was meant chiefly to amuse
her; she appeared to enjoy his company. Deena could also
guess why their mother and Nisha Didi were apt to find fault
with Mrs Khatri, the way she looked and talked. Her habit of
chewing pan (betel) had taken its toll on her teeth and mouth,
and she also seemed a touch hunchbacked; no, that would be
too severe—maybe just a stoop it was—while her speech and
manner, though chirpy and bold, lacked elegance. Yet there
was enough in her to make men like Ram Mohan feel attracted.
Her personality was a far cry from that of Mrs Zaheer, but as
Kanti once muttered, that as long as the form was sufficiently
female, Ram Mohan could compromise on ritualistic notions of
feminine charms. Men such as her husband, according to Kanti,
were able to derive a bit of a romantic thrill from the mere
company of women like Mrs Zaheer and Mrs Khatri, but if it
was someone like their former cleaning woman, nothing short
of copulation would work. Ram Mohan's children however did
not mind his frequenting the house of their new neighbour,
which allowed them not only a little freedom at home but had
made him soften towards Khatri siblings. Though wary of them
coming to his house or his children going to theirs, he would

not react that harshly on catching them together. That could be partly because of Nishant being apparently indifferent to the good-looking girls next door.

Still busy sorting through the issues thrown up by the end of the war, Indira Gandhi had little time for anything else. Sheikh Mujib, the undisputed leader of the new entity Bangladesh, had already been to Delhi twice after his return from Pakistani jail. At about the same time, many Indian states had gone to the polls, producing a Congress landslide. On the other hand, Pakistani leader Bhutto finally hinted at his inclination to resolve peacefully the issues at the core of Indo-Pak animus. Keeping himself conversant with all these developments, Ram Mohan waited to hear from Saansad ji. It was a Sunday morning during late summer when the telephone rang. He was having jalebi at Khatri Sahab's place. When the operator on the other side asked Nishant to hold the line, he wildly gestured to Deena who rushed out. Ram Mohan came running. Saansad ji's PA asked him to wait a second before the former came on the phone. The beam on their father's face was enough for Nishant to sense that things were astir; the moment finally seemed to be here, the moment that would herald a new dawn in their lives. As he replaced the receiver, Ram Mohan was struggling to contain how pleased he was. Telling Nishant he would be back soon and have a chat with them all, he went back to Khatri Sahab's to finish his jalebis. The sudden flurry in Babu ji's room had brought Nisha and Sandhya to the usual spot beside the door in the passageway that led to the big room, from where they had heard the conversation on the phone as well as what Babu ji said to Nishant after hanging up. Excited, they put Kanti wise to the situation at once.

About half an hour later, they all gathered before him. 'It's just a formality now,' he told them straightaway, his voice a blend of glee and gravitas. Saansad ji had confirmed his name was among those cleared by Indira ji for the Rajya Sabha. She was busy preparing for the talks with Bhutto, slated to be held in Shimla. But he would have to go to Delhi sometime soon; Saansad ji wanted him to meet, as a gesture of goodwill, some of Indira ji's aides who she trusted more than most of her Cabinet colleagues, the personages who ran the PM's office and were aware of his candidature.

But before that, there was this question to be settled on the home front, the question that in which college Nishant should study for his BA degree. Ram Mohan was keen on his own college. First of all, Nishant who had a third division in class twelve would be at a clear advantage at D.A.V. College where teachers would be more attentive and generous towards them. Ram Mohan might also be able to give them a hint about the questions to be asked in the exams. 'Didn't I get Sukesh some questions this time almost three weeks beforehand?' said Ram Mohan, 'Then how he had to be rescued! You know the story.' Yes, in one of his exam papers that year, Sukesh was in for a terrible shock. The virtuoso, the ever-boastful of his skill in cribbing in exams, had been caught red-handed. Usually, he would, if spotted, do away promptly with the cheating material in his hand by chewing and swallowing it, but this time when he saw one of the invigilators cast a couple of glances in his direction, he decided to wait for confirmation of his fear. The invigilator was clever; a little later, he surprised Sukesh by suddenly materializing at his side, and before Sukesh could put the ribbon of paper into his mouth, a section of it had already been torn out of his hand. Other invigilators too arrived on the scene. A thorough search of Sukesh's person yielded more such stuff, all of which was fastened to his exam sheet, and he was given a new sheet to begin afresh. He knew the procedure. The confiscated exam sheet carrying the invigilator's remarks plus all the cheating material found on him would be sent to the examiner along with the second sheet. Now an hour and thirty-five minutes were all that Sukesh had left to write his answers; starting over, which he did as best he could, and when the time was up, he, without losing a second, flew out of the exam hall. Luckily, Ram Mohan was at home; his timely intervention had helped Sukesh pass his BA final exams without losing a year.

With his gaze fixed on Nishant who looked unconvinced, Ram Mohan continued, 'You must know the worth of being my son. I have nothing against Christ Church College. It's a good institute; in fact, the best in Kanpur. After all, it was established during the Raj and used to have some Britons as its faculty members, but the problem for you is that it still retains a bit of that old atmosphere, and given your knowledge of English, you might find it hard to cope there.'

'I've passed twelfth board exam with English among my subjects,' said Nishant sounding a bit narked.

'Yes, third division; that too, in two years.'

'I'm willing to work hard. Mahavir Bhaiya has promised me to help with English. He would also help me get admission there.'

'Fine, if you think you can manage . . . Good,' said Ram Mohan. 'Because I don't think you're capable of achieving anything in life without my help. Let's see if you could change this perception of mine.' He stopped and glanced towards Nisha who was sitting with Kanti and Sandhya and said, 'To tell the truth, Nisha is more talented than you, but I didn't see fit to promote her because she is a girl, and a girl, no doubt, is in these modern times, entitled to some formal education before she packs her bags, before she is given away in marriage. That's the best a father can do for a daughter; if you try and help her to an ambition of her own, you have no idea what you're doing. You're interfering with whatever expectations her husband's family might have of her.'

Though happy to be allowed to go to Christ Church College, Nishant resented what Babu ji had had to say about his potential and all. He took it to heart. Nisha however flattered by his acknowledgment, did not like the way he had brought up the question of girls' marriage. She found it ominous. Even for Sandhya, his thoughts on girls' education did not bode well, making her feel downcast. She was now in grade eleven and would in a year's time be eligible to sit the Combined Pre-Medical Test (CPMT) exam, which if cleared would qualify her for admission to undergraduate medical courses in a medical college. She wanted to become a doctor. Later, Nisha in an attempt to assuage her disquiet said, 'Once Babu ji becomes a Rajya Sabha member, he will hardly have time to bother about these things.'

The day Ram Mohan reached Delhi, Saansad ji had some party leaders visiting him; the topic of their conversation was the Shimla Accord signed a few days earlier. Ram Mohan sat listening in the adjoining room. If it was not for 'the statesmanship of our great leader' the talks had all but foundered. Determined not to be outdone, Saansad ji and his visitors were going flat out to lavish plaudits on Indira Gandhi for the way she had got that accord in place. Ram Mohan was amused. It was unlike Saansad ji to be so uncritical in his opinion of something or someone.

'I've never heard you talk in this fashion before,' said Ram Mohan. The visitors had left. 'I know what you mean,' Saansad ji said laughing; and paused as if to work up some gravity for what he was to say next. 'The manner in which we overwhelmed

Pakistan in the war, the way our forces crushed the challenge, should have meant much more than the liberation of Bangladesh. We were in a position to make Pakistan see reason and agree to a resolution of the Kashmir question. What we have got is just rhetoric . . . as far as Indian interests are concerned.'

'But I just heard—'

'Yes, you heard me hailing the Shimla Accord as a historical achievement that should make us all proud of our PM, her leadership and so on. That's because we had in our midst this man, an MP, who reports to Kapur on whatever he happens to hear . . . By the way, why are we carrying on like this, don't we have something better to talk about?'

Ram Mohan brightened up, 'I've had this knot of anticipation in the stomach ever since I got off the train this morning.'

'What anticipation? Didn't I tell you it was only a matter of time?'

Ram Mohan rose and touched Saansad ji's feet as the latter continued, 'It's confirmed. Just the day before yesterday Kapur called and read out all the six names of the Congress candidates for Rajya Sabha. Yours is at number four. And I feel doubly joyous. Firstly, because I have been able to do something for you; secondly, I may not be in her inner circle but now I know Indira ji values my opinion. She hasn't even met you yet . . . Maybe because of her recent preoccupation, but to me it's her way of demonstrating her confidence in my judgement. Of course, you'll meet her, either before or after filing your nomination.'

Later in the afternoon, Saansad ji took Ram Mohan along to his office where he had arranged for him to meet two of Mrs Gandhi's henchmen in addition to Kapur. It was just an introductory meeting confined mostly to polite conversation. Not a word about Ram Mohan's impending Rajya Sabha stint came to be spoken, which—this avoidance—itself was a lucid testament to what had in fact occasioned the meeting; one of them did however talk in the passing of the need for Rajya Sabha to have educated, eloquent people as its members.

The next day they had a brief conversation over breakfast, and just before climbing into the waiting Ambassador—fitted with a red beacon with flasher, the door held wide open by one of the personnel—Saansad ji said, 'You must seek Baran Singh's blessings as soon as your name for Rajya Sabha is announced.'

'Chaudhary Sahab was indignant at my decision . . . But what choice did I have? He's a big leader and can afford to wait for his turn. He should have understood how important it was for me to be made a minister when he became CM the second time. I had stood by him for all I was worth, which he openly acknowledged.'

'He hadn't suspected you could be so disappointed as to look for other options,' Saansad ji said, walking him back, half-way to the portico . . . but I understand your position . . . I had to do the same thing. One has to make these hard decisions in politics sometimes.'

* * *

It had been some months before the war ended. All the stories, anecdotes about the exploits of the Indian soldier in the battlefield—the staple of the two Hindi weeklies for some time—their supply had dried up. Deena had suddenly found himself staring into the same emptiness as when a movie would end, tossing him back into the wretched world, the world outside the cinema hall. This time, however, he was in luck because within no time the void was filled with a more exciting phenomenon. It was like watching movies back to back. For back in the news once again were the legendary Chambal badlands. It transpired that one of the leading lights of Chambal had put out feelers to a

Gandhian active in the region about his wish for a peaceful life. This was none other than Madho Singh, one of the two biggest names at the time, having the highest rewards on their heads, the other being Mohar Singh, who had a bigger gang and was more illustrious and feared of the two and was Deena's favourite. Accused of over five-hundred homicides between them, both were well-known in central India. In Hindi newspapers and magazines, their names tended to be mentioned in tandem.

The Gandhian concurred, seeing in it the opportunity to help those led astray by their circumstances, and if someone like Madho Singh was looking for a way out of the life of violence, there would be others also inclined to explore the same option. The probability of these outlaws surrendering en mass thus was on the horizon. Yet for any such venture to succeed, it was crucial to rope in some big respectable figure with impeccable moral credentials. This locally active Gandhian approached the great Vinoba Bhave—the living caricature of Mahatma Gandhi—who had been involved in a similar exercise years before, but having long retreated to his ashram, he now confined himself to giving his blessings to the powerful who visited him from time to time. He however had directed the messenger to one of his old associates. Jayprakash Narayan, a prominent name in Indian politics, had stood aloof from the trappings of power politics, later devoting his energies under Bhave's influence to social work. JP as he was fondly known was at first reluctant to take up the matter, but then, Madho Singh, the maverick, had in a daring move, travelled all the way to JP's town Patna, wearing a disguise; after listening to the legendary figure from the Chambal ravines, JP had agreed to put his weight behind the cause. Madho Singh and his gang were the first to lay down arms, followed by other big and small dacoits and their gangs, including the one led by Mohar Singh. Both the magazines, *Saptahik Hindustan* and *Dharmyug*, had reported extensively on the subject for weeks. There were detailed profiles and biographies of all the bandits that mattered, the tales of their terror, idiosyncrasies, sometimes their deeds hinting at Robin Hood, tales of their cruelties and compassion. Reading about all this had kept Deena enthralled for days rather weeks. Eventually, the flow of these stories—once the process of the orchestrated mass surrender was over—had also stopped, leaving Deena in the lurch.

One day on leaving school, he had stopped at the familiar roadside book vender, selling old magazines, comics and second-hand Hindi paperbacks of the kind Rajvansh, Deena's cousin, was fond of. What arrested his attention at once was this book, which because of its garishly designed cover, had stuck out in the crowd of other yellowed and tattered stuff. Deena was in raptures. The author was none other than Manmohan Kumar Tamanna, the one who had copiously contributed to the two weeklies during the whole eventful period in the Chambal region. 'Be careful, don't spoil its cover. The book is hot off the press. I received a few copies just yesterday,' had said a wary vendor on seeing Deena picking up the book which offered nothing less than dreamlike reading. Tracing the tradition of banditry in that region back to the British days, the book turned to the recent times. All the familiar names were there, and it discussed at some length the emergence of the contemporary greats like Mohar Singh and Madho Singh, who were in the process of rehabilitation. Deena could hardly wait to read the book. To be able to buy it though, he would have to save his entire daily allowance of one rupee for five days running; that would mean no snacks in school during the period. He had to have that book; if not right then, then the next day. Thinking hard, he had decided with a bit of trepidation on something he had never believed he was capable of. He had stolen candies and sweets his mother would try to hide from him in Parsadpur. But stealing money he would associate with burglars or pickpockets. 'It will be the first and last act of its kind on my part,' he had told himself.

Nisha had been collecting twenty-paisa brass coins for a long time now; the small tin box containing this steadily growing treasure she would openly take out and proudly display, particularly to Deena and Mayank who wanted to count them; she would not let them. She did not want to know until the box became full. Not long after returning from school, Deena had got a chance to open Nisha Didi's suitcase and scoop a handful of the coins out of the tin box, amounting to less than three rupees; after adding his one day's pocket money, he was a little over one rupee short of the sum needed for the book. Sandhya was known to be good at saving among them. She was not a niggard, only careful. When he told her of his need and also that a friend of his in school was willing to share the cost—a lie—Sandhya had lent him the money, which—despite Deena's vociferous assurance—she knew would not be returned.

To put the tin box out of his mind had become rather testing for Deena after Nisha had failed to spot the pilferage. Deena stole one or two coins again in response to the cry from the ice-cream vendor who made the rounds of their neighbourhood in the evening. Then there was this other pull, the bread deliveryman, whose wooden box also contained other, more delicious items. Sandhya and others would have the resources to occasionally buy an ice cream or a bun or a heart-shaped cake, and would hand out to Deena a bit of whatever they had got, enjoining him to learn to set some money aside for such pleasures. Now seeing him get these snacks, Sandhya thought he had taken her advice.

Growing bold, rather reckless, Deena began dipping into the tin box regularly. One day when all of a sudden a wail of anguish issued from the new room—Nisha and Sandhya

now had the room bought from Bade Babu—nobody, barring
Deena, could guess the reason. Fortunately, Babu ji was not
home. Crying inconsolably, Nisha held the nearly empty tin
box in her hand. Everybody gasped. It was not about the
money she had lost, but the years—years of her patience and
effort. Nisha Didi in such distress! Deena felt disgusted with
himself. But what could he do now except to look bewildered
like everybody else. Nishant, being the first to recover from
the staggering blow, declared—giving them another rude
awakening—that the culprit could be none other than one
of them. Deena's sudden edgy look did not escape his notice;
then he said, throwing everybody into a tizzy, 'I'll have the
name by tomorrow.' The pallor on Deena's cheeks needed
no special attention. Kanti pulled him towards her and asked
in a stern voice if he had nicked all those coins. 'No,' he said,
looking furtive. He did not know how to admit to something
so embarrassing, something that would change his image so
drastically at home, as if the notoriety for being hopelessly
poor at studies was not enough. To God he prayed for just
one chance, one last time to be spared, and he would never let
even the thought of stealing enter his head.

When Nishant brought him to the big room and began to
quiz him discreetly, Deena's denial took on a tentative air; before
long Nishant inveigled him into coming clean by promising that
he himself would take the blame just this once. Deena told him
about the book on Chambal outlaws and his other temptations.
Nishant went back and bamboozled them by owning to it; that
he was the offender. He needed the money to help a poor friend
to buy some textbooks; that he would, to make good the loss,
give every 20-paise brass coin coming his way for the tin box.
However, his manner was such that nobody was convinced.
Nisha could detect that twinkle, the smirk adorning his face,
whenever he had something up his sleeve.

Though pulled up by the voice within, Deena thought he was saved. A profound sense of gratitude washed over him. He swore to himself he would never let Nishant Bhaiya down. Sacrifices of this nature were not new to Deena. He knew, from stories and movies, of people capable of saintly acts such as he had just witnessed, but then he also knew that the truth in these stories always came out in the end, usually through the agency of the guilty, the penitent, themselves. He decided that after the threat of being beaten had receded—and after setting an example of good behaviour—he would divulge it all. He did not have to wait that long as Nishant let it fall a couple of hours later. I won't go into details and mention only that considering it was his first offence of the kind, Nisha chose to forgive Deena; holding him close she made him promise he would not do any such thing again. An overjoyed Deena marvelled at Nisha Didi's tender-heartedness. It was also decided to keep it from Babu ji.

When a national daily published the names of the Congress candidates said to have been finalized for the Rajya Sabha, Ram Mohan's name figured prominently among them. Saansad ji called the same morning to congratulate him. VIPs like Shukla ji and others also rang up, and when the local paper put out the same story the next morning, Nishant had to deploy himself by the telephone as calls began to pour in; shortly there was a steady stream of people, friends and acquaintances, alone and in groups, many of them carrying boxes of sweets, some even garlands.

There had never been a bigger occasion for excitement in Ram Mohan's family. Sevak Lal had to start another coal stove to help meet the demand for refreshments; Nisha and Sandhya were busy making tea and lemonade as Kanti sat in front of the stove frying pakoras. The day though overcast was humid, and to get ice, an animated Deena had to now and then cycle down to Parmat. Mahavir Wilson was there to ensure none of the guests felt ignored. A day or two later, Tiwari ji arrived, and as the news spread, people from outside Kanpur, from Lucknow and Fatehpur, also came, Pratap Singh and Deep Narayan being among them. Gulab Singh and Badri were also there.

Ram Mohan stopped going out. He wanted to be around when the call came. The atmosphere of their house was so zestful even his constant presence seemed to add to the air of buoyancy. In a day or two, the filing of nomination papers would begin, the schedule for which had been announced. The names of the Congress candidates from other states had been announced; only UP and a couple of others remained. Saansad ji rang up again. One of the candidates on the current list for the Rajya Sabha had been asked to stand in a Lok Sabha by-poll and was being replaced by somebody else, hence the delay.

Ram Mohan kept waiting to be notified, in vain as it turned out. The Congress's list of its Rajya Sabha candidates from UP, released on the first day of the filing of nominations, did not carry his name. All the other names except his and one other who was to contest a by-poll, were there. Two entirely new names had supplanted theirs. Dazed, Ram Mohan and Tiwari ji could not absorb it at first, the mishap, and the catastrophe, having experienced nothing of the sort before. All those previous ventures had never been without the possibility of setback. That was always part of the deal. More so, those failures were seen to be contributing to Ram Mohan's political capital, and the fact that he could be considered for Rajya Sabha was the result of his three remarkable electoral performances; if it had not been so, even Saansad ji would not have suggested his name to Indira Gandhi.

Ram Mohan had hardly pulled himself together when he felt a pang of regret about leaving Baran Singh. The feeling, however, lasted only a moment. He was liable to get mad about trifles but few could match his composure if faced with a serious situation, and on noticing the headlong drop in the ebullient mood in his house, he quickly assumed his exuberant self. Gathering everybody in the big room, he addressed Tiwari ji, pointing to Kanti and others, 'Looking at their faces one would think we are at the end of our rope; that this is how my political life concludes . . .'

'It's natural to be shocked and upset when something that seemed a certainty fails to materialize,' said Tiwari ji. 'But, yes, this isn't the time to grieve. There remains much to look forward to. We don't know what happened yet.'

'Absolutely, let's wait for Saansad ji's call, said Ram Mohan. 'He'd know the reason; maybe there's something better in it for me. After all, how can we forget I came so close to becoming a Rajya Sabha member?'

'That's why we're so disappointed,' said Kanti.

'Yes, that's the difference between our ways of looking at it. I see an achievement in it, you a failure.' He turned to others, 'I'll go to the ends of the earth to ensure you all lead a good and secure life.' Soon the atmosphere was lightened up; he had everybody laughing at his jokes. Saansad ji phoned rather late in the evening. He had been trying to find out what was behind the disaster. He asked Ram Mohan not to worry, that he would work out something for him as he now knew what had led Mrs Gandhi to make that last-minute change on the list, to explain which and also to discuss the way forward, he suggested a meeting soon. Three days later, Ram Mohan and Tiwari ji were on a train to Delhi.

The day the list was to be made public, Udai Pratap Singh, the Fatehpur MP, had sought an urgent meeting with Indira ji, something not difficult for someone who had been brought into politics by her, and who, prior to Haksar, she used to consult on international issues; but for his aversion to sycophancy she would have made him a minister in the ministry of external affairs. She had also discovered to her discomfort that Udai Pratap Singh, once her favourite, was an independent spirit, given to speaking his mind regardless of who his interlocutor was. Recently when somebody close to her had on his behalf raised the question as to the under-utilized abilities of somebody as intelligent and articulate as him, she had voiced her preference for his younger brother Arimardan Singh, who she thought fitted much better her idea of a follower.

'I'm surprised that she acted on what this man had to say about your political moorings,' said Saansad ji. Udai Pratap Singh had told Mrs Gandhi that Ram Mohan had in the last election been endorsed by the People's Union, the Hindu fundamentalist party, her hatred for which was legendary. She, without caring to double-check or take Saansad ji into her confidence had struck Ram Mohan's name off the list. As soon as a chance presented itself, he would let her know about the lie she had been fed, said Saansad ji. He would tell her that first of all Ram Mohan had fought the election as an independent; since there was no better man to take on Udai Pratap Singh in Fatehpur, the Grand Alliance, of which the People's Union was a junior partner, had decided not to field their candidate, its sole objective being the Congress's defeat. So in a way it said a lot more for Ram Mohan's electoral strength than for the Alliance's unconditional support to him. 'I can't say when but I'll definitely have her realize the mistake,' said Saansad ji, and just as they were taking their leave, he told Ram Mohan that from now on, it would be his headache to find a way to help him to a position of importance.

On the overnight train back to Kanpur, Ram Mohan and Tiwari ji talked to a late hour. One reason for their successive disappointments in politics, they agreed, was that Ram Mohan was not a full-timer.

The silver jubilee of India's Independence was at hand. The government had planned to celebrate it in a big way with enormous amounts of public money made available to hammer home the point that how fortunate India was to have had the Nehru–Gandhi family as its benefactor. To mention anything that clashed with this narrative was anathema to Indira Gandhi and her inner circle. A day or two after returning from Delhi, Ram Mohan too received an invitation to preside over a gathering of poets in Kanpur to commemorate the grand occasion. Sponsored by Lucknow station of AIR, the function was to be broadcast on Independence Day. Ram Mohan poured out his frustration by way of a poem and decided to recite it at the gathering the following day. Titled 'Anomaly', the poem lamented the situation:

Where in every sphere of life, dynamism is mocked and ridiculed,
where all dreams lie worsted and spirit worn down,
whether we are going forward or backwards is hard to know,
where every attempt to rise causes yet another fall,
where seeking respect means its further loss,
where all the jostling for tidying the sheet gets it ripped,
where the lion is on the run and the jackal has his lair,
yet, though conscious of your grief, your inner torment,
Oh silver jubilee of Independence, we hail you.

Tiwari ji was against the poem being recited by Ram Mohan in public. He suggested they book a trunk call to Delhi and ask if it would be appropriate. Saansad ji was not home. Ram Mohan left a message. Hours later, close to the evening, the call was returned, and after listening to a few lines of the long poem, Saansad ji stopped Ram Mohan and forbade him from reciting it himself; then on learning that the programme was to be aired on AIR, he launched into a discourse:

'The only thing expected of All India Radio is to ceaselessly dish out paeans of praise for her government. It's just a tool, a powerful one at that . . . Any talk of India's poverty and corruption in the media would raise her hackles; She regards it as no more than attempts to divert people's attention from all the good work she's doing,' Saansad ji took a breather. 'I don't know whether you're aware but a couple of years ago she came down heavily on BBC for showing a documentary on India by a French director; when the international broadcaster refused to tender an apology, it was sent packing. She was livid at the portrayal in the documentary of so many Indians forced to be living in inhuman conditions. Such misery, such suffering! What's the need to broadcast this to the world?

'It's a good job you called Ram Mohan! My goodness, I can well imagine what would happen if you went ahead and expressed these thoughts from a public platform. She now knows of my close association with you. People like Udai Pratap Singh and his brother and others would grab at an opportunity like this to bring me down.' He also warned Ram Mohan against 'Anomaly' being published anywhere.

Nisha's college like others was also celebrating the occasion, and she, for one, would not miss out on a chance like that, and had already given her name as a prospective participant in the function being planned. Apart from other cultural items, there was to be a debate competition and also a programme to allow students to showcase their individual talents, capturing the spirit of the occasion. To partake in the debate was her obvious choice. She asked Babu ji to write it. He wondered if she could give a recitation of 'Anomaly' that they had heard from him the other day! Though stinging in its assessment of the country's twenty-five years of freedom, the poem should be applauded for its aptness, for calling a spade a spade.

And yes, Nisha's performance was judged one of the best at the function. The best actually, because of it being so different from the usual. The audience was held spellbound by her rendition of 'Anomaly' studded with choice words of Ram Mohan and her ringing voice and flawless elocution. Her spirits rose when several teachers, even the principal, walked up to her to congratulate her; the principal said she had never heard anything like that; that Hindi could sound so robustly pleasing was a revelation to her. Nisha returned home in a state of trance.

But her mood lay ruined by the evening. A reality of which she had had a blurry sentience was made to jump out at her like a flash of lightening, tossing aside the world she had come to believe was her own. Ram Mohan had found a boy whose family was keen to become related to him. 'It's time I fulfilled my duties as a father,' he pronounced, glancing at Nisha, who sitting beside Kanti and Sandhya, shrank back as he continued, 'This boy is suitable for Nisha.' After a degree in electronics from a reputed college of engineering in Allahabad, he had secured a job in the Indian Telephone Industries in Bangalore. 'He comes from a humble but respectable background,' Ram Mohan went on, 'the family has a good social standing in their village. Albeit farmers, his father and elder brother are forward looking men who, despite their limited means, ensured this boy does not end up in the sticks, tending to the fields like them. What better groom can we find in our caste for Nisha,' he paused. 'She'll finish her BA in eight months, after which I want the wedding to take place.'

'You haven't met his family as yet!' said Kanti, who sensing how Nisha—despaired of realizing any of her dreams—must feel. After her BA, she wanted to do an MA in Hindi Literature, which was just an additional option as her main plan was to try and become an announcer with AIR. She had all the qualities required—excellent knowledge of Hindi, sterling voice, impeccable diction. To land this glamorous job should not be that hard given Babu ji's political connections. But for any such enterprise her hardest struggle lay in securing Babu ji's permission.

'No, I haven't seen him, but I know the family. Very nice people . . .!'

'Babu ji, I want to enroll in MA after BA,' Nisha broke in. 'While pursuing it, I can apply for a job at AIR. All my teachers think I should look for a career in broadcasting.'

'After BA, what a girl should or should not do is a decision for her husband to make.'

'I'm asking for only three years . . . Let me at least try and see what I can make of myself!' Nisha was close to tears.

'Your husband willing you can do that after marriage, this MA and broadcasting . . . I might be taken up with politics soon, I have no time to waste, for I must succeed in politics to be able to help you all.'

Nisha kept crying the whole night while her mother, herself in tears, was trying to console her. Kanti related to her again how she had felt forced not to decline when their father had come asking for her hand. 'My father was against the alliance . . . He and your Babu ji did not see eye to eye on women's position in society. I still remember how he had suffered . . . tormented at not having means to send me to college. In a way, Nisha you are lucky to have come this far.'

'I don't want to get married, leave you all behind, go to a totally new place! I want to be independent and stand on my own feet,' said Nisha between the sobs.

'That's our destiny, Nisha. What you can do instead is to resolve that your own daughter or daughters won't suffer the same fate. This, I think, will give you strength to face it.' Then wiping Nisha's face with a corner of her sari, Kanti whimpered, 'You know very well if it were in my power I wouldn't hesitate even for a second to let you do what you want to do in life!' Nisha hugged her mother, weeping bitterly.

In the morning, Nisha sat on her bed, exhausted, with her eyes swollen and features blurred, and Sandhya who too had cried the previous night was preparing to go to school. Deena, also about to leave, stood beside their study table with a sinking feeling, eying Nisha Didi who, looking out of sorts, surveyed the room and said, 'My life here with you all is about to end,' making Sandhya and Deena run to her in floods of tears, to be enfolded in her arms.

Nisha could not wait to see Mahavir Bhaiya for his thoughts on her predicament. On Saturday, when Babu ji left for Parsadpur, she sent for him. He came the same evening. They sat in the big room surrounding him.

'Doctor Sahab came by the other day to tell us what he called the "good news", but I knew what an emotional turmoil you'd be in . . . Look Nisha, you know him, your Babu ji. He's no different from the common run of people in that he thinks the best thing a father can do for his grown-up daughters is to marry them off.'

'But I want only two or three years more for my MA during which, if possible, I'd like to get into AIR as an announcer. I want to take part in an audition at least once to see if I'm good enough.'

'You're more than good enough Nisha . . . though I'd suggest you don't insist on something which would cause you more heartache and bitterness. Doctor Sahab won't agree. First he has already found a boy, an engineer, and second, before

he throws himself into politics, he wants to lighten some of his family worries. So my advice would be that instead of quarrelling with it, you should get yourself attuned to the idea of marriage. Regard it with a positive frame of mind. It might turn out to be a window of opportunity for you, because . . . '
Nisha looked at him, puzzled. 'Yes, your husband might allow you more freedom than your Babu ji. Then you can do your MA and also pursue this goal of yours, the announcing business.'

'I'm completely at sea about this guy!'

'I think he's a regular, normal man, not an authoritarian like Doctor Sahab. The best thing about him is that his family stays in the village, so you would be spared the tyranny of a joint family. He would have his own social circle in the city . . . By the way, Doctor Sahab was saying if you don't like it in Bangalore, he could have him transferred to the Allahabad branch of the ITI. Allahabad is a good city famous for its university and other state institutions and is less than two hundred kilometres from Kanpur.'

'I agree with Mahavir,' said Kanti. 'This new life might make it possible for Nisha to pursue what she seems so keen on.'

'Yes, marriage for Nisha might prove, instead of being an obstacle, a facilitator of achieving her ambition.'

The departure of Nishant from B.N.S.D. bestowed on Deena the freedom to cut classes and go to the cinema at will. The question of money he would solve by stealing from Babu ji's wallet, which had turned out a pretty simple affair as the latter seldom cared to know exactly how much cash he was carrying; a broad idea was enough. With the success of his first two attempts, Deena's nerves were largely settled. He would just have to wait for a chance when there was no one in the big room, where on one of the permanently open doors of his wooden cabinet, Babu ji hung his clothes; gaining access to his wallet was child's play. So Deena was having the time of his life while at school—or while he was supposed to be at school—for to treat himself and his friends to Hindi films and snacks, he would never run out of cash. With Nishant's old bicycle coming to him, the cinema halls located in distant parts of the city were rendered within reach; now he could beat off that sinking feeling at the end of each film by promising himself another flick soon.

Then it all ran up against a snag all of a sudden, this amazing life that Deena was enjoying on the sly. Nishant, who had not kept well for some time, fell seriously ill and would remain lying in the big room, choking off the flow of money from Babu ji's wallet to Deena's pocket. Deena cursed Vaidya ji to whose powdery substances and honey and herbal ointment Nishant's sores would not respond. Of the seemingly superficial ulcers on his member, Nishant had thought nothing at first; when other parts of his body broke out in lesions, he had become scared and gone to Parmat. One look and Vaidya ji had had no doubt as to it being some venereal infection. Left no choice, Nishant had to confide in him. He entreated him not to tell his family; that he would never ever repeat the mistake, but Vaidya ji had sent for Ram Mohan, who on coming back, would not say a word about what he had learnt. Nishant's eyes had also become sore and red. He would have fever and headaches too. Ram Mohan had got an extra bed placed, on which, not far from the front door, Nishant lay almost naked under a sheet.

Plunged into severe austerity, Deena was praying for Nishant's speedy recovery. One day, Tiwari ji blew in; he was shocked to see what confronted him. The figure on the charpoy was not even able to greet him properly. He voiced his displeasure at why a proper doctor had not been consulted, and said, 'We should take him to Fatehpur, to Dr Om Sharma at the district hospital there.' Tiwari ji had tremendous faith in him. To Ram Mohan's contention that Kanpur had much better facilities, Tiwari ji admitted Fatehpur District Hospital was no different from all other decrepit health centres, but things were much better for those who were friends with the head doctor at these state-run holes. What silenced Ram Mohan was Tiwari ji's fear that though Kanpur had much bigger and better hospitals, the chance of people coming to know of Nishant's disease was also high. Ram Mohan asked Tiwari ji to find out what he had done, where he had gone, for according to Vaidya ji, he had been to a woman somewhere.

Soon Tiwari ji blagged how Nishant had got it. He sent for Sukesh, his son; it transpired that he and Nishant had ridden their bicycles to Moolganj, a web of congested narrow passages— dark, squalid, edged with open smelly gutters. Massing about the doors and windows and balconies on either side were heavily made-up girls, in all shapes and sizes. Nervous and shaky, they were about to return as the girls kept calling out, when a thin, untidy, betel-chewing man accosted them. Sukesh had managed to get on his bicycle and ride away, but Nishant could not. The glib pimp, polite but firm in intent, hustled him into accepting his offer. With hardly two or three rupees in his pocket, Nishant was not allowed to mate with either of the young things shown to him; instead, the woman who was in charge had led him into a tiny semi-dark enclosure and let him get his money's worth, asking him to come later with some more cash after which he could savour some delectable piece of ass. After saving some money, Nishant had gone back there once again by himself.

Ram Mohan persuaded Tiwari ji to forgive Sukesh, for whatever they had done could not be undone now. Sukesh looked fazed as Sevak Lal had told him the reason for his being summoned, but to his relief neither Ram Mohan nor his father was mad. They gently got it across to them—Nishant too heard and watched—that such conduct could jeopardize so much that was worthwhile in their lives. 'Now you know the kind of risk one runs by submitting to these temptations,' said Ram Mohan to Nishant specifically.

Nishant's condition and Babu ji and Tiwari ji talking in subdued tones made Nisha and Sandhya go into a huddle with Kanti. Missing out on all of this was Deena who agonized over how long it would take for his finances to be restored. Just then, the same day as Tiwari ji arrived, he was presented with an opportunity to replenish his long dried-up funds. It was late afternoon when Tiwari ji set off with Sukesh to visit some relative in the city; Babu ji went down to the Khatris. The kind of bonhomie he had developed with Mrs Khatri, a chat with her was a must if he was in town. He asked Deena to stay in the big room while he was gone in case the phone rang or Nishant needed something.

Hung on their usual place were Babu ji's khadi trousers, with the thin leather belt still in the loop, which meant they were to be worn again; Deena to his delight could make out the bulge of the wallet in Babu ji's pocket. Nishant seemed asleep with his back to where Deena sat, and could not move his limbs without groaning. The wallet contained several notes of hundred rupees and a few ten-rupee ones. Not sure of a chance like this again anytime soon—especially as Babu ji and Tiwari ji would be taking Nishant to Fatehpur—Deena swiped the big one this time, the first time, unaware that Babu ji had counted them that very day, shortly after the plan of Fatehpur was finalized.

'I don't need to carry out any tests to know that it's syphilis, the second stage of it. But it's curable,' Dr Om Sharma had said. As Nishant was to remain in his grotty messy hospital for about a week, Ram Mohan took the morning shuttle back to Kanpur. And what made Deena catch his breath on his return from school was the news that Babu ji had lost one hundred rupees during the trip. How and where he had no idea. What a close call! Deena could not help breaking out in a sweat!

Nishant returned cured from Fatehpur, bringing Deena's finances back to normal. Deena had not felt so good at school before.

With the work on the link road underway in Parsadpur, Ram Mohan's weekly visits there had become a regular fixture; and what took place during one such visit was something neither Ram Mohan nor anyone else could have imagined. That Padhaiya Bhaiya could be capable of something like that—that he could screw up his courage to threaten Ram Mohan with a country-made pistol—was beyond everybody. But few knew he had of late been consorting with some unsavoury elements, people who could have no influence whatsoever in the area because of Ram Mohan and Gulab Singh. Most of these characters hailed from the villages on the other side of the GT Road to which the link road was to join Parsadpur and other villages on this side. Padhaiya Bhaiya would meet them at a well-screened place in a big grove belonging to one of them where he, the grove owner, had also set up a small distillery that doubled as their bolthole. They mustered there to chat and plan and drink country-made liquor; the most fabulous thing Padhaiya Bhaiya discovered about being tight was that it made you bold. One day when he, after a drinking session, was brought along to commit a murder he had looked on calmly as his friends had shot the man twice in the chest; then a gun was thrust into his hands to take a shot at the supine figure in the throes of death. Without a flutter of disquiet or hesitancy, he had put one more slug into the man.

It would give him a tremendous fillip, a shot in the arm—that murder. He finally had crossed the frontiers of his known behaviour limited up until then to threats of violence and shouting abuse; and then he was let in on something big they were contemplating, the mother of all murders, which would allow them unhindered sway over much of the area. It was fraught with danger, not easy at all, the taking out of Gulab Singh. They had to weigh one plan of action against another before fixing on the most realistic. Though committed to the pledge not to breathe a word about it, Padhaiya Bhaiya could not help his behaviour being influenced by the thought that Ram Mohan's commander-in-chief might well be accounted for before long. So when he shouted at someone a few paces from where Ram Mohan and the man in charge of the construction of the link road were talking, Badri gestured for him to be silent. Paying no heed, Padhaiya Bhaiya kept on speaking loudly. Ram Mohan yelled, 'You must behave yourself when I'm around or be prepared to have your ribs broken.' As a worried Badri led Ram Mohan and his entourage away, Padhaiya Bhaiya left without a word.

During his visits, Ram Mohan stayed in the front room of his former house. Keen as others were to put him up, Kalla Dada would not let go of the privilege and had the room ready for these weekly occasions. Badri would also stay the night in the room. It was the only time when they could go over subjects not possible to discuss publicly, and Gulab Singh, after filling him in on the latest, would go back to Ballamgaon to sleep. It was he who had on Ram Mohan's previous trip told him that some elements in the area viewed their political let-downs as indicative of Ram Mohan's declining clout, to which Ram Mohan had said, 'If they, any of them, are foolhardy enough to let this impression tempt them into something foolish they'd better mind out for the consequence . . . The problem, Gulab Singh, is that some people are so dense as to base their opinions on absolutes. If the Congress made me a Rajya Sabha member,

I'd be everything; if not I'm nothing. Ignorant of reasons behind a particular situation, these people see the final outcome as the only truth . . . To assess a given situation one needs all the details that go into its making. The importance of the fact that a Union minister has been promoting my cause, that my name is known to Indira ji and people close to her, that I almost made it to Parliament . . . all this is lost on these rustics.'

That night when Ram Mohan and Badri lay in bed talking and laughing in their usual fashion, an odd but loud shout outside startled them. They sat up. It was Padhaiya Bhaiya, inebriated, demanding that the door be opened. Without taking his name, he was challenging Ram Mohan to come out. Kalla Dada and his two other sons rushed in from the garret upstairs. In the meantime, Padhaiya Bhaiya fired his pistol into the air. Ram Mohan wanted to go out but Kalla Dada and Badri blocked his way, asking earnestly not to endanger his life in this manner, listening to a swine as drunk as Padhaiya. The gun was let off once again followed by another volley of insults. 'He's out of his senses,' Kalla Dada muttered, looking ashamed and helpless. It lasted till after midnight when Padhaiya Bhaiya became quiet and shortly they heard a woman right outside the door, who Kalla Dada recognized as his daughter-in-law. She took Padhaiya back home.

In the morning, the whole village converged outside Kalla Dada's house. Some were eager to drag Padhaiya Bhaiya out of his house, but Ram Mohan, who along with Badri was occupying his usual place on the chabootra, forbade them. Asking everybody to calm down, Badri said that as Doctor Sahab had to leave for Kanpur, he wanted to address them all briefly. Ram Mohan began, in a voice tinged with sadness, 'For the first time in my life, I've come across something like this. I've fought three elections and who isn't aware of the ever-present menace of violence in electoral politics? Many people get killed and hurt

during every election . . . If anybody thinks I can be intimidated
this way, he needs to have his head examined . . . I won't put
it past people, this kind of conduct, who see in me a dangerous
rival, a threat to their interests or who are openly my enemies.
But this from someone from my extended family, someone to
whom—far from doing any harm—I've done favours, someone
to whom I gave away a plot of land . . . I've more or less ignored
his misdemeanours so far, but last night was the limit, an eye-
opener. So today I want to make it known that from now on
Padhaiya is on his own. I will have nothing to do with him,
with what he does or how he treats others or how others treat
him. Today I sever all ties with him.'

Back in Kanpur, Ram Mohan did not mention the episode.
But the day after his return, Gulab Singh and Badri arrived
unexpectedly. Ram Mohan was out somewhere. Kanti could
not believe what Badri told her. Her facial reaction made Gulab
Singh hurriedly say that since Ram Mohan had announced his
dissociation from him, this scourge would become a thing of
the past soon.

Nisha and Nishant, after coming back from college, were
stunned when Kanti told him what had happened in Parsadpur.
They all had for some time been conscious of their vulnerability
in case something happened to Babu ji, who appeared oblivious
of their fear and would not trouble to have a contingency plan in
place, to make provisions for them. Whatever cash he happened
to have, he would prefer to keep it handy, not a paisa in bank,
no fixed deposits, no savings, nothing. Even their property
in Parsadpur, rather whatever left of it—as Ram Mohan had
already disposed of some cultivable land along with the mango
grove and two isolated pieces of land they owned—had also
been given away. So the ancestral property, consisting only of a
few fields now, Kanti wished her husband to leave alone as an
insurance against any misfortune coming out of the blue. This

anxiety on her part Ram Mohan would laugh off, stating that nothing was going to happen to him, that in the end each of them would have enough to live on comfortably.

Just as he was getting back into the swing of teaching and his visits to Parsadpur, a sudden political development, indeed its force of prognosis swept Ram Mohan along. Kamlapati Tripathi, the man who looked more like a Hindu priest than a politician, the Nehru family loyalist, resigned as CM. Rather he was asked to resign by Indira Gandhi. His family's no-holds-barred approach to spoils of power had become too loud on the grapevine; the CM's eldest daughter-in-law being given full rein to making the most of his position was discussed openly, that those looking for a favour were expected to approach her with corresponding gifts or cash. There was this so-called 'going rate' for everything. Obviously Kamlapati Tripathi's family had overstepped the mark. Otherwise bribery and dishonest dealings had been the norm under the Congress, and Mrs Gandhi, like her late father, tended to view it leniently. There had been unchecked corruption even in the Congress ministries formed in several provinces after the inauguration of direct elections in British India. 'I would go to the length of giving the whole Congress a decent burial, rather than put up with the corruption that is rampant,' was how Mahatma Gandhi remarked in disgust. Nehru and after him his daughter knew that their socialist policies vested politicians and bureaucrats with so much power it would be the height of idiocy to expect them not to use it for personal gain. Yes, they were supposed to act a bit discreetly, for regardless of it being common knowledge any flagrant abuse of authority could still scandalize people. So for the sake of appearances, Mrs Gandhi had to remove Kamlapati Tripathi but would not keep him out in the cold for long, a lickspittle of his calibre; he would soon be accommodated on the Union cabinet. In the wake of his resignation, UP was placed under President's Rule. One day, less than a week later, following a late-night call from Saansad ji's secretary, Ram Mohan and Tiwari ji were en route to Delhi. That call and his rushing to Delhi rekindled the old hopes of his family; beckoning to them once again was the prospect of a privileged lifestyle and a secure future—perks commonly enjoyed by all the families of bureaucrats and politicians. Nisha and Sandhya too, who had lately been sunk in gloom because of Babu ji's pronouncements on their future, felt a little better. With three weeks still remaining of their summer holidays, Deena persuaded Nisha Didi to take them to the pictures as least once; they also visited Naveen Market twice, and had an opportunity for a long chat with Mahavir Bhaiya who, not knowing about Doctor Sahab being in Delhi, had dropped in with cake and pastries to inform him of his imminent move to Christ Church College.

Indira Gandhi might go in for a fresh mandate in UP according to Saansad ji. Election to the Lok Sabha was still a long way off. If things looked favourable, she could advance it too. What was weighing on her mind was that Congress might not win as many seats as it had the last time, and UP—the state with the largest number of Lok Sabha seats—was the key to Congress's strength in Parliament. To head the next government in UP, she wanted to bring in someone with a clean sheet; that someone could be Saansad ji. Ram Mohan and Tiwari ji were exhilarated. They were asked to keep it strictly to themselves. Barring Mrs Gandhi's favourite PA and one or two in her coterie nobody else had a clue about her choice for UP. That's what she had told

Saansad ji. It was not to get out just yet, so she could be spared the usual hassle, the hassle of contingents from UP landing at her door with the request for a rethink of her decision. These were nothing but the machinations of the jealous, angling for being in the reckoning themselves. She knew that and derived an odd pleasure from it.

Ram Mohan announced to all of his family assembled in the big room that at last his career in politics was about to take off. From now on they should look forward to only good things in life. Taking over from him, Tiwari ji held forth about their meeting with Saansad ji who had asked Ram Mohan to gear up for joining his Cabinet in UP after the Assembly polls. 'As I've to ensure a big victory for the Congress in the next Parliamentary vote, you would be aiding in the effort to get my administration off the ground.'

Ram Mohan sent Nishant to Parmat to get mangoes and sweets and made Tiwari ji—who wanted to leave the same afternoon—delay his departure by a day. Everybody loved the way Tiwari ji painted an alluring picture of what Ram Mohan's success in politics would afford his family and friends. On such occasions, he would take on a style—words and sentences delivered in a measured tone with delicious pauses—that would lend a colourful aspect even to most trivial of details. Inspired thus, he was a pleasure to listen to. But this delightful setting—a smug-looking Ram Mohan with Kanti, Nisha, Sandhya, Deena and Mayank being all ears as Tiwari ji dished out a superlative performance—was suddenly transformed into a phantasmagoria, so to speak, when there emerged on the front veranda Sukesh, looking demented and dishevelled. Right behind him was Nishant carrying mangoes and sweets.

Within minutes of hearing the news, Ram Mohan and Tiwari ji hurried off. His elder brother had been shot in the back the previous day in their village. He was first taken to Fatehpur

District Hospital, but Dr Om Sharma and others had rushed him to Kanpur's Hallet Hospital as he needed a big surgery. In a three-hour long operation, the doctors had removed five metal balls from his torso. The sixth one they had not touched. It was embedded at a place difficult to reach. Yes, it was an LG cartridge containing six metal balls, fired from a twelve-bore shotgun. Tiwari ji's family thought he was still in Delhi; Sukesh who had come to inform Nishant and the rest, was surprised to find his father there.

There were people who were jealous of Tiwari ji and felt a rivalry with him for clout in their village, but of an enmity like this he had no knowledge, the kind that could lead to a murderous attack. He had no dispute with the family to which the young man by the name of Mukhiya, who had fired at his brother, belonged. His identity would have remained obscure if not for a Harijan boy who while grazing his master's water buffaloes had seen him hurriedly climb down a mango tree with a shotgun slung over his shoulder. It was just outside their village but the first to reach Tiwari ji's brother who was huddled on the ground, was this Harijan boy, and he was astute enough to keep his mouth shut and play along with others who kept wondering as to the identity of the shooter. He knew whom to tell. It was the man known for his staunch loyalty to Tiwari ji, but that was not the reason for the boy's confidence in Daulat Singh. The reason was that the latter had once saved him from being sodomized by one of his caste men, a Thakur. Few Harijan boys with good features could escape the clutches of some upper caste pederasts. This boy, lucky to have Daulat Singh's protection, had told him about Mukhiya just as they were taking Tiwari ji's brother to Fatehpur.

Daulat Singh and Bholi, a close relation of Tiwari ji, were also with Ram Mohan and Tiwari ji when they returned from the hospital in the evening to discuss the situation, something

not possible at the hospital in the presence of so many people—
an army consisting of Tiwari ji's family members, relations and
friends. Ram Mohan had asked them to come along, because
whatever measures they were to finalize, these two had to be
kept in the loop. Not fully aware of their credentials, Ram
Mohan wanted to call in Gulab Singh or maybe Pratap Singh
but what Tiwari ji told him about them eased his mind. Bholi
it seemed was already a name to reckon with in his area. He
along with his two friends had murdered a notorious figure in
a neighbouring village in broad daylight a year ago; none of
those present had stirred as Bholi to their disbelief had chopped
off this man's right arm before his friends had shot him to death
with their country-made pistols.

Daulat Singh on the other hand had his own reputation as
a strongman. Not in the league of Bholi though—he had not
bumped anyone off yet—his physical strength and fearlessness
were his strong points. Having roughed up many people, some
badly, he was up for crossing that threshold. Smiling at Bholi
and Daulat Singh, Ram Mohan dismissed the idea of giving
Mukhiya's name to the police. 'Mukhiya may have something
important to tell, something you don't know but should
know. It's unlikely he would simply have been overtaken by
a momentary frenzy. Just like that. No, he couldn't have been
acting on his own . . . The best thing is that nobody knows that
you know who shot at your brother. You just have to make
Mukhiya disappear after extracting the truth.'

One of Tiwari ji's sons, the one younger to Sukesh, was
entrusted with the job of bringing Mukhiya to a spot between
the village and the road leading to Fatehpur. Not a difficult
thing given Mukhiya's fondness for the sweet shop on that
road. Tiwari ji's brother would be in hospital for at least two
more weeks. The Mukhiya affair was to be finished before that.
The idea was that Tiwari ji, Bholi and Daulat Singh would

go straight from Kanpur to that spot and come back the next day after spending the night in Fatehpur. Meanwhile, Nishant showed Bholi his Rampuri and said yes when the latter asked if he could borrow it; two days later they set off for Fatehpur. On the way, they bought two lathis, thinking better off using Bholi's country-made pistol, for the place they had in mind was not far from Tiwari ji's village, the place where Mukhiya was to be taken, a wooded area along a Yamuna tributary.

* * *

They returned the next day, tired and unkempt but happy, wearing the same clothes as they had worn the previous day. Ram Mohan asked Nishant to arrange for them to freshen up first, and gave them his clean lungis and vests to wear as they were carrying no change of clothes. Shortly, Tiwari ji gave an account of how the thing had been accomplished.

It would have been the most frightening sight Mukhiya had ever set eyes on, the sight of the three—two with a lathi in their hands—and the moment Tiwari ji's younger son who had brought him to the appointed spot had turned back, Mukhiya had realized his game was up. He had grovelled at Tiwari ji's feet before Daulat Singh had kicked him and pushed him away from his mentor. Asking Mukhiya to stand up, Tiwari ji had said he had a question, which if he answered satisfactorily, he could go; Mukhiya had nodded eagerly; then catching Daulat Singh pointing to a spot a few paces to the right and Bholi saying, 'Who'll carry him from here to the river?' he had fallen at Tiwari ji's feet yet again. Giving the other two a look of annoyance, Tiwari ji had had to reassure him. Once a hundred or so yards into the woods, they came to a halt at a small clearing. A little further ahead was the Yamuna tributary. They all sat down, Tiwari ji cross-legged; the rest on their haunches.

Mukhiya was fond of the shotgun belonging to his father who had taught him how to use it; had also allowed him to fire it into the air during a wedding, and now every so often, he would roam the village with the gun in his hand, prompting some people to jeer that he was just showing off, that he did not have it in him to use it. That would rattle Mukhiya's cage. One day, one of his tormentors had sidled up to him and putting an arm over his shoulder urged him to prove he was for real. They had become friends after this. Soon one of them had suggested that considering Mukhiya's ardour for wielding the shotgun, he should experience the real thing, at least once. But to shoot to kill someone? They had not wanted that, no. Just hurting somebody a little would be enough for Mukhiya to know the lethal potential of the gun, to have a glimpse of its power, which given his interest in the thing, was important to him. They would provide him with an easy target as well as a cartridge used to kill birds. The target was Tiwari ji's brother who went out to his tubewell every afternoon, passing by a clump of trees on the way. There was no visible feud between Tiwari ji and the families to which those three handlers of Mukhiya belonged. Yet it was not a randomly picked target either. Though criticized by his Brahman brethren for aligning himself with a Kurmi, Tiwari ji's political pre-eminence could not be ignored, the pre-eminence that had its source in the very friendship he was accused of, the friendship with a former confidant of Baran Singh and who currently had a political mentor in Saansad ji. Tiwari ji had long been conscious of the feelings of those families towards him, feelings of jealousy or hatred maybe.

'I didn't know it was an LG cartridge. They had said it was meant for birds.' Mukhiya was snuffling.

Then Tiwari ji gave a nod to Daulat Singh who had already got up and was standing behind their man, and when Bholi had grabbed Mukhiya's legs and pulled them towards him, making him fall on his back, Daulat Singh placed his horizontally held lathi across his neck; now Mukhiya, with Bholi sitting on his legs, could not move and had only his terror-stricken, bulging eyes and facial convulsions to convey how he was feeling as Bholi held his legs and Daulat Singh pressed down hard on the lathi with both his hands; Mukhiya's hands, growing limp, tried in vain to get it off his neck.

At that point in the retelling, when Ram Mohan rose and went to the bathroom, Bholi took out the Rampuri from under the pile of their soiled clothes lying on the floor and handed it to Nishant. Its mechanism that made the blade spring from the long handle had conked out. The cutting up of Mukhiya's body had taken a toll on the knife which had severed Mukhiya's head pretty smoothly; when it came to detaching the torso from the rest of the body, it had given up, failing perhaps to deal with some big bone there. Nishant was not upset. He said the basic purpose of a Rampuri was to kill or injure by stabbing, a task it performed wonderfully. It was not meant for dismembering a dead body.

There was no chance of Mukhiya's murder being discovered any time soon, but before his disappearance could be noticed, Ram Mohan wanted at least one of those instigators to be accounted for. He said, 'It should be easy. They don't know you're onto them.' Bholi and Daulat Singh nodded while Tiwari ji seemed lost in thought.

One evening, Ram Mohan called everybody to the big room 'I've something important to share,' he announced sending them euphoric, barring Nisha who, having guessed why he had them assembled in the big room, didn't partake in their eager anticipation. Indeed it had to do with the subject of her wedding.

Yet the reason for his bullish mood that day was not that he had found this engineer boy for Nisha but the resolution of the question of how he was going to raise cash for this expensive affair, the wedding: he had disposed of what was left of their fields in Parsadpur.

Nisha turned pale. Kanti said, 'Now that we have the money we should hold the wedding in our own good time, maybe in a year or so.' She knew the boy's family was in no hurry. They were waiting for Ram Mohan to have him transferred from Bangalore to Allahabad. He glared at her and said she had to be out of her mind. Any delay would make sense only if there were financial difficulties. If not, the sooner the better for he might get wrapped up in politics before long because it had been almost two months since the dissolution of UP Assembly, and according to Saansad ji, Indira ji might change her mind and hold Assembly elections only when they were due, about six months later, in which case Saansad ji was likely to be sent to Lucknow earlier than planned, meaning Assembly polls would take place while he was in charge of the state.

Getting Shekhar, the boy, transferred to Allahabad was no problem said Ram Mohan, asking Nishant to book a trunk call to Delhi. He would talk to Saansad ji. Kanti glanced at Nisha who, fighting back tears, had her mouth tightly shut. Ram Mohan said, 'Don't act as though you're the first girl ever to be getting married. Or am I supposed to give you a lecture on how important it is for a woman to start a family of her own before it's too late? Do I have time to waste on such inanities here? I want to have this done and over with as soon as possible . . . Before I am taken up by the hurly-burly of politics again.' He asked Nishant to get him the pocketbook from the pocket of his shirt hung on one of the doors of his wardrobe, which had particulars of Shekhar's job with the ITI. He also told them of the boy's elder brother's recent communication to him; Shekhar was coming to his village on a two-week vacation the following month and would like to see Nisha. Ram Mohan had on the other hand sounded his brother out about holding the wedding around that time too. Kanti gaped at him in disbelief. He said, 'Now that we have the needed cash a month is more than enough to organize it.'

* * *

The day Shekhar was to visit, Badri turned up, with the news of a fearsome event in Parsadpur/Ballamgaon, the worst possible in an area under Ram Mohan's control—an attempt on Gulab Singh's life; something he could not have thought likely at all. Aware of his movements, three young men had lain in ambush in a sugarcane field near Gulab Singh's tube well, but before they could attack, one of Gulab Singh's men heard them; his loud shout had panicked them into opening fire with no idea of their target's actual position, giving Gulab Singh's men enough time to retaliate. One of the three attackers was shot dead; one had managed to escape; the third one was captured. Ram Mohan dashed off, telling Nishant to inform Mahavir Wilson and have him and his parents present during Shekhar's visit.

Mahavir Wilson along with his parents came two hours before Shekhar and his brother showed up late afternoon. Deena and Mayank who were playing outside in the side yard were the first to see them; the younger of the two—Shekhar—slim and tall, at least taller than his brother, waved to them. Deena ran inside. Thanks to Mahavir Bhaiya and his parents, Nisha looked better and more relaxed than the day before, while Shekhar dressed in a tight pair of trousers and a bush shirt, exuded warmth and confidence. He could well be described as average-looking if it weren't for the scar—rather a large pit—left by a boil on his right cheek in childhood; was nowhere close to Nisha Didi in appearance. Mahavir and his father chatted with him and his brother over tea and refreshments before Nisha, chaperoned by Mrs Wilson, entered the big room, and shortly—to enable them to get acquainted—Shekhar and Nisha were left alone.

After their departure, they all sat down in the big room to talk. Nisha's mournful demeanour prompted Mahavir to speak up. 'Given his rural background the boy is an achiever . . . He's not conventionally good-looking . . . that's true,' then addressing Nisha, 'but this lack is nullified by his other much more worthwhile attributes, and an intelligent girl like you must not assess a person's worth from how they look. Yet he's tall and slim and he talks well. For a person of his extraction, it's quite an attainment . . . to have come this far. It attests to his brilliance and hard work. He can get by in English too,' Mahavir paused. 'No, more than that, his spoken English is quite good, which is good news for you, Nisha. You can learn the language in his company.'

His words steadied Nisha's nerves. Still, she was unable to overcome the fact that a life that had seemed for keeps till a few months ago was drawing to an end.

Lying trussed up in a corner of the shed at Gulab Singh's tube well, the captured assailant was groaning quietly when Ram Mohan arrived. The corpse of the third one, Gulab Singh had disposed of. After being briefed, Ram Mohan asked Gulab Singh to have the police notified. The inspector in charge of the local police station was one of Ram Mohan's loyalists in the state police force; whenever in need of a particular posting, he would seek Ram Mohan's help.

To learn of Padhaiya Bhaiya's complicity, divulged by the injured man, Ram Mohan was shocked. Ever since that night when he had challenged him, Padhaiya Bhaiya had become a marked man; his thuggish behaviour had earned him much animus. What had sheltered him till then was that he was related to Ram Mohan.

It was about to get dark when the police inspector arrived accompanied by several constables. He touched Ram Mohan's feet, looking pleased to be of some help to his patron. To have a quiet word, they walked a few paces away from the tube well. The inspector, having no doubt as to the best course in the situation, explained there was no need to report the attack. The injured man too should be dispatched without delay. The identity of the one who had made off was already known, so was the role of Padhaiya as one of the conspirators. He too would have to be taken out. His continual intransigence—his hostility to Ram Mohan and his hand in the attack on Gulab Singh—would more than justify reprisal. Gulab Singh did not have to have his men involved in the killing; there were people who had been waiting for this very opportunity. Gulab Singh just had to get the message across that nothing, no obstacle, lay between them and Padhaiya now; that they were free to settle whatever score they had with him; the only favour he might ask was to make it brutal. Badri frowned on the idea. He also objected to Gulab Singh's plan to burn the wounded man alive. But the police inspector was all for it. He said these people had brought it all on themselves. A painful remembrance of their deed just before they left this world would do them no harm. He also asked his men, the constables, to help. While the man screaming for mercy was being taken to a field to be set on fire, Ram Mohan told Gulab Singh to have the Padhaiya thing finished in about three weeks. He did not want Nisha's marriage to coincide with a violent death in Parsadpur, in their extended family.

* * *

Rains were almost gone, setting the stage for one of the most agreeable times of the year, which meant little to Nisha. The date for her wedding after Ram Mohan's return from Parsadpur had been set, and every so often she would feel a flutter of anxiety. Shekhar had already sent a telegram to his office in Bangalore for a leave extension. Mahavir Bhaiya and Kanti had, to some extent, helped her become reconciled to the idea of marriage. Yet she had issues with the thought of moving to an alien place alone. She got around it by getting Babu ji to agree to something unusual, that is, after the wedding she would bring Mayank along to her in-laws' house in the village to stay with her till she was due for a brief custom-warranted return to her parents' place. Having Mayank around in strange surroundings was her idea of a defence against feeling cut off from what she had thought was her real family.

Ten days before the wedding, the news of Padhaiya Bhaiya came. He was found close to the railway station with an iron rod driven through his stomach and into a tree trunk with his arms and legs hacked off. No firearms were used. He had died of trauma and blood loss. Ram Mohan went to Parsadpur to be with the shocked and grieving relatives.

* * *

The wedding went well. Ram Mohan's house and its grounds were decorated appropriately. Apart from many a local prominent figure, the wedding was attended by several powerful politicians from Lucknow. Saansad ji could not come; he had asked two members of the state Cabinet to be there on his behalf. Baran Singh had also sent one of his very senior party colleagues. Shukla ji and Liyaqat Argali were there.

To Deena and Sandhya, the morning felt like a shroud over the corpse of the festivity of the previous night. They could not have imagined the heartlessness of the moment of Nisha Didi's departure. Ram Mohan urged Kanti and others to wind up, who hugged and kissed Nisha one last time. For Deena, the sight of Nisha Didi weeping uncontrollably just before being gently pushed into the back seat of a hired Ambassador was soul-searing. He had never felt more envious of Mayank who sat between her and Shekhar in the car. It was, however, some relief for Deena that Babu ji left for Parsadpur the same day; he could be with Sandhya Didi and remember and feel the loss alongside her and their mother; for him, after Gayatri Masi, Gabdu, Nanki, Chhote Baba and his Nana, this was the most excruciating experience.

Just as winter was about to whip across north India, Indira Gandhi sent Saansad ji to UP as CM. He was supposed to take over after the long-expected midterm election but she—unsure of a big win in UP this time—decided to hold polls on schedule i.e. a few months later, in order to buy some time. As a result, the Legislative Assembly after staying dissolved for about four months was reinstated with Saansad ji becoming UP's eighth or perhaps ninth chief minister.

Ram Mohan and Tiwari ji were present at the swearing-in in Lucknow. They looked to have a word with Saansad ji, but thanks to all the hustle around him, he barely managed to ask them to come back after he had moved into the CM's residence. He had to rush to Delhi the very next day to seek Indira ji's blessings and whatever other directions she wished to give before he got down to work. It had become a Congress culture now. No Congress CM was free to choose his ministerial team or make important decisions, permission for which had to be obtained from her personally or through her dreaded coterie.

In less than a week, Ram Mohan got a call from Saansad ji; within hours he and Tiwari ji were in Lucknow. Tiwari ji had been staying in Kanpur for some time, for after the killing of one of the three instigators of the attack on his brother, the enmity between the family of Tiwari ji and that of those three was out in the open. The original idea was to put down all the three one by one on the quiet, without arousing suspicion, but it was no longer easy because Bholi and Daulat Singh had been sighted not far from where the recent killing had taken place. Now the families of the three were not only sure of Tiwari ji's hand in it but in the disappearance of Mukhiya too. Ram Mohan thought his friend had better be seen as politically busy.

Though his bungalow and its grounds were swarming as usual with all types of visitors, political and official both, Saansad ji spent half an hour discussing things with Ram Mohan and Tiwari ji alone in a room. Except for one or two, all his ministers were the same as had held office in the regime of Kamlapati Tripathi. That's what Mrs Gandhi wanted. In some cases, portfolios were also decided in Delhi, and Shukla ji who had got finance, was among the three most powerful ministers under Saansad ji, and Saansad ji told Ram Mohan that after the Assembly poll, he would be allowed to pick a few ministers on his own, by which he meant that Ram Mohan's inclusion—provided things did not take an unforeseen turn—was a sure thing. Then in the same breath, he said he had a good mind to put Ram Mohan in charge of the campaign in Fatehpur that had six Assembly seats. With less than three months to the elections, he suggested Ram Mohan and Tiwari ji put on their campaigners' hat. Leaving the CM's residence, they were on cloud nine.

In Kanpur, Ram Mohan began to identify things warranting attention. Through Saansad ji's good offices, he wanted to get a couple of development projects cleared for Parsadpur before the Assembly ballot, and given the situation in Tiwari ji's village, it was important that the police chief of Fatehpur district and his subordinates were made aware of his closeness to the CM, whereas Bholi and Daulat Singh should kill the remaining two of the three instigators before they could get their act together. A day or two later, Ram Mohan and Tiwari ji launched into a whirlwind of tours, visiting Parsadpur, Fatehpur and Lucknow over and over.

With Nisha and Mayank back and Ram Mohan mostly out of town, their house wore a festive air. Shekhar had gone back to Bangalore to collect his relieving orders. Sandhya and Deena could not have enough of whatever Nisha Didi had to tell them about him and his family. And there was something she shared only with Kanti, something she would not forget, something that had disturbed her to the core, and was one in the eye for her notion of a modern husband like Zaheer or Bhatnagar or Banerjee Sahab or Mr Wilson, the men she had seen at close quarters. Deena was to relate her indignant look to what she would tell him years later. About that he has left a long note. But as I'm making every endeavour to round off the book, a summary of the episode should more than suffice:

She had not slept well during the run-up to her wedding, and in Shekhar's village awaiting the new bride were all kinds of enervating rituals. With her head and face in a veil, she was unable to see much as she sat surrounded by women; the most annoying ceremony of all was the one when all the women present would one by one hunker down before her, lifting the veil, just enough to allow them a close private look at her face, and before getting up, each of them would thrust a little money, one or two folded notes, into her hand. In the meantime, she could hear all kinds of comments, the most hurtful and mortifying being those referring to her complexion, reducing her to tears. However, some were quite generous in acknowledging her sharp features. She was exhausted by the time it had ended. Mayank

was already asleep. After having food, she was led into a narrow
corridor-like space that was their bedroom, obviously a temporary
arrangement. Already drowsy, she had fallen into a slumber by the
time Shekhar could join her. Affronted, he had roused her rather
rudely and had set about acting on his notion of wedding night.
Though appalled, there was nothing she could do. The main shocker
was to come in the morning when Shekhar after changing into fresh
set of clothes tossed her the lungi he had worn through the night,
telling her to wash it.

There was no need to be alarmed, Kanti tried to tell Nisha.
To her, there was nothing abnormal in the way Shekhar had
behaved, as he was someone with no exposure to the lifestyle of
educated urban couples, but once they set up house together in
Allahabad, his outlook would change. Nisha retorted by giving
Babu ji's example. He had lived in the city for so long and known
many such modern families, who once would discuss politics
even with Savitri Devi, Chaudhary Baran Singh's wife. Their
father was a freak, Kanti said, and could not serve as an example
here. Even in villages, there were men who in their attitude
to women were much less feudal than him. Though optimistic
about her mother's prediction, Nisha was not convinced. She
knew the man who could shed more meaningful light on it, but
given the intimate nature of her first encounter with Shekhar,
she could not discuss it with Mahavir Bhaiya.

However, save for his undue attempt to sound 'manly',
Shekhar's behaviour towards his parents, elder brother, sister-
in-law and other elders was very respectful. His fondness for his
nephews, his solicitude for them, the way he seemed keen that
they should not slack off on their studies, all that, she could not
deny, was quite endearing; and the fact remained that it had
been well-nigh impossible for him and her to have some time
alone in the daytime. During the night, his intemperance—

utterly unseemly to her—would not allow her to have a heart-to-heart with him. Once on their own in Allahabad, she would get to know him better. The new life might, as envisaged by Mahavir Bhaiya, afford her some independence of thought and action. Hopeful, Nisha plunged into making the most of Babu ji's absence in the company of Sandhya, Deena and Mayank and their mother.

Hardly had Saansad ji settled himself in the CM's chair than Indira Gandhi embarked on a series of trips to UP; over a span of just two months, she had lavished a great many projects and schemes on the state. Opposition parties were vexed. Baran Singh accused her of misusing the public purse to help her party's cause, while Saansad ji, though privately admitting to her disregard for electoral rectitude, could not but feel glad. To otherwise mitigate the effects of his predecessor, Kamlapati Tripathi's openly corrupt regime would be a tall order. 'Now we have something concrete at which to hammer away during the campaign. We can claim that never before such largess has been dispensed to us by the Centre. In terms of development, UP has been a beacon of neglect since Independence.'

Ram Mohan's political prospects had never looked brighter. He got to meet Indira Gandhi for the first time when she came to address a large public meeting in Kanpur. She seemed to remember his name when Saansad ji introduced him. It hardly lasted a minute before she climbed into her car. What mattered to him though was her intent look as Saansad ji's described him as a well-known Hindi scholar and orator, who was also politically active and had a tremendous following in Fatehpur. She had smiled and said, 'I'm aware of that last bit. Keep it up, Ram Mohan ji.' To him, those words were sheer magic. That evening, he gathered them all in the big room and narrated the whole sequence in great detail. He was in his element, proceeding shortly as usual to tease Kanti, saying she should gear herself up for being a minister's wife soon. Nothing could now stand between them and Lucknow. Then on a rather serious note, he started enquiring about the children's studies and said he was too busy to keep an eye, so they all should behave sensibly and prepare for their exams, because by the time their results were out they would most likely be relocating to Lucknow. For Nishant, it was BA final year and twelfth board for Sandhya while Deena would try to get through class nine. Mayank would soon be done with his time at Hudson school, which only went up to class five for boys.

The day after him meeting Indira Gandhi, Ram Mohan took himself off to Fatehpur where Tiwari ji had set up a meeting with some local Congress leaders. Following Saansad ji's suggestion, they had met Shukla ji and also Liyaqat Argali, their former rival and the sitting MLA from Fatehpur city. They were happy he would be in charge of the Congress campaign in Fatehpur during the Assembly poll; to appreciate the fact that they were now on the same side of the fence, Argali too attended this meeting in Fatehpur. But Ram Mohan who was sure of being made a minister would soon be taken aback by Saansad ji casually suggesting an alternative when he went to Lucknow to see him. No sooner had he briefed him about his rapprochement with Shukla ji and his toady Argali and the way things stood in Fatehpur, than Saansad ji said there was something else, a very prestigious though non-political position to which he would like him to give a serious thought. It was the post of chairman of state Public Service Commission, an autonomous and constitutional body responsible for selecting officials and other professionals for the state bureaucracy and other government-run institutions. Unaware of its importance,

Ram Mohan could not appreciate the offer. Moreover, to him any position lacking in undisguised political authority was no substitute for what he had had in mind, which he now seemed to have come within an ace of achieving. When he asked if there was a hitch in his joining the state cabinet, Saansad ji hastened to assure him, 'The thought occurred to me after I learnt of the vacancy at the top in Public Service Commission; the position has great value in terms of social prestige and influence.'

Because of its being located in Allahabad, Nisha made a pitch for it, and Kanti, Sandhya, Deena and Mayank, they all supported her. Nishant thought otherwise. To him, whatever Public Service Commission was it could not compare with the position of a minister. None of them like their father had previously heard of it, the Commission. The sole reason for the majority in favour of Babu ji accepting the post was that it would allow them to live in the same city as Nisha. 'It only goes to show,' said Ram Mohan, 'how anxious Saansad ji is to do something for me while he can, but to blow a chance of being a minister would be plain folly.' When Tiwari ji—who arrived the following day—was told of Saansad ji's offer, he said a position like this could be of value to a politician only as a last resort. 'Your time for that hasn't come yet.'

* * *

Shekhar had already joined the Allahabad branch of Indian Telephone Industry; anon he wrote to Nisha asking her to come; he had found a house to rent in one of the nicer localities in the city. Ram Mohan told Nishant to accompany her to Allahabad the very next day, the day he was to go to Parsadpur. A rude awakening it was to Nisha, Kanti, Sandhya, Deena and Mayank! With a sweeping sense of melancholy welling up inside them, they kept crying intermittently. A tearful Nisha told them, Deena in particular, to study and do well in their exams, after which she got Babu ji's permission for them to spend summer holidays in Allahabad.

Their exams were still some distance when the dates for the UP Assembly poll were announced. The weather was amiable, a buffer between the extremes of winter and summer. Saansad ji gave Ram Mohan a Jeep with a driver and some cash to spend as he thought fit while overseeing the Congress canvassing in Fatehpur. Ram Mohan's old team got back in action; with no fear of a direct loss, they were relishing every moment of it. To top it all was the fact that this time they were on the side that was likely to win. Ram Mohan was constantly invited to address public meetings across the Fatehpur Assembly segments. All the six Congress candidates including Liyaqat Argali looked forward to these meetings with Ram Mohan firing the audience up.

As expected, Congress secured a comfortable majority in the Legislative Assembly. In Fatehpur, it triumphed in all the six seats. Though Fatehpur had always been a Congress stronghold, this time, it had looked shaky in at least two seats, one of which—in the opinion of many—it was certain to lose. Saansad ji publicly acknowledged Ram Mohan's role in cooking the opposition's goose in Fatehpur, whereas Shukla ji and Liyaqat Argali though appreciative of Ram Mohan's contribution, could barely hide their disquiet about his coming into the political reckoning. It was Shukla ji who had done his political mentoring at a time when Ram Mohan was just an ambitious young man. Of course, it was in recognition of what had happened many years before during a wedding, which they both had attended. Now the thought of him—his former protégé—joining the state cabinet on a par with him was insufferable to Shukla ji, sensing which Saansad ji decided to make a little change in his original plan. He put Ram Mohan's name on the first list itself, the list of prospective ministers to be taken to Delhi for approval.

As it turned out, he had miscalculated even then. The list he got back from Mrs Gandhi had the name of Ram Mohan crossed out. When he tried to plead with her coterie he was told to have patience as madam might agree later. What Kapur told him between themselves was that the Congress' success in UP was attributed entirely to Indira ji's popularity, her political charm and charisma; any suggestion of anybody else having to do anything with it was no less than heresy, and Shukla ji's uncle had mentioned to her that in some quarters Saansad ji was getting the credit for the party's remarkable victory in UP. He also let it be known to her in a little puzzled tone that Ram Mohan— to the chagrin of some old and loyal Congress workers—was being excessively praised for Fatehpur. Saansad ji remonstrated with Kapur, saying it was not true. Whatever appreciation Ram Mohan got was consistent with his efforts during the campaign. 'You know, Saansad ji, that at the end of the day what matters is the way things are portrayed to her,' said Kapur with a grin before going on to say, 'Even then Indira ji might have ignored these complaints which she knows are attributable to jealousy; the argument she found hard to dismiss was that almost all backward castes in UP at present are in Chaudhary Baran Singh's pocket, so what's the point in giving Ram Mohan as critical a position as that of a minister, let alone the fact that it might ruffle some of our upper-caste supporters? As for the symbolic representation of these castes, Congress already has some loyal backward worthies in its fold.' Kapur paused before continuing, 'I won't say making Ram Mohan a minister is not possible. You can try your luck next time. But if you ask for my opinion, Saansad ji, I'd say you give him something else, something not overtly political. Maybe later on, if and when the situation permits, you can bring him back into active politics.'

On coming back, Saansad ji kept this more or less to himself, saying—rather lying—to Ram Mohan that he had been asked to

place his name on the next list of ministers. That might take a
month or two at the most.

Happy he would be made a minister soon, Ram Mohan was
back to his earlier routine, lecturing at his college, enjoying
evening chats with Mrs Khatri and supervising the efforts of
his female PhD students. He also started taking a glass of milk
mixed with the yellow of an egg every day, which Kanti at first
believed to be his attempt at staying healthy. That's what he had
claimed. Then one day she overheard him talking in undertones
with someone on the phone about the beneficial impact of egg
yolk on man's virility. Kanti, from his tone, inferred the identity
of the person on the other side, his favourite PhD student.
Although seething, she decided to let him be and learn to live
with the knowledge of his intimacies with other women. That
was the best and only option according to Nisha, who before
going to Allahabad, had also begged Kanti not to provoke him,
for she could get nothing out of it other than profanities and
physical abuse.

Not as busy as he was during the election, Ram Mohan's
weekly trips to Parsadpur were back to normal, providing some
relief to his family, but to Deena it was preferable to when Babu
ji was away for longer periods. Desperately short of cash he had
had to steal from their Bua who happened to be visiting when
Babu ji was in Lucknow attending the swearing-in ceremony.
Shortly, Nishant had had him confessing. In view of their
upcoming exams, it was decided they would not tell Babu ji,
and in return, Deena had to promise to prepare well for his
exam. In fact, it was to watch movies—all in the course of a few
days left before the school closed ahead of the start of exams—
that he had had to open their Bua's tin trunk. Now he was busy

filling diligently strips of paper with the answers to the questions expected to be asked in almost all his subjects except the one whose question paper he had got in advance. This B.N.S.D. teacher who had set it, was not only a former teacher of Nishant but also a Ram Mohan adherent. He had ticked all the questions in Deena's textbook itself for him to memorize the answers. The most dreadful bit of a year for him was exam-time. The peculiarly austere and grim life at home during the period, he could not bear. No story books, no funny conversations, no Ludo or Snakes and Ladders, no carom board, nothing. He could not wait for the exams to be over. Long gaps between various exams were cause for resentment, because he—unlike others who seemed to always be running out of time—needed just enough time to get his cheating material ready.

Their exams had hardly begun when to Deena's delight an incident regardless of its tragic nature relieved the oppressive atmosphere at home. Tiwari ji's arrival with the news had distracted them. The savage murders of Bholi and the only son of his elder brother shook them all. On their way to the main road to catch the bus to Fatehpur town the previous afternoon, they had been waylaid at a lonely spot; but for their clothes and footwear, it would have been hard to recognize them. They were found tied to a tree with their brains blown out and guts hanging out.

Babu ji was quiet and thinking hard as Tiwari ji declaimed, cursing Bholi for his needless intrepidity. 'I'd been telling him to be cautious and prudent, that his recklessness would tempt their enemies. But he couldn't care less, thinking his infamy was enough to put the fear of God into them . . . Overconfidence did him in.' Then Babu ji cut in, motioning him to stop, 'We'd better figure out what needs to be done now. I wish we had dispatched some more of them, which would have impaired their ability to retaliate . . . Let's not brood over what we did not do, and think instead of what we can do now.'

The next morning Ram Mohan and Tiwari ji left together for Fatehpur. The same day Sukesh wearing a long face dropped in with many more tidbits related to the grisly incident. He like his father was a good storyteller. Ram Mohan was to be gone for several days. In the meantime, the police had rounded up all those Tiwari ji had named in the FIR, but with no evidence to nail them, they were out on bail. Ram Mohan asked Tiwari ji to organize the murders of whoever among his adversaries could be found. It was two days after Deena's exams ended that Sukesh blew in with the news of a strike to take place in Fatehpur, giving him a kick.

Full of nervous excitement, Sukesh had come straight from the bus station. Babu ji had gone to Parsadpur. They all sat in the big room. Sukesh told them his father and brother, and Daulat Singh and his brother, were in Fatehpur to act on the information they had about the visit of the man said to be the chief strategist of their enemies to the district court. He was to be slaughtered within the court precincts. Making it more thrilling was the fact that whether the attempt was successful or not, it could only be known from the newspaper in the morning. According to the plan, Daulat Singh's brother would deliver the blow to the strategist's head with his lathi before Sukesh's brother and Daulat Singh would shoot him dead.

Sukesh was in a state of anticipatory charge. He stayed the night with them; was the first to get hold of the paper in the morning. Within seconds, he read out loud the headline on the second page, 'Two Men Butchered in Broad Daylight near Fatehpur District Court.' After poring over the story, he announced it was not the strategist but his brother and his uncle who had been gunned down. Later that day, Tiwari ji arrived, according to whom either his informant had been mistaken or the strategist could not make it to the court. They were in a quandary—should they go ahead as planned or wait for another opportunity! There was no time to consult Tiwari ji who was at his relative's, waiting for the good news. The strategist's brother and uncle, in the meantime, had got out of the court compound and were about to climb into a rickshaw when Daulat Singh had in the nick of time taken the call—a good one. To throw away a chance like that would have disappointed Tiwari ji in whose opinion the need to swiftly and tellingly avenge the murders of his nephew and Bholi was absolutely urgent. Any act that could hurt and debilitate the enemy camp was in order.

These killings were to be the last of the kind; Ram Mohan had the Fatehpur police chief direct his man in Tiwari ji's area to ensure its end, the end of the ongoing violence. The concerned police inspector sent Tiwari ji's foes the message that they must not aggravate the situation by retaliating, or the police would be forced to take down some of them in staged encounters. The last bit was also meant to make them cough up some money, which to Tiwari ji's glee, they did. However, court cases relating to some of the murders would go on for more than a decade.

The day Nisha reached Kanpur, Ram Mohan received a call from Saansad ji who asked him to come meet him. Something was afoot in Lucknow. As his suitcase was being packed, Nisha asked permission for taking Deena and Mayank to Allahabad for the summer holiday. He agreed; then Nisha decided to extend her stay in Kanpur by a few days; she was also keen to know the significance of Babu ji's Lucknow trip. On returning the next day, he called them all into the big room. Next month Saansad ji would expand his Cabinet, permission for which had been granted by Delhi. He would make one more bid to have his name on the list of new ministers. In case the request was declined yet again, Ram Mohan should be prepared to accept

366   Devesh Verma

whatever else Saansad ji could offer before it was too late. It could well be regarded as a setback, but when he said they would soon be leading a better life, there was nothing in his manner to suggest he was dismayed.

That's what happened in the end. When Saansad ji submitted the list of his prospective ministers to Indira ji, which included Ram Mohan's name, the same people queered the pitch for him again, Shukla ji's uncle, Udai Pratap Singh and some others. A couple of weeks after the new ministers were sworn in, Saansad ji came to attend some function at the Indian Institute of Technology in Kanpur. The venue was milling with who's who of the city, who all watched in astonishment when the CM motioned to Ram Mohan who sat in one of the front rows in the audience to come onto the stage. As he sat beside Saansad ji, in full public glare, the latter whispered into his ear he should resign from D.A.V. College and move to Allahabad as member, Public Service Commission. 'I wish you had accepted the post of chairman. That vacancy has been filled.' To which he added that the position of a member was of equal importance. Two days later the Governor's office informed him of his appointment. Everybody barring Nishant was thrilled. They would now live in the same city as Nisha. Nishant too got over his disappointment as he listened to Babu ji, Tiwari ji and Mahavir Wilson discussing the appointment. 'Albeit not political, the position has a lot of social prestige attached to it . . . and is quite influential,' said Mahavir before going on to elaborate why. Hearing him out, Tiwari ji said, 'I agree . . . and it's just the beginning. Let's regard it that way.'

'Yes, the beginning of something bigger,' said Ram Mohan. 'Given Saansad ji's affection for me it would not be the end.' Deena was to write later: *Once aware of the constraints on his ability to manoeuvre, Babu ji would demonstrate a remarkable capacity to adjust his ambition accordingly.*

ACKNOWLEDGEMENTS

During this long and exhausting journey, during all my problems and predicaments, I have been mighty fortunate to have my wife, Bhavna, in my corner. Without her having my back, I dare say I could not have completed this novel.

I owe gratitude to my friend Mahmood Farooqui but for whose support I do not know how long it would have been before *The Politician* could see the light of day, and it was he who—by spurning a promising career in TV journalism to pursue his passion for theatre and Dastangoi—had inspired me to take the plunge in the first place.

I thank my editor, Anushree Kaushal; she was among those who on reading the manuscript believed it had potential.

Thanks are due to my copy editor, Hina Khajuria; it was a pleasure to work with her. I would also like to thank all those involved, one way or the other, in the production of this book at Penguin Random House India.

I am enormously grateful for the support and good cheer from all the members of my family and friends.

Scan QR code to access the
Penguin Random House India website